Haiti for the Haitians
by
Louis-Joseph Janvier

Haiti for the Haitians
by
Louis-Joseph Janvier

Editors: Brandon R. Byrd and Chelsea Stieber
Consulting Editor: Nathan H. Dize
Translator: Nadève Ménard
With an Afterword by Jean Casimir

LIVERPOOL UNIVERSITY PRESS

First published 2023 by
Liverpool University Press
4 Cambridge Street
Liverpool
L69 7ZU

Copyright © 2023 Liverpool University Press

Brandon R. Byrd and Chelsea Stieber have asserted the right to be identified as the editors of this book in accordance with the Copyright, Designs and Patents Act 1988.

All rights reserved. No part of this book may be reproduced, stored in a retrieval system, or transmitted, in any form or by any means, electronic, mechanical, photocopying, recording, or otherwise, without the prior written permission of the publisher.

Portions of Marlene Daut's chapter were first published as "Caribbean Race Men: Louis Joseph Janvier, Demesvar Delorme, and the Haitian Atlantic," *L'Espirit Créateur* 56, no. 1, Haiti Beyond Commemorations (Spring 2016): 9–23. Yves Chemla's chapter originally appeared as "Louis-Joseph Janvier: Écrivain National," *Francofonia* 49, Lectures et écritures haïtiennes (Autunno 2005): 7–36.

British Library Cataloguing-in-Publication data
A British Library CIP record is available

ISBN 978-1-83764-446-9

Typeset by Carnegie Book Production, Lancaster
Printed and bound by CPI Group (UK) Ltd, Croydon CR0 4YY

Contents

Introduction   1
    Brandon R. Byrd and Chelsea Stieber

Haiti for the Haitians   43
    Translated from French by Nadève Ménard
    Annotations by Brandon R. Byrd and Chelsea Stieber

Critical Essays

1. Louis-Joseph Janvier, National Writer   83
    Yves Chemla
    For Ludovic Janvier
    Translated from French by Nadève Ménard

2. Caribbean "Race Men": Louis Joseph Janvier, Demesvar Delorme, and the Haitian Atlantic   113
    Marlene L. Daut

3. There Is No Odd in Ordinary: Louis Joseph Janvier, Haiti, and the Tropics of Racial Science   141
    Bastien Craipain

4. Haïti farà da se: French Third Republic Colonial Universalism and Louis Joseph Janvier's Haitian Autonomy   163
    Chelsea Stieber

vi   *Haiti for the Haitians* by Louis-Joseph Janvier

5 Louis-Joseph Janvier, the Founding Theorist of the Haitian
   Nation (an Active Reading of *Haïti aux Haïtiens*)   187
     Watson Denis
     Translated from French by Nadève Ménard

6 *Haiti for the Haitians*: A Genealogy of Black Sovereignty   219
     Brandon R. Byrd

Afterword: The Elusive *Habitant*   245
   Jean Casimir
   Translated from French by Chelsea Stieber

Index   257

Introduction

Brandon R. Byrd and Chelsea Stieber

At two o'clock in the morning, well before the sun rose on March 27, 1883, the *Tropic* sailed into the harbor of Miragoâne, one of the principal port towns in southern Haiti. Jean-Pierre Boyer Bazelais and 105 other Haitian exiles from the British colonies of the Bahamas and Jamaica quickly disembarked from their ship and, under cover of darkness, descended upon Miragoâne. They easily took and then barricaded the town, beginning what became known as the Liberal Insurrection of 1883.[1]

A few weeks later, news of the event reached residents of Paris, including Louis-Joseph Janvier. While major newspapers in the French capital reproduced standard color-based clichés about Haitian politics, reporting that the insurgents were uniformily "mulattoes" in revolt against the "negro government" of Haitian president Lysius Salomon, Janvier followed the invasion of Haiti and its ensuing civil war with a far more sophisticated understanding of their root causes.[2] He would watch and interpret the events unfolding in his native country with a growing sense of their profound significance.

---

1 Historical accounts of this event include Louis-Joseph Janvier, *Les Affaires d'Haïti (1883–1884)*, 2nd ed. (Port-au-Prince: Les Éditions Panorama, 1885); Gustave Vigoureux, *L'Année terrible; ou, 1883 à Jérémie* (Jérémie: Imprimerie du Centenaire, 1909); Jean Price-Mars, *Jean-Pierre Boyer Bazelais et le drame de Miragoâne* (Port-au-Prince: Imprimerie de L'État, 1948). More recently, see Matthew J. Smith, *Liberty, Fraternity, Exile: Haiti and Jamaica after Emancipation* (Chapel Hill: University of North Carolina Press, 2014), 224–230.

2 "Haïti," *Le Temps*, April 14, 1883. A note on spellings and translation: on some occasions, Janvier spelled his name with no hyphen. On others, he placed a hyphen between his second and third names. For the sake of consistency, the editors have adopted the spelling he used in *Haïti aux Haïtiens*, with a hyphen between his first and second names. For citations of his other printed works, we have used the spelling as it appeared in print. The spelling of his name in subsequent critical essays reflects the authors' choices. Unless otherwise noted, translations are the editors', authors', or translator's own.

By the time Salomon quelled the rebellion and the routine operations of Haitian governance resumed in early 1884, Janvier had come to see the Liberal Insurrection as a defining moment in Haitian history. It affirmed for him some of the central lessons of the past and clarified the many factors that had contributed to Haiti's current political conflicts. It inspired in him a vision of Haiti's future expressed in a remarkable phrase: *Haïti aux Haïtiens*.

Haiti, the independent state that Janvier would observe, address, defend, and critique, came into being through an unprecedented anticolonial and antislavery struggle initiated by enslaved people.[3] By the late eighteenth century, Saint-Domingue, France's most productive colony, was the apex of the Atlantic plantation economy; there, enslavers held in bondage over 500,000 enslaved people who labored in treacherous, often fatal, conditions. In August 1791, enslaved people in the Northern Province rose up against their enslavers and maintained their insurrection for nearly two years. Their military successes, combined with protracted civil war between French colonists and free people of color and pressure from the rival colonial powers of Spain and Great Britain, led the civil commissioner for the French Republic, Léger-Félicité Sonthonax, to issue a general emancipation decree in the Northern Province on August 29, 1793. It declared "all Negroes and people of mixed blood currently enslaved" free and able to "enjoy all rights

---

[3] Foundational and recent scholarship on the Haitian Revolution includes Jean Fouchard, *Les Marrons de la liberté* (Paris: Éditions de l'École, 1972); C.L.R. James, *The Black Jacobins: Toussaint L'Ouverture and the San Domingo Revolution* (New York: Vintage, 1989); Carolyn Fick, *Making Haiti: The Saint Domingue Revolution from Below* (Knoxville: The University of Tennessee Press, 1990); Leslie F. Manigat, *Eventail d'histoire vivante d'Haïti*, vol. 1 (Port-au-Prince: Collection du CHUDAC, 2001); David Patrick Geggus, *Haitian Revolutionary Studies* (Bloomington: Indiana University Press, 2002); Laurent Dubois, *Avengers of the New World: The Story of the Haitian Revolution* (Cambridge, MA: Harvard University Press, 2004); John D. Garrigus, *Before Haiti: Race and Citizenship in French Saint-Domingue* (New York: Palgrave Macmillan, 2006); Jeremy D. Popkin, *You Are All Free: The Haitian Revolution and the Abolition of Slavery* (New York: Cambridge University Press, 2010); Malick W. Ghachem, *The Old Regime and the Haitian Revolution* (New York: Cambridge University Press, 2012); Ada Ferrer, *Freedom's Mirror: Cuba and Haiti in the Age of Revolution* (New York: Cambridge University Press, 2014); Crystal Nicole Eddins, *Rituals, Runaways, and the Haitian Revolution: Collective Action in the African Diaspora* (Cambridge: Cambridge University Press, 2022).

pertaining to French citizenship."⁴ This emancipation act catalyzed the French Republican government's formal abolition of slavery in its colonies in February 1794. The decree of the National Convention also went beyond abolition, declaring "that all men, without distinction of color, residing in the colonies are French citizens and will enjoy all the rights guaranteed by the Constitution."⁵

Although the actions of enslaved people produced the most expansive notions of freedom and rights in the Age of Revolutions, conflicts over political leadership in Saint-Domingue persisted in the decade preceding Haitian independence.⁶ In the 1790s, Toussaint Louverture emerged as the preeminent military leader of what became known as the Haitian Revolution. A Creole born into slavery in 1743, Louverture rose to the position of lieutenant-governor of Saint-Domingue in 1796. In that post, he possessed an unsurpassed status for a man of African descent in the eighteenth-century Atlantic world.⁷ His power did not come without complications or opposition, however. Beginning in 1799, the War of Knives pitted Louverture's northern army against the southern troops of André Rigaud, the French-educated son of a wealthy French enslaver and a formerly enslaved African woman. Louverture prevailed after two hard years of fighting. He then exiled Rigaud and his generals, including Alexandre Pétion and Jean-Pierre Boyer. They fled to France, though their exile would be brief.

To consolidate his political authority, Louverture addressed the twin issues of labor and land. In an era when the plantation became even more entrenched as the central node of the Atlantic political economy, Louverture tied the survival of what had been France's most profitable colony to its plantation economy. As the governor-general of Saint-Domingue, he promulgated a constitution that abolished slavery

---

4 "The Emancipation Proclamation of 29 August 1793," in *The Haitian Revolution: A Documentary History*, ed. David Geggus (Indianapolis: Hackett, 2014), 107–108.

5 "Décret n° 2262 de la Convention nationale, du 16 pluviôse, an II de la République française, une et indivisible" (https://mjp.univ-perp.fr/france/1794 esclavage.htm). See also Geggus, *Haitian Revolutionary Studies*.

6 Dubois, "An Enslaved Enlightenment: Rethinking the Intellectual History of the French Atlantic," *Social History* 31, no. 1 (February 2006): 1–14.

7 The most recent biographies of Louverture include Charles Forsdick and Christian Høgsjberg, *Toussaint Louverture: A Black Jacobin in the Age of Revolutions* (London: Pluto Press, 2017) and Sudhir Hazareesingh, *Black Spartacus: The Epic Life of Toussaint Louverture* (New York: Farrar, Straus and Giroux, 2020).

but also tried to revitalize his state's agricultural production through a system of compulsory labor that redefined the recently enslaved plantation laborers as ostensibly free *cultivateurs*.[8]

Louverture's insistence on mandatory labor conflicted with the visions of autonomy possessed by his state's formerly enslaved subjects. Like their peers throughout the Americas, the enslaved population of Saint-Domingue drew their political ideologies, including their concepts of freedom, from their recent experience of American enslavement and the West and West Central African cultures from which they were torn. Those ideologies informed their collective resistance to slavery. Beginning in the sixteenth century, from the very moment that Europeans imported enslaved Africans to Saint-Domingue, those enslaved people fled from the colony's sugar plantations to remote areas of its mountains, oftentimes in groups linked by prior social relations or kinship and linguistic ties. Many equated freedom with *marronage*. For maroons, flight was not just a physical act of escape from enslavement. Instead, they attempted a psychological break from the dehumanizing conditions of the plantation towards the complete reclamation of power over their lives, including the terms of their reproduction and governance. Faced with the natal alienation of enslavement, they sought full personhood and belonging.[9]

In the midst of the Haitian Revolution, enslaved people who had long resisted their captivity seized control of the vast estates nourished by their blood and sweat and then used those plantation lands to begin establishing the *lakou* as the basis of their post-slavery society. Analogous to other forms of family landholding that emerged throughout the Caribbean, *lakou* literally translates to "courtyard" or "yard space" but refers more generally to a living arrangement consisting of an extended family whose individual units occupy their own homes but share a common yard where family cemeteries and ritual houses are typically placed.[10] The *lakou* is a space bound by traditions of land inheritance, agricultural practices, kinship ties, and the religion of

---

8 Phillip Kaisary, "Hercules, the Hydra, and the 1801 Constitution of Toussaint Louverture," *Atlantic Studies* 12, no. 4 (2015): 393–411. Louverture built his system upon the existing labor regime introduced by Sonthonax after the emancipation decree of 1793.

9 David Geggus, "Marronage, Voodoo, and the Saint Domingue Slave Revolt of 1791," *Proceedings of the Meeting of the French Colonial Historical Society* 15 (1992): 22–35; Neil Roberts, *Freedom as Marronage* (Chicago: University of Chicago Press, 2015); Eddins, *Rituals, Runaways, and the Haitian Revolution*.

10 On this history of family land in the Caribbean, see Laurent Dubois and

Vodou. In fact, it is a place both produced from and productive of a way of being and knowing that is rooted in an ethics of social care and responsibility rather than the rapacious individualism at the heart of Western liberalism and capitalism.[11] In post-independence rural Haiti, the *lakou* would become the foundation of a new socioeconomic order, the counter-plantation system, which historian Jean Casimir defines as most fundamentally a framework wherein the "autonomous life-styles" of Haitian and Caribbean peasants flourish.[12]

The declaration of a national independence that formerly enslaved people expected would secure their autonomy and end the exploitation of their labor came in defiance of French efforts to reclaim Saint-Domingue. In 1799, Napoleon Bonaparte overthrew the French Directory and established himself as First Consul. He quickly turned his attention to the colonies, first organizing a military expedition to depose Louverture in Saint-Domingue and next re-legalizing and then reestablishing slavery in the French colonies. Though Bonaparte's army was successful in capturing and deporting Louverture and numerous other officers, it failed to retake Saint-Domingue, whose various revolutionary factions joined together as a unified force under Jean-Jacques Dessalines's *armée indigène* and proclaimed the independent state of Haiti on January 1, 1804.[13]

Richard Lee Turits, *Freedom Roots: Histories from the Caribbean* (Chapel Hill: University of North Carolina Press, 2019), 93–136.

11 Myriam J.A. Chancy, *Autochthonomies: Transnationalism, Testimony, and Transmission in the African Diaspora* (Urbana: University of Illinois Press, 2020). In this work, Chancy develops a critical theory of what she calls "lakou consciousness."

12 Casimir, *The Caribbean: One and Divisible* (Santiago, Chile: United Nations Economic Commission for Latin America and the Caribbean, 1992), 78; Jean Casimir, *The Haitians: A Decolonial History*, trans. Laurent Dubois (Chapel Hill: University of North Carolina Press, 2020). On the *lakou*, see also Serge Larose, "The Haitian Lakou: Land, Family and Ritual," in *Family and Kinship in Middle America and the Caribbean: Proceedings of the 14th Seminar of the Committee on Family Research of the International Sociological Association, Curaçao, September 1975*, ed. Arnaud F. Marks and Rene A. Romer (Leiden: University of the Netherlands Antilles and the Royal Institute of Linguistics and Anthropology, 1978), 482–512.

13 On the military expedition and reestablishment of slavery in the French Caribbean, see especially Laurent Dubois, *A Colony of Citizens* (Chapel Hill: University of North Carolina Press, 2004). See also Jean-Pierre Le Glaunec, *The Cry of Vertières*, trans. Jonathan Kaplansky (Montreal: McGill-Queen's University Press, 2020). On Haitian independence, see Julia Gaffield, ed., *The Haitian Declaration of Independence: Creation, Context, and Legacy* (Charlottesville: University of Virginia Press, 2016).

Ideological and regional divisions persisted in the first years of Haitian independence, as elite southern republicans and agricultural laborers alike opposed Dessalines's decision to nationalize plantations and reinstate a rural labor regime akin to that imposed by Louverture. The simmering unrest boiled over when the republican faction orchestrated Dessalines's assassination on October 17, 1806. While the republican partisans characterized their insurrection as Haiti's "true" revolution and intended to bring Haiti under republican governance, their actions initiated another decade and a half of civil war between Henry Christophe's northern state, which he declared a kingdom in 1811, and Pétion and Boyer's southern republic.[14]

From 1807 to 1820, these separate states vied for power, each pursuing different land policies. In the north, Christophe consolidated land under the ownership of his state and its eventual aristocracy, maintaining a system of compulsory labor meant to revitalize sugar production on the large estates formerly owned by French colonists. He also introduced efforts to redistribute those plantations to military officers and soldiers, though only in the last years of his rule. In the south, Pétion relaxed prohibitions against rural inhabitants that tied laborers to one specific plantation and agreed to recognize existing proprietorship of small land parcels so long as they had a legal title and agreed to plant exportable crops. He went further still in 1809 in a decree that made small and medium-sized land concessions (5 to 25 *carreaux*)[15] to officers and soldiers. In 1814, he outlawed the use of bodily force to return cultivators to their plantations.

As Jean-Alix René has recently argued, Pétion's liberal land reforms were a political compromise aimed at molding laborers into republican citizens and gaining their allegiance by integrating them into national politics. Pétion appears to have made some headway towards those goals. Still, as René's analysis of petitions made by small landholders shows, his policies did not persist beyond his tenure as head of state into the years when Boyer united north and south under a republican government and extended the Haitian Republic to the entire island.[16]

---

14 Though these rival governments were centers of power, there remained many insurgent communities throughout the north and south, most notably Goman's (Jean-Baptiste Perrier) independent state in the far southwest. On the civil conflicts in post-independence Haiti, see especially Chelsea Stieber, *Haiti's Paper War: Post-Independence Writing, Civil War, and the Making of the Republic, 1804–1954* (New York: New York University Press, 2020).
15 One *carreau* is equivalent to just over three acres.
16 Jean-Alix René, *Haïti après l'esclavage. Formation de l'état et culture*

As president, Boyer rolled back many of Pétion's liberal land policies, especially with the implementation of the Rural Code of 1826, which sorted rural laborers and landowners into different legal regimes. He also offered state lands and citizenship to black U.S. immigrants. Boyer's immigration policies and domestic laws were meant to revive the production of export crops in Haiti, in part by tying Haitian peasants to the land, denying them rights, and excluding them from active citizenship.[17]

While Boyer attempted to exert state control over rural Haiti, he pursued additional foreign policies that would have a disastrous effect for generations of Haitians. During its first decades of independence, Haiti lacked formal diplomatic recognition from the foreign governments with which it maintained commercial ties. France even maintained its claim to "Saint-Domingue."[18] Confronted with the prospect of continued political exclusion from the international community and faced with the immediate threat of military gunboats, Boyer signed a disastrous indemnity treaty with France that reflected the unequal geopolitical positions and power of the two parties. Under its terms, Haiti agreed to pay 150 million francs—more than $3 billion today—to compensate for

---

politique populaire (1804–1846) (Port-au-Prince: Éditions Le Natal, 2019). See also Johnhenry Gonzalez, *Maroon Nation: A History of Revolutionary Haiti* (New Haven: Yale University Press, 2019) and Robert K. Lacerte, "The Evolution of Land and Labor in the Haitian Revolution, 1791–1820," *The Americas* 34, no. 4 (1978): 449–459. Thomas Madiou provides a detailed account of the events surrounding Boyer's unification of the whole island, see *Histoire d'Haïti*, vol. 6 (Port-au-Prince: H. Deschamps, 1988). On the unification as viewed from the Dominican perspective, see Andrew Walker, "All Spirits Are Roused: The 1822 Antislavery Revolution in Haitian Santo Domingo," *Slavery and Abolition* 40, no. 3 (2019): 583–605 and Anne Eller, *We Dream Together: Dominican Independence, Haiti, and the Fight for Caribbean Freedom* (Durham, NC: Duke University Press, 2016).

17 Claire Payton, "The City and the State: Construction and the Politics of Dictatorship in Haiti (1957–1986)" (PhD diss., Duke University, 2018). See also René, *Haïti après l'esclavage*; Gonzalez, *Maroon Nation*. On the Rural Code on the eastern two-thirds of the island, see especially Frank Moya Pons, "The Land Question in Haiti and Santo Domingo: The Socio-Political Context of the Transition from Slavery to Free Labor, 1801–1843," in *Between Slavery and Free Labor*, ed. Manuel Moreno Fraginals, Frank Moya Pons, and Stanley L. Engerman (Baltimore: Johns Hopkins University Press, 1985), 181–214. Scholarship on black North American immigration to Haiti during the 1820s includes Sara Fanning, *Caribbean Crossing: African Americans and the Haitian Emigration Movement* (New York: New York University Press, 2015).

18 Julia Gaffield, *Haitian Connections in the Atlantic World: Recognition after Revolution* (Chapel Hill: University of North Carolina Press, 2015).

the revenue and property "lost" by French planters during the Haitian Revolution.[19] It also conceded to France the coveted status of "most favored nation," thereby cementing the favorable terms by which France would import Haitian crops and send Haiti its manufactured goods.[20]

In return for these concessions, Haiti gained diplomatic recognition from France and, Boyer hoped, a path towards full and equal integration into the international community. The latter aspiration did not materialize. Instead, opposition to Boyer intensified as some powers, most notably the United States, persisted in the denial of diplomatic recognition to Haiti and, most egregiously, the French indemnity began to accumulate interest and initiate for Haiti a crippling cycle of debt that eroded its economic and political autonomy. Nearly six decades later this debt remained a constant concern for Janvier and one of the major themes in *Haïti aux Haïtiens*.[21]

---

19 According to official documentation, enslaved people were not to be calculated as part of the indemnity payments. However, some correspondence and contemporaneous notes from the period suggest that the number of enslaved people on plantations and their respective positions were taken into account when calculating the overall value of planters' property. See https://esclavage-indemnites.fr/public/Base/1.

20 Julia Gaffield, "The Racialization of International Law after the Haitian Revolution: The Holy See and National Sovereignty," *The American Historical Review* 125.3 (2020): 841–868.

21 Boyer's government immediately took out a loan of 30 million francs from French banks to start making payments on the indemnity. His government then took out a subsequent loan after renegotiating the indemnity down to 90 million francs in 1838. Over the next four decades, subsequent governments paid down the indemnity almost in its entirety, mostly by levying onerous taxes on coffee producers. In 1874, president Michel Domingue negotiated a 21 million franc loan from the French bank Marcuard André et Cie., which was taken over in 1875 by Crédit industriel et commercial (CiC). According to the latter's prospectus, the loan was taken out to settle the remainder of the indemnity debt (roughly 10 million francs) and finance new public works. When the Haitian government paid down the final balance of the indemnity, it was already hobbled by the 1874/1875 loan which, coupled with a drastic drop in coffee prices and changing global economic trends, rendered its situation even more precarious. The 1874/1875 loans were disastrous, a result of a growing appetite in European markets for foreign debt, especially in the Caribbean. The Dominican president Buenaventura Báez would, for instance, finance his many returns to power through foreign loans, which came with hefty conditions for the Dominican state. Haiti took on additional loans in 1896 and by the turn of the twentieth century, half its budget went to paying the French government and the French banks from which it took out loans. On the eve of the 1915 U.S. occupation, Haiti was ensnared in a web of debt controlled not

Boyer's approach to the enduring questions of land, labor, and peasants' rights, in addition to the indemnity, were central causes of opposition to his government. By the 1840s, discontent with Boyer's illiberalism coalesced among some Haitian elites and the masses of small

---

only by France but also by financial institutions in Germany and the United States. Haiti's debt payments took up 80 percent of its annual budget and became a justification for its occupation. In 1914, U.S. secretary of state William Jennings Bryan deployed Marines to Haiti to take $500,000 in gold from the Haitian treasury and deposit it in the National City Bank of New York for "safe-keeping." In November 1915, three months after invading Haiti, the United States forced a treaty upon the Haitian government that permitted a U.S.-appointed official to collect taxes and make debt repayments on Haiti's behalf. The management and financing of Haiti's debt remained a central theme for the rest of the U.S. occupation. In 1922, the United States issued a $16 million loan to Haiti to consolidate Haiti's debt. Even after the withdrawal of the Marines from Haiti in 1934, a U.S. financial adviser continued to oversee payments on Haiti's debt. U.S. control of Haiti's finances lasted until 1947, when Haiti made its final remittance to the National City Bank of New York. This brought to a close a cycle of debt that began in 1825 but the legacies of the indemnity and subsequent debt persist to this day. By the twenty-first century, as the United States, the United Nations, and other international governments and governing bodies initiated new efforts to undermine Haiti's nominal political independence, the Haitian government estimated that the indemnity had cost Haiti the contemporary equivalent of $21 to $40 billion dollars. A recent report in the *New York Times* affirmed an estimate of at least $21 billion dollars while also presenting economic modeling showing that the total costs of the indemnity to Haiti may be as high as $115 billion dollars. On early Haitian foreign relations, the indemnity, debt, and their long-term effects, see especially François Blancpain, *Un siècle de relations financières entre Haïti et la France (1825–1922)* (Paris: L'Harmattan, 2001); Jean-François Brière, "L'Emprunt de 1825 dans la dette de l'indépendance haïtienne envers la France," *Journal of Haitian Studies* 12, no. 2 (2006): 126–134; Guy Pierre, "L'Implantation et l'éviction de la banque française dans la Caraïbe entre la fin du XIXe siècle et le début du XXe," *História e Economia Revista Interdisciplinar* 10, no. 1 (2012): 77–110; Westenley Alcenat, "The Case for Haitian Reparations," *Jacobin*, January 14, 2017, https://www.jacobinmag.com/2017/01/haiti-reparations-france-slavery-colonialism-debt/; Alex Dupuy, *Rethinking the Haitian Revolution: Slavery, Independence, and the Struggle for Recognition* (Lanham: Lexington Books, 2019); Marlene Daut, "When France Extorted Haiti: The Greatest Heist in History," *The Conversation*, June 30, 2020, https://theconversation.com/when-france-extorted-haiti-the-greatest-heist-in-history–137949; Catherine Porter, Constant Méhout, Matt Apuzzo, and Selam Gebrekidan, "The Ransom," *The New York Times*, May 20, 2022. Readers should also note Janvier's condemnations of the indemnity and concern about Haiti's debt in a number of his writings, including *La République d'Haïti et ses visiteurs (1840–1882)* (Paris: Mappon et Flammarion, 1883).

landholders and landless agricultural laborers.[22] Freedom of the press, state investment in public services, a more inclusive political sphere, and the firm protection of Haiti's interests from foreign influence emerged as principal demands of the opposition. So did the equitable distribution of land and the increased availability of capital. As one article in the opposition newspaper *Le Patriote* proclaimed, "[W]e do not conceive of democracy without the division of lands."[23]

In 1843, that discontent transformed into a liberal revolution, which drew upon widespread peasant unrest to depose Boyer from the presidency. The provisional government produced a new liberal constitution, but intense debates about the face and functions of governance demanded resolution after Boyer's removal and exile to Jamaica. In the south, Salomon led a rapidly mounting challenge to the provisional government in Port-au-Prince. Salomon was born into a wealthy landowning family in Les Cayes, a major southern port, where families freed before the Haitian Revolution still held a disproportionate portion of land, wealth, and political power in the mid-nineteenth century. He mobilized his region's peasantry around demands for the full participation of Haiti's black majority in their country's political life. In response to an official delegation sent to Les Cayes by the provisional government, Salomon asserted that "the unjust are those who recognize as citizens only the businessmen, merchants, professionals, capitalists, etc. and who say they were revolted to see men with black skins, tanners, coopers, cultivators by profession, come to vote concurrently with them in the assemblies of the 15th and 16th of June."[24] He adopted a populist stance that, although couched in the categories of color derived from the colonial era, alluded to the lingering relevance of wealth and urban residence as qualifications of formal political participation and markers of citizenship status.

While government troops would suppress armed rebels rallying to Salomon and send Salomon himself into exile in Jamaica, revolutionary currents continued to flow out of the south. In 1844, a former member of the rural police named Jean-Jacques Acaau emerged as the leader of

22 On the democratic revolutions and anti-democratic reactions of the 1830s and 1840s, see especially Mimi Sheller, *Democracy after Slavery: Black Publics and Peasant Rebels in Haiti and Jamaica* (Gainesville: University Press of Florida, 2000) and Michel Hector, *Crises et Mouvements populaires en Haïti*, 2nd ed. (Port-au-Prince: Presses Nationales d'Haïti, 2006).
23 *Le Patriote*, October 19, 1842 quoted in Sheller, *Democracy after Slavery*, 119.
24 Thomas Madiou, *Histoire d'Haïti*, vol. 7 (Port-au Prince: Henri Deschamps, 1988 [orig. 1847–1848]), 512, translation qtd. in Sheller, *Democracy after Slavery*, 129.

a peasant uprising in southern Haiti. His comrades fought as "the army of sufferers" and became known as the Piquets for the wooden sticks with which they armed themselves. At the head of his army of sufferers, dressed in the humble clothing of a peasant, Acaau issued public proclamations demanding the return of Salomon from exile and critiquing the government that had replaced Boyer. He affirmed "respect for the Constitution, Rights, Equality, Liberty." At the heart of the Piquet movement was a far-reaching democratic vision; amid the ascendance of a black general, Phillipe Guerrier, to the Haitian presidency, the Piquets persisted in their demands for a state commitment to public education and assistance for small landholders, who faced the dual burden of high prices for foreign goods and the devaluation of their crops. Their grievances exceeded color, encapsulating a call for land reform and a parallel critique of the unjust political and economic domination of merchants and large landowners in post-emancipation Haiti.[25]

The Piquets won initial victories over government troops but their eventual defeat and dispersal marked a broader blow against the democratization for which they had fought. After a series of short-lived presidencies, Faustin Soulouque was elected to the post in 1847. He was elevated to emperor two years later. Born in Petit-Goâve to an enslaved mother, Soulouque served in the Haitian army under Pétion and Boyer during the early post-independence civil wars and rose up the ranks in the unified republic. As Haiti's head of state, the former general created a more tolerant and inclusive cultural sphere by loosening many of Boyer's repressive laws that had criminalized the peasantry and the practice of Vodou. Yet neither he nor Salomon, who became a senator and then an influential minister under Soulouque after returning from exile, embraced the democratic vision of the Piquets.[26]

---

25 Along with Sheller and Hector, the historical account of Maxime Reybaud offers important insights into the ideas of Acaau and the Piquet movement. Reybaud was the French consul to Haiti and wrote his prejudiced account of Haitian politics under a pseudonym. It was then translated into English. See Gustave d'Alaux, *Soulouque and His Empire*, trans. and ed. by John H. Parkhill (Richmond, VA: J.W. Randolph, 1861). Claire Payton introduces and edits an excerpt of Reybaud's work in Laurent Dubois, Kaiama L. Glover, Nadève Ménard, Millery Polyné, and Chantalle F. Verna, eds., *The Haiti Reader: History, Culture, Politics* (Durham, NC: Duke University Press, 2020): 90–94.

26 Murdo J. MacLeod, "The Soulouque Regime in Haiti, 1847–1859: A Reevaluation," *Caribbean Studies* 10, no. 3 (1970): 35–48. Emmanuel Lachaud, "The Emancipated Empire: Faustin I Soulouque and the Origins of the Second Haitian Empire, 1847–1859" (PhD diss., Yale University, 2021). On Vodou and its historical criminalization in Haiti, see especially Michel S. Laguerre, *Voodoo*

In 1859, Soulouque was unseated, and Salomon was again forced into exile, this time by Fabre Geffrard, a republican military leader from southern Haiti. By then, opposition to Soulouque had mounted in response to the monarch's rejection of republicanism and his violent suppression of political opponents, real and perceived. In office, Geffrard would characterize his political ascendance as a reclamation of republicanism and "civilization" in Haiti. Like Boyer, Geffrard courted diplomatic recognition from foreign powers, namely the United States and the Vatican, and tried to stimulate Haiti's cotton production by recruiting U.S. black agricultural laborers with offers of state lands and citizenship. He advanced a reform agenda, grounded in a colonial vision of modernity and progress, that also entailed a sweeping anti-Vodou campaign and an attempted resurrection of a Boyerist system of repressive labor codes, both of which fell disproportionately upon Haiti's peasantry.[27]

Geffrard's labor codes went largely unenforced due in no small part to the resistance of Haiti's rural masses; the later years of his presidency were marked by uprisings and insurrections until 1867 when, despite receiving substantial support from Great Britain, he was deposed by the northern general Sylvain Salnave.[28] After taking office, Salnave appointed Salomon as Haiti's minister to France and England. He reactivated the populist rhetoric of Acaau and the Piquets, drawing support from nationalist intellectuals, the urban proletariat, and market women alike.[29]

---

and Politics in Haiti (New York: St. Martin's Press, 1989); Patrick Bellegarde-Smith and Claudine Michel, eds., Vodou in Haitian Life and Culture: Invisible Powers (New York: Palgrave Macmillan, 2006); Kate Ramsey, The Spirits and the Law: Vodou and Power in Haiti (Chicago: University of Chicago Press, 2011); Celucien L. Joseph and Nixon S. Cleophat, eds., Vodou in Haitian Memory: The Idea and Representation of Vodou in Haitian Imagination (Lanham: Lexington Books, 2016).

27 Scholarship on the "second wave" of black North American immigration to Haiti includes Chris Dixon, African American and Haiti: Emigration and Black Nationalism in the Nineteenth Century (Westport, CT: Greenwood Press, 2000). On Geffrard's anti-Vodou campaign see Ramsey, The Spirits and the Law, 54–117.

28 Gonzalez, Maroon Nation. See also Marvin Chochotte, "The Twilight of Popular Revolutions: The Suppression of Peasant Armed Struggles and Freedom in Rural Haiti during the US Occupation, 1915–1934," The Journal of African American History 103, no. 3 (2018): 277–308.

29 On Salnave's ascension to and fall from presidential power, see especially Smith, Liberty, Fraternity, Exile, 164–177; Michel-Rolph Trouillot, Haiti, State against Nation: The Origins & Legacy of Duvalierism (New York: Monthly

Despite his initial popularity, Salnave was unable to unify the republic. He enjoyed little support from Haiti's generals or upper classes and, by 1868, Haiti had split into four different separatist states. Salnave desperately tried to cling to power, among other means by essentially offering the United States a protectorate over Haiti. Failing in those efforts, Salnave rigged the presidential palace to explode before trying to escape across the border into the Dominican Republic. In 1870, he was captured and executed in Port-au-Prince.

Salnave's death was an explosive event, a watershed moment in Haitian history. For Janvier, the civil wars of the late 1860s dictated another period of reflection and political reform. "Everything," he wrote, "was to be reorganized after the crisis of 1868–1869."[30]

Janvier's biography is inextricable from this longer history of antislavery and anticolonial revolution, postcolonial frustrations and aspirations, and contested processes of state-building in Haiti.[31] Born in Port-au-Prince on May 7, 1855, Janvier's earliest memories included seeing his father, a coffee merchant, "engaged in casual conversation" with Soulouque before the Haitian emperor went into exile. He later remembered his father talking with Geffrard, the president who deposed Soulouque. For Janvier, those interactions must have affirmed his

---

Review Press, 1990), 92–97; André-Georges Adam, *Une crise haïtienne, 1867–1869: Sylvain Salnave* (Port-au-Prince: H. Deschamps, 1982); Anne Eller, "Raining Blood: Spiritual Power, Gendered Violence, and Anticolonial Lives in the Nineteenth-Century Dominican Borderlands," *Hispanic American Historical Review* 99, no. 3 (2019): 431–465.

30 Louis Joseph Janvier, *Les Constitutions d'Haïti (1801–1885)* (Paris: C. Marpon et E. Flammarion, 1886), 351.

31 Along with the previously cited works, foundational scholarship on nineteenth-century Haiti includes Dupuy, *Haiti in the World Economy: Class, Race, and Underdevelopment since 1700* (Boulder: Westview Press, 1989); Bellegarde Smith, *Haiti: The Breached Citadel* (Boulder: Westview Press, 1990); Michel Hector and Laënnec Hurbon, eds., *Genèse de l'État haïtien (1804–1859)* (La Rochelle: Éditions de la Maison des Sciences de l'Homme, 2009); Laurent Dubois, *Haiti: The Aftershocks of History* (New York: Henry Holt, 2012); Délide Joseph, *L'Etat haïtien et ses intellectuels: socio-histoire d'un engagement politique (1801–1860)* (Port-au-Prince: Société haïtienne d'histoire, de géographie et de géologie, 2017); Jean Casimir and Michel Hector, "Le Long 19e siècle haïtien," *Revue de la Société Haïtienne d'Histoire, de Géographie et de Géologie* 78, no. 216 (2003): 35–64; Brenda Gayle Plummer, *Haiti and the United States: The Psychological Moment* (Athens: University of Georgia Press, 2003).

family's respectable social status and influenced his sense of his own place in Haitian political life. Lessons in family history were equally important in both regards. "My grandfather ... was a personal friend of Pétion," Janvier would later recall. A colonel, he had stood with Pétion against Dessalines.[32]

Like many young Haitian men of the political and professional classes, Janvier received a private education in Port-au-Prince before going to Europe to complete his studies. In the Haitian capital, Janvier attended a primary school operated by English missionaries from the Wesleyan Church. There, he received a religious education that informed his later advocacy for the social, economic, and spiritual benefits of Protestantism for Haiti and, most importantly, Haitian peasants. Like numerous other black intellectuals of the nineteenth-century Atlantic world, his religious upbringing would influence his lifelong association of Protestantism with civilization and modernity and his definition of the "Protestant ethic" as an essential, moral component of individual material success and national progress.[33] Following his education under the guidance of the English Wesleyans, Janvier next matriculated at the prestigious Lycée National before continuing on to the École Médecine de Port-au-Prince. In 1877, having received a scholarship from the

[32] Ertha Pascal Trouillot and Ernst Trouillot, *Encyclopédie biographique d'Haïti*, vol. 2 (Montreal: Éditions SEMIS, 2001), 114. For Janvier's biography, see especially Ernst Trouillot, "Louis Joseph Janvier, le diplomate," *Revue de la Société Haïtienne d'Histoire, de Géographie et de Géologie* 24, no. 90 (July 1953): 39–56; Denis R. Watson, "Louis-Joseph Janvier, 1855–1911," in *Encyclopedia of Race and Racism*, vol. 3, ed. Patrick L. Mason, 2nd ed. (Detroit: MacMillan Reference, 2013): 1–4; Michel Acacia and Carol Macomber, "Louis-Joseph Janvier (1855–1911)," in *Dictionary of Caribbean and Afro-Latin American Biography*, ed. Franklin W. Knight and Henry Louis Gates, Jr. (New York: Oxford University Press, 2016). See also Yves Chemla's essay in the present volume.

[33] The "Clarion Call" essay includes a spirited appeal to modernize Haiti through Protestantism. These writings echo the civilizationist discourses espoused by other Black Atlantic intellectuals of the Victorian era such as Alexander Crummell, James Theodore Holly, and Henry Sylvester Williams. Scholarship on these Afro-Atlantic intellectuals includes Wilson Jeremiah Moses, *Alexander Crummell: A Study of Civilization* (New York: Oxford University Press, 1989); Marika Sherwood, *Origins of Pan-Africanism: Henry Sylvester Williams, Africa, and the African Diaspora* (New York: Routledge, 2011); Felix Jean-Louis, "Double Consciousness and Missionary Work: James Theodore Holly and the Establishment of the Episcopalian Church of Haiti," in *Global Protestant Missions: Politics, Reform and Communication, 1730s–1930s*, ed. Jenna Gibbs (New York: Routledge Press, 2019), 111–133.

Haitian government to continue his education abroad, Janvier started classes at the Faculté de Médecine, Paris. He defended his dissertation on pulmonary tuberculosis four years later and would subsequently obtain additional advanced degrees in political science and law.

Life in France afforded Janvier equally valuable opportunities for intellectual growth and community outside of the university. In 1882, he joined the Société d'anthropologie de Paris, one of the first and most influential anthropological societies in the world. His membership in that pioneering institution offered him a critical opportunity for scholarly exchange and debate; it was a place where he sharpened his ideas about a number of topics, including the intertwined subjects of race and nation. In the process of finding his voice as a scholar and critic, Janvier became a frequent guest at the salon of the poet Leconte de Lisle and an avid reader of writers such as Victor Hugo and Charles Darwin. By the 1880s he was celebrated by some members of the Parisian intelligentsia, who regarded Janvier as a model of assimilation and a testament to French civilization. In the words of one French literary critic, Janvier was "the most remarkable example of the degree of culture that the Black race can attain, this race that France has generously taken in hand and whose case before the high court of justice and of eternal rights France has settled once and for all."[34]

In Paris, Janvier also had a front-row seat to the reformulation of French empire based on the very ideals of culture and civilization for which the French intelligentsia praised him. The 1880s were a watershed moment in which Third Republic France expanded its colonial empire through an idea known as the "civilizing mission" (*mission civilisatrice*). By the early twentieth century, the French empire stretched from old possessions in the French West Indies to the massive confederations of French West Africa and French Equatorial Africa all the way to French Indochina. This imperial republic noted for its brutal treatment of colonial subjects rested paradoxically upon the ideal of French universalism: the right and the duty of "superior" civilizations, and races, to colonize those "inferior" to them.[35] Janvier's professional and intel-

---

34 "La République d'Haïti, par L. Janvier," *La Jeune France*, vol. 5: 1 Mai 1882–1 Mai 1883 (Paris: Bureaux de La Jeune France, 1883), 638.
35 On Third Republic France's "civilizing mission" see Alice L. Conklin, *A Mission to Civilize: The Republican Idea of Empire in France and West Africa, 1895–1930* (Palo Alto: Stanford University Press, 1997) and Dino Costantini, *Mission civilisatrice: le rôle de l'histoire colonial dans la construction de l'identité politique française*, trans. Juliette Ferdinand (Paris: Editions la Découverte, 2008).

lectual maturation came in Paris as Opportunist republicans like Jules Ferry and the colonial lobby took power and set about spreading French universalism simultaneously within the metropole and throughout the republic's expanding empire. Janvier was witness to the invention of the logic of France's "new imperialism," which under the banner of its civilizing mission would at once subjugate and "civilize" peoples in every corner of the globe.

He was attuned to the resurgence of other European imperialisms, too. In the waning decades of the nineteenth century, imperialists across industrializing Europe expressed similar rationales for the exploitation of people in and the extraction of material resources from the Global South. In Germany, Portugal, and especially Great Britain, intellectuals and statesmen cloaked their imperial projects in the language of a civilizing mission or burden. In this guise, rapacious European expansion for the sake of political and economic advantage was simply the means to extend "legitimate" commerce by "liberating" non-European populations from local systems of unfree labor, spread Christianity to "heathen" people, and therefore give the "gift" of "Western civilization" to the world.

The resurgent competition to "civilize" by the Bible and the gun was formalized at the Berlin West Africa Conference of 1884–1885. At the historic conference, twelve European polities, the Ottoman Empire, and the United States discussed the best means of partitioning and pillaging Africa without encouraging violent conflict among themselves. The General Act signed by all participants, with the exception of the United States, which had its own imperial plans, affirmed the need for external oversight of "native [African] tribes and ... the conditions of their moral and material well-being." It cemented the cultural rationale for the European push for guaranteed sources of raw materials, cheap labor, and exclusive markets for manufactured products.[36]

---

[36] The scholarship on European imperialism in the late nineteenth and early twentieth century is too voluminous to cite here but on the causes, consequences, and African responses to the European "scramble for Africa" see especially Steig Förster, Wolfgang J. Mommsen, and Ronald Robinson, eds., *Bismarck, Europe and Africa: The Berlin Africa Conference, 1884–1885 and the Onset of Partition* (London: Oxford University Press, 1988); H. L. Wesseling, *Divide and Rule: The Partition of Africa, 1880–1914* (London: Praeger, 1996); Femi J. Kolap and Kwabena O. Akurang-Parry, eds., *African Agency and European Colonialism: Latitudes of Negotiation and Containment* (Lanham: University Press of America, 2007); John Iliffe, *Africans: The History of a Continent* (Cambridge: Cambridge University Press, 2007), 193–250; A. Adu Boahen,

While Europeans debated the fate of Africa and Asia, the United States initiated its own imperial project, which would have especially dire consequences for Janvier's native country. Following the defeat of the Confederacy during the U.S. Civil War (1861–1865) and a brief flirtation with legal racial equality during the period of Reconstruction (1865–1877), competing regional and political factions of white Americans reconciled through not only a whitewashed memory of the late war but also a shared investment in empire and white supremacy.[37] Some leading U.S. politicians, academics, businessmen, and journalists wedded discourses of scientific racism to a relentless drive for national and corporate expansion, arguing that Anglo-Americans, like their British counterparts, had a unique fitness for self-governance and a singular burden to extend their "free" values and institutions to child-like races in the U.S. West, the Caribbean, and the Pacific.[38]

Haiti and the Dominican Republic were at the heart of their imperial designs.[39] In the years following the U.S. Civil War, well before the

African Perspectives on European Colonialism (New York: Diasporic Africa Press, 2011); Walter Rodney, *How Europe Underdeveloped Africa* (London: Verso, 2018).

37 On the politics of historical memory and reunion, see David W. Blight, *Race and Reunion: The Civil War in American Memory* (Cambridge, MA: Harvard University Press, 2002).

38 Paul Kramer, "Empires, Exceptions, and Anglo-Saxons: Race and Rule between the British and United States Empires, 1880–1910," *The Journal of American History* 88, no. 4 (March 2002): 1315–1353. Eric T.L. Love has offered a compelling reinterpretation of the age of imperialism and Jim Crow, arguing that white supremacist ideologies tempered U.S. expansionism. For his reinterpretation, see Love, *Race Over Empire: Racism & U.S. Imperialism, 1865–1900* (Chapel Hill: University of North Carolina Press, 2004). Although beyond the scope of this introduction, U.S. imperialism was intimately connected both ideologically and materially to the United States' renewed efforts at continental expansion and the military defeat and cultural assimilation of Indigenous people. For a concise overview of those genocidal campaigns and Native resistance to them, see especially Roxanne Dunbar-Ortiz, *An Indigenous Peoples' History of the United States* (Boston: Beacon Press, 2014), 162–177 and Ari Kelman, "For Liberty and Empire," *Common Place: The Journal of Early American Life* 14, no. 2 (Winter 2014), http://commonplace.online/article/for-liberty-and-empire/.

39 On U.S. attempts at expansion on the island, see especially Frank Moya Pons, *The Dominican Republic: A National History* (Princeton: Markus Wiener, 1995); G. Pope Atkins and Larman C. Wilson, *The Dominican Republic and the United States: From Imperialism to Transnationalism* (Athens, GA, 1998), 20–36; Nicholas Guyatt, "America's Conservatory: Race, Reconstruction, and the Santo

United States annexed Hawaii and claimed Cuba, Puerto Rico, the Philippines, and Guam following its victory in the Spanish-American War of 1898, U.S. governments tried to annex the Dominican Republic and secure naval bases through the acquisition of territory on the island. U.S. warships maintained a routine presence off the shores of Haiti. The persistent threat of U.S. military intervention was meant to enforce the economic "rights" of U.S. citizens in Haiti, including businessmen claiming damages from Haitian governments that seized power by force. It gave tangible, terrifying expression to the more aggressive meaning that U.S. imperialists would assign to the Monroe Doctrine—to a presumption of regional hegemony and an ethos of interventionism that would guide the U.S. expansion of empire and, eventually, the U.S. military occupation of Haiti from 1915 to 1934.[40]

Janvier paid close attention to these international developments while observing fundamental changes in Haitian politics. Reflecting on the aftermath of the political crises of the late 1860s, the eminent scholar

Domingo Debate," *The Journal of American History* 97, no. 4 (March 2011): 974–1000; Gerald Horne, *Confronting Black Jacobins: The U.S., the Haitian Revolution, and the Origins of the Dominican Republic* (New York: Monthly Review Press, 2015), 263–315; Eller, *We Dream Together*. For a prolonged explanation of Janvier's condemnations of U.S. empire, particularly president Ulysses S. Grant's efforts to annex the Dominican Republic, see also note 26 to the translation in the present volume.

40 The U.S. occupied the Dominican Republic from 1916 to 1924. Scholarship on the U.S. occupation of Haiti and the years preceding it includes Hans Schmidt, *The United States Occupation of Haiti* (New Brunswick: Rutgers University Press, 1971); Suzy Castor, *L'Occupation Américaine d'Haïti* (Port-au-Prince: Centre de recherche et de formation économique et sociale pour le développement, 1988); Brenda Gayle Plummer, *Haiti and the Great Powers, 1902–1915* (Baton Rouge: Louisiana State University Press, 1988); Mary A. Renda, *Taking Haiti: Military Occupation and the Culture of US Imperialism, 1915–1940* (Chapel Hill: University of North Carolina Press, 2001); Millery Polyné, *From Douglass to Duvalier: U.S. African Americans, Haiti, and Pan Americanism, 1870–1964* (Gainesville: University Press of Florida, 2010); Jeffrey Sommers, *Race, Reality, and Realpolitik: U.S.–Haiti Relations in the Lead Up to the 1915 Occupation* (Lanham: Lexington Books, 2016); Peter James Hudson, *Bankers and Empire: How Wall Street Colonized the Caribbean* (Chicago: University of Chicago Press, 2017); Patrick Bellegarde-Smith, *In the Shadow of Powers: Dantès Bellegarde in Haitian Social Thought* (Nashville: Vanderbilt University Press, 2019); Yveline Alexis, *Haiti Fights Back: The Life and Legacy of Charlemagne Péralte* (New Brunswick: Rutgers University Press, 2021).

of Haiti Michel-Rolph Trouillot would later argue that "Haiti came as close as it ever has to an effective parliamentary experience."[41] It was a transformative moment that inaugurated a transition towards a modern party-based system in Haiti. Two competing political parties emerged out of Haiti's longstanding regional and ideological divisions: Liberals and Nationals. The Liberal Party had support in Haiti's capital as well as in its major southern port cities of Jacmel, Miragoâne, and Jérémie. The party called for "Government by the Most Competent" while espousing a program of financial reform and economic liberalism that, for some Liberals, included the relaxation of Haiti's traditional prohibitions on foreign landownership.[42] Its membership consisted primarily of urban merchants, traders, and prominent elites; it drew support largely but certainly not exclusively from Haitians who would have been considered *milat*.[43] In contrast, the National Party was committed to a program of economic nationalism and drew its support from the rural elite, the peasantry in Haiti's southern peninsula, and the proletariat in Port-au-Prince. Its base was mainly composed of large-scale landowners, planters, and military men—a rural bourgeoisie who tended to be darker-skinned.[44]

Living in France, Janvier was neither engaged in the on-the-ground political operations of the National Party nor involved in

41 Trouillot, *Haiti, State against Nation*, 98.
42 Liberal president Boyer Bazelais apparently adapted the liberal economic formula "laisser faire" into Haitian Creole as "laisser grainnin" (*lese grennen*), or letting things happen as they will (or, more literally, letting seeds spread on their own). Many thanks to Laura Wagner for sharing her expertise on this phrase.
43 *Milat* is the Haitian Creole term used to refer to what has traditionally been a predominantly lighter-skinned Haitian elite. Nevertheless, the term acknowledges both phenotype and class, as expressed in the Haitian proverb "The rich black is mulatto, the poor mulatto is black" ("Nèg riche se milat, milat pov se nèg"). For a discussion of this proverb and the historical nexus of color, class, and social status in Haiti, see Michel-Rolph Trouillot, "Culture, Color, and Politics in Haiti," in *Race*, ed. Steven Gregory and Roger Sanjek (New Brunswick: Rutgers University Press, 1994), 146–174. For further discussion of the term *milat*, see Matthew J. Smith, *Red and Black in Haiti: Radicalism, Conflict, and Political Change, 1934–1957* (Chapel Hill: University of North Carolina Press, 2009), 198.
44 Stieber, *Haiti's Paper War*, 201–226. The divisions between Liberal and National parties that we outline here pertain to the 1870s and early 1880s. In the late 1880s and early 1890s, both parties underwent significant political and demographic transformations. Those changes were particularly pronounced in the Liberal Party under the leadership of Edmond Paul. See Claude B. Auguste, "Réflexions sur l'histoire mouvementée et combien dramatique du Parti Libéral," *Revue de la Société Haïtienne d'Histoire, de Géographie et de Géologie*, no. 237 (2009): 5–37.

Haitian legislation during the period of the party's hegemony, which was achieved in the presidency of Lysius Salomon (1879–1888). Still, Janvier's affiliation with the National Party is apparent across his work. In particular, his essays written after 1883 often focused on Haiti's internal political divisions and critiqued members of the Liberal Party as "les antinationaux" and "les pseudo-libéraux." His expressions of contempt for the Liberal Party and their politics show how Janvier conceived of Haitian electoral politics and the reforms he wished to see in government.

In particular, the question of land reform—that enduring and unresolved issue in Haitian society—became the central node in Janvier's National politics. By the late nineteenth century, Haiti had more equitable access to land than comparable post-slavery societies. By some estimates, a third of Haitian peasants formally owned small plots of land, typically ranging in size from 3 to 10 *carreaux*. The remaining two-thirds either resided on land to which they did not have formal title or worked land owned by others as sharecroppers or tenant farmers. As claimants and workers of the land, the heterogeneous population of Haitian peasants faced similar struggles. Little credit or cash was made available to rural laborers to support their agricultural production while the merchant bourgeoisie and its intermediaries exerted significant control over the process through which cash crops such as coffee were valued and sold at market. Likewise, the production of those crops depended on access to sufficient amounts of arable land but the declining size of the average peasant landholding, along with the problem of soil erosion, tended to diminish crop yields. For some of the most destitute among Haiti's growing population, migration became the key to unlocking a better life. By the turn of the twentieth century, an increasing number of Haitian migrant workers were moving in search of work to foreign countries such as Cuba and the Dominican Republic.[45]

---

45 On the Haitian peasantry and the topic of land reform in late nineteenth-century Haiti, see especially Paul Moral, *Le Paysan haïtien: étude sur la vie rurale en Haïti* (Port-au-Prince: Éditions Fardin, 1978); Mats Lundhal, *Peasants and Poverty: A Study of Haiti* (London: Croom Helm, 1979), 255–296; Lundahl, *The Haitian Economy: Man, Land, and Markets* (London: Croom Helm, 1983), 67–153; Dupuy, *Haiti in the World Economy*, 85–113; Trouillot, *Haiti, State against Nation*, 59–82. Scholarship on Haitian migrant labor in the late nineteenth and early twentieth centuries includes Lundahl, *The Haitian Economy*, 94–152 and Matthew Casey, *Empire's Guestworkers: Haitian Migrants in Cuba during the Age of the US Occupation* (Cambridge: Cambridge University Press, 2017).

For Janvier, "land to the peasant" was thus "the keystone of the edifice of our reconstruction, the cement of the system, the granite foundation upon which we can build everything."[46] Although by the 1880s the Haitian state remained the largest landowner and rentier in Haiti, land redistribution had ceased to be a priority of Haitian governments. Instead, land more often changed hands as a consequence of the rapid political changes at the national level, as a reward for favored partisans and punishment for political enemies. Janvier saw this situation as an untenable continuation of past failures, which included Boyer's 1826 Rural Code. According to Janvier, that onerous set of laws created "two nations within the nation."[47] It was tantamount to "slavery without the whip."[48]

Janvier's commitment to land reform explains not just his critique of Boyer but his support and defense of Salomon. In February 1883, the Haitian president departed from some of the trends of his era, although affirming others, by issuing a law that offered five to eight *carreaux* of public land to peasants. While the law had an article lessening restrictions against foreign landownership in Haiti, it stipulated that peasants would receive permanent title to the land if they cultivated export crops such as coffee on the greater part of their land grants for a period of two to five years.[49]

As scholars such as Gordon K. Lewis have noted, the egalitarianism implied in Janvier's concern for the plight of Haiti's peasant majority should not be overstated or decontextualized.[50] As Janvier wrote in *L'Égalité des races*, he advocated service of "the good of the greatest number, for the honor of all."[51] His understanding of governance resembled that of Demesvar Delorme, another Haitian writer and intellectual, and a contemporary of Janvier, who characterized democracy as government for, not necessarily by, the people.[52] Janvier's political philosophy was no doubt influenced by the ascendant political ideas

---

46 Janvier, *L'Égalité des races* (Paris: Imprimerie G. Rougier et Cie, 1884), 11.
47 Janvier, *Les Constitutions d'Haïti*, 152.
48 Ibid., 149.
49 The program achieved modest success, attracting approximately 1,700 applicants in 1884 and 1885. Janvier, *Les Constitutions d'Haïti*.
50 Gordon K. Lewis, *Main Currents in Caribbean Thought* (Baltimore: Johns Hopkins University Press, 1987), 261–264.
51 Janvier, *L'Égalité*, 8.
52 Ibid. On nineteenth-century Haitian thought, see also Bellegarde-Smith, "Haitian Social Thought in the Nineteenth Century: Class Formation and Westernization," *Caribbean Studies* 20, no. 1 (March 1980): 5–23.

and bodies of the nineteenth-century Atlantic world, including those related to the relationship among international law, property, and national sovereignty.[53] In his understanding, the Haitian government had to assume the form and functions of the liberal democratic state, which would include an investment in education and other public services, ostensibly through taxes, including those on land held through formal titles. The *raison d'être* of Janvier's envisioned state was plain: to support the economic, social, and cultural "development" of Haitian peasants as part of a grander political project of modernization and national progress. Assuring the "productivity" of peasants, Janvier reasoned, was not just in the economic interest of the Haitian state, which experienced a declining gross national product during Janvier's lifetime, but also inseparable from its political sovereignty.

Even as Janvier's statism contained more than a hint of elitism and paternalism born of his class status, self-image, cultural values, and the nature of his education, it rested on a sharp critique of the political and socioeconomic relations born out of colonial systems, old and new. In the final decades of the nineteenth century, foreign capital increasingly penetrated into Haiti, accelerating a trend that would coalesce in the concessions granted to foreign corporations such as the firm Frères Simmond and the railroad company of James MacDonald.[54] Wary of these trends and their logical outcomes—the consolidation of land and property by foreigners—Janvier affirmed the historical opposition to foreign landownership in Haiti, which was a fixture in Haitian constitutions since 1805.[55] He critiqued the

---

53 Jürgen Osterhammel, *The Transformation of the World: A Global History of the Nineteenth Century* (Princeton: Princeton University Press, 2014), 572–633. Janvier would, for example, be a key participant at the international conference in Berne, which resulted in the adoption of the landmark international copyright law, the Berne Convention for the Protection of Literary and Artistic Works (1886). As Haiti's representative at the meetings preceding the convention, he successfully argued for the free reproduction and translation of scientific and medical works on the basis that such knowledge belonged not to the Europeans who currently claimed ownership of it but to all of humanity. See The International Bureau of Intellectual Property, *The Berne Convention for the Protection of Literary and Artistic Works from 1886 to 1986* (Geneva: International Bureau of Intellectual Property, 1986), https://www.legalanthology.ch/t/wipo_berne-convention_1986.pdf, and Sara Bannerman, *International Copyright and Access to Knowledge* (Cambridge: Cambridge University Press, 2016).

54 Dupuy, *Haiti in the World Economy*, 126–142.

55 Ratified in 1805, Haiti's first national constitution prohibited foreigners from purchasing property in Haiti and limited citizenship to "Africans and Indians."

economic proposals of the Liberal Party, which advocated liberalizing trade and exploring new market opportunities, most notably in Europe. In an era when Europe's imperial powers demanded trade monopolies and the type of direct economic control foundational to colonial rule, Janvier supported the building of Haiti's national industries. His opposition to allowing foreign banks into Haiti evinced a shrewd understanding that those institutions would invariably finance foreign companies and expatriate communities while discriminating against Haitians, including peasants who might benefit from more access to credit. As Janvier argues throughout *Haïti aux Haïtiens*, and with particular force in the essay "The Trap," Haiti could not afford to enter into more uneven trade agreements or fall prey to the *laissez-faire* market liberalism championed by some Liberals. Foreign debt meant foreign domination, he concluded. And economic dependence entailed the forfeiture of sovereignty.

Constructed within the changing political and economic environments of Haiti and the late nineteenth-century Atlantic world, Janvier's economic nationalism was not only coherent with his calls for land reform but also insistent on Haiti's territorial integrity. For an observer like Janvier, the threat of foreign intervention in Haiti was all too real. By the late nineteenth century, laws restricting the commercial activities of foreigners in Haiti had been loosened or were simply not enforced. Haitian generals and politicians routinely tried to take or keep power by playing the imperial powers against each other, often by offering economic and even territorial concessions.

In *Haïti aux Haïtiens*, Janvier proclaims that Haitians "cannot abdicate our sovereignty over any point of the territory without shame, without humiliation" and insists that Haiti must reassert its ownership of its satellite islands at a time when the United States and its citizens tried to seize and exploit those guano-rich lands.[56] He even argues

---

Both laws guarded against the return of slavery and colonialism to Haiti. Subsequent constitutions promulgated before 1889 upheld the racial barriers to Haitian citizenship; the ban on foreign landholding in Haiti remained in force until the United States occupation of Haiti (1915–1934). On the constitutional history of Haiti, see especially Janvier, *Les Constitutions d'Haïti*; Claude Moïse, *Constitutions et luttes de pouvoir en Haïti, 1804–1987* (Montreal: Éditions du CIDIHCA, 1988); Julia Gaffield, "Complexities of Imagining Haiti: A Study of National Constitutions, 1801–1807," *Journal of Social History* 41, no. 1 (Fall 2007): 81–103.

56 See Janvier, *Haiti for the Haitians*, 50 in this volume. See also Jimmy M. Skaggs, *The Great Guano Rush: Entrepreneurs and American Overseas*

that Haiti had to reclaim adjacent islands that were then part of the Dominican Republic. According to Janvier, Haiti had never ceded Isla Beata and Isla Alto Velo even after the Dominican Republic declared its independence from Haiti in 1844. He asserted that Haiti had to govern the contested islands because "they are almost situated in our territorial waters, too close to our coasts, too close to Jacmel for us to let any flag fly there other than the one flown in Port-au-Prince."[57]

Janvier's allusion to the threat of foreign intervention—to the inevitable consequences should Haiti permit foreign claims to territories so close to its borders—is part of a much longer political and intellectual tradition in which Haitian political actors tied the anticolonial and antislavery project of the Haitian Revolution to the defense of the entire island. Beginning with Toussaint Louverture's government in 1801, continuing through Boyer's authoritarian republic, and persisting in Faustin Soulouque's monarchy in the 1850s, various Haitian leaders tried to and sometimes did consolidate the island under one unified government.[58] Those men, some formerly enslaved, were fully aware of the close proximity of the Spanish colony of Cuba, the British colony of Jamaica, and the southern United States. Understanding the tenuous nature of black sovereignty in a region dominated by slaveholding nations and empires, they insisted that a politically divided island would enable Europe or the United States to undermine Haiti's sovereignty and undo its antislavery revolution from the island's eastern two-thirds.

This history has often been read as imperial by scholars and publics influenced by the rhetoric of nineteenth-century Dominican elites. In an era of ascendant and imperial European and U.S. nationalisms, at a time when whiteness became entrenched as the measure of civilization

Expansion (New York: St. Martin's Press, 1994); Gregory T. Cushman, *Guano and the Opening of the Pacific World: A Global Ecological History* (New York: Cambridge University Press, 2013); Tao Leigh Goffe, "'Guano in Their Destiny': Race, Geology, and Philosophy of Indenture," *Amerasia Journal* 45, no. 1 (June 2019): 27–49.

57 Janvier, *Haiti for the Haitians*, 72–73.

58 Attempts to unify the island precede Haitian independence. Toussaint Louverture took Santo Domingo in 1800 and in 1801 the Spanish ceded the territory on the eastern side of the island to him. Jean-Jacques Dessalines tried but failed to reunify the east in 1805. When Jean-Pierre Boyer unified east and west in 1822, he relied on a mandate in the constitution that there be only one republic on the island. In 1844, Haitian president Charles Rivière Hérard marched on the east to attempt to thwart Dominican independence and bring the territory back into Haitian control. President-turned-Emperor Faustin Soulouque launched two failed attempts to retake the east.

within the Eurocentric international order, a vocal minority of writers and politicians in Santo Domingo tried to strengthen their nascent national project by criticizing Haiti's. They characterized Dominicans as white, Christian, Spanish, and civilized, and Haitians as black, heathen, African, and barbaric. They recast Boyer's unification of the east as an "invasion" and "occupation" in which Dominicans were subjected to the rule of "savages" from the west. They insisted that the Dominican Republic and Haiti had separate national histories, the former defined by progress, the latter by decline. That revisionist narrative has proven obstinate and influential. It persists in scholarship that emphasizes the ostensibly hegemonic racial conflict between Haitians and Dominicans and in popular understandings of Dominican nationhood, which mythologize the Dominican Republic as the only nation in the Western Hemisphere to win its freedom from another American state.[59]

In contrast, Janvier's claims about the extent and integrity of Haiti's territory invoked a more nuanced history of trans-island solidarity overlooked by his contemporaries and future generations alike. As historian Anne Eller has shown, Haitian-Dominican rural and peasant solidarities developed during the first decades of the nineteenth century. Those solidarities were rooted in the shared experience of colonialism, enslavement, and the common pursuit of land and autonomy. There was a shared struggle, Eller writes, that transcended colonial borders and was "directed to defense of the whole island against outside hostility, which many understood to be constant."[60]

This history of common cause was evident in 1861 when guerrillas from Haiti and the Dominican Republic fought together against Spain, which had annexed the Dominican Republic upon the invitation of Dominican elites. Their resistance was long and hard but ultimately

---

59 Eller, *We Dream Together*, 1–20, 229–236. Samuel Martinez offers a necessary critique of what he calls this "fatal-conflict model" in his review of Michele Wucker's influential book *Why the Cocks Fight: Dominicans, Haitians, and the Struggle for Hispaniola* (New York: Hill & Wang, 1999). See Martinez, "Not a Cockfight: Rethinking Haitian-Dominican Relations," *Latin American Perspectives* 30, no. 3, Popular Participation against Neoliberalism (May 2003): 80–101. In *The Borders of Dominicanidad: Race, Nation, and Archives of Contradiction* (Durham, NC: Duke University Press, 2016), Latinx Studies scholar Lorgia García-Peña offers an excellent theoretical and historical analysis of Dominican racial and national identity. On race, civilization, and the "sisterhood of nations" in the nineteenth century, see especially Gaffield, "The Racialization of International Law."
60 Eller, *We Dream Together*, 15.

successful. At the end of the War of Restoration (1861–1865), the Dominican Republic regained its independence and the Dominican and Haitian governments signed an agreement requiring both parties not to "cede, pledge, or alienate in favor of any foreign power either the whole or any part of their territories."[61]

The ink had barely dried, however, when U.S. president Ulysses S. Grant, with the encouragement of Dominican president Buenaventura Báez, tried to annex the Dominican Republic to the United States and then acquire Haiti, as Grant later admitted. His attempts failed in the U.S. Senate but the Dominican Republic's rural majority rose again against annexation, aided by Haitians. Some dissidents even renewed calls for an anticolonial confederation of Haiti, Cuba, Puerto Rico, and the Dominican Republic.[62]

Janvier hinted at this history of island-wide anti-imperial resistance through his use of toponyms in *Haïti aux Haïtiens*. His references to Haiti and the Dominican Republic as the "Afro-Latin Republics of Haiti" are evocative of the precolonial history of the island and the more recent island-wide struggles against annexationism. His characterizations of himself and his compatriots as "Western Haitians," and thus his implicit invocation of "Eastern Haitians," functioned as both a critique of elite annexationist politics on both sides of the island and an affirmation of the historical island-wide fight against slavery, in defense of popular autonomy and self-rule.[63]

As evident in his appeals to past and present solidarities across the island, Janvier's populism, particularly his advocacy for Haitian peasants

---

61 Atkins and Wilson, *The Dominican Republic and the United States*, 24.
62 Eller, *We Dream Together*, 229–236.
63 Louis-Joseph Janvier, *Haïti aux Haïtiens*, 2nd ed. (Paris: Imprimerie A. Parent, A. Davy, Successeurs, 1884), 22. Janvier's very deliberate choice of geographic place names is worth parsing here. He does not refer to the east as the "République Dominicaine," nor is the entire island referred to as "Hispaniola" (or Española, the imperial toponym bestowed on the island by Christopher Columbus) or "Quisqueya." Instead, he refers to both sides of "Haïti," evoking the shared indigenous Taíno toponym Ayti (or Ayiti), meaning "land of mountains," and the heritage of anticolonial, antislavery independence marked by Jean-Jacques Dessalines's naming of Haiti. Moreover, as Eller notes, independentists in the east declared their state "Spanish Haiti" in 1821, and Dominicans referred to the Island of Haiti during the Boyer period. Janvier is thus evoking the longer shared history of anticolonial independence on both sides of the island. On the naming of Haiti, see David Geggus, "The Naming of Haiti," *NWIG: New West Indian Guide/Nieuwe West-Indische Gids* 70, nos. 1–2 (1997): 43–68. On the various toponyms for the island and their politics, see Eller, *We Dream Together*, 238 n. 5.

and demands for land reform, did not just undergird his economic nationalism and encourage his ideas about territorial integrity. Instead, it nurtured an anticolonial and anti-racist politics that evolved in his public writings. *Les Détracteurs de la race noire* (1882), *La République d'Haïti et ses visiteurs* (1883) and *L'Égalité des races* (1884)—Janvier's earliest attempts at deconstructing imperial projects and racist ideologies in their moment of formation—appeared in essay collections and articles published in French newspapers.[64] These initial public writings were polemical essays that refuted libelous articles and essays published in the French press about Haiti. In *Les Détracteurs de la race noire*, for example, Janvier mobilized a group of Haitian writers living in France to pen letters in response to an article by the French journalist Léo Quesnel titled "Anciennes colonies françaises: Haïti" published in *La Revue politique et littéraire*.[65] In that incendiary piece, Quesnel had argued that Haiti's "failure" to constitute a functioning post-independence society was proof of the inherent inequality of human races. In response, Janvier refuted Quesnel's arguments point by point, offering Haiti's nineteenth-century progress and the maintenance of its

---

64 Janvier published with a variety of different Parisian publishing houses during the 1880s, a period during which print production expanded rapidly with technological innovations and a relaxing of the press laws after the fall of the second empire in France. Janvier's publishers ranged from the mainstream house of C. Marpon et E. Flammarion to lesser-known houses such as Rougier et Cie and A. Parent et A. Davy. Flammarion had founded his new house in collaboration with the bookstore owner Charles Marpon in the 1870s, publishing a broad range of works. A. Parent et A. Davy specialized in publishing medical research, while Rougier et Cie branched out into horticultural and numismatic studies, in addition to medicine, wide-ranging topics. See Roger Chartier and Henry-Jean Martin, eds., *Histoire de l'édition française*, T. 3 (Paris: Promodis, 1985) and Jean-Yves Mollier, *L'Argent et les lettres, histoire du capitalism d'édition (1880–1920)* (Paris: Fayard, 1988). The press was expanding throughout the Americas during the same period. On the press in Haiti, see Jean Desquiron, *Haïti à la une: une anthologie de la presse haïtienne de 1724 à 1934*, 3 vols (Port-au-Prince: 1993–1997) and Max Bissainthe, *Dictionnaire de Bibliographie Haïtienne* (Washington, DC: The Scarecrow Press, 1951). See also note 57 in the translation of *Haiti for the Haitians* below. For a recent study of the nineteenth-century press in Mexico, see Corinna Zeltsman, *Ink under the Fingernails: Printing Politics in Nineteenth-Century Mexico* (Oakland: University of California Press, 2021).
65 Léo Quesnel, "Anciennes colonies française: Haiti," *La Revue politque et littéraire* no. 3 (21 janvier 1882). Quesnel's piece was ostensibly a review of the French travel writer Edgar la Selve's 1881 book *Le pays des nègres*, though it was for the most part a critique of Haiti's "failed state" status.

political independence against colonial and imperial threats as evidence against Quesnel's lies about black inferiority.

In adopting the role of polemical defender, Janvier advanced a well-established nineteenth-century tradition of Haitian writers who defended their country against its many detractors. During the first decades following the declaration of Haitian independence, writers such as Baron de Vastey and Juste Chanlatte championed Haiti's anticolonial, antislavery independence in an Atlantic public sphere that often sought to delegitimize their state and their writing. Vastey was especially influential in establishing what Daut calls "Black Atlantic humanism." As Daut explains, Black Atlantic humanism was an intellectual, discursive practice that challenged colonial slavery and racism and demanded the recognition of black humanity in the print public sphere. It indexes a specifically Haitian, written mode of "challenging color prejudice and the strategies of argumentation deployed to contest the theories and material practices that have supported myriad forms of colonial violence against black people across the Atlantic World."[66]

Yet, even as Janvier took part in that longer, Haitian tradition of Black Atlantic humanism, his work, like that of his forebears, would expand in the wake of an immediate crisis. The civil war of 1883 was in many ways the culmination of the political reorganization that followed the crisis of 1868–1869. The Liberal Party dominated the early 1870s, taking most of the seats in Haiti's parliament and implementing a reformist agenda alongside the Liberal president, Nissage Saget. In 1874, the National Party seized power by boycotting parliamentary sessions and forcing the election of its candidate, Michel Domingue. Prominent Liberals then regrouped in exile in Jamaica and St. Thomas, before returning to power in 1876 and installing a new president, Pierre Théoma Boisrond-Canal.

Their ascension did not resolve lingering political disputes as the remainder of the decade was fraught with divisions within the Liberal Party. In particular, a rift emerged between the faction led by Canal (*canalistes*) and that organized around the party's founder, Boyer Bazelais (*bazelaisistes*).[67] This infighting proved disastrous for the Liberals in the 1879 elections, which established a parliamentary majority for the National Party and cleared the way for the election of Salomon, its presidential candidate, who was once again living in

---

66 Marlene Daut, *Baron de Vastey and the Origins of Black Atlantic Humanism* (New York: Palgrave Macmillan, 2017), xxi.
67 Auguste, "Réflexions."

exile in Kingston. This time it was Bazelais and the Liberal Party who attempted to secure their political interests by boycotting the presidential election. After Bazelais was accused of firing his gun in the chamber of the national assembly, he and his supporters barricaded themselves in his home and for several days exchanged fire with military forces. Bazelais eventually went into exile in Jamaica, arriving in the British colony as Salomon returned triumphant to Haiti.[68]

In office, Salomon faced immediate, violent opposition from Liberals, who opposed his National Party agenda that included the 1883 land reform law. A few weeks after Salomon passed his law, Boyer Bazelais and more than one hundred other Liberal partisans invaded Mirogoâne, a major port town and a Liberal stronghold in Haiti's southern peninsula. The insurgents took control of the town with relative ease; soon their movement spread throughout the southern peninsula and established strongholds in Jérémie in the far southwest, and in Jacmel, just 40 kilometers south of Port-au-Prince. While Janvier attributed the 1883 Liberal Insurrection to Salomon's land reform, subsequent historians, such as Claude Auguste, have argued that Boyer Bazelais and his supporters simply calculated that they could not return to power through any other means.

In the Haitian capital, Salomon's failed attempts to quell the insurrection and his government's accusations that officials and businessmen in Jamaica were aiding the Liberal insurgents fueled diplomatic tensions with the British government. Salomon responded by appealing for U.S. and French assistance against the British and he eventually purchased a U.S. warship, the *Dessalines*, to blockade the Liberal strongholds in Haiti's southern peninsula. His action had minimal immediate effect. Throughout the summer, the Liberals fortified their positions and, by September 1883, their insurrection reached Port-au-Prince. The insurgents then took their fight to the streets of the Haitian capital but ultimately failed to secure popular support from its residents. On September 22 and 23, government troops aided by Port-au-Prince's popular classes marked their victory over the insurgents by setting fire to numerous buildings and businesses in the Haitian capital.[69]

---

68 Ibid., 11. Auguste notes that Bazelais's brothers, a senator, and a hundred other victims died in the fighting. On the shuttling back and forth into exile of Nationals and Liberals during this period, see Smith, *Liberty, Fraternity, Exile*.
69 Janvier, *Les Constitutions*, 496. See also Smith, *Liberty, Fraternity, Exile*, 224–230.

A civil war that implicated the citizens and governments of the United States, France, and Great Britain not only exposed rifts in Haiti's domestic politics but revealed the fragility of its international standing. As flames engulfed Port-au-Prince, imperial powers sprung into action to protect their business interests and members of their expatriate communities. On September 23, 1883, the British consul, along with the representatives of other foreign governments in Port-au-Prince, warned Salomon that they would command their warships to fire upon the national palace if the Haitian president did not or could not quell the disorder in the capital. Taking heed of that dire warning, Salomon managed to restore order to Port-au-Prince. The Liberal uprising ended soon thereafter, when Boyer Bazelais died in Miragoâne in October.

Salomon's victory was hard won and costly; it was cause for celebration in some corners but also reflection. Boyer Bazelais's failed uprising, particularly the destruction to homes and businesses in Port-au-Prince and the consequent impact on national commerce, heightened the stakes for Salomon's government. It clarified the urgency of Janvier's anticolonial, nationalist project. Haiti was tasked with recovering from another civil conflict that had stemmed in large part from the country's unequal integration into the international community and made it even more vulnerable to intensifying pressures from the world's ascendant imperial powers.

Following the events of the 1883 civil war, Janvier's published texts focused more on addressing Haiti's contemporary conflicts and less on its misrepresentations in the French press. He moved from his stringent defense of Haiti abroad towards a more critical analysis of Haiti's politics, culture, and socioeconomic life, assessing them in relation to broader trends and structures in the late nineteenth-century world. As historians Catts Pressoir, Hénock Trouillot, and Ernst Trouillot noted, Janvier's later work is remarkable for its pointed critiques of Haitian society and politics, even as it continued to refute racist characterizations of Haiti. They aptly describe his writings as marked by candor: they went "straight to the point" and offered "the most penetrating critique" of Haiti's "traditional public mores and the country's institutions."[70]

In that regard, Janvier inserted himself into another tradition of Haitian criticism. Decades earlier, Vastey had argued that such public introspection was essential, even if it exposed Haiti to the scorn of its many detractors. Reflecting on the need to address the civil war between

---

[70] Catts Pressoir, Hénock Trouillot, and Ernst Trouillot, *Historiographie d'Haïti* (Mexico City: Pan American Institute of Geography and History, 1953), 259.

Pétion and Christophe, he had asked, "Why expose our wounds out in the open? Must we lift the veil that covers them? Well! How can we heal them if we don't have the nerve to plumb their depths?"[71] Janvier's critical analysis of Haiti in the immediate aftermath of its recent civil war recalls Vastey's argument. It, too, insists on plumbing the depths of Haiti's divisions to resolve its internal conflicts and secure Haiti's sovereignty in a world hostile to its existence.

Janvier wrote the essays in *Haïti aux Haïtiens* in this transitional moment in which he maintained his earlier interest in defending Haiti abroad but identified an immediate and equally urgent need to address the causes and consequences of the recent civil war, as well as the unresolved issues that it had laid bare. First published in June 1884 by the Parisian publishing house A. Parent and A. Davy, *Haïti aux Haïtiens* quickly sold out its first printing. A second edition soon followed. The version of *Haïti aux Haïtiens* published in August 1884 celebrates the success of the first printing and contains an additional essay, "The Trap."

It is in this essay especially that Janvier exposes the late nineteenth-century colonialism of finance and capital and addressed the threat that debt posed to Haitian sovereignty. In "The Trap," Janvier predicts that "seizing upon the first pretext, which they will provoke themselves as needed, helped by unscrupulous legislators or advocates of the extreme colonial policy, they will send ships to our ports to display mizzenmasts bearing the military ensign and scuttle armed with steel canons."[72] His warning that foreign nations would impose an occupation on Haiti to protect their financial interests forewarns of the 1915 U.S. occupation of Haiti with chilling prescience. Even more so than the earlier essays, "The Trap" demonstrates Janvier's enduring role as defender of Haiti and the more critical political analysis that he applied to a fraught moment that, in his view, held two divergent possibilities for Haiti: a progression towards the type of national sovereignty that would fulfill the promise of the Haitian Revolution or a retreat into colonial dependence, which was tantamount to re-enslavement.

This duality helps explain Janvier's positionality and target audiences in *Haïti aux Haïtiens*. In the foreword to that publication

---

71 Baron de Vastey, *Essai sur les causes de la révolution et des guerres civiles d'Hayti* (Sans Souci: Imprimerie royale, 1819), 106.
72 Janvier, *Haiti for the Haitians*, 77.

Janvier proclaims "I am Haitian" and announces that he wrote from a point of view that is "strictly and selfishly Haitian."[73] His self-identification is clear; his audiences are both explicit and implied. Most clearly, Janvier writes to his "brothers from the other side" ("frères de l'autre côté")—his Haitian compatriots with whom he disagrees, his rivals from the Liberal Party. Yet his implied audience is the cosmopolitan lettered sphere in Paris: both the French and the expatriate elite who found themselves in the French capital at the end of the nineteenth century. Even his insistence on his Haitianness and his Haitian addressee seem to be staked out within this cosmopolitan context. Those rhetorical gestures mark Janvier as a capable, even sympathetic, analyst and critic of Haitian politics, rather than a typical outsider, who might observe Haiti through a colonial, anthropological lens.

Haïti aux Haïtiens is therefore coherent with the historical characteristics of Haitian writing. Since Haiti's founding, Haitian writers have had to address—perform for—multiple print publics, both local and foreign, ally and adversary.[74] The fact of Haiti's unequal power relationship to the self-proclaimed "civilized nations" of the world meant that Haitians were keenly aware that they were never just writing for one specific audience but were instead addressing a larger North Atlantic print public that was measuring their "progress" and, by extension, the "progress" of the black race. Janvier was equally cognizant of that context. In writing about Haiti from Third Republic France, he was just as attentive to his multiple audiences.

The content of Janvier's multivalent address is no less complex; it demands explication and analysis, beginning with the very title under which it was published. "Haïti aux Haïtiens" is both alluring and ambiguous. Seemingly transparent, it is an argument about nation and nationalism, about a people and a state, that refuses to reveal the full substance of its claims. It is a declaration that begs more subtle yet substantive questions. Who were the Haitians who had the implied, inviolable claim on Haiti? To whom did Haiti not belong? And what then defined that place declared for Haitians? What was Haiti and what could it be?

73 Ibid., 47.
74 Doris L. Garraway, "Print, Publics, and the Scene of Universal Equality in the Kingdom of Henry Christophe," *L'Esprit créateur* 56, no. 1 (2016): 82–100. On multiple addressees within print publics, see Michael Warner, "Publics and Counterpublics," *Public Culture* 14, no. 1 (2002): 49–90.

This volume, the first critical translation and interdisciplinary interpretation of Janvier and his text, explores these pressing questions. Following the translation of the second edition of *Haïti aux Haïtiens* by Nadève Ménard and preceding an afterword by Jean Casimir, six scholars offer interpretations of Janvier and *Haïti aux Haïtiens*. These scholars come from a range of academic fields, including English, History, Haitian Studies, French and Francophone Studies, and Africana Studies. Their diverse perspectives complement rather than conflict. While this volume differs in scope and aim from a biography of Janvier, the breadth of scholarly viewpoints offered within will hopefully contribute to a more comprehensive treatment of his life and times.

Taken together, the essays offer the type of interdisciplinarity required of Janvier, a Black Atlantic thinker who saw bridges, not barriers, between literary genres and academic disciplines. It endeavors to think with, not simply about, an intellectual who was undisciplined in the service of activist scholarship. In a diverse body of writing that included polemical essays on domestic and foreign politics, historical analyses, sociological observations, and several novels, Janvier moved seamlessly among political economy, race and culture, religion, medicine, constitutional law, diplomacy, and myriad other subjects. His work suggests that acceptance of the disciplinary project of the U.S. and European academies—that conformity to the disciplines that became increasingly hegemonic and detached from one another in the nineteenth century—was inadequate to the present needs, not just the professional study, of Haitian life and culture. It demonstrates a strong tendency towards the sort of intellectual exploration and anticolonial and anti-racist dissent that germinated within post-independence Haitian writing and has since been ingrained in and advanced by Africana Studies and Haitian Studies, two interdisciplinary or even counterdisciplinary projects that have centered the perspectives of black people, challenged racist intellectual categories, and embraced the twin imperatives of study and struggle.[75]

In the spirit of Janvier's work and the intellectual traditions to which he was both indebted and foundational, this volume begins with the

---

75 On Black Studies, see especially Manning Marable, "Introduction: Black Studies and the Racial Mountain," in *Dispatches from the Ebony Tower: Intellectuals Confront the African American Experience* (New York: Columbia University Press, 2000), 1–28; Fabio Rojas, *From Black Power to Black Studies: How a Radical Social Movement Became an Academic Discipline* (Baltimore: Johns Hopkins University Press, 2007); *The Black Scholar* 50, no. 3, Special Issue: What Was Black Studies (Fall 2020); Abdul Alkalimat, *The History of Black Studies* (London: Pluto Press, 2021).

first English translation of "Louis-Joseph Janvier, Écrivain National," Yves Chemla's pioneering article on Janvier. First published in 2005, Chemla's article remains one of the most comprehensive and rigorous treatments of Janvier's life and writings. His careful presentation of each of Janvier's published works remains a vital point of entry for any scholar looking to familiarize themselves with the totality of Janvier's wide range of literary, scholarly, and journalistic production. In particular, Chemla's attention to Janvier's novelistic output offers significant insights, especially for literary scholars and historians. His close reading of Janvier's 1889 novel *Une chercheuse*, for instance, draws important connections to novels published by Janvier's contemporaries and provides a useful point of departure for further explorations of late nineteenth-century Haitian literature.

As Marlene Daut shows in her essay, increased attention to Janvier has the potential to elucidate nineteenth-century Haiti's understudied transnational connections and its intellectual heritage. While Janvier is often overshadowed in critical literature on the period by several of his contemporaries, namely the Haitian intellectual and statesman Anténor Firmin and the Cuban nationalist José Martí, Daut reveals Janvier's equally vital contributions to intellectual history. She draws important, broader conclusions from his overlooked example. In analyzing Janvier's writings alongside those of another oft-overlooked Haitian author, Demesvar Delorme, Daut argues that nineteenth-century Haitian thinkers should be considered "much more as a part of the histories of global 'black nationalism,' as equally as hemispheric American thought."[76] Her reinterpretation of nineteenth-century Haitian intellectual production challenges readers to reconsider established arguments that characterize Haiti as the "peculiar antithesis" of Pan-Africanism, a politics that in its most radical iterations rejected the bourgeois nation-state in support of the cause of transnational black solidarity, and Pan-Americanism, a discourse that ostensibly elided racial difference while affirming an international community composed of nation-states. Daut's key argument that writers such as Janvier were "creating transnational 'black' sovereignty *through* Haiti" encourages readers to situate Janvier's nationalism as also rooted in an ethos of "worldmaking," to use political theorist Adom Getachew's phrase.[77] Ultimately, Daut presents a view of Janvier's oeuvre as exemplary of

---

76 See Daut's essay in the present volume, 140.
77 Ibid., 120, 133. Adom Getachew, *Worldmaking after Empire: The Rise and Fall of Self-Determination* (Princeton: Princeton University Press, 2019).

what she terms Haitian Atlantic humanism, a long-standing way of thinking the world through the nation-state of Haiti in order to combat the twin axes of colonial racism and slavery.

Echoing Daut's emphasis on the anticolonial worldmaking possibilities of Janvier's nationalism, Bastien Craipain argues in his contribution that Janvier promoted "the paradigmatic dimension of the Haitian experience as a way to empower and extend its epistemological potential to all people of African descent in the Atlantic world."[78] Craipain grounds his argument in a social scientific analysis of the dehumanizing rhetoric of post-Enlightenment racial thought, which featured philosophical and scientific debates about the supposed natural inequality of the human races. While it is generally known among historians that Janvier was a member of the Société d'anthropologie de Paris, Craipain reveals that his fellow members of the leading anthropological society possessed a dangerous preoccupation with Haiti. They regarded it as an exceptional post-slavery society—as a laboratory where French physicians, scientists, and social scientists could study black people outside of the debilitating conditions of chattel slavery, measure already assumed racial differences, and thus resolve the "problem of the human races." Craipain's close reading of Janvier's medical thesis on tuberculosis and the proceedings of the Sociéte in the *Bulletins de la Société d'anthropologie de Paris* reveals Janvier's efforts "to turn the discourse of Haitian exceptionalism into what may be best described as a counter-discourse of universalizable particularism" and "challenge the racist teachings and imperialistic musings" of his ostensible colleagues.[79] He offers readers a novel interpretation of an understudied aspect of Janvier's oeuvre and shows its potential to decolonize the genealogy of North Atlantic scientific and anthropological thought.

Just as Craipain insists on situating Janvier within the institutional and intellectual environments of Third Republic France, Chelsea Stieber looks beyond Janvier's response to U.S. imperialism and assesses the significance of his immediate location within Paris, at a time when French intellectuals and political actors were building a colonial project based on the *mission civilisatrice*. Stieber considers the development of Janvier's nationalism in specific relationship to his engagement with the debates about nation, civilization, and empire then roiling Third Republic France. She argues that Janvier's calls for

---

78 See Craipain's chapter below, 145.
79 Ibid., 144, 145.

Haitian sovereignty and self-rule are a reflection of and response to Europe's ascendant imperialisms and France's paradoxical civilizing mission. Janvier's keen awareness of the various imperial projects that were preparing to transform Europe and the world shaped his nationalism; he conceptualized Haiti's sovereignty as its ability to protect itself not only against the mounting threat of France's colonial project but also against a more universal U.S. and European belief in the right and duty of the "superior" races to colonize and subjugate other "inferior" peoples. Ultimately, Stieber demonstrates that Janvier's work is a neglected yet essential part of the history of anticolonial thought. It offers anticolonial dissent from the perspective of the formerly colonized and identifies the violent paradox of Third Republic universalism in its very moment of creation.

In bringing attention back to *Haïti aux Haïtiens*, the principal work under examination in this volume, Watson Denis delves further into the theories of nation and nationalism that Janvier produced alongside his refutations of North Atlantic racism and colonialism. Denis argues that *Haïti aux Haïtiens* is at once a theorization of nationalism and a work that participated in the intellectual construction of Haiti in its first century of independence. His chapter draws particular attention to how Janvier tried to steer Haiti's national development through his assessment of its political economy and shape a shared ideal of patriotism and nationalism, which would then constitute the foundations of Haiti's national community. It elucidates Janvier's understanding of developments within and specific to Haiti, the audience of Haitians to which Janvier addressed *Haïti aux Haïtiens*, and the relevance of that work for scholarly and popular understandings of Haitian nationalism and nation building. Yet, even as Denis returns readers' focus to Haiti, he notes that Janvier was attentive to Haiti's international relations and reconceptualizes the often Eurocentric history of nineteenth-century nationalism by assessing Janvier as a theorist of nationalism on a par with European intellectuals such as Giuseppe Mazzini, Johann Gottfried Herder, and Fustel de Coulanges. In doing both, Denis affirms that Haiti and its thinkers have been fundamentally connected to, not isolated or aberrant from, broader Atlantic histories and intellectual traditions.[80]

---

80 For a critique of the "isolation thesis," the long-standing assumption that the United States and Europe's refusal of formal diplomatic recognition to Haiti was indicative of nineteenth-century Haiti's more universal isolation, see especially Gaffield, *Haitian Connections in the Atlantic World*.

Along with the other contributors to this volume, Denis also offers an interpretation of "Haïti aux Haïtiens" as a phrase and an idea. For Denis, the title of Janvier's collection of essays signals the militant and nationalist overtones of his text. Janvier's nationalism was both affective and intellectual, Denis argues. It emerged from his understanding of Haitians as the inheritors of a black state birthed in an anticolonial and antislavery revolution, whose sovereignty was historic and sacrosanct. Chemla offers a similar interpretation. Stressing Janvier's insistence on Haiti's territorial integrity, he suggests that "Haïti aux Haïtiens" speaks to Janvier's interest in preserving Haiti for Haitians and the black race, in defiance of Western colonialism. Both Daut and Craipain elaborate on that point. According to Daut, "Haïti aux Haïtiens" drew inspiration, both rhetorically and ideologically, from Delorme and Ramón Emeterio Betances, two Caribbean intellectuals who had called for a preservation of the "Antilles for the Antilleans" and opposed U.S. imperialism, which was expressed in the doctrine of "America for the Americans." Drawing on Daut's analysis, Craipain similarly identifies "Haïti aux Haïtiens" as a "logophagic translation of U.S. president James Monroe's apocryphal doctrine [America for the Americans] into an anticolonial watchword." He insists that the phrase "was meant to serve as a powerful reminder of the ever-pressing threat of U.S. control over the country and the Caribbean region more generally."[81] In her essay, Stieber further emphasizes the nationalist impulse behind "Haïti aux Haïtiens" but more firmly locates its genesis within Haiti's intellectual tradition and, more immediately, the ascendant imperial politics of Third Republic France. She shows that "in response to what he witnessed in France [...] and in light of Haiti's long nineteenth century of independence, autonomy, and racial equality, Janvier elaborated a nationalist program based in Haitian autonomy: Haiti for the Haitians."[82]

In the volume's final chapter, Brandon Byrd joins in the interpretation of Janvier's invocation of "Haïti aux Haïtiens" while tracing the varied and often-competing uses and meanings of the phrase across the anglophone and francophone Atlantics, from the nineteenth century to today. As Byrd shows in "Haiti for the Haitians: A Genealogy of Black Sovereignty," some of the earliest documented uses of the phrase emerged among British abolitionists and African American activists during the mid-nineteenth century. Their invocations of "Haiti for the Haitians" betrayed "their hopes and anxieties about Haiti's bearing

---

81 See Craipain's essay in this volume, 141, 142.
82 See Stieber's essay in this volume, 185.

on questions of slavery, abolition, and black potential in the Atlantic world." Decades later, Janvier's concept of "Haiti for the Haitians" announced an anticolonial nationalism predicated on Haiti's absolute political sovereignty, territorial integrity, and economic independence. This concept, Byrd argues, "not only clarified his vision for Haitian governance but also challenged contemporary nationalisms that functioned as imperialism." By the early twentieth century, "Haiti for the Haitians" had gained more widespread use among imperialists and anti-imperialists alike—as a sardonic caricature of alleged Haitian misrule or a subversive demand for Haitian sovereignty, the latter crafted in the mode of Janvier. The phrase would gain increasing urgency during the U.S. occupation of Haiti. As used by Haitian activists and their foreign allies, "Haiti for the Haitians" expressed opposition to the U.S. occupation and advanced the broader anticolonial politics of the World War I era, which are more often associated with the famous cry of "Africa for the Africans." Subversive uses of the phrase, particularly among Haitians, have since addressed one of the ongoing legacies of the occupation—the neocolonial interventions of the so-called international community in Haiti. Accordingly, Byrd insists that the genealogy of "Haiti for the Haitians" reveals "a polyvocal discourse about black sovereignty [...] as it addressed, emerged from, and transcended Haiti."[83]

Looking out from Paris across the Atlantic, visualizing the smoldering ruins of Haitian cities set on fire during the late civil war, Janvier envisioned a new nation rising from the ashes. "Out of all civil war," he would write in the foreword to *Haïti aux Haïtiens*, "a nation should emerge strengthened, wiser, more unified, more courageous in order to hear all truths, all revelations."[84] He was struck by the urgency of the moment. He saw the potential, the need, for Haiti's national renewal.

As all of the authors in this volume note, Janvier's vision has been buried under layers and layers of misrepresentation. In his analysis of late nineteenth-century Haitian politics, David Nicholls depicted Janvier as particularly influential and problematic—as an "ultranationalist" *noiriste* "ideologue" who was both unreliable because of his dogmatism and dangerous because of the groundwork he was supposedly laying for François Duvalier's dictatorship, which weaponized the rhetoric and politics of black consciousness after the United States exacerbated

83 See Byrd's essay in this volume, 222.
84 Janvier, *Haiti for the Haitians*, 47 below.

Haiti's long-standing conflicts of color and class by elevating light-skinned Haitian collaborators to positions of political power during its occupation of Haiti.[85] Yet, as Daut and Claude Auguste have argued, this popular framework exaggerates the salience of color in Haiti, making it the principal, even sole, explanation for Haitian political action and conflict.[86] This interpretive lens was evident in the immediate foreign reactions to the Liberal Insurrection of 1883. It continues to cloud more meaningful analysis of Haitian political philosophies, conflicts, and debates by amplifying a "subjective, reductive, and simplifying vision of [Haiti's] sociopolitical reality."[87]

As this critical translation and volume of essays attests, Janvier articulated a sophisticated politics which, despite its limitations, addressed the evolving challenges of his times, in Haiti and beyond. In *Haïti aux Haïtiens*, Janvier argues that the Haitian state had to help Haitian peasants, and implicitly itself, through a steadfast commitment to reform and the promotion of a robust smallholding economy through wide-scale access to land and credit. Haiti's masses are, and have always been, its future, he insisted. Looking back on Haitian history and evaluating the contemporary politics of Liberal partisans, Janvier concluded that Haitian elites had too often undermined Haitian peasants' rightful claims to the land, which were foundational to Haiti's prosperity and essential its security. He made the parallel argument that Haiti had to insist on its absolute territorial integrity and its economic independence—that the Haitian state could not assume more foreign debt or abdicate parts of its territory without undermining the interests of Haitian peasants, which were

---

85 David Nicholls, *From Dessalines to Duvalier: Race, Colour and National Independence in Haiti* (New Brunswick: Rutgers University Press), 108–141. Matthew J. Smith has offered a critical retrospective on Nicholls's canonical work and his emphasis on color distinctions in Haiti: "*From Dessalines to Duvalier* Revisited: A Quarter-Century Retrospective", *The Journal of Haitian Studies* 13, no. 1 (2007): 27–39. On noirisme, Duvalierism, and post-occupation Haiti, see especially J. Michael Dash, *Literature and Ideology in Haiti, 1915–1961* (London: Macmillan, 1981); Frantz Voltaire, *Pouvoir noir en Haïti: l'explosion de 1946* (Montreal: Éditions du CIDIHCA, 1988); Trouillot, *Haiti, State against Nation*; Matthew J. Smith, *Red and Black in Haiti: Radicalism, Conflict, and Political Change, 1934–1957* (Chapel Hill: University of North Carolina Press, 2009).

86 Auguste, "Réflexions". Marlene Daut, *Tropics of Haiti: Race and the Literary History of the Haitian Revolution in the Atlantic World, 1789–1865* (Liverpool: Liverpool University Press, 2015).

87 Auguste, "Réflexions," 17.

also its own. This concern with foreign influence in Haiti reflected an astute analysis and refutation of the world's emergent colonial order. Janvier equated the condition of the Haitian peasant to that of the Egyptian *fellah*, noting that neither benefited from present or planned projects of national "development" reliant upon and thus beholden to foreign investment. He compared Haiti not to the imperial nations of Europe but to occupied Egypt.

In articulating a nationalism attentive to an international context, in characterizing Haiti as an independent state still struggling to secure the basic conditions of sovereignty as defined in the long aftermath of the Peace of Westphalia, Janvier did not so much affirm those Westphalian or Western notions of sovereignty as reveal the limitations of their historical theorizing and application. He cast Haiti as a political entity that could realize what he conceptualized as the unfulfilled promise of postcolonial statehood—that could advance the emancipatory project of the Haitian Revolution by claiming an equal place in the international order and asserting its right to territorial integrity and non-intervention into its domestic affairs.

Accordingly, although scholarship on anticolonial politics and thought has elided Janvier, his writings affirm the importance of centering Haiti and its people in global intellectual history.[88] As a still modest but growing body of scholarship demonstrates, nineteenth-century Haitian writers and political actors understood that Haiti presented a fundamental challenge to the developing international order in which the racist ideologies and regimes birthed in the development of colonial slavery became the basis of a global hierarchy dominated by "white" nation-states.[89] They knew Haitians not just as the objects of the aspirations and aspersions of foreigners but as central participants in the world's political and intellectual life. Just as Haiti's revolutionaries and its earliest writers articulated radical ideas of human rights and freedom in an age of colonialism and slavery and envisioned an emancipatory humanism that is still unrealized, Haitian writers of the

---

[88] Marlene Daut's work has been particularly important in centering Haiti and Haitian intellectuals in Atlantic and Americanist scholarship. See Daut, *Baron de Vastey*. For an example of Atlantic scholarship that does foreground Haiti and its struggle for sovereignty, see also Karen Salt, *The Unfinished Revolution: Haiti, Black Sovereignty and Power in the 19th Century Atlantic World* (New York: Oxford University Press, 2019).

[89] Anténor Firmin, *The Equality of the Human Races*, trans. Asselin Charles (Urbana: University of Illinois Press, 2002); Daut, *Baron de Vastey*; Gaffield, "The Racialization of International Law"; and Stieber, *Haiti's Paper War*.

late nineteenth century established central pillars of anti-racist thought in opposition to hardening racial ideologies and contested an emergent colonial and imperial order. Janvier and his peers not only defended Haiti but imagined its sovereign future, and in doing so they envisioned a world after colonialism.

Janvier's thinking, particularly about nationalism and the nation-state, remains relevant today. As scholars such as Catherine E. Walsh and Walter D. Mignolo have argued, the bourgeois and secular nation-state emerged as a constitutive part of the worldmaking and world-destroying project of European coloniality. It was the racialized political formation that first expanded to European colonies in the Americas then profited from before regulating the processes of genocide and enslavement at the heart of "modernity."[90] The nation-state is the "modern" form of governance that has since emerged from but also constrained anticolonial struggle. Today, the exclusionary and counter-revolutionary characteristics of this European imposition are evident in the United States, India, and Europe, where far-right governments have consolidated power by promoting religious and ethnonationalisms premised on the refutation of liberal democratic institutions and cultural norms, the expulsion or refusal of immigrants, and the persecution of racial, ethnic, and religious minorities. They are apparent in postcolonial nation-states, including Haiti, where the idealized wedding of the state (the legal and administrative body) and nation (the ethnic and cultural body) failed to materialize. In the recent uprisings against the Haitian government's embezzlement of the billions of dollars provided by the PetroCaribe program, ordinary Haitians have voiced a powerful critique of neocolonialism and the contemporary relationship between states and their citizens, particularly in the ostensibly sovereign Global South. This nation—these "sovereign people," to use the words of Jean Casimir—has persisted in its condemnation of the extractive and exploitative qualities of the state and its articulation of "a new form of sovereignty, one founded on the people's refusal to be vanquished by brute force."[91]

The continued struggle for Haitian sovereignty—the persistent contestation of the idea and practice of self-determination among the Haitian people, the Haitian state, and the world writ large—suggests the immediate relevance of *Haiti aux Haïtiens* in all its complexities.

---

90 Catherine E. Walsh and Walter D. Mignolo, *On Decoloniality: Concepts, Analytics, Praxis* (Durham, NC: Duke University Press, 2018).
91 Casimir, *The Haitians*, 7. See also Trouillot, *Haiti, State against Nation*.

In his collection of essays, Janvier offers a nationalism that was very different from the imperial nationalisms of his day or ours. His nationalism was oriented towards emancipation, not domination. It defied ascendant forms of racism, colonialism, and imperialism and clarified the struggles of the postcolonial state. In fact, it anticipated a dismantling of the lingering racialized hierarchies of the international order through its projection of Haitian sovereignty.[92]

Still, even the most idealistic nationalisms are imperfect and Janvier's was no different, as Jean Casimir makes clear in his afterword to the present volume. While Janvier drew attention and granted some recognition to the ideas of autonomy possessed by the national community born in the Haitian Revolution, his notion of sovereignty prioritized the relationships between states. It assumed the primacy of the state as an administrative, even civilizing, agent at the expense of the "sovereign people," who had crafted their own communal institutions, cultural values, and a praxis of autonomy as non-domination. For instance, in affirming the bourgeois nation-state as the normative form of governance, Janvier celebrated the perceived material and moral benefits of Protestantism. His building of a "better" Haiti required the breakdown of some of the spiritual and socioeconomic structures that had long governed and sustained peasant life.

Ultimately, then, this translation is an invitation to think critically with and even beyond Janvier. What institutions or forms of governance are needed to secure the sovereignty of Haiti *and* its people? What political and economic structures must be abolished in order for Haiti *and* Haitians to thrive? To imagine a "Haiti for the Haitians" requires not just a recognition of the international oppressions that have weighed upon Haiti but a deep consideration of the varied hopes and aspirations, histories and ideologies of Haitians. It entails a decolonial practice of thinking about this world, or dreaming of a different one, from the perspective of Haitian people.

---

[92] Jennifer Pitts, *Boundaries of the International Law and Empire* (Cambridge, MA: Harvard University Press, 2018); Getachew, *Worldmaking after Empire*.

Haiti for the Haitians

Translated from French by Nadève Ménard

Annotations by Brandon R. Byrd and Chelsea Stieber

HAÏTI
AUX HAÏTIENS

PAR

Louis-Joseph JANVIER,

Diplômé de l'École des Sciences politiques.

PARIS
IMPRIMERIE A. PARENT, A. DAVY, Succr.
52, rue Madame et rue Monsieur-le-Prince, 14

1884

Cover of the first edition of *Haiti aux Haïtiens*. This volume is a translation of the second expanded edition, which was published shortly thereafter. (Source: Gallica, Bibliothèque nationale de France)

Haitian Democratic Library

Haiti for the Haitians by Louis-Joseph Janvier

Graduate of l'école des sciences politiques

Second edition (expanded)

Paris

1884

Table of Contents

Dedication

Foreword

The Gluttonous and the Naïve

The Watchword

Our Good Friends

Clarion Call

Our Adjacent Islands

The Trap

PATRIÆ

Tibi Semper[1]

During the torment, when the deniers spit in your face—when the undecided dared not speak a word, I was not afraid to raise my voice in your favor;

Now that calm has returned—and for it to remain—I beg you to again listen to he who comes here to do his duty

As a piously grateful son

Louis-Joseph Janvier

---

[1] Patriæ can be translated as Fatherland. *Tibi semper* is thus Janvier's expression of fidelity to Haiti in Latin, meaning "always for you." Thanks to Sarah Bond for help with this translation.

Foreword

First and foremost, I am Haitian. Circumstances force me to position myself here as strictly and selfishly Haitian. May those who read me and want to discuss or comment upon my opinions not assign to me any thought other than those clearly expressed here.

Especially, may "my brothers from the other side"—to use the expression of the chronicler C. Desroches—who will want to quote me to argue against my ideas please abstain from shortening my sentences or from taking them out of context in order to make me say the opposite of what I have written.[2]

Out of all civil war, a nation should emerge strengthened, wiser, more unified, more courageous in order to hear all truths, all revelations.

These five articles were to appear at long intervals in the newspaper: *La Nation*.[3]

Time is short. I am combining them. With just these words: form and substance, I explain everything.

Lis-Jos-Jver.

June 15, 1884

The first edition sold out in two days.
I offer a second.

L.-J. J.

August 12, 1884.

---

2 Charles Desroches was a participant in the Liberal Insurrection of 1883. Desroches's reflections on what one contemporary called "the terrible year" were published posthumously in *Matières à réflexion pour les révolutionnaires. Notes de l'exilé Charles Desroches* (Port-au-Prince: Imprimerie de L'Oeil, 1884).

3 There were several periodicals entitled *La Nation* in circulation in 1884, including one that was published in Paris and another that was published in Port-au-Prince. Janvier intended his essays for the Paris-based publication.

The Gluttonous and the Naïve

The first are ingratiating, nice, charming. They come to us from all corners of the world or are deserters of Haiti.

They promise the moon and the stars to whosoever takes the pain of listening to them. One asks for la Gonâve;[4] the other has his sights set on la Tortue;[5] this one wants the Haitian subsoil to be left to him; that one dreams of blanketing the country with sugar factories, railroads, dikes, canals, telegraphs, aqueducts, bridges, and beacons.

All, however, are as poor as church mice.

In their private letters or when they are amongst themselves, they call us a people of monkeys, they argue that we are capable of nothing on our own and that foreigners should be placed at the country's head. So and so pushes his impertinence to the point of offering his services as intermediary with the goal of placing Haiti under a foreign protectorate. Such nonsense, these lies, this insolence get our blood up.

We have to be careful; we cannot take any risks, or enter into any contracts by chance, blindly, in the shadows, hastily, or at a gallop.

We must benefit from the hard lesson we have learned over the past four months of the year that just ended. Those who ate at our table the day before, the very ones who, belonging to our race, called themselves our brothers and were treated as such, those very ones insulted us and had us cruelly maligned abroad.[6]

Those are questionable brothers whom we should trust less than anyone. In our days of good fortune, they claim to be more Haitian than us; they drive us to rise up against the Europeans so that we might give everything to them alone, but in our days of misfortune, their attitude towards us changes. Then, too often, the Europeans and the Mainlanders show themselves to be more our brothers than them.

---

4 La Gonâve is a Haitian island located northwest of Port-au-Prince, in the Gulf of Gonâve.

5 L'île de la Tortue (Tortuga Island) is a Haitian island off the northern coast of Haiti.

6 The "brothers" to whom Janvier refers here seem to be the "brothers from the other side" that he addresses in his foreword: his political rivals, the Liberals, and those Haitians whose political and economic interests he considered to be threats to Haiti's sovereignty. See the Introduction to this volume for a more detailed discussion of the internal divisions of politics, class, and color in Haiti.

I am putting aside the foreigners who have married our sisters. Those are half-brothers whom we must flatter but, until the day they naturalize as Haitians, reasonably, politically we can only trust them halfway.[7]

Nothing will stop them at any given time, the ones and the others, from claiming and obtaining an armed intervention on their behalf from their respective governments.

It is then that the naïve would have to repent for their naïvety. It will be too late.

La Gonâve is a strategic position of the utmost importance. It is the most basic of policies that it be leased only to Haitians, exploited only by Haitians.

---

7 As explained in note 55 in the Introduction to this volume, Haiti's first national constitution prohibited foreigners from purchasing property in Haiti and limited citizenship to "Africans and Indians." Both laws were meant to protect against the return of slavery and colonialism to Haiti. Subsequent constitutions promulgated before 1889 continued to uphold race as a factor in determining access to Haitian citizenship; the ban on foreign landholding in Haiti remained in force until the United States occupation of Haiti (1915–1934). Prior to the occupation, foreign merchants sometimes circumvented the landholding provisions in Haitian law by marrying into Haitian families. The history of foreign and "semi-foreign" elites in Haiti receives astute analysis in Brenda Gayle Plummer, "Race, Nationality, and Trade in the Caribbean: The Syrians in Haiti, 1903–1934," *The International History Review* III, no. 4 (October 1981): 517–539 and "The Metropolitan Connection: Foreign and Semiforeign Elites in Haiti, 1900–1915," *Latin American Research Review* 19, no. 2 (1984): 119–142. See also Matthew Casey, "'Haitian Habits' or Occupation Policies? Harris Lifschitz and the Unevenness of State Building in Haiti, 1898–1921," *Journal of Haitian Studies* 21, no. 2, Special Issue on the US Occupation of Haiti, 1915–1934 (Fall 2025): 121–151.

The same goes for La Tortue.⁸ Môle-Saint-Nicolas can be made a free port, never a free city.⁹

Free port, it remains ours; free city, it escapes us.

We cannot abdicate our sovereignty over any point of the territory without shame, without humiliation; we cannot slap ourselves in the face by appearing to admit that it is impossible for us to govern ourselves, that we are unable to guarantee security on our own soil.

Take it or leave it: let those who have no confidence in us stay home.

The naïve shook in their boots during the storm. They are gluttonous in their own way, jumpy gluttons. We must make them understand, the hard way, that the sacred interests of the nation have priority over those of the individual. They should work slowly; save up and wait.

Their pessimism is blind; their simplicity and their gullibility are as childish as they are dangerous. All things considered, our mines and quarries, the forests of our adjacent islands, we will exploit them on our own, later, in the person of our children.

8 In May 1883, Haitian president Lysius Salomon (1879–1888) offered to secretly cede La Tortue to the United States. He explained to John Mercer Langston, the prominent U.S. black abolitionist and activist then serving as the U.S. minister resident and consul general to Haiti, that he had a great fear of Great Britain's antagonism towards his government and was wary of its interests in Haitian territory. The U.S. government did not accept the offer, believing that it departed from a precedent of acquiring only territories contiguous with the United States and could not be accomplished through Salomon's preferred, secretive methods. For more on this episode and U.S.–Haitian relations in this era, see especially Rayford W. Logan, *The Diplomatic Relations of the United States with Haiti, 1776–1891* (Chapel Hill: University of North Carolina Press, 1941).

9 Môle-Saint-Nicolas is a town on the northwestern coast of Haiti. It sits at the northern entrance of the Windward Passage, the strait separating Cuba and Haiti. The location and size of its harbor had long made Môle-Saint-Nicolas one of the most desired prizes for imperial powers in the Western Hemisphere. At the turn of the nineteenth century, one British naval officer even suggested that it had the finest harbor in the world. By the time Janvier wrote *Haïti aux Haïtiens*, the United States had coveted Môle-Saint-Nicolas for decades, in part to undercut European powers hoping to gain a stronger foothold in the Americas. It had become an important bargaining chip. For example, understanding U.S. strategic interests, Haitian president Sylvain Salnave (1867–1869) had offered Môle-Saint-Nicolas to the United States. In exchange, the United States would assume Haiti's debt to France and protect the Salnave government from internal and external threats. The U.S. government declined but soon adopted more aggressive attempts at expansion in Haiti, Hispaniola, and the Caribbean. See Logan, *The Diplomatic Relations of the United States with Haiti*, 315–352.

We have to safeguard the legacy passed down to us by the Haitians of yesteryear, free from any mortgage, free from any humiliating contract, in order to pass it down intact to the Haitians of the future.

May 15, 1884

The Watchword

In the past, Poland was madly determined to trust in foreigners, in the Russians and Prussians. That is what killed it.[10]

Fifty years ago, Egypt still belonged to Egyptians.

Since the reign of Mehmet Ali, the Egyptians have contracted a peculiar disease that we could call the fury of civilization.[11]

Like the word *liberal*, the word *civilization* has been so twisted from its meaning, used so often at every opportunity, that it has become elastic, banal, empty of meaning.[12]

---

10 Here, Janvier alludes to the long struggle for Polish sovereignty, independence, and statehood. Poland became an independent kingdom in the ninth century but ceded much of its territory to Sweden and Russia during the seventeenth century. It lost its independence in the eighteenth century, when a series of military partitions divided it among Russia, Austria, and Prussia. Uprisings ensued but Poland did not become a sovereign state until after World War I. On the history of Poland, see Patrice M. Dabrowski, *Poland: The First Thousand Years* (DeKalb: Northern Illinois University Press, 2014).

11 For Janvier, Egypt was a prime—and recent—example of a nation that had lost its political autonomy because it had submitted to foreign capital in the pursuit of "development." A brief history of Egyptian sovereignty or lack thereof might begin in 1798. That year, the army of French general Napoleon Bonaparte conquered Egypt. It maintained control of Egypt for the next three years. After the withdrawal of French troops, an Ottoman military officer named Muhammad Ali seized control of Egypt and ruled it until his death in 1849. His successors continued to pursue projects of industrialization but they relied on foreign financing, which left Egypt indebted to bankers in London, Paris, and other European financial centers. In 1882, following the construction of the Suez Canal, Great Britain, the principal creditor of that development project, invaded Egypt and effectively claimed it as a protectorate. A principal rationale for the British occupation of Egypt was the ostensible need to secure British investments there. The Kingdom of Egypt (1922–1952) would declare its independence in 1922 but Great Britain maintained a significant influence on Egyptian economics and politics for decades to come. In July 1952, a military coup led by Colonel Gamal Abdel Nassar and animated by anticolonial nationalism finally toppled the foreign-backed monarchy. For a concise treatment of modern Egyptian history, see Afaf Lutfi Al-Sayyid Marsot, *A History of Egypt: From the Arab Conquest to the Present*, 2nd ed. (New York: Cambridge University Press, 2007).

12 As Janvier quipped in his earlier work *La République d'Haïti et ses visiteurs*, "What is civilization, anyway? All pastiche or copy"; *La République d'Haïti et ses visiteurs (1840–1882)* (Paris: Mappon et Flammarion, 1883), 511.

Like children who want to become men in one day, the Egyptians, trying to grow up too quickly, borrowed a lot of money from the Europeans and gave them the right to build in their country. The latter built jetties, docks, beacons, aqueducts, sluices, and railroads; they raised sea walls and dug canals, to the point that one day the Egyptians awoke to find themselves under England's heel.

Long ago, they were whipped in the name of the Qur'an, but at least the pashas[13] who despoiled them were born and lived among them, spoke the same language and practiced the same religion as them. Today their cities have been bombed and burned; they are fleeced and whipped in the name of the Bible. Are they any happier? On the contrary. When will this end? No one knows.

The money extorted from French and English peasants has never served the Egyptian bourgeoisie, has never benefited the Egyptian peasant, the *fellah*.[14]

Haitians have imitated the Polish of the last century only too much. Some would want to encourage them to imitate the Egyptians. I protest.

Haitians have more capital than they realize. The key is to make

---

13 An honorific used to convey "high rank" in the military or a form of lordship.
14 Egyptian peasant agriculturalist. While it is worth noting that Frantz Fanon and Aimé Césaire both invoke the *fellah* in their critiques of colonialism, the most proximate reference for Janvier's discussion here is Ernest Renan's 1871 *La Réforme intellectuelle et morale*, which offered ideas on racial inequality and the regeneration of the inferior races by the "superior" Western races. Renan identified the Chinese as "a race of workers" ("une race d'ouvriers"), Africans as a "race that works the land" ("une race de travailleurs de la terre"), and Europeans as "a race of masters and soldiers" ("une race de maîtres et de soldats"). He assigned the *fellah* an intermediate yet inferior place within this hierarchy: "Reduce this noble race to toil in the workhouse like the negroes and the Chinese and they revolt. Every rebel in Europe is more or less a soldier who missed his calling, someone made for the life of a hero, and who you are asking to do a job that is contrary to his race; bad worker, good soldier. And yet the life that our workers rebel against would make a Chinese, a *fellah* happy—who are not military men in the least. May each one do what he is made for, and all will go well" ("Réduisez cette noble race à travailler dans l'ergastule comme des nègres et des Chinois, elle se révolte. Tout révolté est, chez nous, plus ou moins un soldat qui a manqué sa vocation, un être fait pour la vie héroïque, et que vous appliquez à une besogne contraire à sa race, mauvais ouvrier, trop bon soldat. Or, la vie qui révolte nos travailleurs rendrait heureux un Chinois, un fellah, êtres qui ne sont nullement militaires. Que chacun fasse ce pour quoi il est fait, et tout ira bien") (*La Réforme intellectuelle et morale* (Paris: Michel Lévy Freres, 1871, 93–94)). Césaire cites from this very passage in *Discourse on Colonialism*.

this capital emerge from the hiding places where it is held, beneath the earth. To do so, we must put it at ease by guaranteeing peace, discipline it by creating savings banks, use it via popular banks, purely national credit institutions.[15]

Knowing how to wait is the ultimate wisdom. Counting on oneself is the greatest of strengths.

The Haitian peasant would do well to trust only himself, if he does not want to be eaten, exploited, pressured, and finally one day massacred by the sweet talkers who, running from the four corners of the earth, come now to heap praise upon him, fool him with vain and misleading promises.

And if even Parliament grants land concessions for industrial and agricultural operations, these concessions from the depths of the land must be made in favor of Haitians; and it [Parliament] is in favor of it being expressly stipulated by the contracts that, in no circumstance, in no case, may these Haitians pass them on to foreigners. If these foreigners love us as much as they would have us believe, they should naturalize as Haitians.[16]

We can foresee the future through the past. They sought to humiliate us. They despoil and pillage us. They have held and every day they hold

---

15 In 1880, the Banque Nationale d'Haïti (BNH), was chartered under Salomon's presidency. The bank was technically French: funded by French capital, headquartered in Paris, and chartered through the Société Générale de Crédit Industriel et Commercial. The BNH did establish branches throughout Haiti, stabilize the Haitian gourde, and regularize debt payments to France (see note 21 in the Introduction). Nevertheless, Janvier is asking here for a different kind of national institution, one that is not tied to the interests of the government and international finance but to the interests of those agricultural laborers who could benefit from access to loans and credit. On the Banque Nationale, see the exceptionally rich documentary film produced by Frantz Voltaire, *Une histoire de la banque en Haïti* (Montreal: CIDIHCA, 2014). See also Peter James Hudson, "The National City Bank of New York and Haiti, 1909–1922," *The Radical History Review* no. 115 (2013): 91–114 and Frédéric Marcelin, *La Banque Nationale d'Haïti: une page d'histoire* (Paris: Imprimerie Joseph Kugelmann, 1890).

16 Janvier again alludes to foreign nationals making claims on Haitian citizens and the Haitian state while also asserting their rights as citizens and subjects of other nations. As illustrated in Smith's *Liberty, Fraternity, and Exile* and evident in court cases and diplomatic records from nineteenth-century Haiti, many foreign residents, particularly in Port-au-Prince and other cities, chose not to become naturalized Haitian citizens, even when that status was offered, so that they could benefit from their current national or subject status. Those statuses proved particularly critical when seeking refuge or intercession during episodes of legal dispute or political conflict.

a knife to our throat. They have threatened us and they continue to threaten our very independence because we have a debt of forty million.[17] Everywhere, they have spread the news that we are savages in order to better intimidate us and to better fleece us; those who licked our hand at home called us monkeys in Europe.[18]

Remember to be defiant from now on, Haitian people. Do not forget the September ultimatum and be careful.[19]

Poverty for oneself is better than wealth produced for others. Only the greedy and the naïve, the gluttons and the guileless can claim and believe the opposite.

Haiti for the Haitians. That is what our ancestors intended. It is also what the black race wants.

May 19, 1884

---

17 See note 21 in the Introduction. Like other Haitian intellectuals, Janvier took offense at the economic effects and the moral implications of the indemnity. He recognized that Haitians had to pay an unconscionable price for winning their freedom.

18 Haiti and Haitians had innumerable critics to whom this passage might refer. But it most immediately brings to mind the racist and imperialist propaganda of Spenser Buckingham St. John (1825–1910). After working as the private secretary and commissioner for Sir James Brooke, the so-called White Rajah of Sarawak, St. John became the British consul general to Brunei. He subsequently spent more than a decade in the service of the British Empire in the Caribbean. In 1863, St. John became the British chargé d'affaires in Haiti. He then served as Britain's chargé d'affaires to the Dominican Republic and its resident minister and consul general to Haiti. In 1884, St. John published with a London publishing house *Hayti; or, the Black Republic*. As Jack Daniel Webb notes, the principal arguments of the book included the allegations that Haitian Vodou was an illegitimate and barbarous practice which included rites of infanticide and cannibalism, and that all aspects of Haitian life were regressing from the "civilized" colonial past towards a state of decadence and "savage" African barbarism. His virulently racist caricatures of Haitian life came with more explicit imperial calls for foreign subjugation of Haiti in the second edition of *Hayti*. Thanks in large part to St. John's appeal to common Euro-American notions of civilization, race, and Haiti's relationship to both, *Hayti* became the most widely read anglophone text on Haiti in the five decades after its initial publication. On *Hayti* and its circulation, see especially Webb, *Haiti in the British Imagination: Imperial Worlds, 1847–1915* (Liverpool: Liverpool University Press, 2020), 139–188.

19 A reference to the warning delivered by the British consul in Port-au-Prince on September 23, 1883. See page 30 of the Introduction.

Our Good Friends

They live among us; they are numerous, petty, obsequious, and insipid. They flatter us a thousand different ways, cajole us a thousand different ways. When we need them, they slip between our fingers, then condemn us, ridicule or vilify us the best they can.

They all aspire to dominate us. The contracts they present to us contain thousands of pitfalls and traps into which we fall.

Each contract of general interest should be discussed in the press, should be known to all. The watchword should be: Nothing to foreigners except advisedly. It is best to be informed, to choose, in order to avoid repenting.

We do not have the right to tie the hands of future generations for the pleasure of a few good, yet short-sighted souls too naïve or too eager for a good time.

Haitians have the duty to be serious about matters that can later justify foreign interventions such as those that killed Poland and those that are killing Egypt at this very moment.

When they come, our good friends, honeyed words upon their lips, we will tell them nicely, but firmly: We want to study the contracts in order to better discuss them. We cannot play around with the future of the country; it is not a matter of little consequence. Give us time. We think it dangerous to always entrust ourselves to the formerly bankrupt or swindlers. We want to get to the bottom of things.

They will give Parliament time to gather itself, and the country time to consult its children, who living far from it, by it, or for it, and thinking only of it, do not ignore what is being said about it and what is being conspired against its existence.

And the latter will cry: Be wary of sharks. Trust only yourselves. The Haitian land must be free. Let it be populated. May the nation wait and slowly grow, as waited and slowly grew those that today are great nations.

Our good friends will scream, will shout abuse, and go elsewhere. We will let them. What matters above all is that Haitians be the only masters in autonomous, independent Haiti.

All that is contrary to this doctrine is nothing but danger or chimera.

May 29, 1884

Clarion Call[20]

Since the pessimists and the impetuous, the sentimental and the dreamers are loudly demanding that the country throw open its doors to foreigners, divesting itself of the most sound guarantees that ensure its independence; since financiers with no mandate are going around the world begging for a protectorate or gold for Haiti, it is urgent to draw the attention of altruistic patriots, of educated citizens who care about national dignity, of level-headed and shrewd spirits completely enamored of our collective honor to what is currently happening in the United States.

Mr. Blaine, he who epitomizes and embodies the policies of Monroe, Adams, and Grant, has just been chosen as the Republican candidate by the Chicago Convention to replace Mr. Arthur in the presidency of the Starred Confederation.[21] No one doubts that Chicago's vote will be ratified, that the election will become definitive in Washington.

---

20 Janvier uses this term in his preface to *L'Égalité des races* (Paris: Imprimerie G. Rougier, 1884). In response to the Liberal insurrection, Janvier sounded his clarion call, writing "Aujourd'hui je sonne un coup de clairon pour convier la jeunesse haïtienne au grand combat de l'intelligence pour la lumière" (*L'Égalité*, 5).

21 Here Janvier refers to the foreign policies of U.S. presidents James Monroe (1817–1825), John Quincy Adams (1825–1829), and Ulysses S. Grant (1869–1877). He is specifically alluding to the establishment and enduring effect of the Monroe Doctrine. During the 1810s and the early 1820s, U.S. leaders feared European incursions into the Americas. Russian claims on the Pacific coast of mainland North America and rumors of Spain's attempts to regain its former Latin American colonies exacerbated those concerns. Adams, then the U.S. secretary of state, proposed that Monroe issue a unilateral declaration on European intervention in the Americas. He outlined the message that Monroe would deliver in 1823 during the president's annual message to the U.S. Congress. In that address, Monroe announced that the United States would maintain its traditional policy of non-interference in internal affairs on the European continent and, in turn, would not accept any European attempts to establish new or recover old colonies in the Americas. This policy, the pursuit of hegemony in the Americas, became the cornerstone of nineteenth-century U.S. foreign policy, including in the later presidential administrations of Adams and Grant. As Marlene L. Daut has shown, Haitian intellectuals, including Janvier and Demesvar Delorme, saw the speech or, more precisely, its interpretation by mid- and late nineteenth-century U.S. expansionists, as espousing a racial and imperial policy best described

Mr. Blaine, former Secretary of Foreign Affairs, has always shown himself to be a staunch advocate of the United States' hegemony over all of America.[22] His ardent desire to intervene in the affairs of Peru and Chile forced President Arthur to break with him and to replace him with Mr. Frelinghausen as head of the department of Foreign Relations.[23]

Removed from power, Mr. Blaine never renounced his politics. On the contrary, he accentuated and expanded them.

He is the author of the article of the Republican platform accepted in Chicago and which translates the words of Monroe and Adams: *America for Americans*.[24] This article forcefully and definitively rejects

by the apocryphal phrase "America for the Americans." See Marlene L. Daut, "Beyond 'America for the Americans': Race and Empire in the Work of Demesvar Delorme," *J19: The Journal of Nineteenth-Century Americanists* 6, no. 1 (2018): 189–197. On the history of the Monroe Doctrine, see especially Jay Sexton, *The Monroe Doctrine: Empire and Nation in Nineteenth-Century America* (New York: Hill & Wang, 2011).

22 James G. Blaine was first elected to the U.S. Congress from Maine in 1862 and served as the speaker of the U.S. House of Representatives from 1869 to 1875. He launched two unsuccessful bids for the Republican Party's presidential nomination in 1876 and 1880 but served as U.S. secretary of state under U.S. president Chester A. Arthur (1881–1885) from March to December of 1881. During that time, Blaine tried to negotiate peace among combatants in the War of the Pacific (1879–1884), including Peru and Chile; promoted the doctrine of Pan-Americanism, which he defined as the cultivation of "friendly commercial ties" that would lead to a "large increase in the export trade of the United States"; and called for the construction of a U.S.-controlled canal across Central America. In 1884, Blaine emerged as the frontrunner for the Republican presidential nomination despite the vocal outcry of critics from within his own party who called him "Jingo Jim" due to his aggressive pursuit of U.S. expansionism. Such criticism foreshadowed a messy coronation for Blaine. When the Republican National Convention met in Chicago in June 1884, the assembled delegates failed to select a nominee on the first three ballots. On the fourth, Blaine finally captured the nomination. On Blaine's foreign policy, see especially David Healy, *James G. Blaine and Latin America* (Columbia: University of Missouri Press, 2001).

23 In December 1881, U.S. president Chester A. Arthur replaced secretary of state Blaine with Frederick Frelinghuysen, the former attorney general of and a U.S. senator from New Jersey. In his new position, Frelinghuysen mediated peace negotiations between Chile and Peru that resulted in the Treaty of Ancón and the end of the War of the Pacific. See William F. Sater, *Andean Tragedy: Fighting the War of the Pacific, 1879–1884* (Lincoln: University of Nebraska Press, 2007).

24 While "America for the Americans" entered public usage in the 1850s, Blaine appropriated and popularized the slogan. He helped make it synonymous with the Monroe Doctrine as he interpreted it. As Janvier, several of his fellow Haitian

all interference by European nations in the affairs of the American continent and its dependencies.²⁵

As far as Haiti is concerned, it is to be feared that the future American president, who has always demanded and will demand voting for substantial funds for the Federal Navy, may want to immediately take up the annexation policy of President Grant and Frederick Douglass against the independent Caribbean nation.²⁶

writers, and other Latin American intellectuals and statesmen understood, Blaine considered the Monroe Doctrine not only as a vestige of early U.S. nationalism but as a weapon of U.S. empire to be wielded by the U.S. government amid the rise of new European imperialisms in the late nineteenth century.

25 Janvier is referring to the following plank of the Republican Party's 1884 platform: "the Republican party favors a policy which shall keep us from entangling alliances with foreign nations, and which gives us the right to expect that foreign nations shall refrain from meddling in American affairs; a policy which seeks peace and trade with all powers, but especially with those of the Western Hemisphere." The platform then goes on to demand the "restoration" of the U.S. Navy to its "old-time strength and efficiency" so that it could "protect the rights of American citizens and the interests of American commerce." It also called on the U.S. Congress to remove restrictions on U.S. shipping "so that it may again be true that we have a commerce which leaves no sea unexplored, and a navy which takes no law from superior force." The full platform can be found in Gerhard Peters and John T. Wooley, "Republican Platforms: Republican Party Platform of 1884," *The American Presidency Project* (June 3, 1884), http://www.presidency.ucsb.edu/ws?pid=29626.

26 After entering the White House, U.S. president Ulysses S. Grant (1869–1877) tried to annex the Dominican Republic. While his administration saw the Caribbean nation as an ideal location to station and supply the U.S. Navy and as a potential site of relocation for newly emancipated black southerners, other Republicans, including the abolitionist Charles Sumner, objected to the imperialistic overtones of annexation. Simultaneously, some white Democrats argued that the annexation of the Dominican Republic might erode white supremacy in the United States through the introduction of more citizens of African descent. They assumed, as Grant later confirmed, that expansion would not end with the Dominican Republic—that the United States would eventually try to annex Haiti and thus bring its population into the fold. Influenced by these disparate sources of opposition, the U.S. Senate rejected an annexation treaty between the United States and the Dominican Republic in June 1870. Undeterred, Grant convened a commission, which he tasked with traveling to the Dominican Republic and authoring a report on annexation that might shift public opinion on the issue. Frederick Douglass joined the commission, which did not succeed in its ultimate goal, as its assistant secretary. The most famous black activist and abolitionist in the world, Douglass possessed an idealistic vision of Pan-Americanism. He imagined a network of hemispheric political and economic relationships in which the United States would assume a central role but

60   Louis-Joseph Janvier

It is excellent to point out to the gullible few, who every day bang their heads against Article 6 of the Haitian Constitution,[27] it is fitting to point out to these reckless people who would want us to carelessly and without reason renounce our Liberator's[28] admirable policy, that Mr. Blaine is very popular among his compatriots because, although his country has nothing to fear from Europe, this politician had a clause inserted in the policy platform of the Chicago Convention whereby landownership by foreigners would be forbidden in the States of the Union.[29]

---

all states would participate as equals, in a spirit of racial egalitarianism and mutual cooperation. His progressive view of U.S. history influenced that vision of U.S. foreign policy. Douglass believed that the United States, having defeated the slaveholding Confederacy, was prepared to help the technological, industrial, and cultural advancement of the Dominican Republic and its residents. He also thought that recent amendments to the U.S. Constitution, which ended slavery, introduced birthright citizenship and the equal protection clause, and enfranchised African American men, meant that Dominicans would enjoy the full benefits of U.S. citizenship. Neither the popular classes of the Dominican Republic nor those of Haiti agreed. In fact, Douglass's support of U.S. expansion during the heady days of U.S. Reconstruction drew scrutiny from Haitians later in his career. In July 1889, as Douglass prepared to go to Port-au-Prince as the U.S. minister resident and consul general to Haiti, Stephen Preston, Haiti's minister to the United States, reported that a group of "young Haytiens at Paris [...] were preparing to make war on Mr. Douglass!" Those Haitian expatriates almost certainly included Janvier. In Haiti, Douglass would famously play a pivotal role in the U.S. negotiations for Môle-Saint-Nicolas, in which he developed a more critical stance on U.S. expansion that also reflected the influence of Haitian critics of U.S. empire. See Letter from Ebenezer Don Carlos Bassett to Frederick Douglass, August 14, 1889 in General Correspondence, Frederick Douglass Papers, Library of Congress. For Douglass's assessment of the "Môle St. Nicolas affair," see Douglass, "Haïti and the United States: Inside History of the Negotiations for the Mole St. Nicolas, I," *North American Review* 153, no. 418 (September 1891): 337–345 and "Haïti and the United States: Inside History of the Negotiations for the Mole St. Nicolas, II," *North American Review* 153, no. 419 (October 1891): 450–459. Millery Polyné provides excellent treatment of Douglass's internationalism and diplomacy in *From Douglass to Duvalier: U.S. African Americans, Haiti, and Pan Americanism, 1870–1964* (Gainesville: University Press of Florida, 2010), 25–55.

27 Salomon promulgated the most recent Haitian Constitution (1879). Its Article 6 maintained the prohibition on foreign landholding mentioned in note 7 accompanying "The Gluttonous and the Naïve": "nul, s'il n'est Haïtien, ne peut être propriétaire de biens fonciers en Haïti, à quelque titre que ce soit, ni acquérir aucun immeuble."

28 "Liberator" refers to Dessalines.

29 The Republican platform of 1884 declared that the "public lands are a heritage of the people of the United States, and should be reserved as far as possible for

According to what his electors say, his doctrine and theirs is the only one which conforms to the doctrine professed by the fathers of the independence of the United States.

We have repeated a hundred times, everywhere, in every way imaginable, that the autonomy of the Afro-Latino republics of Haiti has been perpetually threatened by their powerful Anglo-Saxon neighbor.[30]

We, Western Haitians, we have nothing but sympathy and admiration for the federal republic, but not for anything in the world would we want the island of Haiti to become a colony or even a State of the Northern Confederation.[31] We have been masters in our own home for a mere eighty years. We would never want to lose our rank. We do not want to lower ourselves. We want to be neither valets nor vassals.

What are we to do faced with the grave conjecture that looms?

We flatly reject any idea of political protectorate wherever it may come from.

If we offer very considerable political advantages, favors that are too marked to this or that other power, the others will believe we hate and shun them, and will be hostile towards us. That is how we must understand England's current attitude towards us. Let us not push things any further.

On the other hand, if for one reason or another, the authorized powers allowed the Antillean balance to be broken in favor of the United States, they would have implicitly given up on the West Indies, and committed an irreparable error. Within fifty years they would be punished by the loss of their colonies in the Caribbean Sea.

An economic protectorate, as minor as we may wish it to be, and from wherever it may be offered, would not only be humiliating, but also inefficient, dangerous, and certainly ruinous. It does not tempt us in the slightest.

Let us plainly state what must be done. We should withdraw into ourselves; gather ourselves.

We must not enter into commercial treaties with anyone, because even if they bestow the treatment of most preferred nation upon us,

---

small holdings by actual settlers. We are opposed to the acquisition of large tracts of these lands by corporations or individuals, especially where such holdings are in the hands of non-resident or aliens. And we will endeavor to obtain such legislation as will tend to correct this evil."

30 "Afro-Latino Republics" refers to Haiti and the Dominican Republic. See note 63 in the Introduction on Janvier's choice of geographic place names. "Anglo-Saxon neighbor" refers to the United States.

31 The United States, again.

when it comes down to it, these commercial treaties would be onerous for us and profitable for others.

Besides, often these treaties have been used to kill the independence of certain small countries, such as Cambodia for example.[32]

It is not to please our nation that a great commercial power, France, for example, that understands the interests of the greatest number so well that it refuses to protect its colonial and metropolitan sugar at the expense of the French consumer,[33] would rework or shake up its custom tariffs in order to diminish import duties on Haitian coffee, especially given the relatively small amount of this coffee that finds buyers on French markets.

We must keep well in mind that the French market is currently open to all of the countries in the Universe that produce coffee, which was not the case in the eighteenth century, because at that time, the Colonial Pact existed.[34] The products of the colony were sold in all of

---

32 Throughout the 1850s, French interest in Cambodia increased in parallel with its growing involvement in Vietnam and its rivalry with Great Britain, which controlled India and effectively excluded the French from most of southeast Asia. In 1863, the French finalized a treaty with the Cambodian king Norodom, a ruler who had come to power after a series of civil wars and remained unpopular in the eastern *srok* or district of Cambodia. The treaty afforded protection to the Norodom regime while giving the French rights to exploit Cambodia's timber and mineral resources. Further information on French colonialism in Cambodia can be found in David Chandler, *A History of Cambodia*, 4th ed. (Boulder: Westview Press, 2008), 167–232.

33 *The law protecting French sugar has just been voted. According to all serious economists, it is a bad law. It is prejudicial to the interests of the greatest number and only favors a privileged few. It is fundamentally anti democratic. (August 12, 1884).* Footnote in original.

34 Janvier uses the French term "Pacte colonial," which refers to the mercantilist policies established by the French monarchy to regulate trade with its colonial possessions in the seventeenth and eighteenth centuries. Though interchangeable with the term *exclusif*, the latter speaks only to the restrictions on colonial trade, including food, and does not encompass the wider set of restrictions and stipulations laid out in the *pacte colonial*. Manuel Covo provides particularly useful analysis of French trade monopolies in "L'Assemblée constituante face à l'Exclusif colonial (1789–1791)," in *Les Colonies, la Révolution française, la loi*, ed. Jean-François Niort, Frédéric Régent, and Pierre Serna (Rennes: Presses universitaires de Rennes, 2014), 69–89. For additional context and documents that reveal the effects of this policy in colonial Saint-Domingue, see Nathan H. Dize, Kelsey Corlett-Rivera, Abby R. Broughton, Brittany de Gail, *A Colony in Crisis: The Saint-Domingue Grain Shortage of 1789*, https://colonyincrisis.lib.umd.edu.

the metropole's markets, and at the time these products were sufficient for consumption, which was limited, if we want to compare it to that of today.

And even if Haiti were to obtain a reduction in the French tariff for its coffees, although favorable in one way, it would be unfavorable in another. Finding an outlet opened to it under such circumstances, Haiti's coffee would benefit less from the stimulant of competition.

Instead of improving to again become the strong coffee of long ago, the king-coffee of the eighteenth century, the nourishing and strong coffee that warmed the marrow of the Encyclopedia's philosophers, the brains of the fathers of the French Revolution, it would be less and less cared for by its producer, more and more decried, disdained by the consumer.[35] Its reputation would be lost. But in fact, since the Universal Exposition of 1878 and since the one that just ended in Amsterdam, Haiti's coffee is starting to make a name for itself again.[36]

It is the fight that makes the fighter. In order for the Haitian peasant to quickly become a well-rounded man, we must train him to be courageous and put him in a position to look all the peasants around the world in the eye. That is why we must teach him to know his rights and his duties. It is the economic fight that will force the Haitian peasant to work the soil, in order that our country can better compete, on that front, with Brazil, Venezuela, Martinique, Ceylon, and San Salvador.[37]

Here, free trade will beget riches. Monopoly would kill.

---

35 "The Encyclopedia" is a reference to the *Encyclopédie, ou dictionnaire raisonné des sciences, des arts et des métiers*, a general encyclopedia published in France from 1751 to 1772. French philosopher Denis Diderot edited it and Jean le Rond D'Alembert co-edited it until 1759. Contributors included Voltaire, Rousseau, Montesquieu, and other leading *philosophes* (French Enlightenment intellectuals). It is worth emphasizing Janvier's claim: coffee produced by the enslaved people of Saint-Domingue fueled the French Enlightenment.

36 The 1878 World's Fair (L'Exposition Universelle de 1878) was held after the Franco-Prussian War and the downfall of the Second French Empire. Officials of the Third French Republic sought to use the fair to reassert France's position as a global power. Five years later, Amsterdam hosted the International Colonial and Export Exhibition. The event was the first world fair with a colonial theme. It also coincided with an era of heightened European colonialism, preceding by one year the infamous Berlin Conference in which the major European powers partitioned Africa. On Haiti's participation at the world's fairs of the late nineteenth century, see especially Hadassah St. Hubert, "Visions of a Modern Nation: Haiti at the World's Fairs" (PhD diss., University of Miami, 2018), 22–60.

37 Ceylon is the colonial name of the modern state of Sri Lanka. The entire island was united as a British Crown colony from 1815–1948. Residents of the

We cannot introduce monopoly at home in favor of any foreign power, because monopoly, abolished even by the most backwards metropoles, would be an odious measure and childish as well, as vexing as it would be silly; because today everyone knows that we must abandon absolutes, especially in political economy; that we must practice free trade or protection, or both at the same time, according to whether the interests of the country demand it, because, now more than ever, monopoly is contrary to all the healthy ideas of democratic policy and national dignity; because, as far as we are directly concerned, it would kill our commerce, our agriculture, by killing our initiative and our youthful expansion.

Long ago, in the eighteenth century, France fed Haiti with its wheat. Today, France buys a large portion of its wheat from the United States, because a hectoliter of wheat produced in France by French peasants costs 23 francs 50, whereas a hectoliter of wheat produced in the United States by American peasants is worth only 17 francs.[38] The Merchant Marine of the federal republic transports this wheat cheaply: thus, American wheat floods European markets. If Haiti were to stock up on French wheat, it is the Haitian consumer who would suffer due to the ineptitude of legislators who had imposed a monopoly upon him, which, here, would really be senseless, monstrous.

It is also important to take this fact into account: we import hardly any staple foods from France. I am putting aside books: a superior good, almost divine. We mostly import luxury items: fine cloth, fancy goods, toiletries.

Comestibles, cured meats, flours that we consume at home are mainly supplied to us by the United States. The canvas, the cotton fabrics that our peasants and artisans wear, we mostly buy them in the United States, England, and Germany, as well as our plowing implements.

---

nineteenth-century Americas and Europe sometimes referred to the modern state of El Salvador as the "Republic of San Salvador" or the "State of San Salvador."
38 In 1870, one French franc was roughly equivalent to five U.S. dollars. By World War I, it was worth a little more than five U.S. dollars; see R.L. Bidwell, *Currency Conversion Tables: A Hundred Years of Change* (London: Rex Collings, 1970), 19. Converting the contemporary value of historical currency is an inexact science, of course. But inflation calculators show that one U.S. dollar in 1884 was worth between twenty-three and twenty-six U.S. dollars today. Though Janvier correctly identifies the dangers of a trade monopoly for Haiti, he does not anticipate the dangers of U.S. agricultural dumping, which would prove disastrous for Haitian rice production in the late twentieth century. See Sophia Murphy and Karen Hansen-Kuhn, "The True Costs of US Agricultural Dumping," *Renewable Agriculture and Food Systems* 35, no. 4 (2000): 376–390.

Almost half of our importation traffic is with the United States alone.

These facts are the result of laws that are not at all artificial and against which the minor laws blindly voted in Parliament could not prevail.

Here again the monopoly granted to a power that would produce these essential items in lesser conditions, these items that are indispensable to the Haitian inhabitant's[39] existence, this monopoly would be fatal, disastrous for Haiti.

It would be supreme folly to escape from one economic vassalage only to fall into one that is more onerous, heavier, and more limiting.

A country that respects itself can only escape economic serfdom by creating national industries, by providing itself what it used to buy elsewhere.

We must concentrate all our efforts towards this goal. For one can only go from an agricultural phase to an industrial one by perfecting one's agriculture, to first enrich oneself to a certain point, then, to adapt foreign industries at home after having introduced them.

No country evades this evolution because it is natural, necessary. It is the only one that is reasonable and serious.

Besides, the United States' policy towards us is benevolent. We saw it during all of last year, especially on September 23rd.[40] But that is not a reason for us to be sentimental, to remove ourselves from one only to give ourselves to another. Let us implement a scientific policy, a policy based on self-interest. Let us first remain ourselves.

To whom did the Haitian people say they would abdicate? In whom did they confide that they could do nothing for themselves? Our fathers, it seems to me, created the Haitian nation alone, with no loans, they paid with the gold produced by their sweat for the right to live independently; they left us this corner of the earth so that there would be a place in the world where one cannot spit in the face of the black race with impunity. Let us uphold the traditions. Since we knew how to be born and grow alone, physically and intellectually, we can live and grow alone, materially.

It is through the mind that man is conquered. We entrust the minds of our children to France, which it seeds with its ideas.[41] That is enough. It is up to us to do the rest.

---

39 The original text reads "régnicole."
40 Another reference to the British ultimatum to Salomon on September 23, 1883.
41 Here and in the following passages Janvier acknowledges and appreciates the fact that many members of the nineteenth-century Haitian elite received their education, including a wide range of graduate and professional training,

Besides, we must make distinctions. There is a greater Europe: the one continued by Diderot, Condorcet, Grégoire, the Constituent Assembly, and the Convention; it is that of the philosophers, the thinkers and emancipators, that of lovers, of Michelet, Schoelcher, of Pierre Lafitte; that which says to us: We are freeing your minds so that one day you

in France. This trend, which predated Haitian independence, resulted from and, in some ways, exacerbated the obstacles to public education in Haiti. Many Haitian governments did not see themselves as responsible for the education of all Haitians, particularly rural residents. Some, including Salomon's administration, felt more compelled to spend public funds that might otherwise have gone to public education on suppressing opponents, who often had foreign encouragement. While many elites responded by sending their children to Europe for their education, parochial and private schools using French and embracing a French liberal arts curriculum became concentrated in Haiti's cities, particularly Port-au-Prince. These educational trends certainly had cultural implications and encouraged internal debate. Haitian intellectuals of Janvier's era considered whether a vocational or classical education would most benefit Haiti. Some, including Jean Price-Mars, extolled Booker T. Washington's Tuskegee Institute not only as a preferred place to send Haitian students but as a potential model for Haiti's educational system. Later, the U.S. government, with the encouragement of some Haitian politicians and African American educators, would try to universalize vocational education for Haitians during its occupation of Haiti. Haitian Creole (*Kreyòl*), the native language of most Haitians, entered schools for the first time albeit as a tool for creating a more "productive" rural citizenry rather than as part of a progressive reform. At the same time, amid the crisis of the occupation, Price-Mars would famously accuse the Haitian elite of a "collective bovarism." He argued that in seeing themselves as "colored Frenchmen" his compatriots of the professional classes had abandoned the African roots of Haitian peasant culture which were the actual foundations of a sovereign Haiti. While he and other proponents of Haitian *indigénisme* expressed some ambivalence about Haitian Creole their critiques of Eurocentrism, including in Haiti's educational history, certainly contributed to the legitimation of Haitian Creole in Haitian literature, politics, and education. See R.W. Logan, "Education in Haiti," *The Journal of Negro History* 15, no. 4 (October 1930): 401–460; Edner Brutus, *Instruction publique en Haïti, 1492–1945* (Port-au-Prince: Imprimerie de l'Etat, 1948); Job B. Clement, "History of Education in Haiti: 1804–1915," *Revista de Historia de América* no. 88 (July–December, 1979): 33–74; Jean Price-Mars, *La Vocation de l'élite* (Port-au-Prince: Editions, Fardin, 2002); Price-Mars, *So Spoke the Uncle (Ainsi parla l'oncle)*, trans. Magdaline W. Shannon (Washington, DC: Three Continents Press, 1993); Shannon, *Jean-Price Mars, The Haitian Elite and the American Occupation, 1915–35* (New York: St. Martin's Press, 1996); Leon D. Pamphile, "America's Policy-Making in Haitian Education, 1915–1934," *The Journal of Negro Education* 54, no. 1 (Winter 1985): 99–108; Matthew Robertshaw, "Occupying Creole: The Crisis of Language under the US Occupation of Haiti," *Journal of Haitian Studies* 24, no. 1 (Spring 2018): 4–24.

can take your place at the head of the black race.⁴² There is another [Europe]: that of the few small-time traffickers who have insulted us these past months. An altogether different blood than that of the Celts, the Tectosages, and the Burgondes flows through their veins; born near us, within our borders, or far away from us, these fortune hunters would sell the universe to treat themselves to girls.⁴³ To the first we give everything, beginning with our schools; against the second, as Latin as it may be, it makes sense to take the same precautions as we take against the Anglo-Saxons.

Instead of whining and begging, let us be wise, peaceful—and produce.

We should be wary of leasing la Gonâve and la Tortue to foreigners of whose true address we are not even sure. Whatever the nationality to which they say they belong, we cannot place them in these outposts of our nation. Thus is stoked the hope of stealing La Gonâve just as la Navase was taken from us.⁴⁴

42 In celebrating and romanticizing a "greater Europe" that he associates with the French Enlightenment, Janvier alludes to the French philosophers Denis Diderot, Pierre Lafitte, and Marie Jean Antoine Nicolas de Caritat (Marquis de Condorcet); abolitionists Henri Grégoire and Victor Schœlcher; and historian Jules Michelet. The National Constituent Assembly formed during the initial stages of the French Revolution while the National Convention governed France from 1792 to 1795.

43 Here Janvier is claiming a respectable ethnic heritage for his romanticized "greater Europe" and, in turn, denigrating the roots of the "other Europe." The ancient Greeks invented the word Celt (*Keltos*), which they used to designate the tribes situated in various places from the Danube River to the Iberian Peninsula. According to historian Nell Irvin Painter, Celt first "denoted hidden people, painted people, strange people, and barbarians to the west." Self-proclaimed Celts would later associate themselves with a more inclusive racial category—white—and locate their origins in French Brittany and Great Britain while nineteenth-century social scientists came to consider Celtic as a distinct, and distinctly "good," European "racial type." Tectosages and Burgondes (Burgandians) are more obscure products of this period of racial categorization. The former refers to a tribal group of Celts while the latter describes a subgroup of Vandals, a central European tribe most often associated with Germanic identity or "racial stock." See Nell Irvin Painter, *The History of White People* (New York: W.W. Norton & Company, 2010).

44 Navassa is a small island off the western coast of Haiti. Haiti's claim to the island predated its independence and remained a fixture of its post-independence constitutions but in 1857 a U.S. ship captain seized Navassa for the United States. In doing so, he took advantage of recent changes in U.S. law. By the 1840s, U.S. farmers and businessmen had identified seabird guano—excrement—as

We have the strict duty to stop on the slippery slope of concessions of financial or industrial enterprises to individuals who are not or are no longer Haitian, who even seem to have no defined nationality except at the moment of the most unjust and cynical claims.

We need to redouble our surveillance around Môle-Saint-Nicolas. At the very most, we can create a free port at the end of the northwest peninsula; but it would be the biggest of political mistakes to establish Môle-Saint-Nicolas as a free city. A free city is an independent State. We should know this. What need is there to create a State within the State? What reason do we have to break up our national patrimony? And especially to part with the best pieces? ...

Let us borrow neither a penny nor a doubloon either from the United States or from any transatlantic power.

Let us initiate a purely national financial policy. We can and we should. Let us not consolidate our debts. This is extremely important. Along with indirect contributions, let us establish direct taxes. Let us seek Haitian savings for the capital we need by creating savings banks, and through them, popular banks for peasants and artisans.

Let us show that we have faith in ourselves by focusing within. Those who have no confidence cannot inspire any. Let the skeptics and cowards talk, but let us act for the Haitian contingent.

Rather than letting our national fabric be frayed by the poison of cowardly advice, weakened by sacrifices recommended by spineless spirits, let us strengthen it. Let us hold a vivid and clear love for the homeland's interests in our heart. Let us advise each other to be wise, patient, to abstain from petty and surly conflicts. During the course of debates about public affairs, let us set aside all personal friendship, all

---

a uniquely potent fertilizer. The nitrate-rich substance was said to produce massive increases in crop yields. In the midst of what became known as "guano mania," the U.S. Congress passed the Guano Islands Act of 1856, which permitted any U.S. citizen to mine and claim, in the name of the United States, any "uninhabited" or "unclaimed" island containing significant guano deposits. The act resulted in an intensification of U.S. imperialism. Following the enactment of the Guano Islands Act, the United States and its citizens claimed more than one hundred islands across the world, including Navassa. Scholarship on this aspect of U.S. expansionism includes Ludwell Lee Montague, "La Navase, 1857–1917," *Revue de la Société d'Histoire et de Géographie d'Haïti* 12, no. 37 (April 1940): 1–24; Skaggs, *The Great Guano Rush*; Abel Léger, "La Navase dans notre Diplomatie," *Revue de la Société Haïtienne d'Histoire, de Géographie et de Géologie* 53, no. 197 (December 1998); Cushman, *Guano and the Opening of the Pacific World*; Salt, *The Unfinished Revolution*, 113–152; Goffe, "Guano in Their Destiny."

familial influence, all individual pride. Let us see the individual and the family less; let us see only the State, the nation. Let us stifle any thought of insurrection by erasing all traces of civil war, but let us also prepare to manfully and mercilessly repress through scientific means any insurrectional attempt that might occur.

Wealth is the daughter of credit; credit can only be born in the shade of peace, security, stability. What made the prosperity of Saint-Domingue long ago was not loans, nor free cities, nor even free ports, nor monopoly; monopoly on the contrary kept this colony from fully developing and expanding. What made this prosperity was first this: peace and small property, that is to say private initiative, direct farming by the individual owner of the land; personal capital; then, later, at a time closer to our own, peace again, large properties, and slavery.

While the large plantation system was the rule, twenty-five thousand slaves died each year, worn down by beatings or through torture. Without which, during that time, nothing would have been produced, no one would have worked. We have to return to the small property system in the mountains as well as in the plains.[45] In a country like ours, given the climate and the political system, it is the most rational. We have to divide up the large plantations that belong to the State. Before anything else, let us return the land to the peasant's hands. On this point, let us not listen to what retrogrades have to say: here, every minute of delay is an economic error and a political error.[46]

---

45 Janvier's championing of the "system of small property" is evocative of what later scholars identified as the "counter plantation" system. Jean Casimir has defined that system as "a specific social organization encompassing a variety of techniques invented by the workers (enslaved, freedman and indentured labourers) to oppose the owners and their metropolitan countries"; *The Caribbean: One and Divisible* (United Nations: Economic Commission for Latin America and the Caribbean, 1992), 79. See Johnhenry Gonzalez, *Maroon Nation: A History of Revolutionary Haiti* (New Haven: Yale University Press, 2019).

46 Janvier's appeal here affirms Salomon's agrarian law in February 1883, which is discussed in the Introduction to this volume. In this portion of his text, Janvier goes beyond, and perhaps critiques, the terms of that law by proposing the establishment of "popular banks" and the extension of credit from the Haitian state to the Haitian peasantry. According to the economist Mats Lundhal, one reason for the modest success of Salomon's land reform policies was the peasants' relative lack of the resources needed to grow export crops such as coffee at the scale and for the duration required in the law. Lundhal also notes that the Haitian government offered no financial support to the Haitian peasantry, which would have helped resolve the first issue. See Lundahl, *Peasants and Poverty*, 266.

Let us also try to increase the number of Protestants in the country, thus making it undergo a rapid evolution from fetishism to Catholicism to Protestantism, as fast, as transformative as what we see in Sweden from Gustave Wasa to Gustave-Adolphe.[47] The Protestant is frugal, respectful of the law, a book lover, a friend of peace, full of valiant hope, of perseverance. He counts on himself, knows how to capitalize on the material and the immaterial. He eliminates carnival, holidays as numerous as they are costly and which, tiring as they are, weaken his productivity as a worker or father. Catholic wealth is a myth. The dreamy, sleepy, imaginative, quickly discouraged, spendthrift nations are Catholic. They remain poor or are ruined in a short time, are soon decadent.

All that negotiates, cultivates, fabricates, wins, enriches, prospers, is Protestant.

All the great philosophers say so and History proves it, *Heaven helps those who help themselves*, there is the great sword.

Through Protestantism, everyone will learn to recognize their rights and their duties.[48]

---

47 Gustav Eriksson Vasa (Gustavus I) established Swedish independence from Denmark and reigned as king from 1523 to 1560. He also facilitated the beginning of the Reformation in Sweden. The move towards Lutheranism, motivated by an interest in weakening the political and economic power of the Roman Catholic Church, continued during the reign of his grandson, Gustav II Adolf (Gustavus Adolphus). During his reign (1611–1632), Gustav II fought against Roman Catholic resistance to internal reform and Protestantism, what became known as the Counter Reformation. He died fighting in the Thirty Years' War (1618–1648), a series of wars that began as a conflict between Protestant and Catholic states in the Holy Roman Empire. For a concise history of Sweden, see Byron J. Nordstrom, *The History of Sweden* (Westport: Greenwood Press, 2002).

48 Janvier's linkage of Protestantism to economic and social progress and his attendant association of Vodou ("fetishism") and Catholicism with material and moral poverty reflect widespread thinking about religion, race, and civilization that pervaded the nineteenth-century Atlantic World, particularly in an age of ascendant and ostensibly Protestant imperial powers such as Great Britain, the United States, and Germany. Janvier's views are also part of a long-standing political and intellectual tradition in which Haitian intellectuals and political actors proscribed certain religions, particularly Vodou, associated with "backwardness" and Africa while trying to strengthen Haiti's claims to other faith traditions, including Protestantism or, in other instances, Catholicism, deemed more civilized and modern. On this history, see especially David Nicholls, "Politics and Religion in Haiti," *Canadian Journal of Political Science* 3, no. 3 (September 1970): 400–414; Kate Ramsey, *The Spirits and the Law: Vodou and*

That is the policy to adopt. It is that of the healthy and the mighty. It is the great, the good, the scientific one. It is there that we will find salvation and nowhere else.

The Haitian nation is warned. It is threatened on all sides; some do so cynically, others hypocritically. They conspire, they plot, they scheme against it, some in broad daylight, others in the shadows.

Having paid very dearly for its independence—with its blood, with its money, with its resolution to not weaken in the face of slander and insults—it must want to keep it complete, absolute, and whole.

If the Haitian nation wants to live, it must watch over its independence. It must guard it without pause, night and day.

What we are saying here must remain ingrained in the soul of each peasant and each thinker, in the mind of every soldier and every political writer, present in the memory of each deputy, each minister, each senator.

May the citizen perform his duty so that the nation leaves nothing to chance. To put down weapons or to not take up arms at all is to surrender everything to chance, to the unknown.

A nation cannot live autonomously, cannot grow on its own unless at every moment each one of its sons taken in isolation, each one demonstrates individually the haughty, proud, imperious will of the nation.

June 10, 1884

Power in Haiti (Chicago: University of Chicago Press, 2011); Julia Gaffield, "The Racialization of International Law after the Haitian Revolution: The Holy See and National Sovereignty," *American Historical Review* 125, no. 2 (June 2020): 841–868.

Our Adjacent Islands

When you live surrounded by enemies and all kinds of pitfalls, you cannot guard against surprises too carefully.

It is not generally known that there is a law in the United States, dating from August 12, 1856, whereby any abandoned island becomes the property of that citizen of the American union who discovers or takes possession of it.[49]

If that island is rich in guano deposits, instead of being the property of one or several citizens, it can be declared federal property, a Union territory.

This bill was passed at a time when islands rich in guano started to attract the attention of Americans, who needed that dung to manure and fertilize their lands.

All sovereign States that have traditions have always refused to accept the legitimacy of the cavalier claims expressed by the United States. We Haitians do not pay enough mind to the past and not enough to the future. Two errors. And very serious ones at that.

The example of la Navase should have put us on guard, should have woken us up.

Alta-Véla,[50] la Béate,[51] la Tortue, and la Gonâve are guano islands.

Even supposing that, for the moment, immense quantities cannot be exploited, it would be good for the purposes of a protective policy for these islands to be heavily and diligently occupied.

It is said, without sufficient reason, that la Béate and Alta-Véla do not belong to us at all. That is wrong. Long ago those islands were French dependencies rather than Spanish ones, whereas the latter ruled Santo Domingo. From 1844 to this day we have not relinquished them.[52] They

---

49 Reference to the Guano Islands Act of 1856.

50 A small island located off the southern coast of the island. It is now a Dominican territory.

51 A small island approximately 60 miles northeast of Isla Alto Velo. It is also now a Dominican territory.

52 In February 1822, Haitian president Jean-Pierre Boyer launched a successful movement of the Haitian military into neighboring Santo Domingo with strong popular support from its popular classes. He declared emancipation in that part of Hispaniola and governed over a unified island for the next two decades. In February 1844, months after Haitians and Dominicans dissatisfied with Boyer's

are almost situated in our territorial waters, too close to our coasts, too close to Jacmel for us to let any flag fly there other than the one flown in Port-au-Prince.

It would be a wise measure to establish penal colonies [on them] or colonies of political convicts tasked with exploiting them.[53] They would cultivate them, or at least would fish in their waters, so that it would be well demonstrated that we consider them to be ours.

La Gonâve hides the entrance to Port-au-Prince's harbor, guards and defends it. La Tortue looks upon Port-de-Paix, controls the path out of the straits and of the Wind Canal.

Let us not forget that when the buccaneers settled on that island, at the beginning of the seventeenth century, they only did so because it had been abandoned by the Spanish, the only ones who could have claimed legitimate ownership at the time.

The Americans did not hesitate to occupy la Navase, have no shame about refusing to return it, even though they can only extract guano. Now that they are looking to have all the means of access, all the

---

autocratic governance removed the Haitian president from office, a small but influential movement of Dominican elites spearheaded Dominican separation from Haiti. Its independence claimed, the Dominican government proceeded to announce its sovereignty over Isla Beata and Isla Alto Velo, two guano islands also claimed by Haiti and, by the 1860s, the United States. On the intertwined histories of nineteenth-century Haiti and the Dominican Republic, see especially Eller, *We Dream Together*.

53 A subsequent event clarifies the shortsightedness of Janvier's proposal to establish Haitian sovereignty over the guano islands by building penal colonies on them. In September 1889, African Americans working in the guano mines on Navassa rebelled against their white overseers employed by the Baltimore-based Navassa Phosphate Company. The black workers had few other work prospects in the post-Reconstruction United States. On Navassa, they faced brutal working conditions, scarce provisions, and arbitrary punishments. The Navassa Phosphate Company effectively locked them into those conditions akin to slavery by charging exorbitant prices at the company store, the only source of goods on the island. After the rebellion, which resulted in the deaths of five white men, more than forty of the black workers were charged with crimes under U.S. law. The five leaders were all charged with murder and three were sentenced to hang. Citing the slavery-like conditions on Navassa, U.S. president Benjamin Harrison would eventually commute their death sentences to life at hard labor. For more on this event, see especially John Cashman, "'Slaves under Our Flag': The Navassa Island Riot of 1889," *Maryland Historian* 24, no. 2 (Fall/Winter 1993): 1–21 and Jennifer C. James, "'Buried in Guano': Race, Labor, and Sustainability," *American Literary History* 24, no. 1 (Spring 2012): 115–142.

keys to the future Panama Canal in their possession at any price, they would perhaps not back down from the idea of getting their hands on la Tortue.⁵⁴

The Americans have singular ways of understanding things. With a diplomatic dispatch dated June 24, 1881 addressed to the London office, Mr. Blaine, then Secretary, had already made it known that the government of the United States reserved for itself alone the right to protect the interoceanic canal. Based on the thesis he was advancing, the White House's future occupant invoked a treaty made in 1846 between New Granada and the Confederated Republic of the north.⁵⁵

England having responded that it was relying on the stipulations of a treaty signed in 1850 by Clayton and Bulwer, which assured the neutrality of the canal at all times, the Americans made it clearly understood that they would not take the Clayton-Bulwer treaty into account at all, and that the canal would be considered to belong to the coastal territory of the United States.⁵⁶

---

54 The Panama Canal cuts through the Isthmus of Panama, enabling the passage of ships between the Caribbean Sea and the Pacific Ocean. The first attempt to construct the interoceanic canal was begun in the 1880s by the Compagnie Universelle du Canal Interocéanique de Panama but failed due to design flaws, mismanagement of funds, and the high mortality rate among workers. The U.S. government gained the rights to the proposed canal at the turn of the twentieth century. The acquisition of this concession and the completion of the Panama Canal in 1914 further cemented the status of the United States as an imperial, global power. On the history of the United States and the Panama Canal, see especially John Major, *Prize Possession: The United States and the Panama Canal, 1903–1977* (New York: Cambridge University Press, 1993); Alexander Missal, *Seaway to the Future: American Social Visions and the Construction of the Panama Canal* (Madison: University of Wisconsin Press, 2008); Julie Greene, *The Canal Builders: Making America's Empire at the Panama Canal* (New York: Penguin, 2009).

55 On December 12, 1846, the United States and New Granada (present-day Columbia and Panama) signed the Bidlack Treaty (also called the Treaty of New Granada). Under its terms, the United States received an exclusive right of transit across the Isthmus of Panama in exchange for its guarantee of neutrality for and recognition of New Granada's sovereignty over the isthmus. The Bidlack Treaty was thus the rare nineteenth-century agreement in which the United States, then concerned with Great Britain's potential incursions in Central and South America, acknowledged the sovereignty of a Latin American state.

56 On April 19, 1850, Great Britain and the United States signed the Clayton-Bulwer Treaty (named for its principal negotiators, British minister to the United States Henry Lytton Bulwer and U.S. secretary of state John M. Clayton). The treaty dictated that neither the United States nor Great Britain would "occupy,

A Significant fact! A Lesson to be learned!

It would be desirable for Haitians to be the sole concessionaries of la Tortue and la Gonâve; for pastoral or agricultural logging to begin immediately on these islands so that no one can use their relative abandonment to come and seize them.

The future belongs only to those individuals or nations who know how to anticipate, prevent, and act.

June 15, 1884

or fortify, or colonize, or assume or exercise any dominion over Nicaragua, Costa Rica, the Mosquito Coast [the Caribbean coast of present-day Honduras and Nicaragua], or any part of Central America …" and stipulated that they would share control over the planned canal across the Isthmus of Panama. The treaty, prioritizing an ambivalent language of neutrality and shared power, proved unappealing to both parties. It was eventually superseded by the Hay-Pauncefote Treaty (1901), which granted the United States exclusive rights to the construction and control of the Panama Canal, and the Hay-Bunau-Varilla Treaty (1903), which established the U.S.-controlled Panama Canal Zone in exchange for the recognition of Panamanian independence. The United States maintained exclusive control of the canal until the signing of the Carter-Torrijos Treaty (1977), which established a twenty-year period of U.S. withdrawal that culminated in the final transfer of ownership from the United States to the Republic of Panama in 1999. All treaties were named for their principal negotiators or signatories: U.S. secretary of state John Hay and British ambassador to the United States Julian Pauncefote; Hay and Philippe-Jean Bunau-Varilla, a French capitalist who led the Panamanian diplomatic delegation that negotiated the Hay-Bunau-Varilla Treaty; and U.S. president Jimmy Carter and Omar Torrijos, commander of the Panamanian National Guard.

The Trap

They say it everywhere, our dear friends and dubious relatives, that they have obtained important concessions due to your gullibility, and that they can get all the concessions they ask for. They even say it in our own newspapers.[57]

They ask that European governments grab Môle-Saint-Nicolas. They are surprised, indignant even, that in their childish or senile ignorance the accredited diplomats in Haiti have not yet designated this prey to the attention of those for whom they renounce or would renounce their country of origin and the country they want to exploit.

They add, with equal parts impertinence and mockery, that if we give them Môle-Saint-Nicolas, they will pay us a small yearly fee.

They offer to rebuild our cities, the same ones they threatened to burn a few months ago, to lend us money against our harvests and our logging for cabinetmaking and dying.

They especially want to purchase our debt, which they first want to be consolidated.[58]

The gullible, who are shortsighted, the suckers who speak of economic conquest without really knowing what it is, the gluttons, for whom money is everything and national honor nothing, they all take them at their word.

---

57 There were many Haitian newspapers in the late 1870s and early 1880s, thanks in large part to robust regional printing operations. In addition to *Le Moniteur*, Haiti's official state journal, *L'Avant-garde*, *La Nation*, *L'Oeil*, and *Le Peuple* were among the most prominent papers from the period. *Le Constitutionnel*, *Le Démocrate*, *L'Égalité*, *L'Haïtien*, *L'Homme libre*, *Les Mousquetaires*, *Le Patriote*, *Le Ralliement*, *Le Spectateur*, and *Le Vigilant* are also notable Haitian newspapers of the era. Most of these publications were microfilmed from the Saint Louis de Gonzague Collection by the LAMP project and are accessible from the Center for Research Libraries (CRL) and the University of Miami libraries. Unfortunately, the quality of film renders many of them unreadable. For this reason, David Nicholls's meticulous periodical research in *From Dessalines to Duvalier* remains a vital resource for understanding late nineteenth-century periodical culture in Haiti. See also Desquiron, *Haïti à la une* and Bissainthe, *Dictionnaire de Bibliographie Haïtienne*.

58 Janvier is referring to loans taken out in 1874 and 1875. See note 21 in the Introduction.

Until now, we have rebuilt our cities ourselves, without anyone's help, we have plowed our fields, sowed, planted, and harvested. We can continue to manage our own affairs.

And now, may those who desire to get to the heart of things, to know what's what, listen well and retain this: all these gigantic plans (they beg for tens of millions in order to execute them) and all the hypocritical declarations of friendship made to us by overly sentimental financiers, they are all hiding a trap.

When the debt is consolidated—if it is?!—five or ten years later, financial syndicates belonging to some European nation or another will snatch up the Haitian bonds, buying them and clearing out the European and American markets by driving down prices by telegraph. Then, seizing upon the first pretext, which they will provoke themselves as needed, helped by unscrupulous legislators or advocates of the extreme colonial policy, they will send ships to our ports to display mizzenmasts bearing the military ensign and scuttle armed with steel canons.[59]

If we do not resist, our cities will be occupied; and if we resist, they will be bombed like Alexandria was bombed. In both cases, we will be subjected to a political and financial protectorate just like the one imposed upon the Egyptians.[60]

In less than a half-century, the Haitian populations would be civilized, that is to say, they would have disappeared like those of Australia and New Zealand.[61]

---

59 When the French monarch Charles X sent his decree acknowledging Haitian independence in exchange for the indemnity agreement, it was accompanied "by a squadron of 14 brigs of war carrying more than 500 cannons." Daut, "When France Extorted Haiti."

60 See note 11 accompanying "The Watchword."

61 Janvier refers here to the devastating effects of British colonization on the Indigenous peoples of Australia and New Zealand. British settlement of the former began in 1788, while Great Britain established the latter as a crown colony in 1841. Although the Indigenous populations of both British settler colonies declined precipitously over the course of the nineteenth century, Indigenous people in both lands did survive genocide. The Māori people of New Zealand and Aboriginal Australians would both launch powerful protest movements in the mid- to late twentieth century and reclaim significant cultural and political power as part of their respective national renaissances. Demographic growth has ensued. Today, the New Zealand government estimates that the Māori make up approximately 17 percent of New Zealand's population while the Australian government estimated in 2016 that Aboriginal Australians accounted for a little more than 3 percent of its total population. Further reading on this topic includes Richard Broome, *Aboriginal Australians*, 5th ed. (Sydney: Allen

Such would be the certain consequence of the great projects they have the impudence or childishness to not keep quiet, so flexible, simple, and naïve they think us; to the point of imagining that we are honored to be fooled by them.

In any case and any way we want to look at it, from political and financial protectorate to definitive annexation, there is but one step.

For now, our creditors are not really baring their teeth, because the Haitian bonds and the Treasury bonds of our internal debt are scattered among those with private income or French, English, American, German, Belgian, and Italian capitalists.

That is why they are first trying the trick of debt consolidation, precursor to the unspeakable maneuver that succeeded not only in Egypt but elsewhere.

Maneuver of the strong against the weak, of the wise against the ignorant, of those who have known how to prepare for a long time, to combine a political and financial action against those who, abhorring the book, have no brain!

We Haitians have a Parliament before which ministers are responsible. The idea of the homeland that the Muslims and the Orientals hardly possess fills our hearts and brains.

That is enough to make us see clearly.

Sons of courageous men, we are and want to remain free; we do not at all resemble those poor creatures who have been beaten for centuries on the banks of the Nile.

Our deputies and senators are responsible before us. We have the right to speak to each one of them as equals. So that no one ignores it, we are warning them again. They must not pledge that precious entity which we have entrusted to their patriotism and their enlightenment. We beg them to not imitate those foul figures who in 1875 compromised our country, delayed its evolution, humiliated its name with their incompetence, with their thirst for gold and base pleasures.[62] We remind them

---

& Unwin, 2019) and Robert J. Miller, Jacinta Ruru, Larissa Behrendt, and Tracey Lindberg, *Discovering Indigenous Lands: The Doctrine of Discovery in the English Colonies* (Oxford: Oxford University Press, 2010).

62 Janvier seems to be making reference to a series of events during the presidency of Michel Domingue (1874–1876). Before becoming president of Haiti, Domingue had amassed a particularly violent record as a military and political leader during the civil wars of 1868–1869 and gained a reputation for despotism, particularly among Liberals. That reputation proved accurate during his ensuing presidency. In 1874, Domingue signed a 21 million franc loan with Marcuard André et Cie., which was taken over by Crédit industriel et commercial (CiC) in 1875. See note 21 in

that they will have to account for their actions, not only to the Haitians who are coming up, but also to History.

If they want to find money immediately to satisfy the nation's urgent needs, they should impose, during the course of this same session, a personal and real estate tax on the foreigners who are currently despoiling us in complete disregard of all the rules of justice and international law. They should revise the customs tariffs in a few sessions; they are antiquated and vague to the point of absurdity, costing us at least three million per year. They should manfully punish, bloodily even, the reckless or the pillagers who act as accomplices of foreign smugglers; they should chase the latter from the country either by revoking their patents or by imposing large fines upon them. They must place Protestants, honest ones, at the head of all the customs houses. They must impose an economic and financial program in which all the vital reforms will be included; they must reduce the interest of floating debt.

Moreover, we must try everything, anything, have recourse to all financial expedients, even to paper money, the last of them all, rather than consolidate the debt.[63]

---

the Introduction. The disadvantageous terms of the loans put up Haitian territory and sovereignty itself as collateral. Here, Janvier pleads with those government functionaries responsible for overseeing such transactions not to make the same mistakes as Domingue's government and mortgage the country's future for their own gain. Domingue also jeopardized Haiti's sovereignty by fomenting diplomatic crises. In 1875, he ordered the arrests of three prominent Liberals, whom he accused of conspiring against his government. These alleged conspirators included General Pierre Théoma Boisrond Canal. While Domingue's forces killed Boisrond Canal's two affiliates, Boisrond Canal escaped to the U.S. legation just outside of Port-au-Prince. Ebenezer Don Carlos Bassett, the U.S. minister resident and consul general to Haiti, gave him asylum while hundreds of Haitian soldiers surrounded the legation. Bassett's actions resulted in a personal reprimand from the U.S. secretary of state Hamilton Fish, who informed Bassett that the United States did not recognize a right to asylum, and touched off a brief diplomatic crisis between Haiti and the United States. The stand-off ended after several months when a U.S. ship took Boisrond Canal to Kingston, Jamaica. In April 1876, a Liberal insurgency, which had gathered steam in the Cul-de-Sac plain where Boisrond Canal had significant landholdings, succeeded in overthrowing Domingue. Liberal support then coalesced around the election of Boisrond Canal as president. See Matthew J. Smith, *Liberty, Fraternity, Exile: Haiti and Jamaica after Emancipation* (Chapel Hill: University of North Carolina Press, 2014), 201, 210–211 and Logan, *The Diplomatic Relations of the United States with Haiti*, 364–365.

63 The indemnity agreement forced Boyer to issue paper money, which led to a decline in the value of the country's currency. See Victor Bulmer-Thomas, *The*

I say it again, I repeat: behind this consolidation we must see the trap set for us by those who love us so much that in their fervor to enrich themselves under the false pretense of enriching us, they are capable of having us eaten alive.

August 12, 1884

Dr. Louis-Joseph Janvier

Economic History of the Caribbean Since the Napoleonic Wars (Cambridge: Cambridge University Press, 2012), 182. Paper money inflation became a recurring concern in nineteenth-century Haiti.

Critical Essays

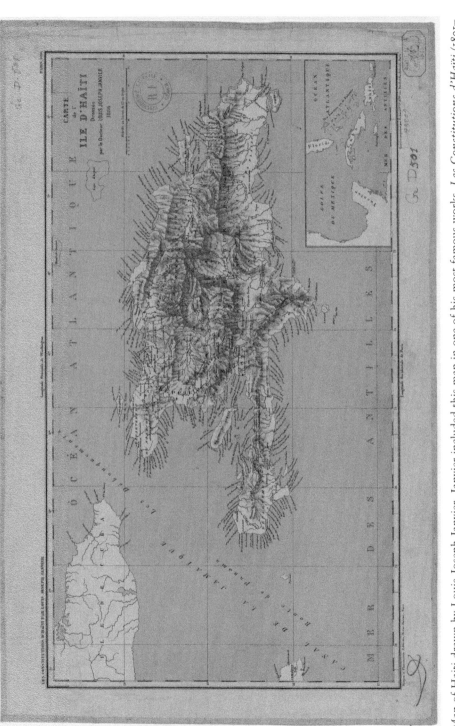

Map of Haiti drawn by Louis-Joseph Janvier. Janvier included this map in one of his most famous works, *Les Constitutions d'Haïti (1801–1885)*, which he published in 1886. It is indicative of the same, close attention to geopolitics displayed in *Haïti aux Haïtiens*. (Source: Gallica, Bibliothèque nationale de France)

CHAPTER ONE

Louis-Joseph Janvier, National Writer

Yves Chemla
For Ludovic Janvier
Translated from French by Nadève Ménard

Louis-Joseph Janvier was born in Port-au-Prince on May 7, 1855. He is considered to be one of the most brilliant essayists of his time and a first-rate thinker. Despite their differences, the essayist Duraciné Vaval wrote of him with marked praise:

> His work embodies the national ideal. Admirable work! Immense! Majestic! A monument adapted to the needs of our people that reflects its aspirations, its miseries, its distress! The man behind the Work enjoyed a great reputation. His books are rare fruit fallen from a tree the roots of which plunge into the depths of our soil.[1]

Of course, for those who are familiar with Haiti, these roots are also those of the Freedom Tree, evoked by Toussaint Louverture when he was being shipped off to France. The image does not stop there: Janvier spent most of his life in Europe. And his work, although often mentioned, seems in fact to be relatively unknown. References to Janvier are usually to the patriotic writer whose work was ill received and is characterized by his sometimes outrageous phrasing. Janvier's literary career demonstrates a limitless appetite for knowledge within the limits defined by the test of rationality. Yes, Janvier's thought has its origins in the Protestant faith, but he always aims to ground his discourse in reason, in essays as well as in his major novel, *Une chercheuse*. Between the 1870s and the 1890s, the anthropological issue was a big one: the works of European anthropological societies cemented scientific dogma on the inequality of the human races. Along with Firmin, Janvier was at the heart of the battle that aimed at deconstructing an ideological

---

1 Duracine Vaval, *Histoire de la littérature haïtienne ou l'âme noire* (Port-au-Prince: Imprimerie Auguste Héraux, 1933), 327.

structure that was very solidly implanted. Here is what Firmin recalled in 1885:

> As for Mr. Janvier, he himself would be enough to prove to what extent the black man's intelligence can reach the highest regions of the mind [...] Mr. Janvier has this special character: it seems he wanted to remain at school his entire life; yet, in his writings, he breathes only action. Some may see an obsession with diplomas pushed to the extreme, but I consider his behavior from another point of view. He probably has the objective of proving, by his own example, the great elasticity of the black man's brain and the facility his mind has to bend to all types of knowledge without fatigue. As such, his experience has a great and incontestable value; and his country has not to regret the expenditures made to sustain him abroad.[2]

It seemed important to recall the most salient traits of this work, the reading of which, it will quickly become apparent, will contribute to a more extensive understanding of Haitian literature. It is also important to constantly reposition Janvier's work within this long ideological tradition which began during the Restoration with Baron Eckstein, propagandist of theses of "Indo-Germanic" civilizational primacy and whose salon would welcome Hugo, Lamartine, Ballanche, Lamennais, Ozanam, Augustin Thierry, Michelet, and so many others.[3] The slow circulation and clarification of these theses would continue until the 1870s through the 1890s, with Quinet, Gobineau, and of course Renan in France. It is against this ideological backdrop that Janvier updates his own critical discourse, which he mixes with that of the political and social perceptions of his country.

Coming from a Protestant family from Morne-à-Tuf, Janvier claimed a visceral grounding in Haiti: his grandfather was close to Pétion, his father to Soulouque and Geffrard. He even writes in *Les Antinationaux*: "my paternal ancestor has Indian blood in his veins." But at the same time, his work reflects a critical distance with regard to the way affairs are conducted in Haitian society and indeed its very form. He spent the majority of his life abroad. He left Haiti in 1877, and studied medicine in Paris, then political science (economics, administration, and diplomacy) and law in Lille. Having become a member of

---

2 Anténor Firmin, *De l'égalité des races humaines (anthropologie positive)* (Paris: F. Pichon, 1885), 464.

3 Nicolas Burtin (O.P.), *Un semeur d'idée au temps de la Restauration, le baron d'Eckstein (1790–1861)* (Paris: E. de Boccart, 1931).

the Paris Anthropological Society in 1882, he successively published *La République d'Haïti et ses visiteurs* (1883), *Haïti aux Haïtiens, L'Égalité des races, Le Vieux piquet, Les Antinationaux, actes et principes* (1884), *Les Affaires d'Haïti (1883–1884)* (1885), *Les Constitutions d'Haïti* (1886), *Une chercheuse* (1888), *Du gouvernement civil en Haïti* (1905). He was thus intensely active during these European years and was a renowned personality. He gave a remarkable speech at the inauguration of Michelet's tomb in 1882. He was a regular at poet Leconte de Lisle's salon. He spent time with François Coppée, Mallarme, Hérédia, Barrès, Reclus. According to Duraciné Vaval, "Judith Gautier […] was intoxicated with his company, as was Elisée Reclus, the geographer."[4] From 1884 onwards he was tasked with various diplomatic missions by the Haitian government. From 1889 to 1904, he was stationed in London, first as legion secretary, then as chargé d'affaires before being appointed resident minister to the court of Saint-James.

He returned to Haiti in 1905, after an absence of twenty-eight years, and unsuccessfully attempted a political career, then went into exile. Although he was appointed Minister Counselor in London, he settled in Paris following a dispute with Duraciné Vaval, the official Minister. He died, exhausted, on March 24, 1911.

Janvier's oeuvre most likely reflects these paradoxes, and foremost, the evocation of Haiti from abroad, from the point of view of the other. Thus, the first important text he published, in 1881, is his thesis, dedicated to pulmonary phthisis. The care put into its publication, the print quality, seems to attest to the importance of this book for its author, although he would never practice as a medical doctor.[5] A large part of Janvier's medical argument consisted in showing that tuberculosis was the result of exhaustion due to debauchery and an unhealthy lifestyle. Yet Haitian peasants suffer from this disease less than others. Thus they lead a healthy lifestyle, founded on strong hygiene. Since in some ways Haitians constitute the vanguard of a proto-negritude, being free since 1804, he could affirm: "From a purely ethnic point of view, from the perspective of pathological anthropology, the black race is not more predisposed than others to tuberculosis."[6] We can always blame Janvier—after the Medical School in Paris—for not having shown sufficient interest in the works of Pasteur and Koch (the bacilli of tuberculosis

---

4 Vaval, *Histoire de la littérature haïtienne*, 320.
5 Louis-Joseph Janvier, *Phtisie pulmonaire. Causes—traitement préventif* (Paris: Imprimerie Antoine Parent, 1881).
6 Ibid., 68.

are only highlighted in 1882), but we must above all retain that this discourse, with its hygienist assumptions, is mostly a discourse to fight against the racism as scientific discourse that was current at the time, including among the members of the Anthropology Society of Paris. It seemed essential then for Janvier to establish a representation of Haiti that was positive and poetic, as if in the mountains where the peasants sought refuge, there remained something of the Paradise transformed into Hell by Columbus[7] and his continuators:

> All these pretty cities that the morning breeze perfumes with the scents of the surrounding mountains and where the night wind, whether it comes from the high sea or the hills, is so fresh and full of delicious fragrances that it intoxicates, all these happy sojourns, when we feel so joyful to breathe and where life is endless enjoyment, know very little of or rather do not know at all the ravages of the cruel illness.[8]

This illness that was still lurking was first of all poverty, however, and it was indeed Europeans who transmitted it. All of Janvier's books resonate with this questioning, and little by little highlight the demonization at work in discourses on Haitians, but also among Haitians themselves, towards the "pays en-dehor."[9]

In 1882, he contributed to a collective volume, *Les Détracteurs de la race noire et de la république d'Haïti*[10] (with Jules Auguste, Arthur Bowler, Clément Denis, Justin Prévost, preceded by letters by M. Schoelcher and Betancès, great figures in the fight against prejudice), in which the authors spoke against the racist and degrading declarations

---

7 "It is most likely voluntarily that Columbus adopted for his name the definitive form of the word colonizer [*cólon*] has the same meaning in Spanish and in French." Christophe Colomb, *La Découverte de l'Amérique, vol. 2: relations de voyage, 1493–1504*, trans. Soledad Estorach and Michel Lequenne (Paris: François Maspero, 1981), 12. We can tie this remark by Michel Lequenne to this reminder: "During his second voyage in 1493 composed of 17 caravels and over 1500 heavily armed men, he would bring among other plants (seeds for orange trees, lime trees, lemon trees and cattle, horses, cows), cutting of sugar cane from the island of Goméra in the Canaries, to be acclimated to the West Indies in Hispaniola." Christian Montbrun, "La Canne à sucre de l'Asie au Maroc au XVIe siècle," in *La Route du sucre du VIIIe au XVIIIe siècle*, ed. É. Eadie (Matoury: Ibis rouge Éditions, 2001), 58.

8 Janvier, *Phtisie pulmonaire*, 32.

9 Rural areas.

10 Louis-Joseph Janvier, *Les Détracteurs de la race noire et de la république d'Haïti* (Paris: Marpon et Flammarion, 1882).

that appeared in certain journals (a response to Léo Quesnel, of the *Revue politique et littéraire*). In his contribution, Janvier responded to the racist arguments one by one, on moral as well as physiological grounds. He deployed a counterargument that relied both on Haitian exemplarity but also on the perfectibility of Haitians that was currently in progress, despite the deprivations imposed by the colonial powers. Thus, he refuted the accusation of laziness with the argument of an appetite for knowledge:

> A people that takes on severe deprivations to have its children raised abroad or who consents to separate from them for several consecutive years thereby proves that it is not at all lazy and that it is not complacent in ignorance.[11]

He also noted from within the scientific racism of the anthropologists of his time the transformations that gradually affected Haitians as they further committed to civilization:

> The law of selection and the doctrine of transformism, so consoling, so comforting for humanity and so true are to receive full confirmation in Haiti. As a first proof, I will cite the improvement of the black type on this island, improvement that is such that the eminent Broca, the most genius of French anthropologists, said, a mere two years ago at Necker hospital, in front of all of his students, that he could recognize a Haitian at first sight, as much from his direct, proud, and sparkling gaze as from his large and rounded forehead and his confident posture, sure signs, he continued of a great capacity of the cranial box and a mind both firm and intelligent.[12]

He also acknowledged the weight of the Debt in this counter-argument. If Haiti is ravaged by civil wars, it is a result of peasant uprisings:

> Haitians had lived impoverished, bled themselves dry to honor their commitments. The revolts that took place in Haiti from 1843, and of which, besides, the importance is always singularly exaggerated in Europe, were almost all caused by the suffering of a people overcharged with taxes and who nonetheless could not substantially improve their economic tools.[13]

---

11 Ibid., 19.
12 Ibid., 18.
13 Ibid., 19.

In 1883, he published a lengthy work, *La République d'Haïti et ses visiteurs*, in which he took on the visitors who likened Haiti to an "island of savagery," in the words of Jacques Stephen Alexis in *L'Espace d'un cillement*.[14] The latest in a long series of publicists who disparaged Haiti, a journalist originally from the Antilles, Cochinat,[15] having published in serial form a series of articles in which he presented a considerably critical and negative tableau of Haitian society, notably of empty forms (generals with no army, admirals with no ship, a council for public education with no high school, etc.), Janvier responded vehemently, point by point, and most importantly, by using irony like a punch against all the atrocities carried out against his country. He thus recalled Haiti's violent origins: "we are not very far from 1804 and we all know where we came from."[16] He did not hesitate to repeat the argument of the Debt, the tactful name for the Ransom that the Haitian people had to pay:

> This piece of land of which we are the masters, and that we keep with such jealous care for our great nephews, we paid for it three times. We first bought it in the person of our ancestors, and paid for it with over two centuries of tears and sweat; then we paid for it with an immense amount of blood, and then we paid for it with 120 million in silver.
>
> One hundred million in silver! From 1825 to 1880! That is a pretty penny! Without counting the hundred thousand francs here, the hundred thousand francs there that you subtracted from us—all of you who ate with us the day before and who said you were one of us, and who the next day came to threaten us from Bismarck, Disraëli, or from Fish, or who said that you were born in Guadeloupe, Martinique, or ... elsewhere.[17]

What is at stake is of course the exemplarity of the Haitian being in the world, and as is often the case in Janvier's paradoxical thinking, this exemplarity is to be interpreted in light of French exemplarity:

> France is the capital of all peoples. Haiti is black France.
> It is the eldest daughter of the loving race that, as it was put by

---

14 Louis-Joseph Janvier, *La République d'Haïti et ses visiteurs (1840–1882)* (Paris: Marpon et Flammarion, 1883).
15 French journalist (1823–1886), especially for the *Figaro*. Cochinat is the author of *Lacenaire, ses crimes, son procès et sa mort* (Paris: Jules-Laisné libraire-éditeur, 1857).
16 Janvier, *La République d'Haïti*, 92.
17 Ibid., 17.

Michelet, that apostle, must renew the world by flooding it with the ocean of love and eternal youth held in reserve within its bosom, that tawny bosom, treasure of sympathy, affection and gratitude.

For the black race Haiti is the sun rising on the horizon.[18]

And it is precisely because of this exemplarity of the heroes of independence, and of this responsibility Haiti has with regard to a proto-negritude, that Janvier teaches Cochinat a lesson, as well as all those who jeer, by recalling the names that are hidden by the History told by Whites:

> Heroes and brave men of 1803 whose names I want to place before your black man's eyes, for you owe to them in large part the ability you enjoy today to insult their sons, and that—no small thing!—in their own home, while you are in their home and eat the crumbs from their tables.
>
> They were named Dessalines and Pétion, Geffrard and Capois, Férou and Toussaint-Brave, Christophe and Cangé, Vernet and Gérin, Jean-Louis François, Magny, Louise Gabart and Boisrond-Tonnerre.
>
> If you had remembered these names instead of making contemporary Haitians laugh, you would have wanted the entire black race to get on their knees to adore the memory of their ancestors [...]
>
> And I say to M. Cochinat: Boor, learn to live and speak with respect of the grandsons of Toussaint-Louverture to whom you owe so much and to whom you all owe so much, children of Africa who reside in America.[19]

One of Janvier's recurring arguments concerning Cochinat is that the latter renounced his brothers, and literally assimilated to the exploiter. He thus highlights the fact that Cochinat is also the object of depreciation, due to his origins:

> Morality:—Some act disgusted and renounce their own to enter into certain circles to which they are only admitted after having suffered all kinds of humiliation and disdain. They are punished for their base acts and their groveling by scorn from up high and further punished by indifference or hatred from below.[20]

The violence of the tone does not fail to surprise. As Vaval declares, "Where a simple sharp bee sting would have sufficed to torment

18 Ibid., 57.
19 Ibid., 55.
20 Ibid., 180.

Cochinat's skin, he is hit over the head with a brick."[21] Reading Cochinat's articles today, published in *La Petite Presse* between October and December 1881, raises more questions than Janvier's booklet would have us believe.[22] The journalist's perception is relatively complex. Yes, Cochinat does adopt a Western gaze on the Haitian social landscape, in which prejudice is heavily embedded. The earliest contacts are grueling:

> We arrived at the pier leading to Customs. There we saw about thirty porters, pretty ragged, mostly black, who started fighting quite brutally over our luggage without having consulted us at all. They were threatening each other with coco macaque blows (trunks of dwarf palms whose knots cover the enormous head).
>
> This horde of agents without IDs, with no fixed fees, and most importantly with no rules, gave us a poor idea of the order that must reign in the city.[23]

The spectacle of the violent and indistinct horde was, however, rapidly mitigated by that of the women, even if the prejudice is still significant:

> When the beautiful indolent mulâtresses emerge from within their dwellings in long and flowing white robes to enjoy the fresh air outside, you might say they were odalisques emerging from the bath. The painting is voluptuous. The black women who sit on the steps to their homes in the afternoons, dressed in ample skirts and white caracos, their heads covered with kerchiefs of the same color, resemble black-faced ghosts.[24]

Little by little, Cochinat's gaze makes distinctions and establishes a chart that is part-sociological, part-touristic in which political considerations take shape. He begins by taking up the argument of the betterment of the black race through freedom, an argument that has in fact become a stereotype:

> Port-au-Prince is a gay and animated city of about thirty thousand inhabitants, but it could hold twice that. Its inhabitants have intelligent and alert faces, and its women are gracious and pretty, especially the mulâtresses with velvet eyes and straight black hair. Blacks constitute three fifths of the population, the mulâtres a fifth and a half and the whites half a fifth. What catches the foreigner's

---

21 Vaval, *Histoire de la littérature haïtienne*, 321.
22 Victor Cochinat, *De Paris à Haïti* (Paris: La Petite Presse, 1881), 5603ff.
23 Ibid., 5603.
24 Ibid., 5609.

attention is usually the beauty of the black type in this country. It would seem that the freedom they have enjoyed for close to a century has largely improved their physique, which, elsewhere, one must admit, leaves much to be desired, for Haiti is none other than our former colony of Saint-Domingue, the biggest and richest of the Antilles, that took the Indian name meaning high land after having shaken off France's yoke, when First consul Bonaparte tried to reestablish there the slavery that the Convention had abolished.[25]

Thus was the initial memory immediately revived, in a context that was also that of Republican France, ten or so years after the fall of Napoléon III and the Commune. Haitians won the right to pride. However, the latter deteriorated into self-esteem then vanity, "which easily becomes annoyed with the being so ill advised as to dare graze it."[26] Cochinat would show that pride, self-esteem, and vanity were no longer relevant: Haiti had become a land of show, eroded by violence, social and often familial. Corporal punishment was frequent: "I have never seen a people more in love with the whip since throwing off its yoke!"[27] The cult of *vaudoux*, to which the poorest and blackest parts of the population, returned to the wild, dedicated themselves, was unspeakable cannibalistic savagery. Public finances were subject to several avowed excesses: lavish spending, corruption, absence of true governance, deficit of citizenship, fighting between clans. The picture was disastrous. The absence of a civil society slowly led to the dissolution of language itself which was no longer able to account for a reality that escaped all understanding:

> We see in Haiti this sublunary thing, which we have never seen in any country in the world and that changes all the facts we have about visible objects, that is to say cavaliers on foot, foot soldiers on horseback, soldiers without uniforms, and curious bourgeois who come to see them maneuver wearing the uniforms meant for those same soldiers.[28]

Cochinat's gaze is very clearly one that contemporary sociologists would define as that of an opinion leader, committed, in France and in his newspaper, to social change that aimed to modernize social structures and thought and which motivated the French State at the

25 Ibid., 5604.
26 Ibid., 5609.
27 Ibid., 5610.
28 Ibid., 5669.

same time. In Haitian foibles and excesses he read the great confusion that was the Commune for him and more generally for the interested community of his social and political class. Renan's *La Réforme intellectuelle et morale* has become, even despite the author himself, the text which articulates the widely shared ideology of reference.[29] Thus, Clémenceau, in his speech on the Egyptian question to the Chamber on July 19, 1882 stated this ideology's impact in politics:

> We should imagine the situation our country has been put into, examine what we are, what degree our reorganization has attained, what we want, what we are capable of, and draw our rule of conduct from all these relevant factors.[30]

The democratic spirit was subject to suspicion because it was an obstacle to modernization, and had to be tempered by solidly established institutions, thanks notably to the ongoing drafting of the legislative apparatus and the rigorous application of laws. The context of Cochinat's touristic trip to Haiti was not devoid of meaning: he would directly evaluate what a revolution that did not end with an established and stable state could produce. This trip to Haiti thus makes sense with regard to the content of *La Petite Presse*, of which he was a distinguished editor.

Well, what Cochinat notes is that Haiti's public institutions are not rooted in efficient operation. They are mere instruments of power, dedicated to a legitimization demanded from abroad. Thus, of the World Expo, pitiful to the journalist's gaze:

> Why at this moment an Expo that is so vain, and that can cost close to a million francs, while farmers lack the most essential roads to bring their goods to the city, while bridges are lacking for Haiti's numerous waterways (which means that the rural dweller who goes to the city is sometimes forced to stay there for a whole week due to an overflowing river), while city streets are not lit at night, and while even Port-au-Prince's great market is not covered due to lack of money?
>
> But we should not be surprised at all by all this nonsense: these acts are deliberately posed by Haitian ministers who are not as simple as one might believe, and who are very well aware of their

---

29 Ernest Renan, *La Réforme intellectuelle et morale*, preceded by Jean François Revel, *Les Origines de la France contemporaine* (Paris: Union générale d'édition, 1967).

30 *Journal officiel de la République française*, 1882, p. 1320.

errors. They do all these things to make the foreigner believe that Haiti—which could still be so rich and so prosperous with an intelligent government—is a country that at this moment has attained the heights of opulence and civilization.

Poor and fertile land! Land that is poor through the narrow vision of its leaders! Land that is fertile through the gifts of nature rendered sterile by masters lacking in patriotism!

For these masters are not administrators: they are directors and, moreover, clumsy directors who are not at all concerned with the returns from the wonders they put on at such high cost, who do not even pay the actors they are forced to hire.[31]

From then on, all social operations in Haiti abandon the field of reality to collapse into a "moral farce" where "tragedy rubs shoulders with the comic and the grotesque."[32] And Cochinat establishes a definitive diagnostic that the majority of essayists, notably Haitian, will take up:

Since Haitians find these methods completely natural, and those aspiring to power even see in them hope for acquiring their own fortune when they hold the keys to the coffers, I do not want, by being indignant about these sinful methods, to seem more royalist than the king, but as much as I say to myself that these things are none of my business, that since those administrated do not buck against these thieveries, and that on the contrary, they bow before those who get rich by putting them into practice, as much as I say to myself that a people definitely gets the government it deserves, I cannot be silent and keep from seeing in this disdain for all political probity, in this space of legitimization of all attacks against public riches, in this aspiration to the posts that allow one to commit them, fatal seeds not only for the future of Haiti, but against its very existence as an independent State. A nation so morally gangrened has lost all the resilience it needs to resist its adversaries, and the first shock it encounters will be fatal.

What have you become, o disinherited sons of those proud soldiers of Independence who, in fighting those who brought slavery to them again, considered lead and iron to be the most precious of metals![33]

---

31 Cochinat, *De Paris à Haïti*, 5624.
32 Ibid., 5684.
33 Ibid., 5685.

After this text, Cochinat's letters become less frequent, then disappear: *La Petite Presse* began to circulate in Port-au-Prince and the author was the object of growing ostracism.

This brief summary of the chronicles against which Janvier protested shows that the real question is not so much that of revealing Haitian reality but rather that of displacing the gaze. This book allows Janvier to clarify his own views on Haiti's future. A series of magisterial texts will thus allow him to construct a true political thought, and to base it on an anthropology as well as on a political science. But this much seems certain, the majority of ruminations highlighted by Cochinat found their reader. And if Janvier's criticism is violent, it is precisely because for him it is a matter of participating in the reconstruction of the Haitian discursive space from within Haitian discourse, of no longer letting Haiti reduce itself to a counterexample, which the country has fatally become.

In 1884, he published *Haiti for the Haitians*,[34] in which he demanded a ban against ceding any part of Haiti to foreigners. The country was living within the context defined by the United States' attempt to take possession of Môle-Saint-Nicolas. Janvier's argument was as follows: the price to be paid for the possession of this land was such that no property should be conceded, especially since that concession would be nothing more than pillaging in disguise, especially in the context of Western colonialist scheming, ultimately based on thinly veiled and willingly duplicitous racism: "[e]verywhere, they have spread the news that we are savages in order to better intimidate us and to better fleece us; those who licked our hand at home called us monkeys in Europe."[35]

Haiti's existence exemplifies the fact that black men can live free and are not inherently doomed to conquest, slavery, and colonial exploitation, which was not universally acknowledged at the time. It is also in this text that an attempt at a program that is both social and religious appears for the first time: the lands of the great properties should be redistributed to peasants and Haiti should be "protestantized": According to Janvier, Concordat Catholicism is a factor of social and economic regression. These two positions will subsequently be repeated many times.

---

34 Louis-Joseph Janvier, *Haïti aux Haïtiens* ("Bibliothèque démocratique haïtienne") (Paris: Imprimerie Antoine Parent, A. Davy, successeur, 1884).
35 Janvier, *Haiti for the Haitians*, 55.

Around the same time, he published *Le Vieux piquet*,³⁶ in which he gives a fictional account of the peasant situation. In this short novel, he establishes ties, within a same continuity, between the state of servitude dating from before Independence and the peasant condition at the time of the civil wars. He poses the separation between the country outside (*en dehors*) and city inhabitants as a definitively established fact and shows how much resentment had accumulated. The text ends with a particularly strong accusation against writers who hide the speech of the excluded by making it illegitimate:

> Our blood was shed in torrents. Once again we were defeated, torn apart, crushed. It is since then especially that in the books they are the only ones to write or which they had commissioned, the sons of the executioners call us wretched, unworthy, looters, and disrespectful! What lying scoundrels and what reprobates!³⁷

Thus, Janvier noted a key issue in Haiti's literature: the novel, when it turned towards Haitian themes, represented beings that were incapable of responding to and criticizing this negative representation. In the twentieth century, a large part of the novelistic question, starting with Price-Mars, Roumain, and Jacques Stephen Alexis would, on the contrary, be to renew this representation in a positive manner. But from then on, and the phenomenon has increased since, the represented subject had even less control over the way he was represented. Around the same time, Janvier founded, and this has been noted too infrequently, the Haitian literary genre of the audience that Justin Lhérisson would claim for his own.

That same year, he published *L'Égalité des races*,³⁸ a response to a declaration by Renan, who had posited their inequality. There again, the ideological context in which France found itself was not incidental to this criticism. He attacked the thinker, a major figure of the French intelligentsia, on the triple grounds of morality, history, and scientific reason. He first criticized Renan for having made his statement in a totally gratuitous manner, and for having failed to live up to his obligations as a man of culture:

---

36 Louis-Joseph Janvier, *Le Vieux piquet. Scène de la vie haïtienne* ("Bibliothèque démocratique haïtienne") (Paris: Imprimerie Antoine Parent, A. Davy, 1884).
37 Ibid., 21.
38 Louis-Joseph Janvier, *L'Égalité des races* ("Bibliothèque démocratique haïtienne") (Paris: Imprimerie G. Rougier et Cie., 1884).

> The more ignorant one is, the more selfish: the more one hides timid, envious, or cowardly thoughts in the depths of one's heart, the more one believes in the success of childish and reprehensible ruses; the more one preaches the excellence, the infallibility of the system of ignominious and vile duplicities, the more one complacently gets caught up in humiliating and dishonorable behavior, the more one excuses shameful capitulations of conscience, villainous moral abjections, the more one accepts inept renouncements; the less one dares speak or act for the good of the greatest number, for the honor of all.[39]

With this accusation, Janvier was criticizing self-righteousness and intellectual leadership; Renan saw his influence grow at the time, especially among young people, in particular thanks to the fundamentally anti-obscurantist aspect of his works. Janvier then criticized his blindness to the true condition of black slaves: Renan considered social inequality to be a natural inequality. The march of history, like the spread of Enlightenment ideas, shows, on the contrary that the slaves emerged from the inhumane state in which they were kept, and that that movement, initiated by French thought, was not about to stop:

> Everywhere, then, the black race performs a true escalation of light. It especially owes this moral ascension to the philosophical France of the eighteenth century, to the resplendent and valiant France of Diderot, d'Alembert, Raynal, and the like, either directly or through indirect influence. Thus, through the centuries to come, and from now on, it will know to never be stingy in its gratitude to the most generous nation of all, the universal emancipator.[40]

Finally, he takes up the argument of evolution towards a perfectibility of the human species that is the very mark of reason in science. And it is Haiti that again becomes exemplary, because it is precisely there that slaves first freed themselves:

> In Haiti where the black man is free, governs himself, and owns the land only since the beginning of this century, an improvement then a true intellectual transformation occurred within him, and moreover a very notable physical selection.
>
> The progression of the large Antillean republic has tripled since about sixty years ago and the evolution of the Haitian nation has

---

39 Ibid., 7.
40 Ibid., 31.

been most rapid, despite the unnecessary and deplorable revolts that have too often bloodied this beautiful country.[41]

This critique of Renanism is in fact completely inscribed within this thought. Unbeknownst to him, Janvier is taking up an essential element of Renan's thought, as demonstrated by Todorov in *Nous et les autres*:[42] the separation of humanity into races is a primary fact, and even *métissages* cannot modify this condition. By deploying his thought within the French language, Janvier offers to our understanding that which constitutes the true factor of civilization within it and through it. But it is precisely through the recall of the anthropological argument that he diminishes the weight of this argument. In the incessant Renanian tourniquet between "physical" and "linguistic" races, Janvier's argument must be appreciated within its context, as was the paradoxical argument of his medical thesis.

What is probably Janvier's major work in terms of political science, *Les Constitutions d'Haïti*,[43] was published in 1886. He published and commented on all those that had been promulgated up until that date. He recalled under what conditions those texts had been conceived, and gradually showed how these fundamental laws progressively attest to Haiti's decline in Haitians' own representations and, in turn, in those by the rest of the world. It is a crucial work, without a doubt one of the most important by the Haitian essayists from the *fin de siècle*; it allows the progressive construction of a coherent political thought that is aware of its assumptions. Thus, Janvier resolutely takes the side of a strong executive power, first, with a view towards installing and stabilizing a State marked by fragility. Dessalines, Christophe, against Pétion are, after Toussaint Louverture, the true political geniuses of Haiti, the only ones capable of having assured, momentarily, a viable economy resting on a solid foundation. The disaster begins with Boyer, especially with the emergence of the "color issue" in the political arena, accepting the Debt settlement, the promulgation of the Rural Code of 1826 that marginalizes the peasant masses, and by the slow establishment of the Catholic Church's stranglehold on the country. From then on, social questions are no longer treated solely from a legal standpoint, and according to the rules of the governing power, the law is

---

41 Ibid., 24.
42 Tzvetan Todorov, *Nous et les autres. La réflexion française sur la diversité humaine* (Paris: Seuil, 1989). See especially pages 195–211.
43 Louis Joseph Janvier, *Les Constitutions d'Haïti* (Paris: Marpon et Flammarion, 1886).

necessarily partisan, because the counter power was never able to find space; notably, it would return in 1905 because power is not, in Haiti, a civilian affair, but rather that of the military, and that has been the case since 1804. Thus, the excluded peasants cannot have any land. They are confined to the social margins whereas the true political issue is the emergence of citizenship, that is to say the project community, and he criticizes the various powers for having ignored "that small property is neither a cause of impoverishment, nor a danger; on the contrary, it offers all sorts of advantages; it uses the land where the large property that only makes agricultural proletarians would have left everything uncultivated; that small property makes peasants independent, foresighted, patriotic, in a word, it forms citizens."[44] The "color issue" is also seen as misguided, because it masks the true issue, which is always social and economic before all else:

> Under Boyer, color prejudice was transformed. It was no longer directed against the *mulâtres* and Black people by the White people who exploited them; it was directed by the *mulâtres* in power against Black people, their economic and political competitors. On that point, Boyer was a miniature Louis XIV. History is not invented, it is told. When Soulouque ascended to the highest seat of power, especially after 1848, it was alleged that he and Black people held color prejudices against the *mulâtres*. No lie is more ridiculous, more insulting to common sense. From time immemorial, Black men have desired intimate contact with *mulâtresses* and white women as one loves forbidden fruit, the same as in Europe, from time immemorial, the commoner, the villein of yesteryear always loved the noblewoman. If Black people in Haiti have often shown loathing for the *mulâtres* who look down on or insulted them, it is because they were also their economic and political competitors, that the former had oppressed them, stripped them of goods that should have belonged to everyone.[45]

That does not stop Janvier from considering how this question of color ended up shaping ridiculous social stances: "the triteness of *mulâtres* that sought to pass for white is incredible: the baseness of Black men who flattered men of color to live amongst them is unspeakable."[46] This unique shift in thought is equally at work in the severe criticism

44 Ibid., 228.
45 Ibid., 291.
46 Ibid., 230.

he levels at Catholicism. It is first qualified as "European fetishism," regarded with the same scorn as "African fetishism." His vision of the very history of the Catholic Church is entirely negative, for the Church threatens Haiti's foundations:

> Catholicism, having practiced the enslavement of black people, remains its accomplice: it is responsible for the abjection in which the black race has languished for centuries. It helped develop the color prejudice of white people against black people; centralized in Rome, it can never become a religion of national policy; and finally, at any given moment, it can compromise the oeuvre of 1804: independence.[47]

The last part of the book is dedicated to a terrible depiction of the civil wars launched after the fall of Geffrard. From that moment on, the succession of presidents would witness the almost systematic opposition of specific interests, temporary alliances, and the crumbling of all constructed and coherent political thought:

> Short term presidencies, bad for a new country where political life is not intense because brains had been left without culture for too long and material interests are concentrated within the hands of a small number of people, will succeed each other. With them, there will be recurrences of the manifestation of the people's wrath, and internecine wars will break out. Both will be preceded, accompanied, and followed by parliamentary clashes utterly deprived of grandeur.[48]

Delorme is the only personality to emerge from these civil wars, notably from the fights between the Piquets and the Cacos. Haiti, in the perception that Janvier now has of it, is reduced to a coveted object for the colonizing powers, and is no longer able to produce anything. Janvier's pessimism thus asserts itself in a particularly sensitive manner: Haiti has become a land from which culture is absent, but where "war lords" proliferate, those district commanders who escape the central power's control. He can only keep his distance from this state of affairs:

> Civil war is the most heinous, despicable, wretched thing there is. Here, we will not praise anyone who showed bravery during the fratricidal battles that bloodied the country from 1868 to 1870.
>
> As brave as one might feel, one is no longer brave when, instead of enlightening their country as to their true interests when one is able, one takes up a gun to kill one's compatriot under the pretext

47 Ibid., 286.
48 Ibid., 297.

of giving him illusory freedoms. For a sentimental people, starving for justice, as are the Haitian people, any question can be resolved through discussion.[49]

The very last part of the essay is devoted to the proposal of a new constitution for the country. In fact, Janvier drafted a true political program and took note of Haitian complexity, of its often cumulative character, rarely treated in the mode of negotiation. For the real issue that Janvier defined was indeed that of the country's necessary modernization. Living in Europe, traveling, he saw imperialisms rising on all sides.

If certain aspects of Janvier's political thought now seem outdated, if sometimes the excess of certain statements raises questions, the reader is nonetheless struck by the will to attempt a real foundation for political discourse, at the same time as he notes the rapid deterioration that affected the State, the few institutions, but especially the absence of a true social space not given to unilateral demonization from the start. The work does not seem to have had the impact it deserved in Haiti, where business was now troubled. However, it interested a few thinkers and essayists in France: the copy consulted at the Bibliothèque Nationale in France belonged to Maurice Barrès. It is not impossible, but this intuition would have to be verified, that the European perception of Haiti became, because of this publication, that of a kind of laboratory of political and social failure, representation that has since become a truism. But it appears especially that Janvier was able to shift the perception of his country, as it had been handled by "travelers" such as Cochinat.

In 1888, he published a surprising novel: *Une chercheuse*. Critics had relatively little to say about this text and the criticism was quite harsh. For starters, Vaval gave it a mixed review:

> It is in 1888 that he published *Une chercheuse*, dedicated to Judith Gauthier [sic]. This magnificent novel, so well constructed, so alertly written, is especially valuable for its sharp analysis of passion. The criticism one could address to *Une chercheuse* is its abuse of archaic and technical words. Mr. Louis Joseph Janvier, being a medical doctor, displays in his book his knowledge of physiology. Which did not prevent him from providing a fine "moral dissection" of his heroine. Such pages on love are found therein that one could believe them excerpted from Stendhal, Bourget, or Balzac, it is all so

---

49 Ibid., 338.

powerful and strong! It is a novel to read and reread and that must be bound for one's library, in crimson with gilt edges, as requested by one of Shakespeare's characters.[50]

It is only evoked by Léon-François Hoffmann, while it is panned by Gouraige:

> [Louis-Joseph Janvier] invents an amoral and cold creature, modeled after liberated women, according to the wish of Dumas fils, deprived of God and socially downgraded.
>
> With that, the novel develops gracelessly and lifelessly. The main character is troubled, repeats experiences in love. But Mimose's heart is dry and her love, which is a perversion of the flesh, lived in spite of morality, with no thought of devotion or abnegation, did not help Janvier to save his work from monotony. Mimose strangely resembles herself in the midst of her multiple adventures. Her deceptions are the responses of the flesh and her gratuitous end seems logical.
>
> The paucity of Janvier's style (elsewhere so dense) adds to the faults of this novel that is deprived of psychological observations, and whose emotional value is more or less null.[51]

We will easily agree: beyond the judgment on the poor style, the main character shows herself to be completely worthy of attention, with regard to modernity.[52]

This novel narrates the life, the joys, and deceptions of Mimose Carminier, who spends her existence in search of a complete love, without giving an inch to mediocrity. The novel opens with a reproduction of the bequest letter with regard to her property, a letter in which she declares she has committed suicide. We learn that she is forty-two years old. Her maid, come to open the windows, discovers her and calls for help. The notables of the village of Bonneuil (near Paris), where the house is located, come running, and take note of her death, all while proffering stereotypical comments, criticized by the doctor who accompanies them. The entire text of the novel is then an anamnesis of Mimose's life, a sort of post mortem hearing. Heiress to

---

50 Vaval, *Histoire de la littérature haïtienne*, 146.
51 Ghislain Gouraige, *Histoire de la littérature haïtienne (de l'indépendance à nos jours)* (Port-au-Prince: Éditions de l'action sociale, 1982), 36.
52 Private conversation with Dany Laferrière on this novel: "But that is exactly what we are looking for, everything beyond the confines of what is morality, beyond conformism!"

a family of goldsmiths and jewelers from Bordeaux, she is seduced by Foncine, a dandy who marries her for her dowry, in order to restore his faded image. Cheated on by her husband, whom she eventually divorces, she has lovers, but they reveal themselves one after the other to be men of moral and intellectual mediocrity. She eventually meets Edriss Gazy, a young Egyptian man, who has come to study medicine in Paris. They live happily in Brittany, then in the Paris area, until, called by his father to participate in the anticolonial struggle, Edriss returns to Alexandria, where he dies when the city is bombed by British battleships in 1882. Pregnant by him, Mimose commits suicide soon after receiving Edriss's last message.

This novel is often associated with those by Demesvar Delorme, *Francesca* and *Le Damné*, and, like them, it has long been left out of discussion of Haitian novels. Jean Jonassaint has well demonstrated that by rejecting them, Haitian criticism tried to describe the national novel through the object it represents: "Haitian criticism [...] is unanimous, the Haitian novel or tale is truly born in 1901, with the publication by Ollendorff, in Paris of *Thémistocle Epaminondas Labasterre* by Frederic Marcelin, subtitled *petit récit haïtien*. Thus, it excludes or sets aside, implicitly or explicitly, *Stella* by Bergeaud (1859), *Francesca* and *Le Damné* by Delorme (1873, 1877), and *Une chercheuse* by Janvier (1889) from the corpus of Haitian novels, at least from those that, worthy of national interest, deserve to be promoted, studied, and established."[53] Yet, given the current process of the deterritorialization of Haitian novels, this exclusion seems less and less justified. Anne Marty also reminds us that in these novels "the events recounted and the characters evoked are closely connected to the country's situation at the time, even when the writers might try to hide it by using a context completely foreign to it: color prejudice, exile, the return to the country to reclaim lost power, are all themes that continue to haunt novelists to the present day."[54]

Indeed, *Une chercheuse* is full of such themes. Exile is a recurring motif, for example. Mimose herself is the daughter of a Spanish political exile and Edriss' return to Egypt to actively participate in the insurrectional movement constitutes one of the novel's dramatic stakes. Here is what he says about political authority:

---

53 Jean Jonassaint, *Des romans de tradition haïtienne. Sur un récit tragique* (Montreal: L'Harmattan and CIDIHCA, 2002), 59.
54 Anne Marty, *Les Personnage féminin dans les romans haïtiens et québécois de 1938 à 1980 (traitement et signification)* (Villeneuve d'Ascq: Presses universitaires du Septentrion, 1997), 24.

The government is rotten with prejudices; it especially hates those who have the misfortune of being young; it hates thinkers and writers. Besides, it doesn't read. It believes in Allah, dervishes, routine, old age and it drinks water. By dint of listening to its bloated and empty sentences, of noting its foolishness and its betrayal, I have become pessimistic and revolutionary. It thinks that old men who have read nothing, nor studied anything and who are incapable of deep thinking have more personal experience than learned young men who have studied all the centuries and who, consequently, possess the accumulated experience of all countries.[55]

Mutatis mutandis, we can apply this diatribe to the Haitian situation as Janvier perceives it from France. But this diatribe is offered obliquely: in some way, Haitians themselves are bearers of political mediocrity, that is to say a deficit of virtue, in Janvier's vocabulary.

In parallel to these themes tied to exile and to the particularly psychological condition of the exiled, there are many signals that, for those who can identify them, refer to Haitian onomastics and geography. Mimose's first name doubtlessly already suggests an "Antillean" space, to use a term favored by Janvier. But in chapter 7, entitled "D'abîme en abîme," the names are explicitly Haitian. Mimose is back from convalescence: her physician, Dr. "Turgeau," who saves her life several times, has sent her to the seaside. Upon her return to Paris, after an emotional disappointment—the fisherman who enables her wanderings on the sea wants only money from her—she goes to the salon of Mrs. "d'Iquiny," meets M. "de Tiburon," who praises the beauty of the "Plateau central" of Auvergne, Mrs. "de Martissant, Mr. and Mrs. "Larcahaie," and Dr. "Limbé." The name of Mrs. "Mancenille" evokes in the salon the tree of the Americas with the venomous sap, the manchineel whose shade is reputed to be fatal. Indeed, there reigns within the salons, in Paris itself, a deleterious atmosphere that ruins one's appetite for life. In the same chapter, the next episode is an encounter with the actor "Jean Rabel," to whom Mimose offers herself, and who leaves her, in a boorish manner, for an actress. Mimose offers a bitter reflection on the character that can be interpreted in several ways: "I could make him my lover; I could not make him a distinguished man. How unhappy I am! When all is said and done, he is a lackey, in spite of all the grand sentences learned by heart that he delivers every night."[56] Yet Jean Rabel's favorite author is

55 Louis Janvier, *Une chercheuse* (Paris: C. Marpon & E. Flamarion, 1889), 348.
56 Ibid., 181.

Victor Hugo, who is also one of Mimose's favorite poets and one of the essential references of the Haitian intelligentsia at the time. The entire chapter seems to function as a Freudian slip, through which Janvier states what separates him every day from a country which, according to him, is no longer able to attain the heights of the destiny it snatched in 1804, and of which the governing and property-owning classes are not worthy. But more than the objective conditions of receptivity of the imperial machinations on the part of the colonized or those in the process of becoming such, the novel paints a picture of the European actors of the former.

Part of Janvier's novel can be read as an anthropological study of the conditions of exercising a power of which the most hidden yet also the most essential object is imperialist scheming. Far from moving radically away from the Haitian theme, it seems rather that the author progressively put it into perspective by inscribing it within the question of colonial expansion, of which Haiti was one potential victim among many. It is also therein that the novelistic project finds its true niche: several authors declare, in fact, that Janvier should have contented himself with writing essays and pamphlets; that *Le Vieux piquet*, for example, has a strictly demonstrative value, and that fiction does not add anything to what we know of the miserable conditions of peasant life. On the contrary, Jean Jonassaint has clearly shown that this short text is probably the starting point of *l'audience* as genre of which Justin Lhérisson is the first heir. In *Une chercheuse*, Janvier tears down the masks of respectability, and fiction is able to point the finger at what cannot be said or thought by political science. The novel showcases a gallery of characters tied to power in some way. They are rarely shown in a positive light.

The first is Mimose's husband, the successive portraits of whom sketch the contours of a washed out "degenerate,"[57] made nondescript by the superficiality of his feelings; he cannot father children and is slowly reduced to a caricature of himself:

> Always dressed with the utmost propriety, gardenia in his buttonhole, flat brimmed hat lightly tipped over his right ear, gold-headed cane in hand, he looked like a walking fashion plate. Aimery de Foncine was one of those descendants of the Crusaders who willingly forget that their ancestors could never have arrived in Palestine had there not been peasants to accompany them [...]

57 This expression should be interpreted in reference to Gobineau, whom Janvier, who knows how to deploy irony, takes at his word this time.

> In truth, the marquis wanted to improve his status. Despite having charged at Marignan at Bayard's side, in the person of one of his ancestors, in this nineteenth century that is so egalitarian, one can find oneself short of money.[58]

Note the social rating that neutralizes the aristocratic origins. Having become the mistress of a deputy who considers her to be a jewel, that he admires but does not touch, Mimose holds court, and welcomes the powerful who make and break the world. Indeed, the following passage, a bit long, describes a veritable menagerie:

> Her salon remained an immense desert in terms of consciousness and character, even when her troop of admirers was there in full. She sometimes called it, jokingly, with a painful smile, my menagerie. Some people from the Stock Exchange attended, pot-bellied, with ruddy faces, spatula-shaped fingers, still numb from the cold of the gold they extorted from the unfortunates who in their cynical language they call suckers; sportsmen absolutely ignorant in all matters, except when women and horses were being discussed [...]
>
> Some doctors also came, some of whom brought shame to a profession that demands such diverse and profound knowledge, such natural finesse and tact, such nuanced science; lawyers who spoke of everything with phenomenal volubility and ignorance; but the bulk was formed by parliamentarians, the occasional or professional politician, who served two or three regimes, collaborated with five or six contradictory revolutions, voted laws, signed senatus consultum, the economics of which will make sensible people snort with laughter a hundred years from now.
>
> Upon seeing this variety of characters, one might think of a zoological collection. This one's body was monstrously heavy, but was of a singularly dexterous mind in the hippo-like mass of his flesh; that one was slight, skinny enough to be transfixed on a pin; yet another who thought himself to be sly and subtle, for having abused the candor of the peasants of his place, was in fact perfectly gullible when it came down to it, because, upon his return, he let himself be duped by the thirty-two pearly whites of a cruel woman encountered on his path. Others, miraculously well-informed on matters of foreign policy or internal administration, but not having climaxed at all as teenagers, were simpletons in sum, letting themselves be taken in by those who were truly crafty and making speeches in three

---

58 Janvier, *Une chercheuse*, 48.

parts, pompous as a fat cow, when they should be shooting off a quick compliment to the socialite who deigned to honor them with her gaze.[59]

A deputy is even compared to a beast of darkness, ready to pounce upon his prey:

> With duplicitous eyes and a sinister expression, a great hulking almost knock-kneed jabberer with a comma torso, twisted legs and feet apart, he walked like a spider and gave one the chills: despite his sluggish ways, one could sense the reprobate within him.[60]

If the evocation of politics stopped at these colorful descriptions, it would border on the anti-parlementarism common in France in the 1880s, less than ten years after the defeat.[61] The narrative equilibrium is more subtle, and traces a reflective path that forces us to nuance this perception. It is the character of Mimose that makes this path possible.

From romantic heroine, she gradually transforms into a woman on a quest for her freedom, enduring multiple experiences. Experiences in society, and as in many novels written by Haitians, permeated by the social, but also sexual experiences, because the tale of her relationship with a woman is recounted in barely veiled terms. Mimose's demand for love does not end in an ethereal ideal. It is a being of flesh, of warmth, and of sweat:

> Oh! My hair, my hair! She continued with growing rage, twisting it with a nervous hand, who will then hold you between fingers trembling and joyous with true passion! Who will then fondle you with no respect for my haughty and majestic self? Who will pull you in the spasm of love, making me cry out with pain and happiness? Who will childishly hide in the depths of your brown locks and will be truly inebriated, drunk to the point of crime, intoxicated to the point of insanity by the perfume that blossoms from you, that perfume made of the finest essence of my flesh and my nerves? ..."[62]

Drawn to the sea, a disciple of a counter-Renanian Brittany, turned towards salt and granite, receptive to scents from elsewhere:

---

59 Ibid., 133.
60 Ibid., 136.
61 Editor's note: *la défaite*, France's defeat in the Franco-Prussian War of 1871.
62 Ibid., 137.

> At the time she was in the splendor of her buxom beauty. In leaving Paris, she had come to die to the world on this Breton beach. Plants from hot countries, the luxurious vegetation that surrounded her had reconciled her with life. Nowhere more than in the surroundings of Concarneau is the earth more maternal [...]
>
> By the moors and the strands, she had again taken up her long walks, her drawn out dreams in the shadow of the oak trees. She had become hot-blooded again under the influence of the air oversaturated with iodine, brome, and alkali chlorides that one breathes on those coasts where the Gulf Stream licks the European continent and excites it with its ardor.[63]

This vague eroticism slowly becomes clearer in the tale of life with Edriss, to the point of the specific evocation of intimate moments. Thus, Mimose gradually deconstructs her initial *bovarysme*, and brings the world to the scale of her resolutely feminine, if not feminist, gaze, always looking to go beyond the conformism in which others try to imprison her.

She responds to this confinement with a progressive passion from indifference to mediocrity, and through a relationship that draws its strength not from the ideal, but from the embrace. For Janvier, who keeps remembering that he is a physician, this constant affirmation has a name, "temperament":

> All of a sudden, without saying a word, she went into her bathroom. She returned, shamelessly sublime and confident in the effect of her barely veiled sculptural beauty. This declaration of love, or desire, if one prefers, is well worth another. It was of a brazenness that repulses women of false mind and body, but of haughty and spicy originality for the valiant ones who rush headlong into passion like a soldier takes up the assault.
>
> Doesn't she seem far preferable to all those who simper, displaying their absence of temperament?[64]

It is through temperament that politics and existence are articulated. Mimose's is constructed with the help of a syntax that is conscious of her demands, and where Gouraige highlights the ease of lust, it is exactly the opposite that is proclaimed by this temperament, and has the haughty character of a demand: "Sir, there is a grammar that is not learned in school: it is the grammar of the heart. Few

---

63 Ibid., 204.
64 Ibid., 204.

people dare or can speak according to its rules or rather its whims. I am one of them."⁶⁵ This existential warning is founded on the demand of a relation to science that is not satisfied with the accumulation of knowledge or erudition without object. The activity of reason is always first that of understanding and the process of understanding, such as classification and categorization, is as essential as knowledge itself. This is indicated from the start of the novel with the long description of Mimose's library and her mode of classification. In a way that one would not guess from a quick reading of the novel, Mimose (and through her, Janvier) takes on a criticism of Renan, who in 1890 returned to his notes of 1848, touching upon *L'Avenir de la science*. As highlighted by Todorov, the Renanian project crumbles into a scientism against which the philosopher wanted to protect himself in his youth. For the later Renan, reason becomes an object of faith, and made him definitively turn his back on science. Thus the whole novel progressively proceeds in the constant critique of a failing yet generalized anthropology. That the point of view adopted is that of a woman is not inconsequential here. Thus, in contrast to the great scientific categorizations of the time which essentialized parts of humanity, Janvier affirms that "woman does not exist": "Each woman is herself, that is to say a nuance. No two are alike."⁶⁶ This declaration, albeit in a minor manner, posits decentering as a mode of thought, and concern with otherness before its time, like a crucial foreboding of what was afoot as far as imperialist policies were concerned.

The last part of the novel depicts Edriss's departure for Alexandria. The last intimate scene is opened by the young man, whistling "Le temps des cerises," a song by Jean-Baptiste Clément still codified in 1882 that refers to the Commune. The lovers separate: "I thank you for loving me so much, me, son of a race that illustrious Westerners, who owe their current civilization to it, believe to be inferior to theirs."⁶⁷ In Egypt, he confronts a political disorganization that looks a lot like that ascribed to Haiti by Janvier in his earlier books. The narrator then speaks, like a voice-over, and moves away from the characters to recall exchanges at the Chamber between Gambetta, advocate for the participation of the French flag in the bombing, and Clémenceau, fiercely opposed. Of course, the economic stakes are the most present (we will recall that it is a matter of controlling the route to Asia), against

65 Ibid., 303.
66 Ibid., 297.
67 Ibid., 337.

the backdrop of the Tunisian affair, which was also taking place. But Gambetta also takes up the British argument that some races can only be governed with a stick. Clémeanceau answers him with criticism of this argument. He displaces it: the true distinction is defined by those who are fit for work and those who are unfit, for example the Indians of America, condemned to disappear. Clémenceau nonetheless calls attention to the terrible social consequences of the European stranglehold on Egyptian finances. Then, finally, follows the description of the bombing itself, like a deluge of fire upon the civilian population:

> The cannonballs of the fleet, weighing close to five hundred pounds, bore into the walls of the entrenchments, pierced the bunkers, exploded on the rocks of the fortifications, sowing death among the combatants. Others were directed at the houses of the city, set fire to several neighborhoods, gutted the women, flattened the children. The Egyptian batteries responded the best they could to the battleships' powerful fire without causing serious damage to those monstrous moving masses that maneuvered six thousand meters away from the fortifications. Instead of a battle, the bombing looked like a crushing perpetrated from a distance.[68]

Janvier thus reveals that the military strategy openly targets the civilian population. In this unworthy world, Mimose no longer feels the need to live, from that moment on Edriss is plunged into the abyss. *Une chercheuse* thus seems to be the novel of Janvier's limits: mirror of the most intimate aspirations, spelled out in the imaginary, the symbolic, and the real, the latter violently demonstrating its oppressive character. In some ways, the novelist puts his own destiny into perspective.

In 1902, Janvier married a British woman, Jeanne-Maria Windsor. In 1905, he returned to Haiti and his return was noticed. He had been away from Haiti for twenty-eight years. Here is how he appeared to Vaval:

> Of above average height, rather large and strapping, a pleasant face, with extraordinarily interrogative eyes, a salt and pepper beard trimmed to a point, à la Napoleon III, always dressed in a frock coat or jacket, head covered with an ever-present top hat, such was Louis-Joseph Janvier, physically, around 1905, after a sojourn of thirty years in Europe. His entire demeanor had something heavy or

68 Ibid., 346.

thick about it. Beneath this heavy envelope was working the finest, most literate, most delicate mind.[69]

In his baggage, he had his latest book, *Du gouvernement civil en Haïti*.[70] Therein he pursues further his reflections on the necessity of finally installing a civilian government founded on parliamentarism:

> The Haitian nation has always been governed by members of the military: general Dessalines, general Pétion, general Christophe, general Boyer, general Charles Hérard, general Guerrier, general Pierrot, general Riché, general Soulouque, general Geffrard, general Salnave, general Domingue, general Boisrond Canal, general Salomon, general Légitime, general Hyppolite, general Tirésias Augustin Simon SAM [sic]. Several of these soldiers came to Power without having received any civilian culture, and consequently, without having any idea of the existence of completely civilian governments.[71]

The entire book is a programmatic description of an alternative organization of institutions, and has the objective of convincing electors to participate in this reform movement, which would see the advent of a State where the president would no longer be responsible, unlike a council of ministers, tasked with defining policy, founded on a party's program. But other aspects capture the modern reader's attention. Janvier demonstrates his grounding in the Haitian land and its history and he recalls his relentless commitment to his country's defense. But it is also a textual machine by which he seeks to make this country a space in which language takes charge of a landscape in which one of the first genocides of modern history took place. Haiti is a widowed land, a land whose conqueror tore off the names and destroyed those who were its carriers and guardians:

> The Spanish changed the Carib names of the island—Haiti, mountainous land; Quisqueya, great land; Bohio, rich in villages—to Hispaniola, Little Spain. Marvelous Hispaniola—that's what Columbus called it when writing to Isabelle—was soon widowed of its indigenous population: used for the exploitation of gold and silver mines, it died out between 1500 and 1540. The Indians dead,

---

69 Vaval, *Histoire de la littérature haïtienne*, 319.
70 Louis Joseph Janvier, *Du gouvernement civil en Haïti* (Lille: Le Bigot Frères, imprimeurs-éditeurs, 1905).
71 Ibid., 50.

the Spanish scornfully refused to cultivate the soil of Haiti. Cortez having conquered Mexico and Pizarro the Incas kingdom of Peru, Marvelous Hispaniola became practically a desert island.[72]

It is indeed a work of mourning that is undertaken in this strange book, which goes far beyond its simply political function. Janvier attempts to describe the various administrative divisions undertaken by Haitian heads of state. With each change, he repeats the list of departments, capitals, districts, toponyms, as though it were necessary to inscribe and again reinscribe these names so that no one could ever erase them. For the danger was getting closer, and Janvier's entire oeuvre shows that he knew from then on that if nothing was done, the country would be invaded.

In Haiti's prevailing political climate, his electoral attempts failed: his discourse had no purchase on the current situation, which was that of the fight between clans. In his *Lettre aux électeurs*,[73] he tried, Pradel Pompilus tells us, to justify his campaign, and to verbally fight the injurious attitudes he was subjected to. But he was forced into exile in 1908. He returned to London. His spouse had died. In London, he clashed with Vaval. He was then appointed to Paris, where he died in 1911, the same year as Firmin. He was survived by a daughter.

Janvier's oeuvre no doubt deserves more than this quick overview that has no other objective than to remind today's scholars how essential it is on at least two levels. First, in the history of ideas, a genre that is not too popular nowadays, it is resolutely inscribed within a critique of ideological patterns that were then common in the Western framework. But its radicalism is constructed gradually. Studying Janvier's oeuvre forces one to get into the history of a conscience that tears away from this framework, to which it actually owes its construction. Vaval remarkably grasped this dynamic and describes it with a grandiose image:

> Colonial ideas are grafted onto our skin to the point where in spite of our apparent autonomy we are like the famous Laocoon group, where the serpents wrap themselves around the priest of Neptune to the point that the god's body can no longer be discerned beneath the vibrant rings that encircle him. Our politicians that seem the most free-spirited unknowingly obey this hereditary impulse. They

---

72 Ibid., 10.
73 Published in Port-au-Prince, references not found.

act under pressure from the dead, who speak within them and guide their will. Doctor Janvier tries to thwart these evil shadows.[74]

We have not mentioned it often enough, but this effort is also, in Janvier's writing, a work on language. It must make audible in French that which that language silences. Janvier's style slows down one's reading, holds one's attention. Then this works says to the Haitians of its time what they cannot hear, and it revisits their history, which is also his, despite the distance. This situation steeped in otherness confers upon him a freedom of tone, a political daring, that cannot be recognized by his peers either. A situation, we know, that lasted, and with which a number of Haitian writers have been confronted. But finally, in a way Janvier also inaugurates the tradition of writers made anxious by the articulation of understanding and knowledge, on the body, disease, health, society, politics, education, and literature and which includes Jacques Roumain, Jacques Stephen Alexis, Jean Métellus, Frankétienne, and Emile Olliver. They plot this articulation in the intimacy of characters, in the knot through which their desires take shape, and through which the body is moved. L'Eglantina, from *L'Espace d'un cillement* is most certainly a relative, albeit distant and fallen, of Mimose, the *Chercheuse*. But when the latter disappears, La Niña Estrellita recovers and goes forth in improbable conquest of the world.

Summary: Born in Port-au-Prince in 1855 and deceased in Paris in 1911, Louis-Joseph Janvier spent most of his life outside of Haiti. Published at the turn of the century, although often cited, his oeuvre, which was not always well received in his country, remains mostly unknown, despite being grounded in Haitian realities, which was exceptional at the time. It is oriented along two axes: on the one hand, a defense of the singular character of Haiti's existence against the imperialist machinations of Western powers; on the other, a critique of Haitian political and sociological discourse. Janvier never stopped exploring the specter defined by this double perspective in different generic registers: his oeuvre unfolds in books about medicine, constitutional law, anthropology, political science, but also concerns history, the novel, even the pamphlet. It definitely seems driven by the will to succeed in grounding his writing within a Haitian discourse not determined by Western frameworks, and to found, in the tradition of his predecessors, a resolutely national writing.

74 Vaval, *Histoire de la littérature haïtienne*, 323.

CHAPTER TWO

Caribbean "Race Men"

Louis Joseph Janvier, Demesvar Delorme, and the Haitian Atlantic

Marlene L. Daut

> We might say that of all the islands of the Caribbean, Haiti is the most advantageously situated, with respect to the connections that it can make with the other islands and with Colombia; those that it can maintain with Europe and the United States do not render less advantageous our geographical position.
> —Louis Joseph Janvier, *La République d'Haïti et ses visiteurs* (1883)[1]

> And who knows, when prosperous, and capable of producing the same economic output that has made other countries powerful, what humanitarian destinies Providence will lead us towards in this archipelago of the Caribbean where we are at the center!
> —Demesvar Delorme, *La Misère au sein des richesses, réflexions diverses sur Haïti* (1873)

This chapter is an extension of ideas and arguments first made by the author in "Beyond 'America for the Americans': Race and Empire in the Work of Demesvar Delorme," *J19: The Journal of Nineteenth-Century Americanists* 6, no. 1 (Spring 2018): 189–197, and in "Caribbean 'Race Men': Louis Joseph Janvier, Demesvar Delorme, and the Haitian Atlantic," *L'Esprit Créateur* 56, no. 1 (Spring 2016): 9–23.

  1 Janvier here quotes the Haitian historian Beaubrun Ardouin. For the original, see Beaubrun Ardouin, *Géographie de l'île d'Haïti: précédée du précis et de la date des événements les plus remarquables de son histoire* (Port-au-Prince: [no pub.], 1832), 51–52.

In his *Cahier d'un retours au pays natal*, Aimé Césaire famously lyricized Haiti's fight for freedom and independence by chanting, "Haiti is where négritude stood up for the first time and proclaimed that it believed in its own humanity" ("Haïti où la négritude se mit debout pour la première fois et dit qu'elle croyait à son humanité").[2] Despite his radical conception of the Haitian Revolution as a potent symbol of black "humanity," Césaire denied the influence of Haitian intellectuals on his development of the concept of négritude. For example, even though he acknowledged them as "parallel movements," Césaire told the Haitian author René Depestre that he was not influenced by the "Negro Renaissance Movement in the United States, *La Revue Indigène* in Haiti, [or] *Negrismo* in Cuba," simply because he "did not know of them."[3] Although Pan-Africanism, black internationalism, and the Harlem Renaissance are other terms that would equally be used to describe the "clear coming to consciousness"[4] that Césaire said had organically, rather than deliberately, led "Negroes" around the world to combat "l'Europe colonialisatrice,"[5] the kind of revolutionary consciousness marked by all of these terms far predates Césaire's invention of the word "négritude" and the "parallel movements" with which it came to be associated.

In his *Mémoires pour servir à l'histoire d'Haïti* (1804) Louis-Félix Boisrond-Tonnerre, secretary of Jean-Jacques Dessalines, wrote that the revolutionary history of Dessalines was itself a mandate for the inevitable liberty and undeniable humanity of "slaves" everywhere:

> Haitians, whom the bravery of a true hero has lifted out of the anathema of prejudice, in reading these memoirs, you will be able to see with your own eyes the abyss from which he has rescued you. And you, slaves of all countries, you will learn from this great man, that every person naturally carries liberty in his heart, and the keys to that liberty are in his own hands.

> (Haïtiens, que le courage d'un héros a relevés de l'anathème du préjugé, en lisant ces mémoires, vous mesurerez de l'œil l'abîme d'où il vous a retirés! Et vous, esclaves de tous les pays, vous apprendrez

---

[2] Aimé Césaire, *Cahier d'un retour au pays natal* (Paris: Présence Africaine, 1983), 24.

[3] René Depestre, "An Interview with Aimé Césaire," trans. Maro Riofrancos, in *Discourse on Colonialism*, trans. Joan Pinkham (New York: Monthly Review, 2000), 86.

[4] Quoted in Ibid., 85.

[5] Aimé Césaire, *Discours sur le colonialisme* (Paris: Présence Africaine, 1955), 27.

par ce grand homme, que l'homme porte naturellement dans son cœur la liberté, et qu'il en tient les clés dans ses mains)⁶

Boisrond-Tonnerre was merely the first in a long line of Haitian historians to use Haitian independence as evidence for what he alludes to as a revolutionary consciousness *vis-à-vis* black "humanity" that would eventually lead to universal emancipation across the Atlantic World. Baron de Vastey, secretary to Haiti's King Henry Christophe, similarly proclaimed in his *Réflexions politiques* (1817) that "the cause of the Haitian people" "involves all of humankind."⁷ In his earlier *Réflexions sur une lettre de Mazères* (1816) Vastey had more forcefully inserted Haiti into transatlantic abolitionism when, referring to enslavers as "enemies of humankind," he wrote, "I hope that Haiti will serve as the point of departure for the philanthropists who can here stake the powerful lever that will be required to lift up the moral world against the enemies of humankind" ("j'espère qu'Hayti sera le point d'appui où les philanthropes pourront poser le levier puissant qui doit soulever le monde moral, contre les ennemis du genre humain").⁸

An antislavery activist connection was more specifically drawn between independent Haiti and the antebellum U.S. later in the nineteenth century by the Haitian historian Joseph Saint-Rémy. Saint-Rémy dedicated his publication of Toussaint Louverture's memoirs, *Mémoires de Toussaint L'Ouverture, écrits par lui-même* (1853), to the U.S. abolitionist "Ms. Harriet Beecher Stowe, author of the philanthropic novel *La Case de l'Oncle Tom, ou Vie des nègres aux Etas-Unis.*"⁹ In his dedication, Saint-Rémy said to Stowe that her novel would help the U.S. to "attack slavery" and in effect "succeed in vanquishing that monster." This was because the abolitionists, in Saint-Rémy's estimation, had "the truth" and Stowe herself—"daughter of the heavens"—on their side.¹⁰ The Haitian dramatist and poet Pierre Faubert also praised Stowe's *Uncle Tom's Cabin* in a note accompanying the publication of his play, *Ogé, ou le prejugé de couleur* (1856),

---

6 Louis Félix Boisrond-Tonnerre, *Mémoires pour servir à l'histoire d'Haïti* (Paris: France Libraire, 1851), 95.

7 Baron de Vastey, *Réflexions politiques sur quelques ouvrages et journaux français concernant Haïti* (Sans Souci: L'Imprimerie Royale, 1817), 1.

8 Baron de Vastey, *Réflexions sur une lettre de Mazères, ex-colon français [...] sur les noirs et les blancs, la civilisation de l'Afrique, le Royaume d'Hayti, etc.* (Sans Souci: L'Imprimerie Royale, 1816), 4.

9 Joseph Saint-Rémy, ed., *Mémoires du général Toussaint-L'Ouverture écrits par lui-même* (Paris: Pagnerre, 1853), 5.

10 Ibid., 6.

first performed at the Lycée National de Port-au-Prince in 1841. Faubert wrote that while a seemingly endless production of pro-slavery novels was being circulated around the world, he was comforted by Stowe's contribution to abolitionist thought and called her epic, "that little volume that moved the two worlds."[11]

Faubert's claim that the two hemispheres of the world could be moved to humanitarian action by abolitionist writing like Stowe's, as equally as by his own, demonstrates a conception widely shared among nineteenth-century Haitian authors that Haitians had a duty to intervene in international antislavery efforts. A later nineteenth-century Haitian author, the medical doctor Louis Joseph Janvier, insisted that Alexandre Pétion had exhibited such a willingness to materially intervene in world affairs when he had given "weapons, money, and soldiers to [Simón] Bolívar," which "had helped the Columbian patriot to deliver his country from Spanish rule" ("des armes, de l'argent et des hommes à Bolívar et aida le patriote colombien à délivrer son pays de la domination des Espagnols"). The ricocheting and longitudinal anti-imperial and antislavery consequences of the Haitian president's collaboration with Bolívar was clear: "It is the independence of Colombia and Venezuela that led to that of Peru and Boliva" ("C'est l'indépendance de la Colombie et du Vénézuela qui a amené celle du Pérou et celle de la Bolivie").[12] Janvier's contemporary Demesvar Delorme also evoked Haiti's historical commitment to combating colonialism and slavery in the Americas when he spoke of the role that the Haitian people had played in various Latin American struggles for independence:

> Right next door to us, in America, on the southern continent, there are people who have, like us, rendered themselves independent from their European metropole, who accomplished this feat a long time after we did, and for whom our fathers, already leaders here at home, still went to fight.
>
> (Il y a tout près de nous, en Amérique, dans le continent méridional, des peuples qui se sont rendus comme nous indépendants de leur métropole européenne; qui se sont constitués longtemps après nous; pour lesquels nos pères, déjà maîtres chez eux, sont allés combattre)[13]

---

11 Pierre Faubert, *Ogé, ou le préjugé de couleur* (Paris: Librairie de C. Maillet-Schmitz, 1856), 41.
12 Louis-Joseph Janvier, *La République d'Haïti et ses visiteurs* (Paris: Marpon et Flammarion, 1883), 16.
13 Demesvar Delorme, *La Misère au sein des richesses, réflexions diverses sur Haïti* (Paris: E. Dentu, 1873), 98.

Yet it is the Haitian ethnographer Anténor Firmin who is probably the most well-known of nineteenth-century Haitian writers to have linked the government of Pétion to the Latin American Age of Independence. In his *De l'égalité des races humaines* (1885) Firmin wrote that in 1811 "the illustrious Bolívar, liberator and founder of five republics in South America" ("l'illustre Bolivar, libérateur et fondateur, de cinq républiques de l'Amérique du Sud"), desperate and out of resources, had turned to "the black republic in order to request help from it to complete the work of liberation" ("la république noire afin d'en tirer les secours pour reprendre l'œuvre de la libération").[14]

Precisely because of Firmin's own collaboration with various revolutionaries across the Americas, and in particular with Cuba's José Martí, J. Michael Dash has written that Firmin's writing demonstrates "important instances of hemispheric crossculturality [that] allow for envisioning a pan-American continuum that reaches back at least to Haitian independence in 1804."[15] Noting, however, that Firmin in particular and nineteenth-century Haiti in general are usually "left out" of such accounts because of "[w]hat a militant poetics once dismissed as Eurocentric," Dash urges that "[c]urrent interest in crosscultural negotiations and suspicion of the nativist impulses of the explosive radicalism of the 1930s should tempt us to look again at what has been stereotyped as an inauthentic, mimetic nineteenth century."[16] Dash's call for scholars to return to the nineteenth century has, in some respects, been heeded, at least with respect to reconsidering the importance of Firmin. Firmin is now firmly located as one of the primary actors in both Pan-Americanism and Pan-Africanism. This resurgent interest in his writings stretches across literary, historical, and anthropological study.[17]

---

14 Anténor Firmin, *De l'égalité des races humaines. Anthropologie positive* (Paris: Librairie Cotillon, 1885), 586.
15 J. Michael Dash, "Nineteenth-Century Haiti and the Archipelago of the Americas: Anténor Firmin's Letters from St. Thomas," *Research in African Literatures* 35, no. 2 (Summer 2004): 45.
16 Ibid., 46.
17 See Paul C. Mocombe, "Reconstructing the Social Sciences and Humanities: Anténor Firmin, Western Intellectual Tradition, and Black Atlantic Thought and Culture," *Insights in Anthropology* 3, no. 2 (April 2019), https://scholarlypages.org/Articles/anthropology/iap-3-018.php?jid=anthropology; Robert Bernasconi, "A Haitian in Paris: Anténor Firmin as a Philosopher against Racism," *Patterns of Prejudice* 42, nos. 4–5 (2008): 365–383; Laurent Dubois, "Frederick Douglass, Anténor Firmin, and the Making of US-Haitian Relations," in *The Haitian Revolution and the Early United States*, ed. Elizabeth Maddock Dillon and Michael Drexler (Philadelphia: University of Pennsylvania Press, 2016), 95–116;

While turning to Firmin's link to Pan-American and Pan-African thought has provided us with new methods of approaching nineteenth-century Haiti's relationship to the broader American hemisphere, Firmin is hardly the only nineteenth-century Haitian author to have been involved in conceiving the kinds of hemispheric solidarity envisioned by Martí, especially with respect to creating a "Caribbean federation."[18] If Firmin's friendship with Martí, forged when the latter visited Cap-Haïtien in 1893,[19] has meant that he could be neatly co-opted into theories of Pan-Americanism, I would like to call our attention to two other Haitian authors—the above-mentioned Delorme and Janvier—neither of whom is ordinarily associated with such "hemispheric crossculturality" or even with négritude, but both of whom made unique and vital contributions to the kind of hemispheric thought now associated with Pan-Caribbean writers like Martí, Firmin, and Puerto Rico's Ramón Emeterio Betances.[20]

Both Delorme and Janvier located Haiti at the center rather than on the margins of not only a Caribbean world system that included the entire archipelago of the Caribbean and the broader continent of South America, but an Atlantic one that included Western Europe and the United States. Indeed, both writers envisioned Haiti as a central part of an interconnected global intellectual tradition of what we might call

---

Asselin Charles, "Race and Geopolitics in the Work of Anténor Firmin," *The Journal of Pan African Studies* 7, no. 2 (August 2014): 68–88; Carolyn Fluehr-Lobban, "Anténor Firmin and Haiti's Contribution to Anthropology," *Gradhivab* no. 1 (2005): 95–108, https://journals.openedition.org/gradhiva/302; Brandon R. Byrd, *The Black Republic: African Americans and the Fate of Haiti* (Philadelphia: University of Pennsylvania Press, 2019); Pierre W. Orelus, *The Agony of Masculinity: Race, Gender, and Education in the Age of "New" Racism and Patriarchy* (New York: Peter Lang, 2010); Celucien L. Joseph, "Introduction: Firmin, Global History and the End of Race," in *Reconstructing the Social Sciences and Humanities: Anténor Firmin, Western Intellectual Tradition, and Black Atlantic Tradition*, ed. Celucien L. Joseph and Paul C. Mocombe (Routledge, 2021).

18 See Stephan Palmié and Francisco A. Scarano, *The Caribbean: A History of the Region and Its Peoples* (Chicago: University of Chicago Press, 2011), 17; Kahlil Chaar-Pérez, "'A Revolution of Love': Ramón Emeterio Betances, Anténor Firmin, and Affective Communities in the Caribbean," *The Global South* 7, no. 2 (2014): 11–36; Jossianna Arroyo, *Writing Secrecy in Caribbean Freemasonry* (New York: Palgrave Macmillan, 2013), 88.

19 Chaar-Pérez, "A Revolution of Love," 31.

20 Yves Chemla, however, has read Janvier as espousing "une négritude avant la lettre"; "Louis-Joseph Janvier, écrivain national," 13.

Haitian Atlantic humanism: a long-standing way of thinking about eradicating the problems of racism and slavery *through* and *from* the nation-state of Haiti, but also *in collaboration* with Western European and intra-American world powers.

In the early nineteenth century, producing a Haitian Atlantic humanism seems to have specifically entailed speaking the languages, cultures, and histories of the Haitian revolutionists' radical exhortation to fight for "liberty or death," and in so doing to "avenge America" like Dessalines, thereby ensuring the growth and spread of Toussaint Louverture's apocryphal "tree of liberty" throughout the world, each of these being iconic phrases repeated throughout nineteenth-century transatlantic abolitionist literature.[21] Yet for Janvier and Delorme, Haiti was more than an important symbol to be proverbially evoked by the oppressed of the Atlantic World. In Delorme's and Janvier's respective theorizations, Haiti remained a decisive player in the ongoing struggle for the liberation of enslaved people across the hemisphere, especially in Cuba, where Janvier lamented that slavery was still in existence in 1883.[22] Delorme, for his part, saw himself as exposing the continuation of domestic racism on U.S. soil after the Civil War when he wrote that after having traveled to "North America," "where for a long time slavery in name has no longer existed" ("où depuis longtemps l'esclavage de fait n'existe pas"), he had to confront the fact that "men of our race are obliged to resign themselves to living in that country as the Jews had everywhere lived in the Middle Ages, tolerated, but persecuted" ("[l]es hommes de notre race sont obligés de résigner à vivre dans ce pays-là comme vivaient partout les Juifs dans le moyen âge, tolérés mais persecutes").[23] Such evocations of slavery and color prejudice as Atlantic World problems that deeply involved Haitians demonstrate how writing both *from* and *through* Haiti to get to the other islands and continents of the Americas could produce what Wai Chee Dimock calls in another context "input channels, kinship networks, routes of transit and forms of attachment."[24] In fact, turning to nineteenth-century Haitian intellectual history as a part of a larger continuum of both

21 Marlene L. Daut, "The Franco-Haitian Grammar of Transnational African American Writing," *J19: The Journal of Nineteenth-Century Americanists* 3, no. 2 (2015): 387–389.
22 Janvier, *La République*, 89.
23 Delorme, *La Misère*, 124, 127.
24 Wai Chee Dimock, *Through Other Continents: American Literature across Deep Time* (Princeton: Princeton University Press, 2006), 3.

hemispheric anticolonial and transatlantic antislavery thought plainly demonstrates what we miss when our conception of these intellectual traditions is limited to western European and U.S. American metropolitan centers. That is to say, turning to the writings of Janvier and Delorme can help us to develop a better history of the transatlantic abolitionist and anticolonial movements of the nineteenth century, one that instead of isolating and excluding Haiti, locates it as deeply enmeshed in both the rhetorical and material struggles of anti-imperialism as well as abolitionism.

The language and terminology of both Pan-Americanism and Pan-Africanism surfaced in cultural studies largely in order to make space for understanding the anticolonial discourses of early twentieth-century activists from the African diaspora and Latin America. Brenda Gayle Plummer has attempted nevertheless to understand the distinction between the two movements, noting, "[i]f Pan-Africanism was a way of stepping out of a discourse that did not privilege blackness, Pan-Americanism was a way of subordinating that and other particularisms in a manner that left the nation-state system intact." For her, nineteenth-century Haiti, therefore, "does not represent the nexus of Pan-Africanism and Pan-Americanism, but, rather, a peculiar antithesis of both."[25] Yet it seems to me that the simultaneously Pan-African and Pan-American vision put forth in Janvier's and Delorme's writings do not really suggest the "antithesis" of these formations. Instead, these works beg us to find a new vocabulary that can reveal not the limits but rather the expanses of Pan-African and Pan-American thought. That is to say that nineteenth-century Haitian intellectuals often privileged blackness at the same time that they centered, and even promoted, the nation-state.

Using a Caribbean frame of reference to think about the storied idea of the "race man,"[26] a concept normally associated with the post-Civil

---

25 Brenda Gayle Plummer, "Firmin and Martí at the Intersection of Pan-Americanism and Pan-Africanism," in *José Martí's "Our America": From National to Hemispheric Cultural Studies*, ed. Jeffrey Grant Belknap and Raoul A. Fernandez (Durham, NC: Duke University Press, 1998), 223.

26 In her iconic work, *Race Men*, Hazel Carby conceives of the "race man" as a "black" man who actively seeks to prove that he is not inferior to "whites" and that his achievements, as a person of color, stand as evidence of the facile nature of theories of racial superiority circulating in the Atlantic World. Carby is critical of such "race men," however, noting that "[her] position [...] is an outright rejection of male centered assumptions at work in such claims of representativenenss." Although it is beyond the purview of this essay to entangle the

War U.S., with this essay I hope to reinsert Delorme and Janvier into the kinds of transnational debates about colonialism, slavery, racism, and nationalism that inform both Pan-Africanism and Pan-Americanism. In so doing, I want to reconsider the path-breaking positions of both writers in having developed what we might think of as a comparative critical race theory that was both black nationalist and anti-imperialist. Both Janvier's and Delorme's publications specifically depended upon collaboration with black writers from the Americas in order to contribute to efforts to uplift "the race," on the one hand, and on the other to use the fact of Haitian sovereignty as an argument against the spread of U.S. imperialism in the American hemisphere.

Yet even though both Delorme and Janvier believed that Haiti represented the very sign and symbol of black American sovereignty, neither appears to have seen any conflict in recognizing either European or U.S. thought as central to the development and continuation of discourses of Haitian sovereignty. Janvier, who lived the majority of his life abroad in Europe,[27] had this to say about "noble France":

> I give thanks to noble France, that teat of the world, which has nourished my brain for about six years, and has made it possible to this day for me to pick up the pen in defense of my country, of my race, which is being attacked, injured, and slandered by a few men from the Middle Ages who evidently find themselves lost among us here in the nineteenth century, and by several individuals who do not wish to understand that just as the sun cannot be forced to retreat, neither can the sublime French Revolution, nor can Haiti, daughter of the one, and godchild of the other, nor can the black race, which is awakening and emerging at last from the intellectual and physical prison where it has been trapped for centuries.
>
> (je remercie la noble France, cette mamelle du monde, qui me nourrit le cerveau depuis tantôt six ans, et qui permet, par ainsi, que je tienne aujourd'hui la plume pour la défense de ma patrie, de ma race attaquées, injuriées, calomniées par quelques hommes du

undoubtedly masculinist inflections in the works of Janvier and Delorme, it is worth thinking about how both Haitian authors positioned themselves as *men* whose primary expression of masculinity was to deconstruct racism and colonialism (Hazel Carby, *Race Men* [Cambridge, MA: Harvard University Press, 1998], 4, 5).
27 Yves Chemla, "Louis Joseph Janvier," *Île en île*, June 12, 2005, http://ile-en-ile.org/janvier/.

Moyen-Age égarés au milieu du XIXe siècle, par quelques individus qui ne veulent pas comprendre que l'on ne peut faire reculer ni le soleil, ni la sublime Révolution française, ni Haïti, fille de l'un et filleule de l'autre, ni la race noire qui s'éveille, sortant enfin du bagne matériel et intellectuel où l'esclavage l'avait maintenue prisonnière pendant des semaines d'années)[28]

Delorme, too, while highly critical of the United States' continuous attempts to acquire the Dominican Republic's Bay of Samana,[29] counseled U.S. politicians to follow the example of George Washington and Benjamin Franklin, whom he claimed did not have such imperial designs. He writes: "That was not what Franklin and Washington desired. They wanted, these men, to create a great country for themselves out of independence; but they said at the same time that this should not be done by despoiling the others" ("Ce n'était pas cela que voulaient Franklin et Washington. Ils voulaient, eux, avec l'indépendance, la grandeur de leurs pays; mais ils disaient en même temps qu'il ne fallait point songer à dépouiller les autres").[30] If Dash has observed that Firmin's "*Letters from Saint Thomas* [1910] belong to a new geographic imaginary where metropolitan France and postindependence Haiti," as well as "postcolonial Haiti are no longer opposed,"[31] the same could be said to characterize the works of Delorme and Janvier, particularly in relation to the United States. Neither Haitian writer saw any contradiction in defending against European and U.S. American imperial attempts in the West Indies by critiquing and praising France or lauding and lambasting the United States. Janvier praised the citizens of the United States, speaking to the fiction of "Anglo-Saxon blood" in one breath,[32] while in another he

---

28 Janvier, *La République*, xvi.
29 The U.S., looking to secure a naval station in the Caribbean, leased the bay from the Dominican Republic beginning in 1868. Haitians widely viewed the United States' presence in the region, and their attempt to acquire Haiti's Môle-Saint-Nicholas, as foreboding of U.S. imperial interests. See Patrick Bellegarde-Smith, "Overview of Haitian Foreign Policy and Relations: A Schematic Analysis," in *Haiti: Today and Tomorrow: An Interdisciplinary Study*, ed. Charles Foster and Albert Valdman (Lanham: University Press of America, 1984), 265–281; G. Pope Atkins and Larman C. Wilson, *The Dominican Republic and the United States: From Imperialism to Transnationalism* (Athens: University of Georgia Press, 1998).
30 Delorme, *La Misère*, 131.
31 Dash, "Nineteenth-Century Haiti," 51.
32 Janvier, *La République*, 92–93.

provided this damning critique of what he described as a U.S. imperial mindset. According to Janvier, Americans have "only one fault: that of believing that all of America should be one big colony or outpost of the United States" ("qu'un défaut [l'Américain]: celui de croire que toute l'Amérique ne doit être qu'une vaste colonie ou une succursale des États-Unis").[33] In the works of both Haitian writers, France and the U.S. could be venerated in the service of arguing for Latin America's— and specifically Haiti's— right to sovereignty and critiqued in concert with the larger goal of combating color prejudice around the world. Delorme tells us, in fact, that the Haitian Constitution of his era was modeled after the U.S. Constitution,[34] even though later he notes:

> In that country, things do not have the same meaning that they have elsewhere: for them, in other words, republic and democracy do not mean what they mean in other nations. There is, we know only too well, a strange but very great difference between what we call Republicans and Democrats and what is meant by these denominations in their country. There, freedoms and rights are not for all, but only for some. Justice is limited by ethnic considerations. Reason is circumscribed by prejudice.
>
> (Dans ce pays-là, les choses n'ont pas le sens qu'elles ont ailleurs: ainsi, république et démocratie n'y signifient point ce qu'elles veulent dire chez les autres nations. Il y a, on ne le sait que trop, une différence bizarre mais très grande entre ce qu'on appelle républicains et démocrates et ce qu'on entend par ces dénominations dans les autres pays. Là, les libertés et les droits ne sont pas pour tous, mais pour une partie. La justice est limitée par des considérations ethnologiques. La raison est circonscrite dans le préjugé)[35]

A Haitian Atlantic, in contrast, or, in Janvier's words, "the irregular triangle formed by the Atlantic, the Caribbean Sea, the Lucayes, and the Gulf of Mexico" ("le triangle irrégulier formé par l'Atlantique, la mer des Antilles, les Lucayes et le golfe du Mexique"),[36] while necessarily opposed to a slaveholding "French Atlantic triangle"[37] and an imperialist American hemisphere, was at the same time one where ideas of democracy

---

33 Ibid., 105.
34 Delorme, *La Misère*, 81–82
35 Ibid., 127–128.
36 Janvier, *La République*, 120.
37 Christopher Miller, *The French Atlantic Triangle: Literature and Culture of the Slave Trade* (Durham, NC: Duke University Press, 2008).

and republicanism that were ordinarily associated with Europe and the United States could be restored to their more metaphysical rather than distinctly French enlightenment or U.S. national meanings. As interpreted through the works of Janvier and Delorme, once wrested free of their specifically nationalist implications, democracy and republicanism could be put to the service of black sovereignty as well as inter-American and transatlantic political and economic alliances.

Neither Pan-African, nor Pan-American, yet both

Although both Janvier and Delorme theorized a simultaneously hemispheric and afro-diasporic Americas long before such thinking became common in more modern scholarly circles, neither Haitian writer has readily been associated with Pan-American or Pan-African thought. Jean Price-Mars, for example, whom Robert Cornevin once called "in the black world, the equivalent of what Dr. William Burghardt Du Bois is for anglophone black people" ("dans le monde noir francophone l'équivalent du Dr. William Burghardt Du Bois pour les noirs anglophones"),[38] regularly collaborated with Marcus Garvey, Claude McKay, and Réné Maran on *Le cri des nègres*.[39] However, Price-Mars's writings have not readily been connected to these movements in many of the most prominent works on black internationalism, such as in that of Paul Gilroy in *The Black Atlantic: Modernity and Double Consciousness* (1993), Brent Hayes Edwards in *The Practice of Diaspora: Literature, Translation, and the Rise of Black Internationalism* (2003), Penny Von Eschen in *Race Against Empire: Black Americans and Anticolonialism, 1937–1957* (1997), Ralph Posnock's *Color and Culture: Black Writers and the Making of the Modern Intellectual* (2000), or Michelle Stephens's *Black Empire: The Masculine Global Imaginary of Caribbean Intellectuals in the United States* (2005). Moreover, while it is true that, in the words of Michelle Stephens, "certain black leaders and intellectuals of Caribbean descent chose to imagine African Americans as part of a global political community during the early years of the twentieth century,"[40] those leaders and intellectuals were not solely located in the anglophone Caribbean.

[38] Robert Cornevin, "L'Oncle n'est plus: Jean Price (1876–1969) Champion de la Négritude," *France-Eurafrique* 205 (1969): 3–7.
[39] Quoted in Depestre, "An Interview with Aimé Césaire," 71.
[40] Michelle Ann Stephens, *Black Empire: The Masculine Global Imaginary of Caribbean Intellectuals in the United States, 1914–1962* (Durham, NC: Duke University Press, 2005), 1.

Not only did Price-Mars immediately reference the influence that the writings of Booker T. Washington had on his own agricultural theories in *La Vocation de l'élite* (1919), the Haitian ethnographer describes having collaborated for at least a fortnight with the "powerful American orator" in the early years of the twentieth century. Price-Mars praised Washington: "[a]t last, the American negroes have produced the most powerful orator of our time: Mr. Booker T. Washington" ("Enfin, les Américains nègres ont produit le plus puissant orateur américain de nos jours, M. Booker T. Washington").[41] Moreover, referring to what he perceived as an enviable "social solidarity"[42] that stretched across lines of class among black people living in the United States, Price-Mars wrote that Haiti could learn from such cross-class unity. Specifically, the Haitian ethnologist believed that Haiti's educated class should play a formative and collaborative role in the country's agricultural industry,[43] merging the work of Du Bois and Washington in an unusually complementary rather than diametrical way.

Yet before Price-Mars's simultaneous creolization of Washington's agricultural theories and co-optation of Du Bois's idea of the "talented tenth," Janvier had proffered an internationalist political vision that would make Haitians, rather than black U.S. Americans, the leaders of a broader social justice movement for not only the "Africano-Américains" of the U.S., but for "negroes" and other "Americans" of color across the hemisphere. He wrote, "[f]or the black race, Haiti is the sun rising over the horizon. Shame upon anyone, whatever his nationality may be, who, having even a single drop of the noble and generous blood of an African, would attempt to deny this; and blinded, three times blinded, would be any African-American who did not have the eyes to recognize this" ("Pour la race noire, Haïti c'est le soleil se levant à l'horizon. Honte à celui, quelle que soit sa nationalité, qui, ayant dans les veines une seule goutte du noble et généreux sang africain, tenterait de le nier; et aveugle, trois fois aveugle, serait tout Africano-Américain qui n'aurait pas d'yeux pour le voir").[44] Aside from providing a very distinct precursor to the contemporary term, African American, like many of the later Pan-Africanists discussed in the works of Gilroy, von Eschen, Stephens, and Posnock, Janvier envisioned people of African descent around the globe as linked

---

41 Jean Price-Mars, *La Vocation de l'élite* (Port-au-Prince: Imprimerie E. Chenet, 1919), 237.
42 Ibid., 127.
43 Ibid., 93–99.
44 Janvier, *La République*, 57.

to one another not only because he believed they shared the same skin color or "race," but because they shared the same interest in combating colonialism and slavery—and, therefore, the same interest in the sustenance of Haitian sovereignty. He wrote:

> It is the independence of Haiti that led to the emancipation of the slaves in the English colonies, to the founding of Liberia, and to the emancipation of slaves in Martinique and later, in the United States. It was our independence, which had an influence that has not even been acknowledged [...] it was the independence of Haiti and the sovereignty of Haiti that put an advantageous pressure on certain governments and that led to the emancipation of slaves in Puerto Rico and Brazil.
>
> (C'est l'indépendance d'Haïti qui a déterminé l'émancipation des noirs dans les colonies anglaises, la fondation de Libéria, l'émancipation des noirs à la Martinique et, plus tard, aux États-Unis [...] c'est cette indépendance et cette autonomie d'Haïti qui ont exercé une pression salutaire sur certains gouvernements et qui ont déterminé l'émancipation des noirs à Puerto-Rico et au Brésil).[45]

Later, Janvier essentially argued that all black people in the Americas were the figurative descendants of Toussaint Louverture. He therefore admonished people of color around the world "to learn to live among and speak with respect about the grandchildren of Toussaint-Louverture to whom [...] you owe so much, all of you, the children of Africa, living in America" ("apprends à vivre et parle avec respect des petit-fils de Toussaint-Louverture [...] auxquels vous devez tant, vous tous, enfants de l'Afrique qui habitez l'Amérique").[46]

Despite Janvier's own conception of what Césaire would later refer to as "our condition as Negroes,"[47] such linkages among nineteenth-century Haiti and Europe, the U.S., or the broader circum-Caribbean have been ordinarily tied to twentieth-century Haitian writers like Jacques Roumain, whose novel *Gouverneurs de la rosée* was famously translated into English by Mercer Cook and Langston Hughes.[48] Yet in many

---

45 Ibid., 56.
46 Ibid., 56.
47 Quoted in Depestre, "An Interview with Aimé Césaire," 85.
48 See Martha Cobb, *Harlem, Haiti, and Havana: A Comparative Critical Study of Langston Hughes, Jacques Roumain, Nicolás Guillén* (New York: Three Continents Press, 1979); Vera Kutzinski, *The Worlds of Langston Hughes* (Ithaca: Cornell University Press, 2012).

respects, Janvier and Delorme were just as connected to an Afro-diasporic and inter-American world of activism as Firmin, Martí, Price-Mars, and Roumain. Janvier, for example, was a French-trained medical doctor who was a part of a burgeoning Parisian Latin American expatriate community, which included Betances (also a medical doctor), who had translated U.S. abolitionist Wendell Phillips's famous speech, "Toussaint Louverture," into Spanish in 1869.[49] In 1882 a letter from Betances would appear in a collection of essays published in Paris and co-edited by Janvier, entitled *Les Détracteurs de la race noire et la république d'Haïti* (1882). In this volume, Betances defended Haiti, and Janvier in particular, against the charge of "sterility" made by the latter's racist "detractors."[50] Moreover, in March of 1874, Betances, who was known under the pseudonymn El Antillano, the moniker that he also used to sign the above-mentioned letter, reviewed Delorme's *La Misère au sein des richesses* for the Parisian journal *El Americano*.[51] Betances translated the title into Spanish as "Miseria entre riquezas" and went on to call the work "an important volume published by a Haitian" ("un importante folleto publicado por un haitiano"), referring to Delorme himself as a "bueno américano."[52]

However, it is in fact Delorme's earlier *La Démocratie et le préjugé de couleur aux Étas Unis/Les Nationalités américaines et le système Monroë* (1866) that had perhaps the most measurable influence upon the shape that Janvier's hemispheric thought would take on in the antislavery and anticolonial movements of the latter half of the nineteenth century. Delorme's very title was radical in that it affirmed that U.S. color prejudices ("le préjugé de couleur") must be understood alongside U.S. expansionism in the Americas ("le système Monroë"), indicating the mutually reinforcing nature of racism and empire. For Delorme, the fact that the United States had not immediately outlawed color prejudice after the Civil War, as Haiti had done in its first constitution in 1805, issued one year after independence from France, signaled a lack of seriousness about integrating formerly enslaved Africans into the nation. Delorme wrote that despite "a long and fierce civil war" ("une guerre civile, longue

---

49 Janvier would in fact quote from Betances's translation (in Janvier's own French translation of Betances's Spanish) in *La République*, 454–458.
50 Ramón Emeterio Betances, "Lettre de M. le Dr. Betances," in *Les Détracteurs de la race noire et de la république d'Haïti* (Paris: Marpon et Flammarion, 1882), 10.
51 Paul Estrade, *Les Écrits de Betances dans la presse latino-américaine de Paris* (Paris: Publications de l'Équipe de Recherche de l'Université de Paris VIII, 1988), iv.
52 Betances, rpt. in Estrade, *Les Écrits de Betances*, 11, 15.

et acharnée") the elimination of color prejudice "has not been accomplished by the great struggle that the government of the Union has just so gloriously supported against the States of the South, in the name of the liberty of the blacks" ("n'a pas été accomplie par la lutte imense que le gouvernement de l'Union vient de soutenir avec tant de gloire contre les États du Sud au nom de la liberte des noirs").[53] Delorme's argument that eliminating slavery would not be enough to rid the United States of its corresponding "slavery of color prejudice" (*"l'esclavage du préjugé"*)[54] implies that equality needed to be supported by an actual legal policy requiring it. Alongside this observation Delorme identified ongoing domestic racism as indelibly connected to U.S. colonial conquest by his evocation of the phrase "America for the United States."

While the post-independence Haiti of Dessalines, as equally as those of Christophe, Pétion, and Boyer, positioned its past under colonial domination in direct opposition to any future potential as an empire, according to Delorme, the United States, under President James Monroe, exhibited a more fraught relationship not only to its tardy elimination of slavery, but between its past as a colony and its future as an empire. In his December 1823 presidential message to Congress, Monroe gave a speech asserting, as Dessalines had earlier done, that "European world powers" should abandon any imperial designs on the Americas,[55] claiming that the United States would actively resist such incursions not only on its own territory but anywhere in the hemisphere.[56] Although Monroe's words are often cited as evidence of early national U.S. imperialism, the speech did not become the mantra for either westward expansion or U.S. American hemispheric protectionism until closer towards the middle of the century. In 1845, President James Polk used Monroe's words to "defend the rights of the United States to the Oregon territory."[57] From that point forward, Monroe's speech would have lasting influence in the U.S. political sphere. Its longitudinal implications for hemispheric American intellectual history, however, can be demonstrated by the continuous engagement

---

53 Démesvar Delorme, *La Démocratie et le préjugé de couleur aux Étas Unis/ Les Nationalités américaines et le système Monroë* (Brussels: H. Thiry-Van Buggenhoudt, 1866), 18, 24.

54 Ibid., 24; emphasis original.

55 All quotations of this speech taken from http://millercenter.org/president/monroe/speeches/speech-3604.

56 For an analysis of this speech, see Gretchen Murphy, *Hemispheric Imaginings: The Monroe Doctrine and Narratives of U.S. Empire* (Durham, NC: Duke University Press, 2005), 6.

57 Ibid., 27.

of Caribbean writers like Delorme with the apocryphal phrase, "America for the Americans," which has become a synecdoche for the kinds of racial-imperial policies that would later be associated with the speech, even though these words were not a part of the actual address.[58] Delorme's 1866 book, in fact, constitutes perhaps the earliest response from the Caribbean to the speech, which Delorme saw as evidence of an "equivocal laconism that troubles Europe and America at the same time: *America for the Americans*" ("un laconisme équivoque, qui inquiète à la fois l'Europe et l'Amérique: *l'Amérique aux Américains*").[59] Delorme later explained that the phrase could be more accurately translated as "America for the United States" ("l'Amérique aux Etats-Unis").[60]

Latin American and Caribbean engagements with the original apocryphal phrase continued throughout the nineteenth century. Betances also sought to counter the idea of "American for the Americans" with his own iconic phrase, "[t]he Antilles for the sons of the Antilles" ("les Antilles pour les fils des Antilles"), which he uttered for the first time at a speech he gave at a masonic lodge in Port-au-Prince.[61] In fact, it is likely that Betances was well acquainted with the works of Delorme even before he reviewed Delorme's *La Misère au sein des richesses*, since he lived in exile in Port-au-Prince from 1870 to 1872.[62] Betances's later idea of a "Confederación Antillana" ("Confederación Antillana"), too, then, may have been influenced by Delorme, who had theorized in *La Misère* that a "North American Confederation," represented in his mind at that time by the U.S. alone, could be conceived of less in terms of the nation-state and more in terms of a full-scale inter-American political organism that could benefit all of the Americas. Delorme wrote:

> The citizens of the great Republic of the United States should not allow themselves to become drunk on their own prosperity. Wisdom consists largely in not getting a big head in the midst of success. The role of the mighty North American Confederation should be, instead of coveting the territory of these young nations that have formed themselves next

---

58 An article titled "German Rage at the Monroe Doctrine," for example, begins, "The Monroe Doctrine is founded on the catch-phrase 'America for the Americans'"; *Literary Digest* 44 (January–June 1912): 978.
59 Delorme, *La Démocratie et le préjugé*, 44.
60 Ibid., 45.
61 For both Janvier's engagement with the term and Betances's connection to Delorme, see Daut's essay in this volume.
62 Ibid.

to it in the New World, to protect, defend, and form with them a great confraternity of societies in solidarity in an independent America.

(Les citoyens de la grande République des États-Unis ne devraient pas se laisser enivrer par les prospérités. La sagesse consiste en grande partie à ne pas perdre la tête au milieu des succès. Le rôle de la puissante Confédération de l'Amérique du Nord devrait être, au lieu de convoiter le territoire de ces jeunes nations qui se sont formées à côté d'elle dans le Nouveau-Monde, de les protéger, de les défendre, de former avec elles une grande contrafraternité de sociétés solidaires dans l'Amérique indépendante)[63]

Delorme's desire for separately sovereign, yet connected, states is not entirely dissimilar to the inter-Caribbean political organizations imagined first by the Puerto Rican writer Eugenio María de Hostos, then extended by Betances, and further modified by Janvier.

The Caribbean Confederation dreamed up by Hostos and Betances was at first imagined between the three Spanish-speaking Caribbean islands: Cuba, Santo Domingo (the Dominican Republic), and Puerto Rico. This was in concert with Hostos's novel *La peregrinación de Bayoán* (1863) where political solidarities are metaphorically represented in characters personified as Cuba, Santo Domingo, and Puerto Rico, respectively. Yet as Betances continued to develop his idea for a "Confederación Antillana," the vision for this alliance deepened and became more inclusive, to the point where Betances could even imagine an alliance with Haiti (unlike in Hostos's vision).[64]

Betances's now characteristic motto—"the Antilles for the sons of the Antilles"—was a will to inter-Caribbean solidarity in the face of U.S. attempts to annex various islands in the Caribbean even before the war of 1898.[65] But in the speech, Betances implored his Haitian collaborators to aid the Cubans in their ongoing fight for independence from Spain:

> Where are the people who, more than any other, have the right to take into their own hands the defense of the oppressed? Your heart has already told you: they are in Haiti; it is you. You are masons, you are Haitians, you are men of equality, you are the sons of those

---

63 Delorme, *La Misère*, 131
64 Josianna Arroyo, *Writing Secrecy in Caribbean Freemasonry* (Basingstoke, UK: Palgrave Macmillan, 2013), 161.
65 Marlene L. Daut, "Antillean Sovereignty in Pan-Caribbean Writing," in *Caribbean Literature in Transition*, vol. 1, ed. Timothy Watson and Evelyn O'Callaghan (Cambridge: Cambridge University Press, 2021), 215–230.

first great citizens who knew how to achieve civil and political rights for their race. You are therefore suited to understand better than any other people this valiant Liberating Army, which is composed of all the races mixed together, and which fights to proclaim, by supporting Cuba against Spain, the honor of raising the same standard of liberty that you made triumphant in Haiti against the power of France. There are no longer in Cuba any slaves or masters; there are only citizens; there are no longer any distinctions, no more privileges separating the whites and the blacks, there are only Creoles. Everyone is fighting for the same principles. It is a war of independence that is taking place alongside a social war, and both of them are devoted, with the most perfect alignment, to the fight against the tyranny of the government and against the tyranny of the slave-master that the Spanish European personifies.[66]

(Quel est donc le peuple qui, plus que tout autre, a le droit de prendre en mains la défense de ces opprimés? Votre cœur vous l'a déjà dit: c'est Haïti, c'est vous mêmes. Vous êtes maçons, vous êtes haïtiens vous êtes les hommes de l'égalité, vous êtes les fils de ces grands citoyens que les premiers surent conquérir pour leur race les droits civils et politiques. Vous êtes donc dignes de comprendre mieux que les autres hommes, cette vaillante armée libératrice où toutes les races confondues se disputent aujourd'hui l'honneur de soutenir à Cuba, contre l'Espagne, le même drapeau que vous avez fait triompher à Haïti contre tout le pouvoir de la France. Il n'y a plus dans la république de Cuba des esclaves et des maîtres; il n'y a que des citoyens; il n'y a plus de distinctions, plus de privilèges entre les noirs et les blancs, il n'y a que des créoles. Tous, ils combattent pour les mêmes principes. C'est une guerre d'indépendance qui marche à côté d'une guerre sociale toutes deux sont menées, dans le plus parfait accord, contre la tyrannie du gouvernement et contre la tyrannie du maître que l'espagnol européen personifie)

Such cross-pollination of ideas that led from Haiti to Cuba to Puerto Rico and back to Haiti can be immediately glimpsed in the title of Janvier's *Haïti aux Haïtiens* (1884). Janvier was almost certainly influenced in this titular position by both the works of his contemporary Delorme and by Betances's exhortation in the Delorme review that Haiti was an absolutely central player in "our archipelago," specifically

---

[66] Translated from Ramón Emeterio Betances, "A.L.G.D.P.A.D.L.U.," in *Betances*, ed. Luis Bonafoux y Quintero (San Juan: Instituto de Cultura Puertorriqueña, 1970), 110–116.

when it came to preserving "The Antilles for the Antilleans" ("Las Antillas, para los Antillanos").[67] But Janvier explained the much more deliberately nationalist logic behind his phrase "Haïti aux Haïtiens" by speaking directly to the Haitian people themselves:

> What is important above all is that in autonomous, independent Haiti, Haitians remain the only ones in charge. Anything contrary to this doctrine represents only danger or chimera.
>
> (Ce qu'il importe avant tout, c'est que dans Haïti autonome, indépendante, les Haïtiens soient les seulent maîtres. Tout ce qui est contraire à cette doctrine n'est que danger ou chimère)[68]

The intertextual similarities to be found among the writings of Betances, Delorme, and Janvier are perhaps unsurprising when we consider that each was educated in Paris and lived there in exile, a situation that was apparently common enough for Latin American *émigrés* in the late nineteenth century. Paul Estrade writes that:

> Paris had become a site of meetings and exchanges between Latin Americans, and it was also a kind of "center of operations" where politically, economically, culturally, North American incursions in Latin America could be thwarted in the interest of Latin America.
>
> (Paris est devenu un lieu de rencontres et d'échanges entre Latino-Américains et un "centre d'opérations" d'où politiquement, économiquement, culturellement, les visées nord-américains sur l'Amérique latine peuvent être contrecarrées dans l'intérêt de l'Amérique latine)[69]

The Latin American Paris described by Estrade is the locale where Delorme wrote and published almost all of his major works. Yet the more common story told of Delorme's Paris is that in the 1870s he frequented the salons of French writers Alphonse de Lamartine and Victor Hugo, as well as Alexandre Dumas.[70] The innermost circle of Janvier is similarly described as having been made up of primarily French writers, such as Charles Leconte de Lisle, Judith Gautier,

---

67 Betances, rpt. in Estrade, *Les Écrits de Betances*, 16.
68 Louis-Joseph Janvier, *Haïti aux Haïtiens*, 2nd ed. (Paris: Imprimerie A. Parent, A. Davy, Successeurs, 1884), 18.
69 Estrade, *Les Écrits de Betances*, vii.
70 Chemla, "Demesvar Delorme." See also Raphaël Berrou and Pradel Pompilus, *Histoire de la littérature haïtienne illustrée par les textes*, 3 vols. (Port-au-Prince: Édition Caraïbes, 1975–1977), 1:545.

François Coppée, and Stéphane Mallarmé.⁷¹ I wonder if it is the linkage of both men to a circle of French Parisian literati, rather than a Latin American one, that has until now obscured and excluded both Haitian writers' involvement in Latin American and hemispheric American intellectual circles?

Both Delorme and Janvier wrote novels that have been used as examples of what Price-Mars called "bovarysme collectif," or the imitation of French forms and subject matter.⁷² However, instead of viewing their veneration for France and usage of the French language (which was not at all dissimilar from Betances's in both regards) and their penchants for classical forms in their fiction as examples of *bovarysme*, perhaps we should see their claims that Haiti's history, literature, culture, and politics were indelibly intertwined with that of France, and Europe in general, as a part of the tensions involved in creating transnational "black" sovereignty *through* Haiti in an often hostile postcolonial Atlantic World. Neither writer sought to isolate Haiti from its European past or to isolate it from a future that might include the United States. This tendency to turn simultaneously towards and away from colonialist powers might reflect, as Raphael Dalleo has written, "the shifting tension between these two demands—of being oppositional to power yet representing the nation," which he says "is crucial to periodizing Caribbean literature."⁷³ Dalleo argues that "[t]he persistently peripheral location of the Caribbean in relation to the centers of global power means that one consistent structural element of the Caribbean public sphere is the contradictory push and pull of consolidation and oppositionality."⁷⁴ Part of what makes the work of Delorme and Janvier so crucial for thinking about the relationship of nineteenth-century Haiti to a Latin American Age of Independence is the argument that Haiti stood at the "center," not at the periphery, of the archipelago of the Caribbean.⁷⁵ This strategic placement in the middle of North and

---

71 Yves Chemla, "Louis-Joseph Janvier, écrivain national," *Francofonia* 49, special issue: Lectures et écritures haïtiennes (2005): 8–9.
72 Jean Price-Mars, *Ainsi parla l'Oncle: Essais d'ethnographie. Un volume avec 10 gravures et une carte par l'auteur. Un document produit en version numérique par Jean-Marie Tremblay, bénévole, professeur de sociologie au Cégep de Chicoutimi* (New York: Parapsychology Foundation, 1954 [1928]), 10, 192; Chemla, "Louis-Joseph Janvier, écrivain national," 30.
73 Raphael Dalleo, *Caribbean Literature and the Public Sphere: From the Plantation to the Postcolonial* (Charlottesville: University of Virginia Press, 2011), 5.
74 Ibid., 8.
75 Delorme, *La Misère*, 133.

South America, Africa, and Europe meant that Haiti had just as much to teach as it had to learn from transnational cultural, political, and intellectual histories. In describing the language of Haiti, Janvier wrote that while it was officially French,

> Among the people we speak a patois that is a mixture of words from the French, English, and Spanish languages, along with words from various African dialects. In our schools we also teach English and Spanish.
>
> (Dans le peuple on parle un patois qui est un mélange de mots de langues françaises, anglaises et espagnoles et de mots provenant des dialectes africains. Dans les écoles on enseigne aussi l'anglais et l'espagnol)[76]

Thus, the strength of Haiti was that even while it was determined to be a separate and distinct nation, it remained Creole like the Atlantic.

Creole nationalism as humanism

In their famous 1989 manifesto, "L'Éloge de la créolité," written in part as a diatribe against négritude, Jean Bernabé, Patrick Chamoiseau, and Raphaël Confiant criticized twentieth-century Haitian indigenist literature and its connection to négritude. Bernabé et al. wrote that Caribbean life "ought not to be described ethnographically, nor ought there to be a census-taking of Creole practices after the fashion of the Haitian indigenists, instead we ought *to show what, in these practices, bears witness to both Creoleness and the human condition.*"[77] The trio propose, therefore, that "Creoleness encompasses and perfects Americanness because it involves a double process:—*the adaptation of Europeans, Africans, and Asians to the New World; and—the cultural confrontation of these peoples within the same space, resulting in a mixed culture called Creole.*"[78] Nevertheless, while Bernabé, Confiant, and Chamoiseau, as subjects of France, all of them hailing from Martinique, have the luxury of operating with an affective statelessness, defined by them as *créolité*, all the while enjoying citizenship rights as ancillary members of a powerful nation-state, no such position was available to nineteenth-century Haitians. Haitians lived and continue to live in a state of material precarity that

76 Janvier, *La République*, xxi.
77 Jean Bernabé et al., "In Praise of Creoleness," trans. Mohamed B. Taleb Khyar, *Callaloo* 13, no. 4 (Autumn 1990): 898.
78 Ibid., 894.

makes recourse to the aesthetic imaginings of a conglomerate and utopian culture of *créolité* much less attractive, let alone useful.

In a milieu in which such transnational citizenship was not only proclaimed, but regarded as the only path towards moving beyond what Bernabé et al. conceived as the limitations of *négritude*, *Americanness*, and *Caribbeanness*, it is easy to see why Haitian authors like Janvier and Delorme can so often be left out of accounts of the critical intellectual and historical trajectory of *créolité*. Janvier minced no words when it came to the protection of Haitian sovereignty. Observing U.S. imperial designs in the West Indies, Janvier repeated Delorme's interpretation of the Monroe doctrine by saying it had amounted to one thing: "America for the Americans, *which means America for the United States*" ("l'Amérique aux Américains, *lisez l'Amérique aux États-Unis*").[79] Even before the publication of *Haïti aux Haïtiens* in 1884, Janvier's response to this was if "[t]he Yankees happily say: America for the Americans," "let us Haitians never forget to shout even louder: 'Haiti for Haitians! ...'" ("Les Yankees disent volontiers: 'l'Amérique aux Américains' [...] Que les Haïtiens n'oublient pas de crier bien haut: 'Haïti aux Haïtiens! ...'").[80]

Janvier's statement, "Haïti aux Haïtiens," seems at first glance like a political position that many *créolistes* might describe as a part of the same "essentially nasty ideological formation" that constitutes European and U.S. nationhood. Yet in Simon During's words, it is important to "remember that nationalism has different effects and meanings in a peripheral nation than in a world power," and was often "a mode of freedom" that was "developed *against* imperialism."[81] Faith Smith has similarly cautioned that "[t]he elaboration of a diasporic context that uncritically renders all nationalisms equally essentialist and hegemonic can further marginalize [...] nationalist and anti-imperialist struggles."[82] Indeed, in Janvier's formulation, Haiti is for the Haitians because a nation-state is not necessarily a *bad* political organization. Instead, it is the imperialist tendency of nations, their drive to conquer, that must be

---

79 Janvier, *La République*, 122. The Monroe Doctrine, signed by James Monroe in 1823, allowed the U.S. to intervene in other nations and territories in Latin America, allegedly to protect them from the colonial designs of Western Europe.
80 Ibid., 122.
81 Simon During, "Literature–Nationalism's Other? The Case for Revision," in *Nation and Narration*, ed. Homi K. Bhabha (London: Routledge, 1990), 139.
82 Faith Smith, *Creole Recitations: John Jacob Thomas and Colonial Formation in the Late Nineteenth Century* (Charlottesville: University of Virginia Press, 2002), xviii–xix.

quelled. The problem with the United States, then, was not that it was a nation, but rather that it sought to be an empire.

For historical context, we should observe that Janvier published the essays that make up *Haïti aux Haïtiens* in haste to express his displeasure at the news that James G. Blaine, former secretary of state under U.S. president James Garfield, was chosen as the Republican candidate at the 1884 Chicago Convention.[83] Janvier's dismay at the Republican nominee was directly related to the fact that not only did Blaine openly support and defend the so-called Monroe Doctrine, he was known to have repeatedly and publicly uttered the phrase, "America for the Americans."[84] Of Blaine's nomination, Janvier wrote:

> Mr. Blaine, former secretary of state, has always shown himself to be one of the greatest advocates of the hegemony of the United States over all of America [...] He is the author of the Republican plan accepted in Chicago and that has translated the words of Monroe and Adams to mean: *America for the Americans.*
>
> (M. Blaine, ancien secrétaire des Affaires Etrangeres, s'est toujours montré grand prôneur de l'hégémonie des Etas-Unis sur toute l'Amérique [...] Il est l'auteur de l'article du programme républicain accepté à Chicago et qui traduit le mot de Monroë et d'Adams: *l'Amérique aux Américains*)[85]

Janvier clearly understood Blaine's co-optation of the phrase to mean that the United States sought control over the entire American hemisphere. However, even "westernized Haitians," Janvier said, "do not want anything in the world to do with the idea that Haiti would become a colony or even a state [of the U.S.]" ("nous autres, Haïtiens occidentaux... nous ne voulons pour rien au monde que l'île d'Haïti devienne une colonie ou même un État de la Confédération du Nord").[86] "To whom have the Haitian people said they will abdicate?", he asked:

> Our fathers, so it seems to me, created the Haitian nation by themselves, all alone, without loans, which they paid for with the

---

[83] Janvier, *Haïti aux Haïtiens*, 19. [Editor's note: regarding Daut's citation and analysis of Janvier's *Haïti aux Haïtiens*, see also the translation of "Clarion Call" in the present volume.]

[84] James Gillespie Blaine, "Mr. Sprague of Monson," in *Memorial Addresses on the Life and Character of James Gillespie Blaine* (Augusta: Burleigh and Flynt, 1893), 42.

[85] Janvier, *Haïti aux Haïtiens*, 20.

[86] Ibid., 22.

gold that they procured through the sweat of their labor, precisely in order to have the right to live independently; they left us this little corner of the earth so that there would be at least one place on the globe where no one could spit upon the black race with impunity.

(A qui le peuple haïtien a-t-il dit qu'il abdiquait? [...] Nos pères, il me semble, ont créé tout seuls la nation haïtienne; tout seuls, sans emprunts, ils ont payé de l'or qu'avait produit leurs sueurs de droit de vivre indépendants; ils nous ont laissé ce coin de terre afin qu'il y eût un endroit dans le globe où l'on ne peut cracher impunément à la face de la race noire)[87]

If Janvier wanted "Haiti for Haitians," then, as a protection against U.S. imperialism and global white supremacy, Delorme went even further in his criticism by warning Haitians not to be seduced by the ostensive stability that could be offered by the U.S. if Haiti were to become its protectorate, and thus a part of its empire of racism:

Now, we must admit that we are aware that those who oppose our sovereignty have been stating very loudly that our country has not been productive in the realm of agriculture in order to challenge our autonomy by questioning our ability to govern ourselves.

(Or, on doit le savoir, les ennemis de notre nationalité arguent tout haut de l'improductivité actuelle de notre sol pour nous contester notre autonomie en contestant notre aptitude à nous gouverner)[88]

But if Haiti were to become a protectorate of the U.S., not only would Haitians lose their all-important national sovereignty, they would be subject to the kinds of racism experienced by all people of color in the U.S. He warned, to that end, "[t]hey will have nothing but scorn for you, they will mistreat you, just as they scorn and mistreat the men of our race who live in the United States" ("On vous méprisera, on vous maltraitera, comme on méprise et maltraite les hommes de notre race aux Etas-Unis").[89]

Delorme did not just fear that Haitians might consent to U.S. "protection." He also feared that Haitian citizens might want to emigrate to the U.S. Warning them away from such a fatalist project, which he said would doom them once again to subjugation, Delorme critiqued U.S. racism and imperialism by way of capitalism. Delorme essentially argued

87 Ibid. 30
88 Delorme, *La Misère*, 119.
89 Ibid., 124.

that the term "civilization" itself had merely monetary, rather than philosophical or humanistic meaning for U.S. Americans:

> Everywhere else, civilization means humanity striving towards its moral, intellectual, and physical improvement all at once; in [the United States], civilization means money. It's all about making dollars; no matter the cost.
>
> (Partout ailleurs, la civilisation signifie les efforts de l'humanité vers son amélioration morale, intellectuelle et physique tout à la fois; dans ce pays-là, civilisation signifie dollar. Il s'agit uniquement de faire de l'argent; coûte que coûte)[90]

Delorme is even more insistent when he notes that in the U.S.,

> Every idea of justice and duty is subordinated to this dominant idea: having millions. A person is appreciated, esteemed, considered of value, if he does not have black skin, of course, according to the sum of money that he has in his possession.
>
> (Toute idée de justice et de devoir est subordonnée à cette idée mère: avoir des millions. On est apprécié, estimé, considéré, quand on n'a pas la peau noire, bien entendu, suivant la somme d'argent qu'on a en sa possession)[91]

He continues:

> Of a man who has sixty thousand dollars, it is said: *He is worth sixty thousand dollars.* "He is worth," that is to say the amount by which he is valued. The language of a people reveals its spirit.
>
> (On dit d'un homme qui a soixante mille piastres: *He is worth sixty thousand dollars*. He is worth, c'est-à-dire *il vaut*. La langue d'un peuple dit son génie)[92]

This drive to have more and more, and therefore to be *worth* more and more, leads Delorme back to U.S. imperialism. Delorme describes imperialism as an outgrowth of the same sense of capital that dominates U.S. American life when he likens it to a desire to possess geographical and political sovereignty over more and more regions of the world. He asks why the U.S., which had a large part of an entire continent to itself, constantly sought to extend its borders:

90 Ibid., 128.
91 Ibid.
92 Ibid.

You have become a great power, one of the richest, most powerful countries in the world; you have all to yourselves almost the entire northern continent of America, essentially half of a world; and that is not enough for you; you would like to take from a small people who have done nothing to harm you the tiny part of the earth that belongs to them!

(Vous êtes devenus une grande puissance, l'une des puissances les plus riches du monde; vous avez à vous tout le nord du continent de l'Amérique, toute la moitié d'un monde; et cela ne vous suffit plus; et vous voulez encore ravir à un petit peuple qui ne vous nuit pas le coin de terre qui lui appartient!)[93]

Echoing Baron de Vastey's question, "[t]he blacks, have they ever crossed the seas in order to invade, enslave, and destroy whites?" ("Les noirs ont-ils jamais traversés les mers pour envahir, enchaîner et détruire des blancs?"),[94] Delorme returns to the philanthropic project of racial uplift and solidarity that informs so much of his work, asking, "Is it in the name of justice that you crossed the sea in order to attack the rights of the inhabitants of Hispaniola?" ("Est-ce que au nom de la même justice que vous traverseriez la mer pour aller attaquer les droits des habitants d'Hispaniola?").[95] This passage presciently questions what would become the logic of U.S. imperialism throughout the rest of the nineteenth century and continuing today: spreading U.S. notions of democracy and capitalism to places ravaged by forms of dictatorship, political unrest, and poverty that can very often be directly linked to the U.S. and other world powers. Janvier noted as much when he wrote:

If we were truly to look into the matter, behind every insurrection that has taken place in Haiti from 1843 to our day, we would always see that a foreign hand has been pulling the strings and making the puppets dance.

(Si l'on cherchait bien, derrière chaque insurrection qui a eu lieu en Haïti depuis 1843 jusques [sic] à nos jours, on trouverait toujours une main d'étranger qui tient les fils et qui fait mouvoir les pantins)[96]

---

93 Ibid., 130.
94 Baron de Vastey, *Notes à M. le Baron de V.P. Malouet [...] en réfutation du 4ème volume de son ouvrage, intitulé: Collection de mémoires sur les colonies, et particulièrement sur Saint-Domingue, etc.* (Cap-Henry: P. Roux, 1814), 13.
95 Delorme, *La Misère*, 130.
96 Janvier, *La République*, 18.

Instead of pursuing the enlargement of its territories, Delorme, for his part, wondered why the U.S. did not just settle for being a beacon for the other states of the Americas. He wrote that if the U.S. were to follow his advice to be content merely with the already magnificent *largesse* of its terrain, the country "could become, like its president has said he desires, *the star that will guide* the other Republics" ("pourra devenir, comme l'a dit son président, *l'étoile qui guidera les autres Républiques*").[97]

This brief excursus into the worlds of Delorme and Janvier represents merely a meager call for the works of these writers to be considered much more as a part of the histories of global "black nationalism," as equally as hemispheric American thought. Both men put into effect the kind of discourse analysis more immediately associated with the thought of later Pan-African writers like Du Bois, Césaire, and Frantz Fanon. And their visions of the world were, in some ways, just as cosmopolitan as Martí's and Betances's contributions to Pan-American intellectual history. Janvier and Delorme believed that Haitians could remain Haitian and be citizens of the world since making Haiti, unlike making the U.S., did not mean becoming an imperialist state. Vastey, who in many respects marks the origins of such a Haitian Atlantic humanism, had sought to remind his transnational audience that "The revolution did not transfer from the whites to the blacks the question of control over the Antilles. Haiti is one of the islands of this archipelago, and is not itself the Antilles" ("La révolution n'a point transplanté des blancs aux noirs la question de l'empire des Antilles. Hayti est une des îles de cet Archipel, et n'est point les Antilles").[98] Perhaps a policy of "nationalities" rather than the *créoliste*'s dream of global citizenship is at the heart of humanistic thought. After all, it was Aimé Césaire who told us that Europe, in order to save itself from the "sheet of mortal darkness" ("drap des mortelles ténèbres") represented by its colonialist practices, needed to undertake all on its own "the initiative of a politics of *nationalities*, the initiative of a politics founded upon respect for people and cultures" ("l'initiative d'une politique des nationalités, l'initiative d'une politique fondée sur le respect des peuples et des cultures").[99]

---

97 Delorme, *La Misère*, 132, emphasis original.
98 Baron de Vastey, *Notes à M. le Baron de V.P.*, 7.
99 Césaire, *Discours*, 74.

CHAPTER THREE

There Is No Odd in Ordinary

Louis Joseph Janvier, Haiti, and the Tropics of Racial Science

Bastien Craipain

> From the past, we can prejudge the future. They have sought to humiliate us; they are robbing and pillaging us; [...] they have threatened and are still threatening our independence because we have a debt of forty million; they have peddled the news everywhere that we were savages, in order to better intimidate us and to better hold us at ransom; those who licked our hand at home called us monkeys in Europe.
>
> Remember now not to confide, people of Haiti [...]
>
> Poverty for oneself is worth more than the wealth one produces for others [...]
>
> Haiti for the Haitians! It is thus that our ancestors understood it. It is also what the black race wants.
>
> —Louis Joseph Janvier,
> *Haïti aux Haïtiens* (1884)[1]

How may we read these words beyond their performative assertion of Haiti's national sovereignty in the face of an uncertain political future? Clearly, Louis Joseph Janvier's logophagic translation of U.S. President James Monroe's apocryphal doctrine into an anticolonial watchword—"Haiti for the Haitians"—was meant to serve as a powerful reminder of the ever-pressing threat of U.S. control over the country

---

1 All translations are mine unless otherwise indicated.

and the Caribbean region more generally.² Modern readers of *Haïti aux Haïtiens* (1884) may be tempted, in that regard, to overlook the larger historical backdrop of nineteenth-century racial thinking to focus instead on the author's explicit critique of North Atlantic imperialism and (neo)colonialism. Yet, as the above epigraph illustrates, the specter of external dominion—whether in the form of political annexation or through the means of economic predation—was undergirded by a dehumanizing rhetoric which, over the centuries, had fueled philosophical and scientific debates over a so-called natural (in)equality of the human races.³ In other words, if Janvier wished for the "people of Haiti" to remain a free, self-governing polity, it was *also* because he was convinced they had something to prove to themselves and to the world, both in memory of their "ancestors" and on behalf of the entire "black race."

The origins of this idea had already surfaced a year prior in Janvier's *La République d'Haïti et ses visiteurs* (1883). In this major rebuttal of racist stereotypes and degrading clichés on contemporary Haitian society, Janvier stated unapologetically that, when "Yankees readily say: 'America for the Americans,'" then in turn, "Haitians should not forget to shout loud and clear: 'Haiti for the Haitians!'" because, "as the black Latin civilization," Haiti "must exist and develop to assert this truth, namely: that the black race is perfectly sociable [...] and that it can perfectly govern and administer itself."⁴ Thus understood, the issue of Haitian independence was both a question of political sovereignty and a matter of heuristic necessity. "Haiti is an argument," Janvier proceeded to claim in a stroke of aphoristic witticism, "an argument [...] that troubles and upsets."⁵ As a standard-bearer for all people of African descent around the world, the country was invested with what Janvier

---

2 Janvier was not the first Haitian intellectual to critically engage with the "America for the Americans" of the so-called "Monroe doctrine." See Marlene L. Daut, "Beyond 'America for the Americans': Race and Empire in the Work of Demesvar Delorme," *J19: The Journal of Nineteenth-Century Americanists* 6, no. 1 (2018): 189–197.

3 According to Jeremy Popkin, "Revolutionary Saint-Domingue was one of the birthplaces of modern, pseudoscientific racism"; *Facing Racial Revolution: Eyewitness Accounts of the Haitian Insurrection* (Chicago: University of Chicago Press, 2010), 25.

4 Louis-Joseph Janvier, *La République d'Haïti et ses visiteurs (1840–1882). Réponse à M. Victor Cochinat (de la Petite Presse) et à quelques autres écrivains* (Paris: Marpon et Flammarion, 1883), 122–123.

5 Ibid., 123.

saw as a fundamental and radical mission: that of enabling the adoption of a new anthropological paradigm within which the "truth" of racial blackness—at once scientific and political—could be finally demonstrated and recognized.

Eager to advance his nascent antiracist agenda, Janvier joined the Société d'anthropologie de Paris (SAP) in 1882, just a year and half after completing his studies at the Faculté de médecine de Paris.[6] At the time, the SAP was not only the gatekeeping institution of a discipline responsible for upholding theories of polygenic human origins and inherent racial inequalities; as advocates of the Third Republic's "civilizing mission," the members of this prestigious circle also saw themselves as agents of a particular brand of universalistic progress whose duty was to contribute to the French imperial effort with a heavy apparatus of speculative and empirical knowledge.[7]

In *La Colonisation scientifique et les colonies françaises* (1884), for example, medical geographer and anthropologist Arthur Bordier would state that the success of France's renewed wave of colonial expansion in the tropics was highly dependent on the "teachings of medical climatology, anthropology, and ethnology."[8] Like many of his colleagues, Bordier was convinced that "*colonization* [could] only succeed through *science*," and that the study of "acclimatization—that of animals and plants, [...] of the colonizers to the colony, and finally of indigenous people to the new civilization we bring them—comprise[d] nearly all of the science of colonization."[9] From that point of view, the scientific observation of racialized others in occupied territories around the globe constituted an essential part of the French project of imperial worldmaking.

Despite its independence, Haiti held a rather special place in this political-scientific project. In 1878, Bordier had penned on behalf of the SAP a set of "Instructions to a hospital physician in Port-au-Prince" in which he underlined the "unique" opportunity that Haiti presented

---

[6] For a relatively brief yet rather exhaustive discussion of Janvier's life and oeuvre, see Yves Chemla, "Louis-Joseph Janvier, écrivain national," *Francofonia* 49, special issue: Lectures et écritures haïtiennes (2005): 7–36.

[7] See Alice L. Conklin, *A Mission to Civilize: The Republican Idea of Empire in France and West Africa, 1895–1930* (Palo Alto: Stanford University Press, 1997); and *In the Museum of Man: Race, Anthropology, and Empire in France, 1850–1950* (Ithaca: Cornell University Press, 2013).

[8] Arthur Bordier, *La Colonisation scientifique et les colonies françaises* (Paris: C. Reinwald, 1884), xiv.

[9] Ibid., xiv–xv.

in the field of "comparative racial pathology" in large part due to the racial makeup of its population: "Creole negroes, but negroes of all African origins, who can consequently be taken as providing *average* data on each question related to the negro race."[10] Reportedly allowing for a scrutinization of the black body outside of the "vicious conditions" of slavery and colonial rule, Haiti was coveted as an "experiment that offer[ed] all the scientific guaranties."[11] Indeed, according to Bordier, it provided a sort of large-scale laboratory in which hospital physicians—among other specialists and observers—could collect reliable "information on the pathological immunities of the black race and on its special pathological aptitudes" as well as study the "physiology of a race whose anatomy […] ha[d] thus far exclusively preoccupied anthropologists."[12] Tropic among the tropics, Haiti was thus construed as the proverbial *exception* confirming the *rules* of racial science.[13] It served, in other words, as an ambivalent trope for figuring (out) and seeing (through) what was then referred to as the "problem of the human races."[14]

To be sure, the narrative of an "exceptional Haiti" was not new at the time, and neither is my present attempt to draw attention to its othering logic and objectifying language. In his foundational essay "The Odd and the Ordinary: Haiti, the Caribbean, and the World," Michel-Rolph Trouillot critiqued with forceful rhetoric the "myth of Haitian exceptionalism," pointing to the presence of a "most potent antidote" in the "classics of nineteenth-century Haitian social thought."[15]

Following Trouillot's insight, I argue that Janvier built on his training as a physician and social scientist to turn the discourse of Haitian exceptionalism into what may be best described as a counter-discourse of universalizable particularism. In his scientific practice, he promoted the

---

10 Arthur Bordier, "Instructions pour un médecin d'hôpital à Port-au-Prince (Haïti)," *Mémoires de la Société d'anthropologie de Paris* 2, no. 2 (1882): 209.
11 Ibid., 235.
12 Ibid., 209–210.
13 On the relationship between the tropological and the tropical in the context of discourses on Haiti, see Marlene Daut, *Tropics of Haiti: Race and the Literary History of the Haitian Revolution in the Atlantic World, 1789–1865* (Liverpool: Liverpool University Press, 2015), 5.
14 Arthur Bordier, "Cours de géographie médicale," *La Gazette médicale de Paris* 50 (1879): 190.
15 Michel-Rolph Trouillot, "The Odd and the Ordinary: Haiti, the Caribbean, and the World," *Cimarrón: New Perspectives on the Caribbean* 2, no. 3 (1990): 11.

paradigmatic dimension of the Haitian experience as a way to empower and extend its epistemological potential to all people of African descent in the Atlantic world. To do so, he invoked the scientific theories and concepts of his time, transforming them in relation to the lived conditions of Haiti's social and material reality. Looking at Janvier's medical thesis on tuberculosis, I will show how his championing of a romantic vision of Haiti and the black body through the figure of the maroon-turned-peasant allowed him to challenge the racist teachings and imperialistic musings of medical geographers and colonial physicians. Further, by examining his various interventions at the SAP, I will demonstrate how his attempt to depart from a North Atlantic approach to the discipline of anthropology—that is, as a site of racial imagining and racist authorization—led him to formulate an early postcolonial understanding of the concept of creolization. Finally, in an effort to further amplify his voice within the silences of the archive, I will turn to some of the underlying causes of his current anonymity in the francophone (scientific) canon.

Marooning medicine: *Phtisie pulmonaire* and the mountains of Haiti

It is no coincidence that Janvier chose to dedicate his doctoral thesis to the study of pulmonary phthisis, a disease more commonly known today as tuberculosis. When he left Port-au-Prince to enter the Faculté de médecine de Paris in 1877, the disease had reached epidemic proportions in France, where over the course of the century it had become gradually associated with an urban geography of miasmas, overcrowding, pauperism, excessive behaviors, and poor hygiene.[16] About a decade earlier, Jean-Antoine Villemin had taken a crucial step towards understanding the pathogenesis of tuberculosis by demonstrating its transmissibility and bringing contagiousness into its long-debated etiology. One of the earliest opponents of the contagionist doctrine in France was Michel Peter, a physician and professor at the Faculté de médecine de Paris who, according to historian David Barnes, "viewed contagion as a prejudice that inspired fear among the populace, pitted citizen against citizen, and stigmatized the sick as enemies of the healthy."[17] Incidentally, it was the same Peter who, a few years later,

---

16 For a brief history of tuberculosis, see Thomas M. Daniel, "The History of Tuberculosis," *Respiratory Medicine* 100, no. 11 (2006): 1862–1870.

17 David Barnes, *The Making of a Social Disease: Tuberculosis in Nineteenth-Century France* (Berkeley: University of California Press, 1995), 41.

would become one of Louis Pasteur's most vocal and notorious critics, denouncing the antisocial excesses of an emerging "microbic furia."[18] But more importantly, it was the same Peter who in 1881 would serve as Janvier's academic mentor and preside over the jury of his doctoral thesis, "Phtisie pulmonaire. Causes—traitement préventif."

Following Peter's lead, Janvier proposed an etiology of pulmonary phthisis that would become antiquated a year later when German physician Robert Koch managed to isolate the tubercle bacillus, thereby confirming the contagious nature of the disease. It would be a mistake, however, to discard the young physician's work on the sole basis of his obsolete diagnosis.

In a way, Janvier's adherence to the anticontagionist reaction allowed him to articulate a very valuable argument against some of the racist theories upheld by his contemporaries. As Yves Chemla contends, "Janvier's discourse, with its hygienist assumptions, is above all a discourse of combat against racism as scientific discourse, which was common back then, including among the members of the Parisian society of anthropology."[19] Just as Peter rejected the social stigma associated with contagion, so did Janvier contest the pathological branding of a racial susceptibility to the disease. "From a purely ethnic point of view," he argued, "from the point of view of pathological anthropology, the black race is no more predisposed than the others to tuberculosis."[20] With hindsight, this statement may appear as one of the first instantiations of Janvier's life-long struggle against the discursive fabric of scientific racism. Yet in order to comprehend how the study of tuberculosis led him to these later political engagements, we must first understand how science and empire worked hand in hand to pathologize the black body through the racialization of diseases.[21]

---

18 Bruno Latour, *The Pasteurization of France*, trans. Alan Sheridan and John Law (Cambridge, MA: Harvard University Press, 1988), 29–30.

19 Chemla, "Louis-Joseph Janvier," 10. Janvier's exhaustive survey of the myriad causes and agents responsible for the disease is indeed reminiscent of what Bruno Latour has identified as the main features of French hygienist rhetoric, namely: its cumulative economy and lack of a central argument (20).

20 Louis-Joseph Janvier, *Phtisie pulmonaire. Causes—traitement préventif* (Paris: A. Parent, 1881), 68.

21 See Marion M. Torchia, "The Tuberculosis Movement and the Race Question," *Bulletin of the History of Medicine* 49, no. 2 (1975): 152–168, and Aro Velmet, *Pasteur's Empire: Bacteriology and Politics in France, Its Colonies, and the World* (New York: Oxford University Press, 2020).

The second half of the nineteenth century marked a paradoxical moment in the history of French imperialism. While engaging in a new wave of colonial expansion in the tropics, French medical authorities had come to seriously question the sustainability of life in those faraway regions of the globe, the hot and humid climates of which had long been thought to accelerate or even provoke physical and moral degeneration.[22] The emergence of tropical medicine and germ theory in the 1870s and 1880s, far from alleviating these fears, further supplemented the ideology of a "white man's grave" with a renewed scientific discourse on the pathological nature of tropical environments.[23] As germs gradually replaced miasmas in the medical imaginary, certain areas of the globe came to occupy an increasingly prominent position in the French epidemiological geography, and the joint Pasteurian and hygienist project of national regeneration and sanitization traveled from the metropole to the colonies with a newly germocentric yet clearly race-specific agenda.[24] Bluntly put, colonial physicians and administrators were now in charge of enacting a "pasteurization" of the French empire by ridding its overseas territories of their ills and diseases—that is, by targeting those populations whose pathological symptoms were considered to be signs of an essential "barbarism" or "backwardness."[25]

While this revived enterprise of scientific colonialism was still in its infancy when Janvier composed the text of his medical thesis, depictions of the Caribbean as a hotbed of miasmatic diseases were already circulating widely among colonial physicians and administrators. Tuberculosis, which was commonly associated with the maritime professions, figured prominently among said diseases.[26] According to Jean-Christian-Marc Boudin, a former military surgeon often credited with founding the discipline of medical geography, tuberculosis was "incomparably more frequent in the islands of the Gulf of Mexico than in the portions of the torrid zones belonging to the ancient continent."[27] Likewise, for naval

---

22 Eric T. Jennings, *Curing the Colonizers: Hydrotherapy, Climatology, and French Colonial Spas* (Durham, NC: Duke University Press, 2006), 36.
23 For an in-depth analysis of the rise of French tropical medicine, see Michael A. Osborne, *The Emergence of Tropical Medicine in France* (Chicago: University of Chicago Press, 2014).
24 Latour, *The Pasteurization of France*, 156–161.
25 Pratik Chakrabati, *Medicine and Empire, 1600–1960* (Basingstoke: Palgrave Macmillan, 2014), 166–176.
26 Osborne, *The Emergence of Tropical Medicine in France*, 63.
27 Jean-Christian-Marc Boudin, *Traité de géographie et de statistique médicales et des maladies endémiques*, vol. 2 (Paris: J.-B. Baillière et fils, 1857), 629.

physician Auguste-Frédéric Dutrouleau, the spreading of tuberculosis was "fostered rather than impeded" by the climate of the Caribbean archipelago, where "one encounter[ed] it among all classes, although the class of color [was] more affected by it."[28]

Eager to provide tangible evidence against such ideas of an intrinsic Afro-Caribbean morbidity, Janvier retorted to both Boudin and Dutrouleau—especially to the latter—that "in Haiti [...] a mountainous island *par excellence*, large and elevated enough for its coasts only to be swept by sea winds, phthisis is very rare in the countryside."[29] Indeed, according to his survey of the global and regional distribution of tuberculosis, Haiti was a kind of safe haven where, due to a series of environmental and topographic factors, the disease was virtually nonexistent. After a detailed description of these "small cities [...] sitting by the seashores and at the mountains' feet," Janvier thus concluded that, "phthisis is very rare in Haiti [...] because Haiti is [...] a land of mountains."[30]

There are two sides to this environmental discourse. On the one hand, there is the fact that, in the absence of a definitive treatment for the disease, aerotherapy or the *cure d'air* remained the primary "known remedy" to tuberculosis at the time.[31] In that respect, Janvier's comments on the curative qualities of Haiti's reliefs are well in accordance with the perceived physiological functionality of their "rarified air [...] forcing the lung to a perpetual gymnastic."[32]

On the other hand, there is a particular vision of the natural that draws and expands on this hygienist discourse. In the *mornes* or mountains of his estranged island, Janvier sees the "spectacle of a nature at once lavish and exceptionally endowed by the hand of the Creator";[33] he sees what "[t]hose poor people who swallow the dust of littoral cities cannot fathom," that is, "the calm, happiness, and poetry of existence in the mountains."[34] He sees, in short, a Romantic nature whose moral virtues permeate the people growing and flourishing in her bosom. "After having lived for a month in the *mornes* of Anse-à-Veau

---

28 Auguste-Frédéric Dutrouleau, "Antilles," in *Dictionnaire encyclopédique des sciences médicales*, vol. 5, ed. Amédée Dechambre (Paris: Victor Masson et fils, 1886), 339.
29 Janvier, *Phtisie*, 30.
30 Ibid., 33.
31 Barnes, *The Making of a Social Disease*, 100.
32 Janvier, *Phtisie*, 33,
33 Ibid., 31.
34 Ibid., 261.

There Is No Odd in Ordinary   149

(January 1876), we can knowingly praise the experience of life in the mountains," Janvier writes before immediately adding in a footnote:

> Sorry for speaking about myself. I know Pascal's words.
> I have always loved peasants and envied their way of life. I adore mountains. Could it be moral atavism? Maybe so!
> I keep a deep and durable memory of gratitude to the mountaineers and mountains of the Valley of the Asile in Anse à Veau [...] They are my friends, the men as well as the things, and I love them as though I had been born among the former and in the midst of the latter [...]
> The mountains of Anse à Veau have been my road to Damascus. Since I left them, I have been converted to hygiene. As I am writing these lines—Paris, May 1881—I am overflowing with blood and health. Five years ago, I had no health and I had even less blood than I did health.[35]

Those familiar with the writings of Jules Michelet—to whom Janvier constantly refers in his oeuvre, including in this text—will not fail to recognize the Romantic historian's influence on the young physician's imaginary.[36] Michelet's mystical tribute to *La Montagne* (1867), a place where the "Rise of the Earth" acts as a metaphor and mediator for the future "regeneration of the human species,"[37] certainly played a role in reinforcing Janvier's visceral attachment to the mountains of Haiti.[38] Yet there is something more intimately Haitian here in that Janvier's praise of the Haitian countryside and its people echoes a kind of bucolic Romanticism intricately rooted in the works of past and contemporary Haitian poets such as Coriolan Ardouin, Ignace Nau, or Oswald Durand, all of whom would figure prominently in Janvier's later writings on Haitian literary history.[39]

---

35 Ibid., 260 n. 1.
36 For an analysis of Janvier's engagement with history and historiography, see Chelsea Stieber, "The Haitian Revolution and the Myth of the Republic: Louis Joseph Janvier's Revisionist History," in *Remembering Early Modern Revolutions: England, North America, France and Haiti*, ed. Edward Vallance (New York: Routledge, 2019), 145–157.
37 Jules Michelet, *La Montagne* (Paris: Librairie Internationale, 1868 [1867]), 119, 364.
38 On Michelet's Romanticism and its participation in the emergence of a so-called "religion of the mountains," see François Dagognet, "La cure d'air: essai sur l'histoire d'une idée en thérapeutique médicale," *Thalès* 10 (1959): 78–85.
39 In 1884, Janvier published "L'Evolution littéraire en Haïti" in the French journal *La Revue universelle internationale*, and "La Poésie française d'outre-mer" in the Parisian weekly *Le Papillon*. While the first of these two texts was

At odds with the scientific writing conventions of his time, Janvier conjured in his medical thesis the imagery of an untainted New World nature and the old myth of Noble Savagery it engendered in order to invoke—and perhaps contribute to—Haiti's long-established tradition of Romantic poetics and politics.[40] Premised on the historical vindication and symbolic reconstruction of an imagined Haitian community, Janvier's participation in this tradition bears desires of a historical—if not genealogical—continuity between the long-decimated indigenous populations of the Caribbean and the formerly enslaved African people of Haiti. In that sense, Chemla is right to present *Phtisie pulmonaire*'s "positive and poetic" representation of Haiti as an illustration of the author's eagerness to show that, "in the *mornes* where peasants have taken refuge, there may be something left of the Paradise turned into hell by Columbus and his followers."[41] Yet Janvier's indigenist and black Romantic prose also surpasses this merely symbolic necessity to heal the wounds or cover the scars of a history marked by colonial violence and racial exploitation.

Confronted with the specter of a (neo)colonialism in white coats, Janvier exceeds the *therapeutic* dimension of his poetic discourse to propose what I suggest may be a *prophylactic* remedy to the theories and practices of imperial medicine and their impending consequences. By depicting a black body overflowing with life and in symbiosis with its surrounding environment, he composes a Romantic-scientific narrative aimed at protecting and defending—both poetically and proleptically—the continued sovereignty of the Haitian nation. And to blow the *lambi* of anticolonial resistance, Janvier finds a most suitable protagonist in the figure of the Haitian mountaineer.

Heir to the rebellious maroons who brought about the revolution, this (male) character becomes the hero of a new emancipatory epic. He is the synecdochal embodiment of collective resistance against a North

---

meant to offer—over multiple installments—a diachronic study of Haitian literature since the first years of independence, the second was specifically dedicated to Durand and would be in fact reproduced the following year under the title "Oswald Durand" in Janvier's collection of essays and articles entitled *Les Affaires d'Haïti (1883–1884)* (Paris: C. Marpon et E. Flammarion, 1885).

40 On the "poetics of Romanticism" and its "wedded[ness] to a politics of historical analyses in nineteenth-century Haiti," see Marlene L. Daut, "'Nothing in Nature Is Mute': Reading Revolutionary Romanticism in *L'Haïtiade* and Hérard Dumesle's *Voyage dans le nord d'Hayti* (1824)," *New Literary History* 49, no. 4 (2018), 497.

41 Chemla, "Louis-Joseph Janvier," 9.

Atlantic gaze that insists on seeing in him—and in Haiti—the reminiscences of a purported "African barbarity."⁴² Defined by the circular temporality of his daily tasks and activities, Janvier's mountaineer is "always lively and cheerful, strong and intelligent, working as he pleases"; he is "free, the master of his own land [...] Barely affected by morally depressing causes"; he is "always in the open air, partial to dancing, horseback riding, hunting, and fishing, [...] living fully and well at last"; and for all these reasons, Janvier concludes, "he almost never dies of phthisis."⁴³ His bourgeois-paternalistic vision notwithstanding, Janvier constructs the mountaineer as an archetypal figure for the nation, a metaphor for the past and present of black masterlessness as well as for the future of Haitian sovereignty and self-sufficiency. He is, in short, the individuated projection of what Johnhenry Gonzalez calls the "maroon nation."

This may explain, in part, why the portrait of this naturally healthy, resilient body is that of a virtually timeless, invincible silhouette evolving in the margins of the "West's geography of imagination."⁴⁴ Beyond the metaphorical level, the Haitian peasantry is meant to provide a counter-argument and corrective to the colonial-racist discourse according to which Haiti's eighty years of national independence amounted to nothing more than a failed experiment in postcolonial modernity. Aware of the direct correlation between tuberculosis and poverty, Janvier sees the near absence of the disease in the island as irrefutable proof that "Haiti is [...] a country where misery is unknown."⁴⁵ That is, a country whose very conditions of existence and development, contrary to the theories of environmental and racial determinism, defy the *necessity* of a so-called "civilizing mission," whether it be couched in a medical, hygienist rhetoric⁴⁶ or in a paternalistic, economic discourse.⁴⁷

Janvier's struggle against the colonial, scientific, racist status quo would not end with the publication of *Phtisie pulmonaire*. The following year, he collided with French journalist Léo Quesnel after the latter had claimed in the Parisian *Revue politique et littéraire* that, "if the theory of racial inequality required confirmation, it would find it

---

42 Laënnec Hurbon, *Le barbare imaginaire* (Port-au-Prince: Éditions Henri Deschamps, 1987), 59.
43 Janvier, *Phtisie*, 30.
44 Michel-Rolph Trouillot, *Global Transformations: Anthropology and the Modern World* (New York: Palgrave Macmillan, 2003), 8.
45 Janvier, *Phtisie*, 33.
46 Osborne, *The Emergence of Tropical Medicine in France*, 64.
47 Hurbon, *Le barbare imaginaire*, 64.

in the inanity that the blacks of Haiti have shown in their century-old efforts to constitute a society."[48] In the conclusion of his article, Quesnel had even gone so far as to gesture to a providential U.S. annexation of the country, declaring that "Negroes [would] never make anything out of Saint Domingue," which "'[lay] fallow' on the social, commercial, industrial levels, as well as on the agricultural level," and would "remain so up until the moment the growing influence of the United States extends to the Antillean archipelago."[49] As students of Haitian intellectual history know, this decisive clash with the French chronicler led to a pivotal moment in the entangled genealogies of social-scientific and antiracist thought in Haiti: namely, the landmark publication of *Les Détracteurs de la race noire et de la république d'Haïti* (1882), a collective volume for which Janvier was largely responsible.[50]

An underestimated work in the "black vindicationist" tradition, *Les Détracteurs* would prove highly instrumental in Janvier's introduction into the Parisian anthropological sphere.[51] Just a few months later, on December 7, 1882, French physician and anthropologist Léonce Manouvrier addressed his colleagues at the SAP to provide a brief description of the volume, claiming it would "be of interest to many a member of the Société" as it contained "a series of letters and articles written by several authors in order to refute various assertions related to the black race."[52] As Manouvrier noted, "Dr. Janvier belongs himself to that race: he is originally from Haiti"; furthermore, he "is a highly

---

48 Léo Quesnel, "Anciennes colonies françaises: Haïti," *La Revue politique et littéraire* 3, no. 3 (1882): 84.

49 Ibid., 87.

50 Although largely responsible for channeling the voices of this collective outcry into a single publication, Janvier was by no means the sole contributor to *Les Détracteurs*. The volume includes texts by Jules Auguste, Arthur Bowler, Clément Denis, and Justin Dévot, all of whom were Haitian expatriates living, working, and/or studying in France at the time. Aside from Bowler, they had all participated in the first wave of protest against Quesnel's article, and had come together—following a second article by the journalist—to further debunk his racist and imperialistic claims.

51 According to David Scott's definition, "black vindicationism" is "at once a practice of providing evidence to refute a disagreeable or incorrect claim and a practice of *reclamation*, and, indeed, of *redemption* of what has been denied. This is why moral indignation—indeed, outrage—is most often the tone of black vindicationist discourse"; David Scott, *Conscripts of Modernity: The Tragedy of Colonial Enlightenment* (Durham, NC: Duke University Press, 2004), 83.

52 Léonce Manouvrier, "Ouvrages offerts, Séance du 7 décembre 1882," *Bulletins de la Société d'anthropolgie de Paris* 5 (1882): 742.

educated physician who will certainly contribute to the development of anthropology" and "has asked to be a part of the Société."[53] Janvier would not wait long before seeing his request granted. Two weeks later, on December 21, 1882, an election was held, and he officially became a "full member" of the prestigious, nearly all-white institution.[54]

Creolizing anthropology: A Haitian at the SAP

Since its creation in 1859, the SAP had become the hallmark institution of a discipline originally premised and primarily fixated on the "scientific study of the human races."[55] Paul Broca, its founder and life-long secretary, had set the tone for the decades to come when, following the presentation of his 1861 essay "On the Volume and Shape of the Brain According to Individuals and Races," he responded to one of his critics that, "[i]n general, the brain is larger [...] in superior races than in inferior races."[56] In his view, taxonomies and hierarchies of racially discrete aptitudes and dispositions were natural truths waiting to be confirmed by the tools of craniometry and phrenology—i.e., the measuring and indexing of the cognitive and moral qualities of individuals or racial groups based on the volume and shape of their craniums. After Broca's death in 1880, this penchant for physical measurements and physiological arithmetic began to lose currency among the members of the SAP.[57] But the so-called "problem of the human races" remained at the center of the field.[58] So much so, in fact, that we may be tempted to describe the era's "French School of Anthropology" in much the same way as Lee D. Baker has described the "American School of Anthropology" of Josiah Clark Nott, Samuel Morton, and Louis Agassiz—that is, as a seemingly "reliable narrator in the story of white supremacy."[59]

53 Ibid.
54 "Élections," *Bulletins de la Société d'anthropologie de Paris* 5 (1882): 792.
55 "Statuts," *Bulletins de la Société d'anthropologie de Paris* 2 (1861): i.
56 Paul Broca, "Sur le volume et la forme du cerveau suivant les individus et suivant les races," *Bulletins de la Société d'anthropologie de Paris* 2 (1861): 304.
57 See Claude Blanckaert, "La crise de l'anthropométrie: Des arts anthropotechniques aux dérives militantes (1860–1920)," in *Les politiques de l'anthropologie: Discours et pratiques en France (1860–1940)*, ed. Claude Blanckaert (Paris: L'Harmattan, 2001), 95–172.
58 Laurent Mucchielli, "Sociologies versus anthropologie raciale. L'engagement décesif des durkheimiens dans le contexte 'fin de siècle' (1885–1914)," *Gradhiva* 21 (1997): 77–78.
59 Lee D. Baker, *Anthropology and the Racial Politics of Culture* (Durham, NC: Duke University Press, 2010), 3.

Janvier, of course, had come to the discipline with another objective in mind. Unlike most of his new colleagues, he was eager to demonstrate that the story of white supremacy rested on a misconception and misconstruction of the historical and cultural realities of race. Before entering the sphere of anthropology proper, he had already engaged with various notions and concepts pertaining to the field of social-scientific epistemology. In *Les Détracteurs*, most notably, he had ventured onto the "terrain [...] of anthropology and social physiology" to present Haiti as "a field of sociological experimentation" where "the physical, intellectual, and moral selection of a race [was] happening [...] with a wise gradation, an admirable progression."[60] At a time when Charles Darwin's idea of natural selection was being mobilized to reaffirm the natural origins of social forms and cultural phenomena, Janvier's deployment of evolutionary theory as a tool for dismantling the racial hierarchies supported by past and contemporary (social) scientists granted him significant exposure and recognition.[61] More importantly, it gave specific relevance to his participation in what Marlene L. Daut calls the discourse of "Black Atlantic humanism."[62] By understanding evolution *in relation* to the Caribbean context, Janvier would not only

60 Louis-Joseph Janvier, *Les Détracteurs de la race noire et de la République d'Haïti* (Paris: Marpon et Flammarion, 1882), 32, 76.
61 In addition to its endorsement by French abolitionist Victor Schœlcher and Puerto Rican revolutionary exile Ramón Emeterio Betances, *Les Détracteurs* drew accolades from French physician and historian Jean-François Robinet—a former disciple and close collaborator of Auguste Comte—who described it as "a strong, indignant, thrilling piece, which we recommend all of our friends to read" ("Haiti," *La Revue occidentale, philosophique, sociale et politique* 8, no. 94 [1882]: 415). Robinet's laudatory comments carried all the more weight as they appeared in the *Revue occidentale philosophique*, a positivist journal founded and directed by French philosopher Pierre Laffitte whom many saw as Comte's intellectual successor. The following year, Robinet would go on to extend his praises to another of Janvier's works, *La République d'Haïti et ses visiteurs* (1883)—which I will discuss shortly—celebrating the author as "the eloquent, erudite, and ever so competent apologist of the black race, the historiographer and ever so truthful, authorized, and convinced panegyrist of the Haitian Republic" ("Bibliographie," *La Revue occidentale philosophique, sociale et politique* 10 [1883]: 266). On Robinet as a successor of Comte, see Alice Gérard, "Les disciples 'complets' de Comte et la politique positive (1870–1914)," in *Auguste Comte. Trajectoires positivistes, 1789–1998*, ed. Annie Petit (Paris: L'Harmattan, 2003), 285–302.
62 According to Daut, the expression describes "an intellectual endeavor begun in the eighteenth century on both sides of the Atlantic with the principal aim to prove that black people were equal to the white people that were enslaving

unearth some of the deeply rooted contradictions of the field but also help creolize the anthropological imaginary *from within*.

At the time of his inauguration, Janvier was immediately faced with the duality of his condition. As a black anthropologist, he had to assert himself as the *subject* of a discipline that failed to recognize the humanity of its *object*. Looking back, this would place him in a radically new vantage point, allowing for a rearticulation of the "problem of the human races" into a much-needed questioning of its underlying assumptions. Daut is right, in that regard, to call attention to his "pioneering position [...] with respect to what we might think of as a comparative critical race theory."[63] Janvier's engagement with anthropology was indeed entirely structured and motivated by the comparative perspectivism and critical intentionality of his approach to the concept of race. To the members of the SAP, however, this would not be clear until January 18, 1883, when Janvier took the floor to introduce another of his major vindicationist works:

> I have the distinguished honor to submit today to your eminent appreciation a work entitled: *La République d'Haïti et ses visiteurs*.
>
> Many of the questions which I had only touched upon in [*Les Détracteurs*] have been more clearly exposed and more thoroughly explored in my second study on the evolution of the Haitian people.
>
> I have demonstrated at length the harmful influence of *color prejudice* in America, and I have characterized the philosophical and political movement which has taken place and continues to occur to make it soon disappear, in Haiti as well as in the French colonies of the Gulf of Mexico and in the southern states of the star-spangled Confederacy [...]
>
> In a word, [... this book is] an apology for the Ethiopian race as well as a work of comparative sociology, which can be productively consulted by all of those who want to study seriously and impartially the Antillean civilization in contact with the Western one, by all of those who want to be exactly aware of the selection, of the psychological transformation that the black individual's brain can undergo, just like that of individuals belonging to other families of humankind.[64]

them"; Marlene L. Daut, *Baron de Vastey and the Origins of Black Atlantic Humanism* (New York: Palgrave Macmillan, 2017), xviii.
63 See Daut's essay in this volume.
64 Louis-Joseph Janvier, "La République d'Haïti et ses visiteurs," *Bulletins de la Société d'anthropologie de Paris* 6 (1883): 63–64.

Evidently, introducing the content of *La République d'Haïti* to the SAP amounted to much more than a simple gesture of self-promotion. As Janvier took it upon himself to explain, the book proposed to tackle two complex issues and achieve two explicit goals: first, to analyze, compare, and critique the distinct regimes of racial prejudice and pigmentocracy in the Caribbean and the United States; and second, to further vindicate and celebrate the "Ethiopian race" in light of its historical achievements in Haiti. Regardless of the actual content of the book, then, we must read Janvier's introductory remarks as an epistemological provocation whose aim was to exhort anthropologists to overcome the limitations of North Atlantic raciology in order to approach their solidifying field of knowledge through a different set of questions. By drawing attention to the "contact" between an "Antillean civilization" and a "Western one," he was effectively calling for the consideration and recognition of cultural formations and exchanges as necessary objects of anthropological investigation.

Somewhat subtle at the time, this intention to move the discipline towards a more culture-focused approach became clearer the following year when Janvier participated for the first time in one of the SAP's discussions.[65] Among the many items on the agenda that day was a presentation by Armand de Quatrefages—one of France's most revered anthropologists—titled "Observations on a Passage of a Letter by M. Paul Lévy, Relative to the Influence of the American Milieu on the Races of the Ancient Continent." After reporting that in a "long conversation" Lévy had provided him with some "rather curious details on the Creole Negro race" of the Caribbean, Quatrefages summed up the traveler's comments on the "maroon Negroes" of Guyana, noting that they had been "free for several generations [...] liv[ing] in the forests [... where they had] never mixed with indigenous people," and that, despite these conditions, they had seen their "characters [...] deeply transformed" and "gotten closer to indigenous races."[66] Of particular interest to Quatrefages was the passage in which Lévy called for "the study of what, for lack of a better term, [he would] name *creolization* [...] without

---

65 As it so happens, this was also the day that one of his fellow countrymen, Anténor Firmin, became himself a member of the Parisian institution, thanks in part to Janvier's introduction and official sponsorship. One of Haiti's most influential intellectual and political figures, Firmin is mostly known today for his monumental *De l'égalité des races humaines: anthropologie positive*.

66 Armand de Quatrefages, "Observations à propos d'un passage d'une lettre de M. Paul Lévy, relatif à l'action exercée par le milieu américain sur les races de l'ancien continente," *Bulletins de la Société d'anthropologie de Paris* 7 (1884): 579–580.

the study of which all studies on the *métissage* of human races seem[ed] to [him] necessarily sterile, for nearly all mixed-race individuals," he added, "are produced between creolized races rather and more often than between pure races."[67]

Picking up on Lévy's neologism, Quatrefages proposed that the term "creolization" be universally adopted to describe the "ethnic" transformations that a change of environment provokes on "the White individual from Europe as well as on the Black individual from Africa." This was all the more important, in his opinion, for it confirmed what he had already "long contended in stating that each race from the ancient continent, from Europe in particular, was represented in the colonies by a *derivative race*."[68] Understood as a phenomenon akin to acclimatization, creolization was thus to enter the anthropological lexicon to provide evidence for the theory according to which all human races were not only capable of adapting to the conditions of a new climate and environment, but also resulted from physiological and environmental variations occurring within the same original human species.[69] For Lévy, however, this concept was meant to advance the study of a much more specific question, namely: the process of *métissage* or miscegenation.

Above all else, the focus on racial mixing is what seems to have caught Janvier's attention and led him to intervene in the discussion. As he proceeded to underline the potential value of this new concept, he turned again to Haiti and presented its evolution as a paradigmatic example of creolization, the reality of which extended far beyond the realm of climatological or biological phenomena:

> I would only like to add one word to all the very profound and very true things Mr. de Quatrefages has just said about *creolization*.
>
> One could maintain that, in Haiti, the black race has transformed as much under the influence of the climatological environment as it has under that of ethnic mixings and intellectual work [...]
>
> Since Haitians have become independent, only eighty years ago, public education has singularly progressed in the country and, as a consequence, has instigated notable changes in the population's general physiognomy [...]
>
> It is also necessary that we take into account the mixings of black blood with that of peoples belonging to the white race who have

---

67 Ibid., 580.
68 Ibid., 581.
69 On the relationship between Creoleness, acclimatization, and the debate on monogenism versus polygenism, see Jennings, *Curing the Colonizers*, 8–14.

successively colonized Haiti. These mixings occur indefinitely, in such a way that, under some entirely black skin, there may also flow some Indian blood, some Spanish blood, or French blood.

Finally, the decisive influence of politics, of the struggle for power must not be forgotten [...]

It is above all in Haiti that we can observe the creolization of the black race. From a physical point of view, every day it tends to form a particular, original human group; from an intellectual and moral point of view, it comes closer to the nations taking part in what philosopher Pierre Lafitte calls "the Western group."[70]

Undoubtedly, there was more to the concept of creolization than the mere description of a series of physical transformations.[71] Janvier conceived of it as natural and cultural changes and exchanges resonating in many ways with what we have come to understand today as a dynamic process of ceaseless and unforeseeable interactions between people(s), ideas, experiences, and sensibilities.

There is indeed a resounding echo between Janvier's final declaration on the observability of creolization in Haiti and Edouard Glissant's depiction of the "Caribbean [...] as one of the places in the world where Relation presents itself most visibly."[72] In his philosophical meditations, Glissant describes creolization—which he assimilates to "the idea of Relation"—as a "new and original dimension allowing each person to be there and elsewhere, rooted and open, lost in the mountains and free beneath the sea, in harmony and in errantry."[73] Admittedly, the Martinican poet refused the unidirectional movement inherent to the universalistic projection of a "Western group" asserting itself as the necessary and ultimate point of reference and realization.[74] At the core

70 Louis Joseph Janvier, "Discussion, Séance du 17 juillet 1884," *Bulletins de la Société d'anthropologie de Paris* 7 (1884): 582–584.

71 In his account of the event, Jean-Luc Bonniol did point to Janvier's participation in the discussion. Yet he failed to recognize the originality of Janvier's contribution, implying instead that he reiterated what Lévy and Quatrefages had already said on the subject. Jean-Luc Bonniol, "Au prisme de la créolisation. Tentative d'épuisement d'un concept," *L'Homme* 207–208 (2013), 139–141.

72 Édouard Glissant, *Poetics of Relation*, trans. Betsy Wing (Ann Arbor: University of Michigan Press, 1997), 33.

73 Ibid., 34.

74 On the foundational relationship between Comtean positivism and the idea of "the West," see Georgios Varouxakis, "The Godfather of 'Occidentality': Auguste Comte and the Idea of 'the West,'" *Modern Intellectual History* 16, no. 2 (2019): 411–441.

There Is No Odd in Ordinary 159

of Glissant's conception of creolization lies indeed a process of cultural "intervalorization" that negates the idea of a "Western civilization" altogether. Moreover, creolization is by no means equivalent to *métissage* in the Glissantian "All-World"; rather, it amounts to "*métissage* with an added value which is unpredictability."[75] Somewhat counterintuitively, that "added value" is key to understanding how Janvier may have addressed questions only later raised by twentieth-century postcolonial thinkers of creolization like Glissant.

In the ellipses of the long excerpt quoted above, Janvier complicated his teleological model of creolization by revealing the very principle of unpredictability inscribed at its core. "By way of a particular natural selection," he claimed, "under the influence of cerebral work, some muscles atrophy or decrease in volume, while others become denser, their fibers tighter."[76] Rather than pointing to a rigid understanding of Darwin's theory of natural selection, this claim illustrates how Janvier's observation of its "particular" unfolding in Haiti allowed him to articulate a rather original interpretation of the process of creolization. In his Caribbean reading of the Darwinian world-text, Janvier came to understand creolization as a perpetual interaction between the "cerebral" and the "physical"—or, in the words of Nihad M. Farooq, as the "always-already there and elsewhere of intellectual and organic matter."[77] It is no coincidence that Janvier was both able and eager to envision it in such a way. As Farooq contends in her study of Darwin's thought and writings, it was in the second half of the nineteenth century that creolization "was first articulated systematically in and as scientific practice, and eventually given a name: evolution."[78]

Therefore, contrary to many of his contemporaries, Janvier understood that Darwin's story of origins was above all, as Elizabeth Grosz has since argued, a story in which "being is transformed into becoming, essence into existence, and the past and the present are rendered provisional in light of the force of the future."[79] By translating this conception of temporal becoming into a dynamic vision of creolization in Haiti, Janvier quite literally creolized the theory of evolution at a moment

75 Édouard Glissant, *Introduction à une poétique du divers* (Paris: Gallimard, 1996), 19.
76 Janvier, "Discussion," 583.
77 Nihad M. Farooq, *Undisciplined: Science, Ethnography, and Personhood in the Americas, 1830–1940* (New York: New York University Press, 2016), 17.
78 Ibid.
79 Elizabeth A. Grosz, *The Nick of Time: Politics, Evolution, and the Untimely* (Durham, NC: Duke University Press, 2004), 7.

when it was largely being used to reify socio-racial hierarchies. Resisting the deterministic inflection of *fin-de-siècle* social Darwinism, he stood as a forebear to all those Caribbean thinkers who, half a century later, started to perform what Farooq describes as a "creolization of the human sciences themselves."[80]

On silencing and/as sciencing

In his struggle for black sovereignty in Haiti and beyond, Janvier helped transform the social sciences in ways which, paradoxically, may only be grasped in light of his virtual anonymity in the disciplinary canon today. It is indeed no accident that his name has practically vanished from the archive of social-scientific thought and practice outside of Haiti. The need for an uninterrupted and uncontested narrative of development and progress may run too deep in the genealogy of North Atlantic anthropology for its history to remain free of certain erasures. Since the 1970s, efforts to decolonize the discipline have led to a long-overdue recognition of its colonial underpinnings as well as a timely rediscovery of some of its silenced practitioners. Yet there is still much to be done to break away from what Faye V. Harrison once identified as an "anthropology [that] remains overwhelmingly a Western intellectual—and ideological—project" and to critically restructure a discipline founded upon the "underlying assumption [...] that cultural, epistemological, and theoretical perspectives outside of the Eurocentric canon are less adequate, less 'universal', and less 'scientific'—in other words, inferior."[81] In other words, to complete a "decolonization project [that] is still in effect," as Gina Athena Ulysse warns us, we may want to go back and listen to the cohort of Haitian intellectuals who initiated such a project nearly a century and a half ago.[82]

---

80 Farooq, *Undisciplined*, 9.
81 Faye V. Harrison, "Anthropology as an Agent of Transformation: Introductory Comments and Queries," in *Decolonizing Anthropology: Moving Further Toward an Anthropology for Liberation*, ed. Faye V. Harrison (Arlington: American Anthropological Association, 2010), 1, 6. For a particularly insightful analysis of the work done by Harrison and other agents of the "decolonizing generation" to tackle the colonial heritage of anthropological theory, methodology, and pedagogy, see Jafari Sinclaire Allen and Ryan Cecil Jobson, "The Decolonizing Generation: (Race and) Theory in Anthropology since the Eighties," *Current Anthropology* 57, no. 2 (2016), 129–148.
82 Gina Athena Ulysse, "Homage to Those Who Hollered before Me /

Janvier, as I have attempted to show here, was one of these insurgent figures. Both in his writings and in his interventions at the SAP, he raised his voice to defend Haiti's position in the modern world, accounting for the particularities as well as the universalizable potential of the Haitian experience. By addressing the "odd" as a another kind of "ordinary"—to use the language of Trouillot's unforgettable title—he has left us with invaluable insights to tackle what Kaiama L. Glover and Alessandra Benedicty-Kokken have recently described as the "dialectic of exemplarity and alterity" integral to the ways in which "Haiti has long been framed discursively."[83] It is therefore my hope that, as we embark on a new reading of his political writings with the present translation of *Haïti aux Haïtiens*, some of these insights will be recognized more widely for their critical value, and Janvier will finally be acknowledged as a foundational figure in the history of the social sciences.

Meditations on Inheritances and Lineages, Anthropological and Otherwise," *Anthropology News* (8 April 2019), www.anthropology-news.org.
83 Kaiama L. Glover and Alessandra Benedicty-Kokken, "Editor's Introduction," in *The Haiti Exception: Anthropology and the Predicament of Narrative*, ed. Alessandra Benedicty-Kokken, Kaiama L. Glover et al. (Liverpool: Liverpool University Press, 2016), 3.

CHAPTER FOUR

Haïti farà da se[1]

French Third Republic Colonial Universalism and Louis Joseph Janvier's Haitian Autonomy

Chelsea Stieber

Louis Joseph Janvier was in the room when Ernest Renan gave his famed lecture in the great room of the Sorbonne on the evening of March 11, 1882 that asked, "What is a nation" ("Qu'est-ce qu'une nation?"). Renan's speech engaged nascent Third Republic debates about nationalism and argued for an idea of national belonging based in will and sacrifice over the essentialist concepts of race, language, and territory. It is in this speech that Renan famously proffered the formula for French nationalism as a collective forgetting and a daily commitment to national belonging—"a daily plebiscite" ("plébiscite de tous les jours").[2] It is fair to say that Renan's concept of plebiscitary nationalism remains canonical in French republican historiography and in studies of the rise of nationalism.[3] Yet the near-mythic status of Renan's putatively universalist plebiscitary republican nationalism stands in stark contrast to the French philologist-philosopher's earlier writing on morality, human nature, and goodness in which he proffered the racist and anti-universal belief that European civilization was superior, and that races were unequal: "men are not equal, races are not equal" ("les hommes

---

1 "Haiti will do it on her own." From "Italia farà da se," King Charles Albert of Sardinia's proclamation in the war of Italian independence against Austria, in which he expressly refused the French Second Republic's intervention in the war. Many thanks to Kenyse Lyons for her expertise on this context.

2 Ernest Renan, *Qu'est-ce qu'une nation?* (Paris: Calmann Lévy, 1882), 27.

3 See Benedict Anderson, *Imagined Communities: Reflections on the Origin and Spread of Nationalism* (London: Verso, 1983).

ne sont pas égaux, les races ne sont pas égales").[4] While critics have wrestled with Renan's conception of "race" and his evolving views on "civilization" and colonization, few have paid attention to the real-time critiques of Renan's conflicting views as they were unfolding in the French press in the 1880s.[5] More specifically, few have paid attention to Louis Joseph Janvier's critiques of Renan and the broader race-based logic of civilizational inferiority that the Third Republic government was deploying to justify its new colonial project.

The period 1879–1885 was a watershed moment in France in which the culture, symbolism, and politics of the Third Republic took shape. One of the lasting—and most contradictory—legacies of French republicanism that emerged in this period was the creation of a new republican imperialism through a renewed idea of a civilizing mission (*mission civilisatrice*) and French universalism: the right and the duty (*devoir*) of "superior" civilizations, and races, to colonize "inferior" civilizations in order to modernize them and set them on the path to progress and eventual "equality" with the "superior" civilizations. The civilizing mission thus rested on a belief in the fundamental inequality of peoples—articulated interchangeably as race, civilization, and ethnicity—and the fundamental superiority of French civilization to correct that inequality.[6] Having arrived in France in 1876,

---

4 Ernest Renan, *Dialogues et fragments philosophiques* (Paris: Calmann-Lévy, 1876), xvi–xvii. He proffered similar statements on racial inequality and European ("occidental") supremacy in *La Réforme intellectuelle et morale* (1871) and *L'Avenir de la science* (written in 1848–1849 but published in 1890).

5 Aimé Césaire famously took French republicanism to task for its investment in Renanian canonical nationalist thinking in *Discours sur le colonialisme* (Paris: Imprimerie des Éditions Réclame, 1950), reproducing full paragraphs of unattributed racist writing and asking, "Hitler? Rosenberg? No, Renan." See also Edward Said, *Orientalism* (New York: Pantheon, 1978). For an excellent synthesis of the reception of Renan's work and especially the problem of "race," see Robert. D. Priest, "Ernest Renan's Race Problem," *The Historical Journal* 58, no. 1 (2015): 309–330.

6 On the civilizing mission and its long French history, see Dino Costantini, *Mission civilisatrice: le rôle de l'histoire colonial dans la construction de l'identité politique française*, trans. Juilette Ferdinand (Paris: Éditions la Découverte, 2008). See also Alice Conklin, *A Mission to Civilize: The Republican Idea of Empire in France and West Africa, 1895–1930* (Stanford: Stanford University Press, 1997). As Eugen Weber's work has shown, France carried out its civilizing mission within the Hexagon as well. Third Republic France's civilizing mission was thus a parallel program of the republicanization and "civilization" of French men and women within France's borders and of indigenous inhabitants of North

Janvier effectively witnessed the full ascendance of the Third Republic universalist civilizing mission and its paradoxes, embodied in Renan's writing but also in the language and policies of the government more broadly. He and a community of other Caribbean writers in Paris—Anténor Firmin, Ramón Emeterio Betances, Clément Denis, Justin Dévost, Jules Auguste, Dantès Sabourin, and Arthur Bowler, among others—engaged in the formation of public opinion in France around questions of race, civilization, equality, and called into question the very discursive foundations of France's new imperialist project.[7] The real-time arguments these Caribbean black thinkers made in refutation of France's contradictory stance on humanism and universalism have largely gone unremarked in the historiography of French Third Republic universalism, silenced by the mythologizing of what Tyler Stovall calls the "myth of the liberatory republic."[8]

Janvier's 1880s writing in particular is crucial to uncovering the central paradox of Third Republic universalism and its limits. He sounds a clear voice of dissent and critique from the formerly colonized point of view, offering lessons from Haiti's long nineteenth century of postcolonial independence, and drawing upon a long heritage of Haitian polemical textual practices and anticolonial refutation. Janvier's witnessing of France's neoimperial republican universalism is also central to contextualizing his insistence on Haitian autonomy above all else, which he expressed in many formulations throughout his oeuvre—"Haïti doit être aux Haïtiens!", "Haïti farà da se," "Haïti se fera d'elle même," and "Haïti aux Haïtiens."

This essay considers Janvier's Haitian nationalist thinking via his engagement with the Third Republic's debates about nation, civilization, and empire in France. For, while Janvier's early work took aim at individual racist detractors of Haiti, his later work evinces a realization that French republicanism itself was invested in an idea

---

and West Africa and parts of Asia. Eugen Weber, *Peasants into Frenchmen: The Modernization of Rural France, 1870–1914* (Stanford: Stanford University Press, 1976).

7 On Janvier, Betances, and Firmin, see Marlene Daut's contribution to the present volume. On Firmin, see Daniel Desormeaux, "Le Facteur littéraire dans *De l'égalité des races humaines* d'Anténor Firmin," *L'Esprit créateur* 56, no. 1 (2016): 24–39. See also Robert Bernasconi, "A Haitian in Paris: Anténor Firmin as a Philosopher against Racism," *Patterns of Prejudice* 42, nos. 4–5 (2008): 365–383.

8 Tyler Stovall, "The Myth of the Liberatory Republic and the Political Culture of Freedom in Imperial France," *Yale French Studies* 111 (2007): 89–103.

of nationalism based on a "civilizing mission" that extended France's empire over other, "uncivilized" peoples. Ultimately, this essay argues that Janvier identified the fundamental contradictions in French republicanism's universal nationalism that underwrote the Third Republic's imperial nation-state as they were unfolding in real time. This keen awareness of the neoimperial project that was gearing up to transform Europe in turn shaped Janvier's Haitian nationalism: a conceptualization of Haitian autonomy that protected itself against not only this growing imperial French republican civilizational program, but a more widespread US-European-white supremacist belief in the right, and duty, of "superior" races-civilizations to colonize other "inferior" peoples.

French universalism and the paradox of the colonial republic

In order to take stock of Janvier's critique of France's Third Republic imperial project it is necessary first to establish the terms of a very French concept: universalism. Universalism is the cornerstone of French republican identity, politics, and culture and can be understood broadly as the idea that equality is a natural right of all human beings. Yet this universal belief is particularly French in its implementation: equality is achieved in France today "by making one's social, religious, ethnic, and other origins irrelevant in the public sphere; it is as an abstract individual that one becomes a French citizen."[9] Put in this context, universalism in its specifically French usage is less about a global idea of equality and more about the specific cultural and political practices in France; universalism carries with it the implication "that all peoples can (and should) aspire to French models of citizenship and liberal egalitarianism."[10] The origins of France's particularistic universalism are often located in the events surrounding the French Revolution, where liberal egalitarianism found its most identifiable expression in the Declaration of the Rights of Man and later a more radical instantiation with the Convention's abolition of slavery throughout the colonies on February 4, 1794 that

---

9 Joan Scott, *The Politics of the Veil* (Princeton: Princeton University Press, 2010), 11. Scott offers an excellent overview of the intricacies and paradoxes of French universalism for a reading audience unfamiliar with French republicanism and the universalist myth. See also Naomi Schor, "The Crisis of French Universalism," *Yale French Studies* 100 (2001): 43–64; Stovall, "The Myth of the Liberatory Republic."

10 Stovall, "The Myth of the Liberatory Republic," 90.

declared all men, without distinction of color, French citizens with all the rights assured by the constitution. Of course, we must not obscure the fact that the radical liberal egalitarianism of the nascent French Republic was initiated by the *liberté générale* proclaimed on the ground in colonial Saint-Domingue by Légér-Félicté Sonthonax, then civil commissioner, himself responding to the uprising led by slaves throughout the colony and their demands for freedom.

Yet to place French universalism's origins in the liberal egalitarianism gained (and later lost) by the First Republic is misleading or, at best, only a partial accounting. Indeed, French universalism has never been solely about equality; it is bound up in colonialism and imperialism as well. A longer view of the history of French universalism shows that the concept is entangled with French imperialism before and after 1789, tied to efforts to evangelize and "civilize" peoples and civilizations outside of Christianity and the West. As Naomi Schor has argued, French universalism is tied intimately to the history of the Catholic Church and its "founding reputation and mission as a disseminator of a universalist creed."[11] What is understood today as French secular universalism has conceptual roots in Ancien Régime Catholicism and missionary imperialism. Viewed through its longer history, and to borrow René Rémond's terminology, France has always been a "missionary nation."[12] It follows that French universalism has always been a fundamentally colonial concept. There is thus a continuity in France's Catholic colonial missionary projects from the Ancien Régime and the colonial *mission civilisatrice* of the post-revolutionary period. What changed was the content of the mission: from "civilizing" through evangelization to "civilizing" through republican universal nationalism. Crucially, however, Third Republic colonial universalism was secular: it displaced the Christian principle of a universal brotherhood of man and replaced it with the idea of a universal civilization that France alone possessed, and had the duty to bestow upon inferior civilizations and inferior races.

The specificity of the Third Republic's *mission civilisatrice* that Janvier witnessed unfold and its particularistic embrace of this longer heritage of missionary universalism warrants additional contextualization here. First and foremost, the particular republican form of France's nineteenth-century colonial empire (the "strangest of political

---

11 Schor, "The Crisis of French Universalism," 44.
12 Rémond, "La Fille aînée de l'Eglise" qtd. in Schor, "The Crisis of French Universalism," 44.

formations")[13] was not the result of some inexorable march towards progress. The republic was far from inevitable: the First Republic itself lasted little more than a decade, from 1792 to 1804, with its final years under Napoleon's Consulate taking on an increasingly military authoritarian and undemocratic form, most notably with the May 20, 1802 revocation of the 1794 abolition of slavery in the French colonies and the official proclamation of the First Empire in 1804.[14] In fact, the first seventy years of the nineteenth century in France saw sixty-six years of monarchy (the First Empire, the Bourbon Restoration, the July Monarchy, and the Second Empire) and only four years of a Second Republic. Yet even this Second Republic, which in 1848 fulfilled the universalist egalitarianism of 1794 with the second, belated but definitive abolition of slavery in its colonies, helped usher in a new wave of French imperialism. Republican France deployed its successful (again, belated) abolition as evidence of its moral virtue and superior civilization, which in turn became the basis upon which France justified its colonial expansion against "uncivilized" peoples who had yet to achieve this enlightened republican state form. As Gilles Manceron argues, republican abolition became an "alibi" for colonization:

> an alibi for colonization, in the service of a "right of colonial intervention" held by "civilized people to fight against the barbarism of slavery."
>
> (un alibi de la colonisation, au service d'un "droit d'intervention colonial" que détiendraient les "civilisés pour lutter contre cette barbarie qu'est l'esclavage")[15]

---

13 Tyler Stovall, *Transnational France: The Modern History of a Universal Nation* (Boulder: Westview, 2015), 206. On the paradoxes of this colonial republican construction, see also Gary Wilder, *The French Imperial Nation State: Negritude and Colonial Humanism between the Two World Wars* (Chicago: University of Chicago Press, 2005); Nicolas Bancel, Pascal Blanchard, and Françoise Vergès, *La République coloniale: essai sur une utopie* (Paris: Albin Michel, 2003).

14 Indeed, independent Haiti remained the only site where the aspirational models of French citizenship and liberal egalitarianism found fertile ground—and even then, these models of citizenship and equality remained unequal in their application. See Chelsea Stieber, *Haiti's Paper War: Writing, Civil War, and the Making of the Republic (1804–1954)* (New York: New York University Press, 2020). See also Jean Alix René, *Haïti après l'esclavage: formation de l'état et culture politique populaire (1804–1846)* (Port-au-Prince: Éditions Le Natal, 2019).

15 Gilles Manceron qtd. in Costantini, *Mission civilisatrice*, 58.

By the time Louis Napoleon's Second Empire came to an end in 1870, the reestablishment of monarchy seemed much more likely than the implementation of a robust universal colonial republic. Historians agree that for the first years of the provisional Third Republic government, monarchists made a strong showing and many expected their eventual return to dominance.[16] Internal divisions among monarchists and the refusal to compromise among various *prétendants* allowed the fledgling Third Republic to hold on. It was only after a constitutional crisis in May 1877 that republicans emerged dominant and set about establishing the institutions and political culture of French republicanism that we know today: the Marseillaise once again became the official national anthem, Bastille Day became the official national holiday, Marianne became the official symbol of republican liberty and reason, and so on. As Schor asserts, the Third Republic was the "golden age of French universalism, coinciding with what Pierre Nora, borrowing from the British Marxist historian Eric Hobsbawm, has called the 'invention' of France."[17]

The period 1879–1885, what is known as the "Opportunist Republic," saw moderate republican ministers play upon the divided leftist coalitions to achieve a series of laws and programs to secularize (*laïciser*) state institutions and centralize the administration of France. Jules Ferry, the most prominent member of the Opportunist coalition, had a particularly large role in shaping the period as prime minister and minister of public instruction. Yet if the 1879–1885 period marked a watershed in the creation (invention) of secular French universalism within the metropole, it was simultaneously a turning point in French colonial expansion. This expansion, referred to as France's "new imperialism," took France's long heritage of Catholic missionary universalism and translated it into the service of republican universal nationalism. Under the banner of the *mission civilisatrice*, Ferry, Opportunist republicans, and the "parti colonial" (colonial lobby) argued for the expansion of France's colonial empire throughout Indochina, Africa, and Oceania, all territories for which rival European powers "scrambled" in the late nineteenth century.[18] Ferry and the Opportunists cast it as their mandate and their duty—their *mission*—to "civilize," both within metropolitan France and in the vast "unclaimed" territories in Africa, Asia, and Oceania.

16 Stovall, *Transnational France*, 174–175.
17 Schor, "The Crisis of French Universalism," 47.
18 See Costantini, *Mission civilisatrice*. See also Conklin, *A Mission to Civilize*.

The terms upon which the Opportunists defended this civilizing colonial expansion reveal the paradoxes of the republican colonial project. In his (in)famous speech to parliament on July 28, 1885, entitled "The foundations of colonial policy" ("Les Fondements de la politique coloniale"), Ferry made an economic and political case for the expansion of France's empire: it would be good for trade and industry, and it was necessary to maintain France's status as a European power as other rival nations like Germany scrambled for more territory.[19] He argued that because of the interest in colonial expansion among other rival European powers, a policy of passivity or abstention in this period of European colonial expansion was the fast track to decadence. Yet it was in what he deemed the "humanitarian and civilizing side of the question" that Ferry exposed the paradox of Third Republic universalism. His approach to humanism and civilization was based in the logic of biological racism and in the dominant racist conceptions of Western "civilization" and "progress" that developed and sharpened over the course of the nineteenth century.[20] As Ferry argued,

> superior races have a right *vis-à-vis* inferior races [...] a right because they have a duty. They have the duty to civilize the inferior races [...] [France] must spread this influence across the world and carry everywhere that it can its language, its mores, its flag, its weapons, its genius.
>
> (les races supérieures ont un droit vis-à-vis des races inférieures [...] un droit, parce qu'il y a un devoir pour elles. Elles ont le devoir

---

19 Assemblée Nationale, "Jules Ferry (28 juillet 1885)," http://www2.assemblee-nationale.fr/decouvrir-l-assemblee/histoire/grands-moments-d-eloquence/jules-ferry-28-juillet-1885.

20 There is a massive body of Anglo-American scholarship on the invention of the concept of race, and whiteness specifically, as it emerged in the eighteenth century and sharpened and narrowed in the nineteenth. See Theodore Allen, *The Invention of the White Race*, 2 vols. (London: Verso, 1994–1997); Bruce Dain, *A Hideous Monster of the Mind: American Race Theory in the Early Republic* (Cambridge, MA: Harvard University Press, 2002). On the association of whiteness with the notion of personhood and the human, see Alexander Weheliye, *Habeas Viscus: Racializing Assemblages, Biopolitics, and Black Feminist Theories of the Human* (Durham, NC: Duke University Press, 2014). On the specific racialization of the concept of "civilization" in the Atlantic World as it related to Haitian diplomatic recognition in international law, see Julia Gaffield, "The Racialization of International Law after the Haitian Revolution: The Holy See and National Sovereignty," *The American Historical Review* 125, no. 3 (2020): 841–868.

de civiliser les races inférieures [...] [la France] doit répandre cette influence sur le monde, et porter partout où elle le peut sa langue, ses mœurs, son drapeau, ses armes, son génie)[21]

Ferry's logic rests first and foremost on the *inequality* of "races"—here meaning, vaguely, peoples, cultures, civilizations but also ethnic groups. Second, Ferry conflates the notions of France's "rights" (*droit*) and its "duties" (*devoir*), which both derive from the premise of superior/inferior races. Third Republic French colonial policy was based in France's *right* to civilize inferior races, a right that is based in *obligation*: because France is a superior "race," it has a duty (*un devoir supérieur de civilisation*) and thus a right, to colonize those "races" it deems inferior.

France's colonial Third Republic was a paradox: it drew on a conception of universalism that was rooted in a longer history of missionary colonialism, and based its neoimperial expansion on the logic of biological racism and Western conceptions of "civilization." Paradoxical also because French revolutionary values of liberty and equality were at once universal (the rights of all humans) *and* imposed, or "granted," in the form of a colonial empire that instituted itself through military force and the creation of colonial *subjects* out of otherwise "free" inhabitants of these colonized lands. I have developed this Third Republic historical context at length here because I believe it is crucial to understanding the context within which Janvier was advocating for the Haitian Republic, the black race, and his project of Haitian autonomy.[22] Janvier was in France during this precise moment of French Republican ideological formation, watching these paradoxes unfold in the halls of institutions of higher learning, learned societies, and the press. By revealing how the Third Republic's stated values of progress were fundamentally inconsistent with the civilizing mission as it has been articulated by Opportunists and the colonial lobby, Janvier argued against France's new imperialism and in defense of the autonomy and territorial integrity of "other," non-European civilizations.[23] Not

---

21 Assemblée Nationale, "Jules Ferry (28 juillet 1885)," http://www2.assemblee-nationale.fr/decouvrir-l-assemblee/histoire/grands-moments-d-eloquence/jules-ferry-28-juillet-1885.
22 See the Introduction to the present volume for a discussion of Janvier's conception of Haitian autonomy.
23 While I am most interested in this essay in Louis Joseph Janvier's refutation of the logical premises upon which Ferry's entire colonial policy is constructed, it is important to note here that the colonial lobby's specious logic did not go

only did Janvier shine a light on the Third Republic's imperial universalist logic and the idea of a French colonial republic, Janvier articulated his own Haitian nationalist program in the shadow of France's new republican imperialism, which he did through his privileged medium: the polemical essay.

"Race," "civilization," and the press debates of the 1880s

> Then Haitians (the only negroes in the world who did not have a fond memory of French domination) will see if they did the right thing by not looking, right from the start of their independence, for a foothold to climb on, a force to grow alongside their friends, their former masters!

unchecked. Republican Radicals like Georges Perin and Georges Clemenceau, among others, accused Ferry of abdicating the universalist principles of human rights that the French Revolution championed. Clemenceau especially took issue with a central component of Ferry's argument, the inequality of races that foregrounded Ferry's specious "duty" argument. In a speech given a few days after Ferry's, entitled "La Colonisation est-elle un devoir de civilization?," Clemenceau roundly rejected the thesis that there were superior and inferior races. He concluded that the colonial lobby's arguments were a thinly veiled attempt to alienate those very human rights upon which the French Republic was founded and rule by the primacy of force, which was anathema to the values of 1789: "I do not wish to adjudicate on the merits of the thesis that has been brought before us and which is nothing other than the proclamation of the rule of might over right; France's history since the Revolution is a living protest against this heinous claim" ("Je ne veux pas juger au fond la thèse qui a été apportée ici et qui n'est pas autre chose que la proclamation de la primauté de la force sur le droit; l'histoire de France depuis la Révolution est une vivante protestation contre cette inique prétention"); Georges Clemenceau, "La Colonisation est-elle un devoir de civilization?", http://www.assemblee-nationale.fr/histoire/7ec.asp. Indeed, even Georges Clémenceau and the Radicals' objections are a footnote in the victorious Third Republic historiography of imperial expansion under the banner of the *mission civilisatrice*. One need only look to the visual propaganda from the Third Republic to see just how successful the myth of the liberatory republic was. Take, for example, the *Supplement illustré* of the *Petit Journal* from November 19, 1911. The cover illustration portrays a larger-than-life Marianne, her head crowned by the sun's rays, bringing a literal cornucopia full of gold to a flock of impoverished, downtrodden brown men half her size. The caption reads "France will be able to freely bring Morocco civilization, wealth, and peace" ("La France va pouvoir porter librement au Maroc la civilisation, la richesse et la paix"). The use of the adverb "librement" captures the central paradox still operating at the heart of the civilizing mission.

(Alors les Haïtiens (les seuls nègres du monde qui n'aient pas gardé un souvenir affectueux de la domination française) verront s'ils ont bien fait de ne pas chercher, dès le début de leur indépendance, un point d'appui pour monter, une force pour grandir, auprès de leurs amis, leurs anciens maîtres!)

—Léo Quesnel

Haiti will do it on her own.

(Haïti farà da se)

—Louis Joseph Janvier

Janvier took part in the boom in newspaper, journal, and mass edition production in Third Republic France. As the Opportunist ministry repealed restrictive laws on freedom of expression and press censorship, Janvier participated in this new press sphere with enthusiasm and purpose: to refute libelous claims made about the black race and the Haitian Republic in the French press. His early articles are notable for the form and style that they take: the refutation essay, a polemical piece designed to disprove (through writing, evidence, and argumentation) the main thesis of the original detractor's essay. Janvier's use of the refutation mode places him in dialogue with a long heritage of nineteenth-century Haitian writers whose writing he drew upon, notably those anticolonial polemists from the early post-independence period.[24] By engaging this form, Janvier enacted a textual performance that addressed multiple publics at once: his French detractors (the explicit addressee in his text), his French supporters (who wished to see him denounce the specious claims made against in him in his own terms), as well as his Haitian brothers (friend and foe), for whom his writing stood as a representation of all Haitians. Janvier's polemical texts make clear that he was aware of this performative dimension: he was performing a certain role for his European readership as a representative and an example of Haitians and black people more broadly

24 On the legacy of the refutation pamphlet in Haiti, see Stieber, *Haiti's Paper War*. On early Haitian writing's engagement of multiple print publics see Doris L. Garraway, "Abolition, Sentiment, and the Problem of Agency," in Baron de Vastey, *The Colonial System Unveiled*, ed. Chris Bongie (Liverpool: Liverpool University Press, 2014); Doris L. Garraway, "Print, Publics, and the Scene of Universal Equality in the Kingdom of Henry Christophe," *L'Esprit créateur* 56, no. 1 (2016): 82–100.

living and studying in France. He nevertheless staked out a position that set him apart from earlier generations of Haitians living in France, whom Janvier derided as cosmopolitans eager to renounce Haiti's intellectual legacy. As he wrote elsewhere of his role as a defender of Haiti,

> so often I see the care of representing [my country] abroad given either to people who have not been back since 1848, when it was considered good form to renounce Haiti, or to others who boast loudly about never reading works published by Haitians.
>
> (je vois si souvent confier le soin de le représenter [mon pays] à l'étranger, soit à des personnes qui l'ont quitté depuis 1848, alors qu'il était de bon ton de le renier, soit à d'autres qui se vantent tout haut de ne jamais lire les écrits que publient les Haïtiens)[25]

In place of these earlier Haitian representatives abroad, Janvier presented himself as a champion of Haitian thought in Haiti and of the fundamental interests of Haiti's inhabitants.

Janvier's debut in the French press (aside from his medical thesis) was a refutation of an inflammatory article written by the French journalist Léo Quesnel that presented Haiti's nineteenth-century failure to constitute a functioning post-independence society as proof of the inequality of races.[26] Quesnel's article was ostensibly written as a review of the French travel writer Edgar la Selve's 1881 book *Le Pays des nègres*, which Selve had written based on his time living and teaching theology in Haiti at the Lycée Pétion in Port-au-Prince in 1872.[27] While Selve's book offers a degrading portrait of Haitian civilization, it is not as aggressive and overtly political as Quesnel in its portrayal of Haiti. Quesnel's main objective was to offer proof of racial inequality and France's superiority in moral and intellectual realms, proof that he drew from Haiti's so-called "failed state" status:

---

25 Louis Joseph Janvier, ed., *Les Constitutions d'Haïti (1801–1885)* (Paris: C. Marpon et E. Flammarion, 1886), 619.

26 Léo Quesnel, "Anciennes colonies française: Haiti," *La Revue politique et littéraire* no. 3 (January 21, 1882). For a discussion of Quesnel's article see Desormeaux, "Le Facteur littéraire."

27 Edgar la Selve, *Le Pays des nègres: voyage à Haïti, ancienne partie française de Saint-Domingue* (Paris: Hachette, 1881). On Selve see Deborah Jenson, "Jean-Jacques Dessalines and the African Character of the Haitian Revolution," *The William and Mary Quarterly* 69, no. 3 (2012): 615–638.

If the theory of racial inequality needed to be confirmed, it would be by the futility of the efforts to constitute a society made by the negroes of Haiti over the last century.

(Si la théorie de l'inégalité des races avait besoin d'être confirmée, elle le serait par l'inanité des efforts que font depuis un siècle des nègres d'Haïti pour constituer une société)[28]

Quesnel's use of the conditional "if" here is particularly inflammatory: for him, and others like him, the theory of racial inequality was already proven fact. The rest of his argument works through a compendium of racist tropes about Haiti and its inhabitants: the country was beautiful during the colonial period ("What a beautiful country in the time of French rule! What rich harvests, what noble buildings, what prosperity!" ("Quel beau pays au temps de la domination française! Quelles riches cultures, quels nobles édifices, quelle prospérité!"); there was less crime and violence under colonial domination than in Haiti's postcolonial independence; black people exhibit an "natural inferiority [...] the negro is a child that does not grow up" ("infériorité native [...] le noir est un enfant qui ne grandit pas"); and so on.[29] Quesnel also cites approvingly from Maxime Raybaud's racist, fantastical reading of Haiti under Emperor Faustin Soulouque (1849–1859), which portrayed Haiti as descended into violent debauchery and barbarism under the black emperor.[30] Quesnel concludes that to survive and progress, Haiti must accept to mix with white civilization: "the negroes will never make anything of Saint-Domingue; it 'lies fallow' from a social, commercial, and industrial point of view, as well as from an agricultural point of view" ("jamais les nègres ne feront rien de Saint-Domingue; elle est 'en jachère' au point de vue social, commercial, industriel, aussi bien qu'au point de vue agricole").[31] Quesnel threatens that Haiti will remain in its "fallow state" until the U.S. eventually extends its influence over the Antilles, in a prescient reading of the United States' geopolitical interests and inevitability of U.S. tutelage in the region. Quesnel closes

---

28 Quesnel, "Anciennes colonies," 84. It bears noting that white supremacist arguments that turn on Haiti's "failed state" status as proof remain at work today, as evidenced by the former U.S. president's "shithole country" comments in 2018.
29 Quesnel, "Anciennes colonies," 84, 85.
30 Raybaud served as the French consul general in Haiti under Soulouque. He penned his *L'Empereur Soulouque et son empire* (1856) under the pseudonym Gustave d'Alaux.
31 Quesnel, "Anciennes colonies," 87.

with the preposterous claim (cited in epigraph above) that Haitians are the only black people in the world who do not express a fond memory of French colonialism—a claim that is pure Third Republic imperial universalist propaganda. He adds to this claim a vindictive taunt: assuring Haitians that when another superior white nation eventually does extend its colonial influence, Haitians will see how wrong they were to have refused French supervision and civilizational stewardship. Quesnel's tract is certainly more polemical and sensationalist than Ferry in its activation of the protocols of the Third Republic's new imperialist discourse: there is no talk of rights or duty, but rather a malevolent comeuppance dedicated to proving Haitians wrong for having so brutally expelled the French from their newly formed independent nation. Quesnel's argument is nevertheless part and parcel of the same discourse based in racial inequality and the superiority of the French "race" that underwrote the Third Republic's *mission civilisatrice.*

Quesnel's aggressive tone and tenuous "proof" of the inequality of races provoked a press polemical: Janvier penned a letter to the editor of *La Revue politique et littéraire* (the very next day), refuting Quesnel's claims and defending Haiti's independence. Perhaps unsurprisingly, the *revue* refused to publish Janvier's response and so Janvier published it in two separate letters in the French newspapers: *Union républicaine* and *Sauveteur.*[32] Next, he and his fellow Haitians in Paris mobilized. They asked Victor Schœlcher, the celebrated French abolitionist then serving as an elected senator in the Third Republic, and Ramón Betances, the Puerto Rican doctor and abolitionist activist, to write letters in defense of Haiti and Haitians that they could use as introductory pieces to a volume they were putting together, *Les Détracteurs de la race noire et de la république d'Haïti.* Both men obliged, providing letters within a month of Quesnel's original article. Janvier included his letter and article in refutation of Quesnel in the volume, alongside essays from prominent Paris-based Haitian intellectuals Clément Denis, Justin Dévost, Jules Auguste, and Arthur Bowler.[33]

The collected volume also included reprints of several supportive French press articles that lauded their endeavor and

---

32 *La Revue politique* did, however, publish a short, two-paragraph response from Quesnel addressing the complaints levied against the journal for its publication of Quesnel's earlier article, entitled "Les Haïtiens à Paris" (February 4, 1882). It was even more condescending, racist, and injurious than his original article.

33 Ertha Pascal Trouillot and Ernst Trouillot, eds., *Encyclopédie biographique d'Haïti,* vol. 1 (Montreal: Éditions SEMIS, 2001).

criticized Quesnel's racist arguments. Of note among these reprints is an article that appeared in Pierre Lafitte's *La Revue occidentale: philosophique, sociale et politique* in May 1882 by the psychiatrist and positivist Jean-François Eugène Robinet. Robinet's article lauded the young Haitians' defense in their collected volume, calling it a "strong, indignant, thrilling work" ("oeuvre forte, indignée, palpitante"), and criticized *La Revue politique et littéraire* for publishing Quesnel's opinions based in racial prejudice. In refutation of Quesnel's position, Robinet reiterated the positivist stance that there was no inherent physiological or biological difference between the human races:

> the founder of Positivism, rejecting inept and barbaric prejudices, accepts only differences of development and not an intrinsic, physiological inequality between the diversity of human races, including the black race.
>
> (le fondateur du Positivisme, repoussant des préjugés ineptes et barbares, n'admet, entre les diverses races humaines, y compris la race noire, que des différences de développement et non pas une inégalité intrinsèque, physiologique)[34]

In addition to refuting Quesnel's position on race, Robinet's essay engaged the history of French colonialism that evinced a keen understanding of the Haitian Revolution and Haiti's long nineteenth-century heritage of anticolonial thought deployed against a French pro-colonial lobby. For example, Robinet derided Quesnel for assuming the language of the pro-colonial lobby in his article—"said like a true planter!" ("veritable propos de planteur!")—and being arrogant and audacious in his belief in racial superiority—"so imbued with racial prejudice and with the organic superiority of the one to which he belongs" ("tellement imbu du préjugé de race et de la supériorité organique de celle à laquelle il appartient").[35] What is more, Robinet roundly dismissed Quesnel's criticism of Haitian revolutionaries' ferocity and bloodshed, calling it heroic instead:

---

34 Jean-François Eugène Robinet, "Haiti," *La Revue occidentale, philosophique, sociale et politique* 8, no. 94 (1882): 413. Jean Robinet is a fascinating Third Republic socialist and positivist about whom relatively little has been written. For more on Robinet, see Alric Mabire, "Entre orthodoxie positiviste et histoire universitaire," *Annales historiques de la Révolution française*, no. 374 (2013): 3–23.

35 Robinet, "Haiti," 415.

He criticizes them for their barbarity, their ferocity in the terrible war—heroic in our opinion but without mercy—by which they had to conquer their independence and extricate themselves from the most monstrous enslavement.

(Il leur reproche leur barbarie, leur férocité dans la guerre terrible, héroïque selon nous, mais sans merci, par laquelle ils ont dû conquérir leur indépendance et se sortir de l'esclavage le plus monstrueux)[36]

Indeed, Robinet seems to be endorsing the language of Dessalinean anticolonialism with his use of the term "to avenge" ("venger") to describe Janvier and his fellow Haitians' righteous, legitimate defense of their race and their country in their volume *Les Détracteurs*.[37]

Janvier based his own refutation of Quesnel's arguments in the century of Haiti's progress since independence. He pointed to the Haitian people's development and evolution as a society and a nation throughout the nineteenth century. Through an extended metaphor of sterility and virility, he denied the premise of Quesnel's biological argument: that Haiti was fallow, sterile, or unable to *progress* physically, intellectually, morally, or culturally without the influence of the white, European "race." In essence, Janvier offered a case study of how Haitians and the Haitian republic progressed *on their own* in order to disprove Quesnel's racist premise, but also to advocate for Haiti's long tradition of autonomy in a world marked by increasing neocolonial incursions among the powers of the North Atlantic.

Janvier performed a similar refutation of the thesis of racial inequality in his essay "M. Renan et l'égalité des races," published first as a polemical in the review *La Jeune France* and later republished in 1884 with an extended introduction under the title *L'Égalité des races*. That Janvier would refute Renan's statements of racial inequality is entirely in keeping with his earlier refutation of Quesnel. Yet his refutation of Renan came after Janvier had initially lauded the French philologist-philosopher for his 1882 speech at the Sorbonne and his statements of sacrifice and devotion, and for his compelling formulation of national identity beyond race, ethnicity, language, or religion. Indeed, the front cover of the 1882 essay collection *Les Détracteurs de la race noire et de la république d'Haïti*, which Janvier co-edited, includes an epigraph

---

36 Ibid., 416.
37 Ibid., 414.

Haïti farà da se 179

from Renan's 1882 conference, "Man does not improvise. The nation, like the individual, is the result of a long history of efforts, sacrifices, and devotion" ("L'homme ne s'improvise pas. La nation, comme l'individu, est l'aboutissant d'un long passé, d'efforts, de sacrifices et de dévouement").[38] While Renan's 1882 articulation of a plebiscitary nationalism had spoken to Janvier's own conceptions of Haitian nationalism, Janvier found them impossible to square with Renan's earlier statements of racial inequality and European civilizational superiority. Janvier thus heavily criticized Renan for his contradictory stance on race and nationalism in his essay "M. Renan et l'égalité des races: Bretons et nègres," highlighting Renan's statements of belief in racial inequality, natural hierarchy, and the superiority of French morality and intellect as untenable with the idea of France as a beacon of *progress* and modern civilization.[39]

It is worth briefly revisiting Renan's statements of inequality before highlighting Janvier's refutation of them. Renan articulated an anti-egalitarian worldview in the 1876 preface to his *Dialogues et*

---

38 Louis-Joseph Janvier, ed., *Les Détracteurs de la race noire et de la république d'Haïti* (Paris: C. Marpon et E. Flammarion, 1882).
39 Aimé Césaire also called out Renan's pro-European colonialism and anti-democratic arguments in his 1950 anticolonial essay, *Discours sur le colonialisme*, though this aspect of Césaire's text has received little attention. Césaire takes issue therein with the canonical (pantheonic) status that Renan held—and still holds—in French philosophical and national-political history as the "the Western *humanist*, the idealist philosopher" ("*humaniste* occidental, le philosophe 'idéaliste'"), which effectively obscured Renan's stated belief in the inequality of human races and his very definition of "humanism" as rooted in Western, European moral and intellectual superiority; Césaire, *Discours*, 15. Césaire quotes this contradictory stance directly from Renan's *La Réforme intellectuelle et morale*: "The regeneration of inferior or degenerate races by superior races is the divine order of humanity" ("La régénération des races inférieures ou abâtardies par les races supérieures est dans l'ordre providential de l'humanité"). Césaire expressed astonishment and shame at the lack of protest, the lack of indignation at such statements from Renan, who was held in such high regard in postwar France. Yet long before Césaire, Janvier was performing a refutation of Renan's contradictory humanism in real time. There remains much more to explore in Césaire's indebtedness—and possible drawing upon—his anticolonial Haitian predecessors. See Marlene Daut, "Un-Silencing the Past: Boisrond-Tonnerre, Vastey, and the Re-Writing of the Haitian Revolution," *South Atlantic Review* 74, no. 1 (2008): 35–60. Jean Jonassaint, drawing upon earlier arguments made by Daut, has suggested Césaire's indebtedness to Janvier's refutation-style rhetorical essay in the construction and style of *Discours*—both of which, Jonassaint notes, are linked to earlier Haitian pamphlet writing from Vastey and others. See Jean Jonassaint, "Césaire et Haïti, des apports à évaluer," *Francophonies d'Amérique* 36 (2013): 135–165.

fragments philosophiques, with statements on the existence of a natural hierarchy, a divine order of things in which each being has his place and rank. While Renan maintained that all men had rights, and that all beings should be treated with love and respect, this belief nevertheless co-existed with "the ironclad hierarchy of nature" ("la hiérarchie de fer de la nature") and "a divine order where everything has its place, its rank, its utility, even its necessity" ("un ordre providentiel, où tout a sa place et son rang, son utilité, sa nécessité même").[40] In this, Renan saw the fundamental inequality of men, and of races: "Men are not equal, races are not equal. The negro, for example, is made so that he may be of use in the great things willed and designed by the white man" ("Les hommes ne sont pas égaux, les races ne sont pas égales. Le nègre, par exemple, est fait pour servir aux grandes choses voulues et conçues par le blanc").[41] Based on this natural inequality of men, Renan argued that Europeans had a duty to the black race: "one must do well by them, spoil them, one most console them with the harshness required by nature" ("il faut leur faire du bien, il faut les gâter, il faut les consoler des rudesses obligées de la nature").[42]

Drawing upon the strategy of reproducing arguments from the original text and refuting them line by line, Janvier reproduced Renan's earlier statements on natural hierarchy and racial inequality in his own text. He made the point that it was precisely this idea of a duty to civilize, a duty based in the supposed unequal nature of man and France's supposed racial superiority, that undergirded the practice of slavery, and continued in the post-abolition era in France under the form of color prejudice that justified French Third Republic new imperialism. As Janvier put it:

> It is with the help of such doctrines that they made the abominable trade in human flesh last for so long, and it is behind such doctrines that they continue to entrench themselves so that they might give an appearance of purpose to stupid color prejudice.
>
> (C'est à l'aide de pareilles doctrines qu'on a fait durer pendant si longtemps l'abominable trafic de la chair humaine, et c'est derrière

---

40 Renan, *Dialogues et fragments philosophiques*, xvi. On Renan's aristocratic, anti-egalitarian writing, see Priest, "Ernest Renan's Race Problem." Renan wrote most of these philosophical dialogues in May 1871 from Versailles, having escaped the tumult and bloodshed of the most violent episodes of the Paris Commune.
41 Renan, *Dialogues*, xvi–xvii.
42 Ibid., xvii.

elles qu'on continue de se retrancher pour donner une apparence de raison d'être au stupide préjugé de couleur)[43]

To disprove Renan's premise of racial inequality, Janvier employed a rhetorical trope common to refutation: he used Renan's own language (and identity) against him. Janvier reminded Renan—and his readers—that during Roman times, the *Britones* (ancestors of the modern-day Bretons) were considered the most barbarous and unintelligent of all men under the Roman empire. Yet, Janvier argued, Bretons evolved, and now comprised the majority of "this battalion of elite men who are leading France, that is, who are leading the civilized world" ("ce bataillon d'hommes d'élite qui marche à la tête de la France, c'est-à-dire du monde civilisé").[44] He gave the example of prominent Frenchmen who claimed Breton heritage: Le Chapelier, Lamennais, Hugo, and of course, Renan himself. In light of this history, Janvier concluded that Renan could not in good conscience continue to promote the idea of an inherent, immutable inequality between races. Further, Janvier argued that France could not continue to promote itself as a beacon of progress and civilization if it did not first acknowledge the fundamental equality of all races and civilizations.

It is worth reflecting further here on Janvier's use of polemical rhetoric and the refutation pamphlet genre, as it connects him to a longer line of Haitian anticolonial writing that he was surely activating with his texts. Janvier wrote to shine a light on the pro-colonial machinations of the Opportunists and the colonial lobby, not unlike the work undertaken by Baron de Vastey and other Haitian writers of the 1810s who refuted Restoration France's colonial lobby. A focus on Janvier's form and rhetoric also provides an important distinction to the work his compatriot Anténor Firmin was doing to refute these same theses of racial inequality in the French public sphere. In 1885, Firmin penned a massive essay with a similar title to Janvier's: *De l'égalité des races humaines*.[45] While the two men were friends and even colleagues, each vindicating Haiti by refuting the logic of racial inequality that underwrote France's Third Republic colonial project, they did so through different forms, genres, tropes, and styles of argumentation.[46] Janvier's

---

43 Louis-Joseph Janvier, "M. Renan et l'égalité des races," *La Jeune France* no. 6 (May 1, 1883–May 25, 1884): 211.
44 Ibid., 209.
45 Joseph-Anténor Firmin, *De l'égalité des races humaines (anthropologie positive)* (Paris: Librairie Cotillon, 1885).
46 Work remains to be done comparing the oeuvres of Janvier and Firmin and

polemical, journalistic texts did not appeal in any great detail to nascent social scientific schools of thought, scientific doctrine, or extant anthropological theories and debates. In this, his *L'Égalité des races* differs from Firmin's *De l'égalité des races humaines*, a 650-page tome that engaged nascent anthropological thought and social scientific theories to promote his own kind of positivist study of human progress, or what he called "anthropologie positive."[47] In this sense, Janvier's essays are more rhetorical than empirical, but always in the service of a much larger, much more radical commentary on Haiti's place in the world as an independent, sovereign black antislavery state.

In sum, Janvier recognized the stakes for Haiti in the new imperial transformations of the 1880s: the scramble for Africa among Western European countries, the paradoxical arguments of republican universalism and the "duty" to civilize the "uncivilized," and the precarious position in which Haiti found itself in this era of new imperialism. He recognized that Haiti could not remain isolated or closed off ("une terre fermée") from European influence. Nevertheless, he maintained vehemently that it was up to Haitians to decide how to open up their country, to whom, in a way that would allow them to maintain their autonomy as an independent nation and an independent people. He insisted throughout his responses, in a number of different formulations, on the same idea: Haitian autonomy. It was an idea of autonomy based first and foremost in Haiti's self-emancipation from foreign servitude and on Haiti's own self-sufficiency. As he argued in his response to Quesnel:

> We have emancipated ourselves and want to move through the world on our own. Some find us pretentious and wish to place us under their care. No thank you! We've already been through that.
>
> (Nous nous sommes mis hors de page et nous voulons aller par le monde tout seuls. D'aucuns nous trouvent prétentieux et nous voudraient mettre en tutelle. Merci! Nous sortons d'en prendre)[48]

---

understanding their relationship. See Marlene Daut's essay in the present volume. See also Michel Acacia, "Firmin et Janvier, entre convergence et divergence," *Le Nouvelliste* (December 28, 2011).

47 See Bastien Craipain's contribution to this volume.

48 Janvier, *Les Détracteurs de la race noire*, 53–54. The phrase "mettre hors de page" translates in eighteenth-century English as "to unboy," or to emancipate from a role of servitude or guardianship. Abel Boyer, *Boyer's Royal Dictionary Abridged* (London: Printed for Messrs. Longman, Law, 1797).

Elsewhere, he declined France's offer of the riches and prosperity that its civilizing mission promised, arguing that Haiti's autonomy and freedom from enslavement has always been more important than its economic prosperity:

> If we are happy to be unhappy [... it is] because we want to maintain our autonomy! ... Poverty in the midst of luxury, so be it, but poverty with independence!
>
> (s'il nous plaisait d'être malheureux [... ce serait] pour garder notre autonomie! ... La misère au milieu des richesses soit, mais la misère avec l'indépendance!)[49]

Haitian self-sufficiency and Haitian autonomy were the crux of his response to France's new imperial project: "Haiti must be for the Haitians! ... And I will add with pride and with confidence: Haiti will do it on her own. Haiti will do it on her own" ("Haïti doit être aux Haïtiens! ... Et j'ajoute avec orgueil et confiance: Haïti se fera d'elle-même. *Haïti farà da se*").[50]

Conclusion: Haitian autonomy in *Haiti for the Haitians*

> Haiti for the Haitians. That is what our ancestors intended.
> —Louis Joseph Janvier

Janvier's call for the preservation of Haitian autonomy is a thread we can trace throughout his essays and polemical articles in the 1880s. Given the rise of the new imperialism that he witnessed taking shape in France, his focus on Haitian autonomy and self-sufficiency was a direct response to the emergent neocolonial discourse among the great powers of the North Atlantic. It is within this late nineteenth-century context that we must also understand the articulation of the idea of *Haiti for the Haitians*. We see this especially in the "Clarion Call" essay, which sounded the trumpet of nationalism in the face of impending neocolonial incursions that threatened Haiti's autonomy. Janvier called upon his fellow Haitians to turn inward, to focus on their Haitianness first and foremost: "We should withdraw into ourselves; gather ourselves."[51] He goes further still,

---

49 Janvier, *Les Détracteurs de la race noire*, 59. Janvier is making a reference here to Demservar Delorme, *La Misère au sein des richesses: réflexions diverses sur Haiti* (Paris: E. Dentu, 1873).
50 Janvier, *Les Détracteurs de la race noire*, 75. See n. 1 above.
51 Louis-Joseph Janvier, *Haiti for the Haitians*, 61 above.

concluding the essay with a rousing call for the maintenance of Haiti's autonomy. Echoing Dessalines's "imperious" will (*impérieux vouloir*) to defeat the French and create the independent, anticolonial, antislavery state of Haiti, Janvier warned his fellow countrymen that Haiti would only remain autonomous, would only mature by her own force if Haitians chose, individually, in their own isolation, at every moment of every day, to show the pride and imperious will to remain independent: "A nation cannot live autonomously, cannot grow on its own unless at every moment each one of its sons taken in isolation, each one demonstrates individually the haughty, proud, imperious will of the nation."[52] Here, Janvier does not cite but rather adapts and redeploys the idea of Renan's plebiscitary nationalism to a Haitian national context in order to stave off, to protect against precisely the kind of imperial universalism that Renan's race-based arguments of superior civilizations justified. It is as if Janvier inoculates Haitian nationalism against French universalist imperialism by building aspects of Renan's doctrine into his own Haitian nationalism.

If Janvier's call for Haitian autonomy was made in response to the immediate threat of neoimperialism from France and, increasingly, the U.S., he articulated it as part of a much longer heritage of Haiti's long nineteenth century of independence and autonomy. It is hard to overstate the singularity and the importance of what Haiti represented as an anticolonial, antislavery black republic in the world. Measured from the 1880s, Haiti had enjoyed (at least nominally) a republican government for much longer than France had up until that point, and considered its political legacy as a beacon for enslaved and recently emancipated black people in the Atlantic World.[53] Janvier evoked this longer heritage in his call for Haitian autonomy in *Haiti for the Haitians*, casting it as Haitians' duty, and legacy, to transmit the heritage of the Haitian Revolution—anticolonial, antislavery independence—intact to Haiti's future generations: "We have to safeguard the legacy passed down to us by the Haitians of yesteryear [...] in order to pass it down intact to the Haitians of the future."[54] Indeed, his clarion call to Haitians to defend their autonomy is itself an interpretation, a transmission of Dessalinean anticolonial, antislavery independence (cited in epigraph above): "Haiti for the Haitians. That is what our ancestors intended."[55] The longer

---

52 Ibid., 71.
53 See Brandon Byrd, *The Black Republic: African Americans and the Fate of Haiti* (Philadelphia: University of Pennsylvania Press, 2019).
54 Janvier, *Haiti for the Haitians*, 50–51.
55 Ibid., 55.

heritage of Haiti's radical independence is central to making sense of the importance Janvier placed on Haitian autonomy, and what the threat of a neocolonial invasion or tutelage-conservatorship—based on specious race-based claims of superior/inferior civilizations—meant to a Haitian people who had been independent since 1804. The threat was real and it was deeply offensive; it ignored the legitimate state that Haiti had maintained since independence in the face of Atlantic World powers who were continually hostile to its existence, and trotting out new and ever-evolving reasons to refuse its legitimacy. It is Janvier's investment in this legacy and his devotion to transmitting it to future generations, coupled with the knowledge of hindsight that what he feared would come to pass a mere thirty years later with the U.S. Occupation of Haiti (1915–1934), that makes *Haiti for the Haitians* all the more powerful and troubling to read.

To be sure, the threat of the U.S. is pressing and present in Janvier's texts, as Brandon Byrd's chapter in this volume attests. By considering the U.S. and European neoimperial projects in parallel, we gain a better understanding of the genesis of *Haiti for the Haitians* and especially Janvier's calls for autonomy as a reflection of Europe's new imperialism and France's paradoxical Third Republic civilizing mission. In response to what he witnessed in France—the evolution and institutionalization of the "strangest of political formations: the republican empire"—*and* in light of Haiti's long nineteenth century of independence, autonomy, and racial equality, Janvier elaborated a nationalist program based in Haitian autonomy: Haiti for the Haitians. Therein, he refuted the thesis of racial inequality and superior/inferior civilizations in order to defend the Haitian Republic's independence in an increasingly hostile neoimperial environment. Janvier shined a light on the paradox of Third Republic universalism in the 1880s, but his insights are still relevant for us now. They help us make sense of the contradictions inherent in French universal republicanism and its investment in a civilization and language that it once proclaimed, and continues to proclaim today, superior to all others.

CHAPTER FIVE

Louis-Joseph Janvier, the Founding Theorist of the Haitian Nation (an Active Reading of *Haïti aux Haïtiens*)

Watson Denis
Translated from French by Nadève Ménard

Introduction

Louis-Joseph Janvier is considered to be one of the four or five most important authors, thinkers, and social theorists of the long Haitian nineteenth century.[1] His work is simultaneously polemical, anti-establishment, provocative, constructive, and programmatic. He wielded his pen like a weapon to expose the gravediggers of his beloved nation, to show his compatriots the light and propose public policies he thought to be closer to political emancipation for peasants and farmers, "the wounded social class," as well as beneficial to the development of the country into which he was born.

From 1881 to 1883, this maverick author already counted three essays to his name that were discussed in the Haitian public sphere.[2] During 1884, he published five texts one after the other, among them *Haïti aux Haïtiens*,[3] a book we can categorize among his programmatic

---

1 On this period, see Michel Hector and Jean Casimir, "Le Long XIXe siècle haïtien," *Revue de la Société Haïtienne d'Histoire et de Géographie* 78, no. 216 (October 2003–March 2004): 35–64.

2 They are: *Phtisie pulmonaire. Causes—traitement préventif* (Paris: Asselin), his doctoral thesis in medicine published as a book in 1881; *Les Détracteurs de la race noire et de la république d'Haïti. Réponses à Léo Quesnel* (Paris: Marpon et Flammarion), a volume of texts he edited in 1882; *Haïti et ses visiteurs (1840–1882)* (Paris: Marpon et Flammarion, 1883), a tremendous text that gives the full scope of the author's vision for Haiti and its relations with the outside world.

3 Louis-Joseph Janvier, *Haïti aux Haïtiens*, 2nd ed. (Paris: Imprimerie A. Parent, A. Davy, Successeurs, 1884). See the translation *Haiti for the Haitians* in the present volume.

works. It is a pamphlet in which the author lays out his opinions, issues watchwords, and guides public opinion.

The essay's very title, considering the topics and issues Janvier had already considered in his first writings, as well as his ideological inclinations, indicated the possible problems he might deal with. The title suggested an activist work with nationalist accents. Yes, the work could be considered within the nationalist framework the author was known for, yet, beyond this nationalism, readers discovered a thinking Janvier, who wrote a work tinged with political economy for Haiti. In this work, a 48-page pamphlet, he touched upon economic and political questions, he considered matters relating to history, sociology, to Haiti's international relations, to wealth creation, to national heritage assets and their conservation in optimal conditions for "future Haitians." In sum, *Haïti aux Haïtiens* is a digest of political, patriotic, autonomist, and nationalist ideas and an endogenous treatise of political economy with a view towards compelling Haitian society onto the path to nation building.

I presume that Janvier placed this work in the wake of State formation for the construction of the Haitian nation.[4] At the time of the

---

4 Today, several scholars in the social sciences and humanities, Haitians and foreigners alike, are considering this fundamental question of Haitian nation building. They especially analyze the formation of the Haitian state, the establishment of the Republic, and the existing relations between the Haitian Revolution, national independence, freedom, and citizenship. On this matter, see, among Haitian authors, Jean Casimir, "La Révolution de 1804 et l'État," in *Genèse de l'État haïtien, 1804–1859*, ed. Michel Hector and Laënnec Hurbon (Port-au-Prince: Éditions des Presses Nationales d'Haïti, 2009), 79–96; Michel Hector, "Une autre voie de construction de l'État-nation: l'expérience christophienne (1806–1820)," in *Genèse de l'État haïtien, 1804–1859*, ed. Michel Hector and Laënnec Hurbon (Port-au-Prince: Éditions des Presses Nationales d'Haïti, 2009), 255–281; Jean Alix René, *Haïti après l'esclavage. Formation de l'État et culture politique populaire (1804–1846)* (Port-au-Prince: Imprimerie Le Natal, 2019), Prix d'Histoire 2017 of the Société Haïtienne d'Histoire de Géographie et de Géologie. Among the foreign authors, see François Blancpain, *La Condition des paysans haïtiens: du code noir aux codes ruraux* (Paris: Éditions Kartala, 2003); Carolyn Fick, "La Révolution haïtienne dans l'Atlantique révolutionnaire. Les enjeux contradictoires de la liberté, de la citoyenneté et de l'indépendance nationale," *Revue Histoire Haïtienne* no. 1 (2019): 151–188; Mimi Sheller, "The Army of Sufferers: Peasant Democracy in the Early Republic of Haiti," *New West Indian Guide, Nieuwe West-Indische Gids* 74, nos. 1–2 (2000): 33–55; Chelsea Stieber, "The Haitian Revolution and the Myth of the Republic: Louis Joseph Janvier's Revisionist History," in *Remembering Early Modern Revolutions: England, North America, France and Haiti*, ed. Edward Vallance (London and New York: Routledge, 2019), 245–257. Furthermore, it would be useful to read

book's publication, the author had understood that the Haitian state existed, but the nation was still an illusion, an empty shell, at the very least a fundamental objective to be achieved by the state power elite. In other words, taking note of the persistence of the State's structures of domination to the detriment of the social class of the "wounded" since the country's independence, he proposed a new structural arrangement between the political, the economic, and the social with a view towards finally building the nation. This project of nation building certainly had contours. The contour which was most important to him was the integration of the "wounded" into the country's political and socioeconomic life. He dreamed and imagined an independent Haitian nation, integrated, sovereign, free from social prejudices and discrimination based on epidermal nuances.[5]

There are not too many kilometers between the problematic of the nation and nationalism. For as much as Janvier posed the necessity of nation building in Haiti in his text *Haïti aux Haïtiens* he also exposed a certain vision of Haitian nationalism at the end of the nineteenth century. Janvier wrote this work at a time when he saw the imperialisms of the world rising; this imperialism was of major concern to the Republic of Haiti, euphemistically referred to as the "black republic"[6] in the travel literature of the time. For me, *Haïti aux Haïtiens* is the culmination of thought built upon the Haitian state's evolution and the national community's future. The author presents his conception of Haiti's place within international relations, especially in its political and diplomatic relations with the international powers, including France and the United States of America.

Reading or rereading the work *Haïti aux Haïtiens* today, we clearly get the impression that Janvier wrote it for posterity. In this essay, I

Michel Hector's well-known article "Classes, État et Nation dans la période de transition," in *La Révolution française et Haïti. Filiations, ruptures, nouvelles dimensions*, vol. 1 (Port-au-Prince: Henri Deschamps—Société Haïtienne d'Histoire et de Géographie, 1995), 112–129 and Tadeusz Lepkowski's good old book, *Haïti. Les débuts de l'État et de la nation*, trans. Serge Rousseu (Montreal: Numérilab, 2018 [1964]), which was already raising this much-talked about set of themes over fifty years ago.

5 For a preliminary consideration of this question, see Watson Denis, "La Nation comme projet d'intégration socio-économique. La vision de Louis-Joseph Janvier relative à une nation intégrée, moderne et souveraine," *Revue de la Société Haïtienne D'histoire, de Géographie et de Géologie* no. 240 (July–December 2010): 36–76.

6 See Spenser B. Saint-John, *Hayti or the Black Republic* (London: Smith, Elder & Co, 1884) for illustration.

will try to unpack the principal ideas that the author conveyed around nation building in Haiti. To do so, I will undertake an active reading of the text.[7]

Historical context and presentation of the book

Janvier's work *Haïti aux Haïtiens* was published in Haiti within a context of political turmoil and tensions between the international powers of the time.[8] These powers were looking to strengthen their

---

[7] There exist different types of possible readings of a text or an essay, as is the case here. There is analytical reading, cursory reading, methodical reading, concise reading, selective or spot reading, and active reading. Here, I envision active reading like a dialogue between the work's author and myself, the critic or analyst. In that sense, I give the floor to the author in my own work to better broadcast his thinking. On essay analysis, see Jérôme Roger, *La Critique littéraire* (Paris: Armand Colin, 2001 [1997]); Catherine Fromilhague, *Les Figures de style* (Paris: Armand Colin, 2007 [1995]); José Luis Gómez Martínez, *Teoría del ensayo* (Mexico City: Universidad Nacional Autónoma de México, 1992); Charles E. Bressler, *Literacy Criticism: An Introduction to Theory and Practice*, 3rd ed. (Upper Saddle River: Pearson Prentice Hall, 2003); Edouardo Villarreal Cantú and Victor Hugo Martínez González, eds., *(Pre) Textos para el análisis político. Disciplinas, reglas y procesos* (Mexico City: FLACSO, 2010).

[8] Janvier lived in Paris when his pamphlet was published. Like the young students and others who received grants from the Haitian government in France, he was involved in his country's politics. He defended President Lysius Félicité Salomon's regime. In my opinion, *Haïti aux Haïtiens* was primarily aimed at the Haitian public, but the author also wanted to address international public opinion indirectly, especially the French public. (France maintained a trusteeship relationship with the Republic of Haiti, its former colony). The book had two successive editions in 1884, which suggests that the author, an affable man, prodigal son, young social theorist, found the desired success in local bookstores, the literary salons, and amongst the Haitian colony living in Paris and within intellectual circles and the political milieu in Haiti. Janvier was well aware of his opuscule's possible impact. In general his texts caused a sensation due to their polemical nature; they were read, commented upon, and criticized by liberals and the enemies of the National Party, and especially by President Salomon. One should recall that the Paris-residing Janvier was not the only one publishing in France. The intellectuals and novelists of the time who were great apologists of "local color" in their works, Haitian literati of all stripes, whether residing in Paris or not, afforded themselves the luxury of publishing the works of their lives in France. The most well-known social theorists, such as Edmond Paul, Demesvar Delorme, Anténor Firmin, Frédéric Marcelin, and of course Janvier, also published the majority of their works in the former motherland, which they generally considered to be "Haiti's cultural metropole."

influence in certain geographic areas, through capital investments to capture markets as well as through military might to impose their domination. Haiti was very much sought after due to its enviable position in the Caribbean Sea. Naval demonstrations in its territorial waters really set the country on this path. Indeed, for every little thing, the powers of the time sent their fleets into Port-au-Prince's harbor at will with a view to having their desiderata respected. From the 1860s through 1880, Haiti suffered the weight of these powers' authority. Serious concerns were accumulating, to the beat of political threats and diplomatic disputes that were often to the country's disadvantage. Figures from the Haitian power elite thought Haiti's independence was compromised, despite the formal diplomatic recognition it enjoyed on the international stage.

Haiti's independence, object of national pride, was sometimes, either due to the reprehensible actions of Haitian politicians, or due to repeated aggressions by the great powers, a major source of concern in various sectors of national life. There were thus apprehensions in the national public opinion about the country's future. Janvier interpreted these concerns, rightly writing in *Haïti aux Haïtiens*: "The Haitian nation is warned. It is threatened on all sides; some do it cynically, the others hypocritically. They conspire, they plot, they scheme against it, some in broad daylight, others in the shadows."[9] This work marks a time of great anxiety in the evolution of the Haitian state and it also represents a breviary of resistance to consolidate the gains of national independence and build the Haitian nation on the foundations of the integration of the "wounded social majority" (the peasants).

Now we have only to ask ourselves what are the main ideas that Janvier expounded upon in this pamphlet that has grabbed our attention. In my opinion, in this work, Janvier revealed to the public, if it was still necessary to do so, the ideological, nationalist, and *classist* leanings of his thought. Moreover, he tackled a new theme in the political debate of the time that, on the one hand, shocked not a few people and, on the other, opened new prospects for social coexistence in the evolution of the Haitian people. He took on the important question of the nation at a time of political conflicts and social turbulence in Haiti.[10]

9 Janvier, *Haiti for the Haitians*, 71.
10 This turbulent period was marked by the civil war pitting the Liberals, led by Jean-Pierre Boyer Bazelais, the main leader of the Liberal Party, against the regime of the Nationals, led by President Lysius Félicité Salomon between May and September 1883. On this topic, see Max A. Antoine, *Louis-Etienne Lysius Salomon, jeune* (Port-au-Prince: Imprimerie Henri Deschamps, 1968); Jean

A strident literary critic, Dr. Duraciné Vaval, who was not always well disposed towards Dr. Louis Joseph Janvier, went as far as to write that the latter's work embodied the national ideal:

> "His work embodies the national ideal. Admirable work! Immense and majestic! It is a monument adapted to the needs of our people and reflects its aspirations, its hardship, its distress! The man who executed the work enjoyed great renown. His books are rare fruit fallen from a tree whose roots plunge into the depths of our soil."[11]

Vaval did not know how well he spoke. Indeed, *Haïti aux Haïtiens* is among those of Janvier's works that plunge their roots into Haiti's depths. The author was careful to expose the motivations that guided him in its publication. Indeed, he wrote in the Foreword: "Out of all civil war, a nation should emerge strengthened, wiser, more unified, more courageous in order to hear all truths, all revelations."[12]

All truths, all revelations, that is saying a lot! The author's choice is based on his involvement—through his pen—in the turbulent sphere of politics. In that sense, one year after the publication of the text *Haïti aux Haïtiens*, he revealed:

> I lived my first twenty-two years in my country, in immediate and daily contact with artisans, peasants, the literate. They told me everything: their struggles and defeats, their hopes and their despair, their joy and their pain [...] I feel it is my duty to fight against the doctrines of their former exploiters. I feel that I am wholly a man of the people, a peasant; I am the culmination of a long series of oppressed and wounded people.[13]

The book's title, *Haïti aux Haïtiens*, is a direct reference to the Monroe Doctrine: "America for Americans."[14] Janvier paraphrased

---

Price-Mars, *Jean-Pierre Boyer Bazelais et le drame de Miragoâne, 1883–1884* (Port-au-Prince: Imprimerie de l'État, 1948).

11 Duraciné Vaval, *Histoire de la littérature haïtienne ou l'âme noire* (Port-au-Prince: Imprimerie Auguste Héraux, 1933), 327.

12 Janvier, *Haiti for the Haitians*, 47. Janvier was referring to the recent civil war (May–September 1883) pitting Salomon's government against the Liberals led by Jean-Pierre Boyer Bazelais.

13 Louis Joseph Janvier, *Les Constitutions d'Haïti (1801–1885)* (Paris: Marpon et Flammarion, 1886), 620.

14 The Monroe Doctrine was the international policy of the United States promoted by President James Monroe. The doctrine was launched with a

this American doctrine and put it in Haitian nationalist style. Thus, it is to be expected that in its content, the book would reflect the nationalist sentiment of certain social groups of the time, particularly the subalterns, the peasants, the social class of the dominated that the author, in his world vision and political ideology, tried to transcribe in this book.

The book is comprised of five essays. The first four ("The Gluttonous and the Naïve", "The Watchword," "Our Good Friends," "Clarion Call," "Our Adjacent Islands") were planned to appear in the newspaper *La Nation* in Haiti. The fifth and final essay, "The Trap," was to be published elsewhere. In the heat of the moment (at the turning point of the civil war between the Nationals and the Liberals), the author decided to unite them and to publish them in a pamphlet entitled *Haïti aux Haïtiens*. This pamphlet is in fact a militant work, Janvier's way of defending the cause that seemed to him just and that was in the interest of the national collective.

Upon analysis, Janvier took on several matters of general interest in this text. I present four of them:

a) The vision of an autonomous political economy founded on national production;

b) National sovereignty and a critical gaze on the United States of America;

c) The matter of capital, wealth production, political stability as guarantor of economic development;

d) The project of nation building or the fundamental questions relative to the territory, to the population, and to agrarian reform.

---

speech given in 1823. In this historic speech, the North American head of state warned the European powers, after the declaration of independence of numerous countries and territories of South America, not to intervene in the affairs of the new independent states. The Monroe Doctrine could be summed up as America for Americans. At the time, this doctrine meant that the American continent should belong solely to inhabitants of the Americas. With time and the rise of the United States' power in the affairs of the continent and the world, the Monroe Doctrine has been interpreted, in certain political and diplomatic milieus, as America for the U.S.A. On the Monroe Doctrine, see, among others, Reginald Stuart, *War and American Thought: From the Revolution to the Monroe Doctrine* (Kent, OH: Kent State University Press, 1982); Ernest R. May, *Making of the Monroe Doctrine* (Cambridge, MA: Belknap Press of Harvard University Press, 1975).

These four issues will be expounded upon in turn.[15] I draw attention to the fact that two of them are economic in nature (the first and the third), the second has to do with politics, and the fourth analyzes the problem of the nation, strictly speaking.

The vision of an autonomous political economy based on national production

The matter of political economy in Janvier's work refers to his conception of politics, of the economy, and of the intrinsic relations that exist between them. This vision can be seen on two levels; better yet, it refers to a scalable methodology. Indeed, the author established two successive phases: one of agriculture production, intense even, to enrich the country, and an industrial phase, by adapting foreign industries into the national economy. On this matter, he wrote: "one can only go from an agricultural phase to an industrial one by perfecting one's agriculture, to first enrich oneself to a certain point, then, to adapt foreign industries at home after having introduced them."[16] Elsewhere, wanting to show the justice or the soundness of this vision of economy by stages, he states peremptorily: "[n]o country evades this evolution because it is natural, necessary. It is the only one that is reasonable and serious."[17]

This scalable political economy had a strong nationalist accent. On this matter, Janvier wrote: "[l]et us borrow neither a penny nor a doubloon either from the United States or from any transatlantic power."[18] To have the means for such a policy, he recommended that "[a] purely national financial policy" be put into place:

---

15 My essay contains several quotations from *Haïti aux Haïtiens*. I believe quotations are necessary in this type of exercise. Must I emphasize that I am myself an advocate of storytelling? It is with great pleasure that I note that some time ago now there was a return to narration in the Western intellectual and academic world, influenced by postmodernism. See on this topic, Lawrence Stone, "The Revival of Narrative: Reflections on a New Old History," *Past & Present* no. 85 (1979): 3–24. At home in Haiti, we maintain this devotion to the tale, life histories, and stories of life that are told to others orally. It is also to respond to this tradition of "oraliture" we practise in the country that is translated into literature, linguistics, history, and anthropology, and even in everyday life that I include quotations. For us, the storytellers pass the speech on to actors in their path. Janvier wrote his thought like he spoke to his audience, so there is no better interpreter of his ideas than the author himself.

16 Janvier, *Haiti for the Haitians*, 65.

17 Ibid.

18 Ibid., 68.

Founding Theorist of the Haitian Nation 195

We can and we should. Let us not consolidate our debts. This is extremely important. Along with indirect contributions, let us establish direct taxes. Let us seek Haitian savings for the capital we need by creating savings banks, and through them, popular banks for peasants and artisans.[19]

Janvier reaffirmed his nationalist doctrine based on the autonomy and independence of Haiti, on which he indicated: "[w]hat matters above all is that Haitians be the only masters in autonomous, independent Haiti."[20] That is what he summarized with the slogan: *Haiti for Haitians!* Moreover, he emphasized: "[t]hat is what our ancestors intended. It is also what the black race wants."[21] In his view, in order for Haiti to remain independent, it had to promote the State's neutrality, if not that of the entire island of Haiti, composed of the Republic of Haiti and the Dominican Republic, on the international scene.[22] In addition, and it may surprise some, this scalable political economy had a religious consonance. Janvier himself, raised in his father's Protestant faith, imagined that Haiti would adopt the Protestant faith for its full material and spiritual evolution. On this, he declared:

Let us also try to increase the number of Protestants in the country, thus making it undergo a rapid evolution from fetishism[23] to Catholicism to Protestantism, as fast, as transformative [...] All that negotiates, cultivates, fabricates, wins, enriches, prospers,

---

19 Ibid.
20 Ibid., 56.
21 Ibid., 55. We are to understand that Janvier justified his nationalist ideology by basing himself on the separatist vision of the founding fathers, drawing especially close to the stature of Dessalines, whom he would rehabilitate a year later in *Les Constitutions d'Haïti*. On the other hand, we should note that this nationalist ideology of Janvier's followed a straight line from the liberation of the peoples of the black continent who were at the time, in the great majority, under the colonial domination of the European powers.
22 We should recall that Janvier had already promoted Haiti's neutrality on the international scene in order to guarantee its independence: see *La République d'Haïti*, 597–614.
23 He is most likely referring to Vodou, a set of sacred rituals and religious practices originating in Africa. In Janvier's time, Vodou was practiced in Haiti by a lage number of people, including peasants and city folk. However, continuing a colonial-era tradition, the practice of Vodou was often criminalized by the Haitian political authorities. See on this topic Kate Ramsey, *The Spirits and the Law: Vodou and Power in Haiti* (Chicago: University of Chicago Press, 2011). Today, Vodou is emerging from its historical confinement.

is Protestant [...] Through Protestantism, everyone will learn to recognize their rights and their duties. That is the policy to adopt. It is that of the healthy and the mighty. It is the great, the good, the scientific one. It is there that we will find salvation and nowhere else.[24]

We find here, in the Protestant Janvier, the pretty speech spread by the followers of Anglo-Saxon ideology, notably in the United Kingdom and the United States of America, making Protestantism a major vector of capitalist development.[25] However, on the political and economic levels, Janvier's vision of political economy went hand in hand with the project of an endogenous economy, even approaching autarky. He asked his compatriots to have faith, to trust in themselves in order to defend the homeland's interests. "Let us see the individual and the family less; let us see only the State, the nation."[26]

Despite Janvier's fierce defense of national sovereignty, he had in a way mellowed his thought, knowing that there are no absolutes in political economy. In that way, he claimed that if the country still had to sign contracts with foreigners, those contracts should be discussed in the press and known by all, for there was a risk of them containing traps and "thousands of pitfalls."[27] Finally, his directive was to concede nothing to foreigners, except advisedly, in order not to tie the hands of future generations:

24 Janvier, *Haiti for the Haitians*, 70–71.
25 This discourse was systematized by the German thinker and sociologist Max Weber, especially in his *Éthique protestante et l'Esprit du Capitalisme*. In that work, Weber defends the idea that Protestant countries such as the Netherlands, England, Scotland, and Germany have attained a higher level of capitalist development than others. He added that even in countries with other religions, businesses led by Protestants have more success than others. One might remark that the great theorist Max Weber does not have exclusive ownership of this thesis. Janvier had already spread such ideas in 1884; the first edition of Max Weber's work appeared in 1904–1905, and the first translation into French in 1930. That is to say that well before Weber, Janvier had linked success and economic development with Protestantism. He had even asked that Haiti be "Protestantized." On the other hand, the request to "Protestantize" the country (at the time, Protestants were an exogenous element of Haitian society, or at least a minority) reveals an ambiguity in his political thought. That is to say a mix of "endogeneity" and "exogeneity." This ambiguity is not completely surprising on the part of a thinker of a former French colony, Saint-Domingue, now Haiti. It is the ideological framework of postcoloniality, as expressed in the important works of authors from the independent states emancipated from European powers!
26 Janvier, *Haiti for the Haitians*, 69.
27 Ibid., 56.

[T]oday everyone knows that we must abandon absolutes, especially in political economy; that we must practice free trade or protection, or both at the same time, according to whether the interests of the country demand it, because, now more than ever, monopoly is contrary to all the healthy ideas of democratic policy and national dignity; because, as far as we are directly concerned, it would kill our commerce, our agriculture, by killing our initiative and our youthful expansion.[28]

National sovereignty and a critical view of the United States of America

Janvier's nationalist ideology has historic origins; it goes back to the time of the proclamation of national independence and the formation of the Haitian state under Emperor Jacques I. Meaning around 1804–1806. In his work, the author promotes the Dessalinian ideal. More precisely, in the pamphlet *Haïti aux Haïtiens*, Janvier restores strength and vigor to Dessalines's ban. This political principle, which became a nationalist credo adopted under Dessalines's regime, which consisted of not according even a parcel of land in Haiti to any foreigner. He maintained that the country should continue to evolve and prosper without the help of those foreigners who were on the lookout for the Haitian people's weaknesses in order to enslave them for their sole benefit.

Faced with the siren song coming from all sides (especially from the U.S.A. and Germany at the time), Janvier proposed an autonomist policy for Haiti. Indeed, he recommended that no treaty be concluded with any power. According to him, even if those powers pronounced themselves in favor of Haiti and accorded to it the privilege of most favored nation, in the end, those treaties would turn out to be prejudicial to the country and beneficial only to them. He thought that such treaties were used for deception, to "kill the independence of certain small countries" like Haiti.[29]

Janvier declared himself in favor of keeping Haiti's natural resources for Haitians. Consequently, it goes without saying that he was against any idea of according foreigners any role in the country's affairs. He insisted upon the idea of neither leasing nor ceding the country's strategic points to foreign powers. On that subject, he wrote peremptorily:

28 Ibid., 64.
29 Ibid., 62.

> We should be wary of leasing La Gonâve and La Tortue to foreigners of whose true address we are not even sure. Whatever the nationality to which they say they belong, we cannot place them in these outposts of our nation. Thus is stoked the hope of stealing La Gonâve just as la Navase was taken from us [...] We need to redouble our surveillance around Môle-Saint-Nicolas [...] What reason do we have to break up our national patrimony? And especially to part with the best pieces? ...[30]

Further, he denounced the behavior of certain foreigners he called gluttons, who seem nice and charming towards Haiti and Haitians, but in reality are hypocrites and disrespectful. He emphasized that when amongst themselves, they call us "a people of monkeys." "Everywhere, they have spread the news that we are savages in order to better intimidate us and to better fleece us; those who licked our hand at home called us monkeys in Europe."[31]

Moreover, Janvier added that foreigners promise all kinds of wonders to Haiti, some asking for La Gonâve island, others showing interest in La Tortue island, and still others asking for Haitian subsoil. They promise to cover the country in sugar factories, railroads, canals, telegraphs, bridges, lighthouses, and aqueducts. In truth, they have nothing to offer: they are "as poor as church mice."[32] According to him, these foreigners, gluttons and opportunists, are only interested in Haiti with the objective of arranging their own affairs, often through scams, rather than creating wealth for the country.

Going from the general to arrive at the specific, Janvier had warnings against the United States of America. In fact, Janvier's critical position towards that country, an emerging power at the time, was already announced in his *La République d'Haïti et ses visiteurs*. Indeed, in that book, he had written:

> The Yankees readily say "America for Americans." May Haitians not forget to loudly cry: Haiti for Haitians! We should say it for a hundred thousand reasons, the least of which is this: Haiti is a Black Latin civilization. It must exist and develop to affirm this truth, that the black race is perfectly sociable [...] and that it can perfectly govern and administrate itself.[33]

---

30 Ibid., 67–68.
31 Ibid., 55.
32 Ibid., 48.
33 Janvier, *La République d'Haïti*, 122–123.

Founding Theorist of the Haitian Nation 199

In the same work, Janvier had noted that the American had a (big) fault: "that of believing that all of America should be a vast colony or branch of the United States."³⁴ We can understand that two years later, in 1884, the anxious gaze he had cast upon the northern colossus had not changed. In this text, *Haïti aux Haïtiens*, Janvier demonstrated his concerns about seeing the Haitian Republic fall under the domination of its North American neighbor. His concerns were expressed on both the political and economic levels.

On the political level, Janvier emphasized: "it is to be feared that the future American president, who has always demanded and will demand voting for substantial funds for the Federal Navy, may want to immediately take up the annexation policy of President Grant and Frederick Douglass."³⁵ On the economic level (notably in the chapter on commercial exchanges), Janvier specified that "[a]lmost half of our importation traffic is with the United States alone [...] It would be supreme folly to escape from one economic vassalage [with France] only to fall into one that is more onerous, heavier, and more limiting [with the USA]."³⁶ He continues: "[a] country that respects itself can only escape economic serfdom by creating national industries, by providing itself what it used to buy elsewhere."³⁷

Nonetheless, we must understand that Janvier was not necessarily anti-American as is claimed today; he was a Haitian patriot who promoted national sovereignty. To that end, he emphasized:

> We, Western Haitians, [the Republic of Haiti], we have nothing but sympathy and admiration for the federal republic, but not for anything in the world would we want the island of Haiti to become a colony or even a State of the Northern Confederation. We have been masters in our own home for a mere eighty years. We would never want to lose our rank. We do not want to lower ourselves. We want to be neither valets nor vassals.³⁸

Janvier knew how to make allowances. Did he recognize that in the turbulent political conjuncture in which he published his text, American policy was favorable to the government of President Lysius

---

34 Ibid., 105.
35 Janvier, *Haiti for the Haitians*, 59. The author was referring here to the attempt by the Grant administration to annex the Dominican Republic to the United States in 1869–1871.
36 Ibid., 65.
37 Ibid.
38 Ibid., 61.

Salomon, as attested by its attitude during the events in Port-au-Prince on September 23, 1883? He signaled that that was no reason to be sentimental, to take something away from one power and give it to another. In sum, he repeated to his compatriots: "[l]et us implement a scientific policy, a policy based on self-interest." So saying, he wanted to enjoin his compatriots to not give in to the bribes and pressures of foreign powers, to put the country's interests first according to an elaborated plan, a well-defined program.[39]

Janvier was consistent. In defending Haiti's national sovereignty, he took on the problem of the capital necessary for production and the country's socioeconomic development.

The matter of capital, wealth production, political stability as guarantor of economic development

The matter of capital formation and wealth creation is a central theme in Janvier's nationalist discourse. He had recommended to his compatriots that they not engage in foreign loans. He had promoted instead asset and capital formation on the national market. He heavily emphasized: "[c]ounting on oneself is the greatest of strengths." He further emphasized that the Haitian soil is full of capital; the crux of the matter is to generate it and make it fructify:

> Haitians have more capital than they realize. The key is to make this capital emerge from the hiding places where it is held, beneath the earth. To do so, we must put it at ease by guaranteeing peace, discipline it by creating savings banks, use it via popular banks, purely national credit institutions.[40]

---

39 Janvier wanted to be as precise as possible in his warning. In the chapter of *Haiti for the Haitians* entitled "Watchword" he signaled that since 1862, the year it recognized Haiti's independence, the first republic of the Americas (the U.S.A.) had been looking to exert political influence over the second independent republic of the American continent. This will to subjugate Haiti was repudiated by Janvier. This manifest will of the U.S.A. went even further, during the 1880s the United States was looking to appropriate strategic points in Haiti, including the lease of the much-discussed Môle-Saint-Nicolas, located in the Caribbean Sea, in order to establish a coaling station and a replenishing port for American Navy ships. On this topic, see Watson Denis, "Miradas de mutua des confianza entre dos repúblicas americanas: el expansionismo estadounidense frente a la francofilia haitana (1888–1898)" (PhD diss., University of Puerto Rico, 2004; published by University of Michigan Microfilms, Ann Arbor, 2005).

40 Janvier, *Haiti for the Haitians*, 53–54.

As far as exploitation of the country's natural resources was concerned, Janvier indicated that there was no rush. Haiti could evolve according to its own rhythm, its own interests. He was convinced that Haitians could build a solid economy capable of getting them prosperity, happiness, and the material wealth necessary for the population's fulfillment. Basing himself on the past, he stated: "[u]ntil now, we have rebuilt our cities ourselves, without anyone's help, we have plowed our fields, sowed, planted, and harvested. We can continue to manage our own affairs."[41] In line with this vision of a Haitian economy fortified by itself, the author pronounced himself against the consolidation of Haiti's national debt that was strongly encouraged by the financial sectors of the outside world. He indicated that foreign powers proposed the consolidation of its debt (interior and foreign) with a view towards the country attaining economic prosperity, but in fact they only wanted to get rich on Haiti's back. For him, once Haiti's debt was consolidated, financial syndicates, belonging to such foreign powers, would immediately appear to take over the country's economy and impose a political and financial protectorate upon it. From political and financial protectorate to definitive annexation, there is but one step.

Living with the fear of one day seeing Haiti succumb to the domination of one of the world's powers, he heavily emphasized that "our mines and quarries, the forests of our adjacent islands, we will exploit them on our own, later, in the person of our children."[42]

The author of *Haïti aux Haïtiens* also imagined the application of his autonomist economic policy in a stable and prosperous Haiti. Thus, he strongly recommended that his compatriots take the road of political stability in order to achieve the economic prosperity they dreamed of: "[l]et us stifle any thought of insurrection by erasing all traces of civil war, but let us also prepare to manfully and mercilessly repress through scientific means any insurrectional attempt that might occur."[43] To ground his governing principle in stability, he added a strong argument: "[w]ealth is the daughter of credit; credit can only be born in the shade of peace, security, stability"[44]

The matter of political stability in Haiti was thus an essential theme in Janvier's thought. In fact, he scrutinized different aspects of it. He approached it from the angle of political debate, negotiations between

41 Ibid., 77.
42 Ibid., 50.
43 Ibid., 69.
44 Ibid.

competing parties for the exercise of political power and from the angle of resolving the causes that generate it, repeatedly. Let us say that he approached it from the structural and circumstantial angles.[45] On the structural angle, he explained that:

> The Haitian nation will only be happy when it is peaceful, peaceful when it is enlightened, enlightened the day when to sentimental politics, which foment conspiracies, it prefers scientific policy, which prevents them; it will be rich and respected above all the day it instills democratic policy, the policy of the majority of interests, the policy of the greatest number. Outside of that, there will always be waste or even chaos, stagnation or even regression.[46]

On the circumstantial angle, he wrote:

> Civil war is the most hateful, the most ignoble, the most wretched thing there is. Here it is to no one's glory to have shown bravery during the fratricidal battles that bloodied the country [...] As brave as one might imagine oneself to be, we are no longer brave when, being able to, instead of shedding light on the country's true interests, one takes up arms to kill one's compatriot on the pretext of giving him illusory freedoms. For a sentimental people starving for justice, such as the Haitian people, all matters can be resolved through discussion.[47]

Whichever angle one considers, it is clear Janvier strongly condemned the series of civil wars that had Haitian national life in mourning. He promoted political stability, conducive, according to him, to helping the country advance in the production of capital, wealth, and socioeconomic development.

Of nation building or matters related to the territory's defense, to the population's well-being, and agrarian reform

Everything I have identified so far in *Haïti aux Haïtiens* on political economy, national sovereignty, capital formation, and wealth creation as well as on political stability is tied to the project of nation building in

---

45 The author expounded on this theme in one of his pivotal works, *Les Constitutions d'Haïti*.
46 Janvier, *Les Constitutions d'Haïti*, 264–265.
47 Ibid., 338.

Haiti. This Haitian nation, dreamed of, imagined by Janvier, was based on at least three levels:

- Defense of the territory (the political aspect or the projection of the Haitian state in the concert of nations);
- The population's well-being (the social aspect or a fundamental indicator which defines the relations between inhabitants of the same State);
- Agrarian reform (the economic aspect or the projection of the State's economic development itself).

a) *Defense of the national territory*

On the matter of Haiti's territory, Janvier wrote:

> This piece of land where we are masters and that we keep with such jealous care for our great-nephews, we have paid for it three times. We first bought it in the person of our ancestors, and paid with two centuries of tears and sweat, then we paid for it with an immense amount of blood, and then we paid for it with 120 million in silver [...] One hundred twenty million in silver, from 1825 to 1880! That is a pretty penny![48]

Janvier thus showed that Haiti belonged *de jure* and *de facto* to the Haitians. The territory so dearly acquired by them could not be handed over to foreigners for a mess of pottage. In his words, "[w]e have to safeguard the legacy passed down to us by the Haitians of yesteryear, free from any mortgage, free from any humiliating contract, in order to pass it down intact to the Haitians of the future."[49]

The matter of the adjacent islands and strategic points of the country, lusted over by the great powers of the time, also captured his attention. Once more his thoughts were of the order of safeguarding the Haitian patrimony, which should be managed by Haitians:

> La Gonâve is a strategic position of the utmost importance. It is the most basic of policies that it be leased only to Haitians, exploited only by Haitians [...] The same goes for La Tortue [Island]. Môle-Saint-Nicolas can be made a free port, never a free city.
>
> Free port, it remains ours; free city, it escapes us.[50]

---

48 Janvier, *La République d'Haïti*, 17.
49 Janvier, *Haiti for the Haitians*, 50–51.
50 Ibid., 49–50.

b) *The population's well-being, especially the social emancipation of the peasants*

Janvier took up the cause of the peasants in every circumstance. Their social flourishing and their economic ease constituted an important element of his political vision. He returned several times to the important matter of peasants and farmers in their relationship with the state power elite. He pled for their integration to the fullest extent possible into the nation in the making. He thought mere political freedom without economic freedom was insufficient. Rather, he believed that the economic liberation of this "wounded social majority" would allow it to better work the land, make it fructify as much as possible, and live with the appropriate comfort and amenities. On this matter, his thought was expressed in these terms:

> It is not enough to cry: Freedom! Freedom! We must guarantee that freedom by ensuring the independence of the greatest number, that of the peasants, the artisans. It is social liberties that allow the flourishing of political freedoms. If the former are only enjoyed by a small number of individuals from the middle classes, their existence is precarious; it remains at the mercy of the first popular tyrant, the first corporal to win a riot.[51]

Along the same lines, he thought economic liberation would stimulate the peasants, that it would, for example, allow them to compete with peasants in America:

> It is the fight that makes the fighter. In order for the Haitian peasant to quickly become a well-rounded man, we must train him to be courageous and put him in a position to look all the peasants around the world in the eye. That is why we must teach him to know his rights and his duties. It is the economic fight that will force the Haitian peasant to work the soil, in order that our country can better compete, on that front, with Brazil, Venezuela, Martinique, Ceylon, and San Salvador.[52]

c) *The promotion of agrarian reform*

Janvier had entered into a true battle for the distribution of land to peasants, the very people who worked it day in and day out:

> We have to return to the small property system in the mountains as

---

[51] Janvier, *Les Constitutions d'Haïti*, 530–531.
[52] Janvier, *Haiti for the Haitians*, 63.

well as in the plains. In a country like ours, given the climate and the political system, it is the most rational. We have to divide the large plantations that belong to the State. Before anything else, let us return the land to the peasant's hands.[53]

It is worth noting that Janvier was not a simple proponent of land distribution to the peasants; as he argued at one point: "[t]he division by head of conquered lands over the former landholders."[54] He spoke out for true agrarian reform in the country.[55] He tirelessly wrote on this fundamental matter, not only to influence Lysius Salomon's government, but also to sensitize the members of the National Party, its supporters, and public opinion. Thus, he criticized the fact that after the independence proclamation, "[w]e stopped at a hybrid stratagem which created a land aristocracy in favor of the big farmers and large property owners, a rural proletariat to the detriment of the former slaves. This stratagem would later unfailingly bring about civil war, class struggle, and hatred of the exploiters on the part of the exploited."[56]

---

53 Ibid., 69.
54 Janvier, *Les Constitutions d'Haïti*, 483.
55 After Haiti's proclamation of independence, the majority of slaves turned farmers ardently wished for agrarian reform, or at least land distribution, the principal means of production at the time. Their hope was vain, their wait ignored. Yes, General Alexandre Pétion (1806–1818), after having satisfied the gargantuan appetite for landed property of the generals from the western and southern departments who surrounded him in power, had started a distribution of land to some middle cadres of the army and to a few soldiers, but this policy of cooptation was biased and partial. Later, within the context of the political crisis of 1843–1848, the Piquets of the south took up arms in 1844–1845 to invite the power elite to undertake reforms at the level of the state and in society more generally, but they were defeated and the agrarian reform they demanded was postponed indefinitely. Nonetheless, under Lysius Salomon's government, the matter of agrarian reform returned to the forefront. This government had even adopted a law on land management and exploitation, in 1882; however, there was no follow-through on the initiative, of which Janvier wrote that he had been the instigator. What is certain is that in 1886, in *Les Constitutions d'Haïti*, he had asked the government of Lysius Salomon, like him a member of the National Party, "to operate the most just, the most economic, the most opportune, the best of reforms by granting freehold land to this interesting being, who is however so slandered by his traditional exploiters, so deprived of true belongings: the peasant" (*Les Constitutions d'Haïti*, 421). To my knowledge, no renowned personality other than Janvier raised this important matter of agrarian reform.
56 Janvier, *Les Constitutions d'Haïti*, 482–483. I take the liberty of quoting Janvier's other works besides *Haiti for Haitians*. These quotations attest to his position in favor of the peasants and farmers. If we willingly admit that an

Janvier firmly believed that agrarian reform remained the primary political option to resolve Haiti's notorious social question. For him, agrarian reform could emancipate the peasants from an economic standpoint and socially democratize the country once and for all. His demand, the claim he was making in the name of peasants and farmers, was revealed as a cry of alarm:

> The great reform, the primary one, the one which should be the base and the backbone, the one without which no other can be seriously realized, concerns [the peasants] and should concern them more than anything else. They want to see it through before all else. Land to the peasants, that is the keystone of the reconstruction, the cement of the general system, the granite foundation on which we can build everything else, construct everything, scaffold everything. It is the essential evolution. All else will follow.[57]

To justify his demand for agrarian reform, he emphasized that since the country's independence, peasants had always lived a situation of semi-bondage. Although they represented the nation's bedrock, the nation still treated them like pariahs.[58] In this, the author sympathized with the peasants and farmers of the post-independence period involved in the protest movement for land appropriation led by Goman (real name Jean-Baptiste Perrier), from 1804 to 1820 to the Piquets movement (1843–1848) under the name of the Army of Sufferers and under the leadership established by Jean-Jacques Acaau. These two protest

---

author writes only one work during his life, that is to say that he is driven by a great problem that he can describe in several works, in various ways, spread out over several years, Janvier carried the flame of the redemption of peasants and farmers in Haitian society through several texts. He remained true to his political and ideological choices in favor of the wounded social class. In other works following *Haiti for Haitians*, he again took up his emancipatory message in favor of peasants. In a reflection on "the social question," he also argued that peasants represented the social question in Haiti. See Louis-Joseph Janvier, *Les Affaires d'Haïti (1883–1884)* (Paris: C. Marpon et E. Flammarion, 1885), 56.

57 Louis-Joseph Janvier, *L'Égalité des races* (Paris: Imprimerie G. Rougier et Cie., 1884), 11.

58 Janvier, *Les Affaires d'Haïti*, 56. Janvier referred to the system of semi-bondage in which the political elite maintained the peasants and farmers: placed in service of the state and in service of those who enjoyed state benefits. This social domination was systematized in 1826 with the rural code adopted under the presidency of Jean-Pierre de Boyer, who imposed a taxation regime on agricultural work that fell upon the social class of the wounded.

movements, in different historical contexts, demanded agrarian liberation and the participation of the wounded social class in the country's affairs.

Janvier's critics condemned him for his promotion of *minifundia* (small property) in Haiti to the detriment of *latifundia* (large property); he replied that in Haiti it was necessary to have a community of citizen owners; landownership is the thing that ties them to the country, to the State, and to their compatriots. According to Janvier, what formats the citizen's soul is the property of the great majority of the population, that is to say the peasants:

> Small property is neither a cause of impoverishment nor a danger; on the contrary it offers all sorts of advantages, it uses the soil where large property which only creates agricultural proletarians would leave everything fallow; small property renders peasants independent, foresighted, patriotic; in a word, it shapes [the soul of] citizens.[59]

In fact, Janvier never stopped claiming land for peasants and farmers, more specifically, agrarian reform, which according to him was a vital economic reform to concretize the project of nation building. He did so before the publication of *Haïti aux Haïtiens* and continued to do so after.[60]

Janvier: Thinker of the Haitian nation

Since the social movement (1843–1848), the Haitian power elite, worried about the continuity of its political domination, began trying to find a path through State consolidation.[61] It thus offered a project of top-down power. It was a political project that was both elitist and conservative, centered around the State. Then Janvier came along, and shifted the focus of the political debate, moving it from the State to the nation.

---

59 Janvier, *Les Constitutions d'Haïti*, 228.
60 Indeed, in *Le Vieux piquet (scènes de la vie haïtienne)* (Paris: A. Parent, 1884) and *Les Constitutions d'Haïti* (1885), Janvier continued his plea for agrarian reform, or at the very least for land distribution to peasants. Nevertheless, agrarian reform is a structural or fundamental political reform that has never taken place in Haiti.
61 See Michel Hector, "La Participation populaire dans la crise 1843–1848," in *Crise et mouvements populaires en Haïti* (Montreal: Éditions du CIDIHCA, 2000), 99–155.

Janvier's pamphlet *Haïti aux Haïtiens* is a militant book that promotes his vision of Haiti as much on the political level as on the economic and social. It is a patriotic work, written by an author with a nationalist vision of things; at the same time, he took it upon himself to promote a sovereign and integrated project of a Haitian nation yet to be built. Without a doubt, the civil war (1883–1884) that opposed the Nationals in power and the Liberals in search of power showed Janvier that Haiti had to progress differently than before. The country had to move towards the constitution of the nation.

This polemical text, written in the heat of a great political crisis, still marks a turning point in the period's historiography, if not in Haitian social thought in general. Before this work, discussions focused on State reform; indeed, political discourse prioritized the State's political power through the military institution or the State's capacity to intervene within society. On the whole, historians, writers, and ideologues of both political parties of Janvier's time, the Liberal party and the National party, knew how to discuss the Haitian state's formation, its reconstruction; debating the specific issue of the nation was unusual. Moreover, discussing it from the angle of the political and economic inclusion of peasants and farmers was even rarer.

From the point of view of the movement of ideas or the history of social thought in nineteenth-century Haiti, we can certainly find writers who pled for changes to be instituted in the country, but they did not directly tackle the question of the nation. I am thinking specifically of Baron de Vastey, the brain of President Henry Christophe's regime in the north (1907–1811), then of the kingdom of Henry I (1811–1820) and Baron Émile Nau, the official intellectual figure of the newspapers. Vastey's texts tackle a variety of subjects, from politics to anthropology, from literature to history, and from the need for Haitians to unite against the racism of Whites, social prejudices, and foreign enemies, but the question of the nation is not specifically considered. An overview of the studies undertaken by the best specialist of Vastey to date, Marlene L. Daut, confirms that he did not consider the question of the nation in Haiti as Janvier did.[62]

---

62 See Marlène L. Daut, *Baron de Vastey and the Origins of Black Humanism* (New York: Palgrave Macmillan, 2017). By the same author, see *Tropics of Haiti: Race and the Literacy History of the Haitian Revolution in the Atlantic World (1789–1865)* (Liverpool: Liverpool University Press, 2015). Also see the introduction and preface, respectively, by Michel Hector and Jean Casimir of Baron de Vastey, *Le Système colonial dévoilé*, new ed. (Port-au-Prince: Société Haïtienne d'Histoire, de Géographie et de Géologie, 2013).

Perhaps that prolific thinker, gone too soon, in 1820 during the political events that did away with Henry I and his kingdom, had not yet analyzed the matter in all its complexity. As for Émile Nau, he was a thoughtful theorist who launched several newspapers and press outlets in Republic during the 1830s, including *L'Union*, *Le Républicain*, *Le Manifeste*. He most often took on the role of columnist and editor-in-chief of his newspapers. He formed the "Cenacle of 1836" with his brothers, the Ardouin brothers, and other friends belonging to Port-au-Prince's golden intellectual youth. This Cenacle composed of poets, playwrights, and future historians gave a romantic orientation to Haitian literature as well as an esthetic based on local color. We owe to Émile Nau that flavorful turn of phrase: "[w]e must darken the French language beneath the tropical sun." From 1842 to 1858, he had a political life crowned with success and he held high functions in public administration. In 1859, having fallen into political disgrace, he co-founded the newspaper *Le Patriote* and at the same time ran *La République*. Nau's known works do not permit us to consider him as an eventual theorist of the Haitian nation, as was Janvier. He no doubt awaits the historian who will eventually unearth his writings from the various newspapers he founded and with which he collaborated to define or establish his conception and eventual vision of the Haitian nation.

Starting in 1860, a new generation of poets, thinkers, writers, novelists, and men of letters emerged onto the country's literary and intellectual scene. This new generation stimulated a new aesthetic in Haitian letters; at the same time, it developed new political and economic concerns. What role would the specific theme of the nation play among the subjects raised?

From 1860 to the 1880s, authors and political writers including social theorists tackled a great variety of questions, subjects pertaining to the State, to the political system, and to national production. For example, Edmond Paul, in his three-volume book, *Questions politico-économiques*, studied the Haitian power elite's sensibility with regard to matters inherent to the population's education and the country's industrialization.[63] On his end, Demesvar Delorme, in his *La Misère au sein des richesses*,[64] analyzed the matter of national production and the outsized role accorded to the State in order to arrive at economic prosperity. For

---

63 Edmond Paul, *Questions politico-économiques*, 3 vols. (Paris: Meyris et Cie/Bourdier et Cie, 1861–1863).
64 Demesvar Delorme, *La Misère au sein des richesses, réflexions diverses sur Haïti* (Paris: E. Dentu, 1873).

his part, Anténor Firmin insisted in a chapter of his *Monsieur Roosevelt et la République d'Haïti* on the role of the State and national production via agro-industry.⁶⁵ In sum, there were very good reflections and propositions that highlighted the future of Haitian society. However, they did not take up the specific matter of the nation. In that sense, it seems to me that among the principled social theorists of Haiti's long nineteenth century, Janvier was the only one who approached it in stark terms. Surprisingly, he had posed the problematic of the nation in Haiti with regard to national production, the Haitian state's sovereign relations with foreign powers and in the context of socioeconomic relations within the country. He even went as far as to identify the social class in Haiti's social structure that could emancipate itself, to promote the production of national wealth, and to facilitate through work and social harmony the political stability necessary to the country. He named the wounded social class of peasants and farmers whom he associated with the fundamental interests of the nation. We can thus understand the opinion of Janvier's biographer, Gracia F. Isidore, who wrote that he was "the reasoned and thought-out expression of true national interests":

> Through his republicanism, he was the spokesperson of the national bourgeoisie rejected from the national combat [...] By his reformism, that of the class of artisans and rudimentary workers incapable of developing at a rapid rate; by his agrarian socialism, that of free and precarious owners and poor peasants languishing in misery with no other perspective than subsistence.⁶⁶

In sum, to my knowledge, no personality of renown other than Janvier raised this important question of agrarian reform.

Janvier, the writer, the thinker believed in the country's progress; he was a reformer, a man of ruptures, and a visionary. He dreamed of solidity, something that could really be used as a weapon. As explained by the North American historian Chelsea Stieber, Janvier rejected the republicanism established in Haiti in 1806 by Alexandre Pétion. That republicanism was a fiction, the proclaimed ideals of liberty and democracy did not match the reality of things, specifically as pertained

---

65 Anténor Firmin, *Monsieur Roosevelt, Président des Etats-Unis et la République d'Haïti* (New York and Paris: Hamilton Bank Note Engraving and Printing/F. Pichon et Durand-Auzias, 1905).

66 Isidore, Gracia F. Garcia, "Un patriote et un homme de parti: Louis Joseph Janvier," *Louis Joseph Janvier*, ed. Michel Soukar (Port-au-Prince: C3 Éditions, 2016), 43.

to the existence of peasants.⁶⁷ No doubt to remedy the situation, Janvier proposed a political project from the bottom up, a complete social revolution; he envisioned a socioeconomic integration capable of building the Haitian nation.

He dreamed of a strong and prosperous Haiti, politically and economically independent, a country in which peasants would finally be masters of their destiny and owners of the land made fruitful by their daily labor. He discerned that there would never be political stability without the satisfaction of the fundamental claims of the majority of the population, if appropriate political measures towards the satisfaction of peasants and farmers were not taken. For him the construction of the nation was a powerful beacon for the rupture of the social relations inherited from the counter-revolution begun in 1806 following the assassination of the emperor (Jean-Jacques Dessalines) and the economic and political emancipation of the subordinated classes.

Janvier is thus definitively the appointed theorist of the nation in Haiti. From a theoretical point of view, he did for Haiti what Giuseppe Mazzini did for Italy within the context of the Risorgimento or Italian unification, what Herder and Fichte established for Germany in the context of German unification, and Renan and Fustel de Coulanges systematized for France in the context of the new construction of the French nation at the end of the nineteenth century.⁶⁸

---

67 Chelsea Stieber, "The Haitian Revolution and the Myth of the Republic: Louis Joseph Janvier's Revisionist History", in *Remembering Early Modern Revolutions: England, North America, France and Haiti*, ed. Edward Vallance (London and New York: Routledge, 2019), 146.

68 The example of Italy is revealing. Although united by geography, language, and religion, the Italian peninsula was divided into several states from the end of the Roman empire. It was not until the late nineteenth century, not until the year 1870 that Italian unification became, after countless pangs, reality. And that was thanks to prominent figures such as Camillo Benso, Conte di Cavour and Giuseppe Garibaldi. See Giuseppe Mazzini, *I sistemi e la democrazia. Pensieri* (Milan: Greco & Greco, 2005) and Giuseppe Mazzini, *Duties of Man and Other Essays* (London: J.M. Dent & Sons, Ltd., 1992). In addition, on the Risorgimento, refer to Sergio Romano, *Histoire de l'Italie. Du Risorgimento à nos jours* (Paris: Seuil, 1977). Regarding Germany, Johann Gottlieb Fichte published *Les Discours à la nation allemande*, trans. Alain Renaut (Paris: Imprimerie Nationale, 1992 [1808]) and Johann Gottfried von Herder published *Traité sur l'origine des langues*, trans. Lionel Duvoy (Paris: Allia, 2010 [1771]). Finally, for France, Ernest Renan is the author of the famous speech "Qu'est-ce qu'une nation" given March 11, 1882 at the Sorbonne. For his part, Numa Denis Fustel de Coulanges published *La Cité antique* (Paris: Durand, 1864). It is important to emphasize

Janvier held the country close to his heart; he defended it tooth and nail and proposed the constitution of the nation as a remedy for the ills from which it suffered. In his words, he loved Haiti with a "furious love." In his understanding, "[l]ove of country is also a religion. From it can follow every grandeur, every virtue. It is the first and most vigorous source of honesty and honor."[69] Ah, that Janvier, always true to himself! He was a true Haitian! He was that writer, that thinker, that polemist, that social theorist, that ideologue, that doctrinarian who had a vision of the nation that included, amongst other things, defense of the territory, the preservation of natural resources, which he presented as a sacred legacy, the inclusion of peasants and farmers in the national economy, and was a defender of political stability. In a few words, Janvier can be considered the thinker, and even the (theoretical) founder, of the Haitian nation. He was that social theorist who pleaded for the true integration of the wounded social class into the economy. He also pleaded for political stability and for the country's modernization.

The man, the style, and his battle's destiny

Janvier's work leaves no one indifferent. If in some ways his thought captivates through its originality or his opinions provoke through their boldness, his writings sometimes shock some readers and disturb the narrow-minded.

In *Haïti aux Haïtiens*, Janvier revealed himself to be simultaneously a polemicist, a theorist, an ideologue, and a doctrinaire. He was a polemicist for polemics were part of his skill set as a writer and a seasoned opponent. He was a theorist because after study and considerations he arrived at precepts and conclusions on the socioeconomic realities of his milieu. He was an ideologue because he inscribed his oeuvre within the context of a political ideology he thought to be in line with the causes he was defending. That is why he specifically addressed the segments of Haitian society that he wanted to sensitize and place on the ideal path for national recovery. He was a (party) doctrinaire in offering to the members of the National Party, to which he adhered, his vision of Haiti and the ideological orientations that the party should

that Janvier opposed the great Renan, prominent intellectual figure of the time, when the latter seemed to take position in favor of the idea of the inequality of human races. Janvier then wrote his text *L'Égalité des races*, in which he criticized Renan on moral and historical grounds as well as on that of scientific reason.

69 Janvier, quoted by Marie Edouard Lenoir, "Biographie du Dr Louis-Joseph Janvier," *Le Biographe* 7, no. 5 (1884), 71.

Founding Theorist of the Haitian Nation 213

adopt in its management of State affairs. Well aware of his work's reach, he wrote: "[w]hat we are saying here must remain ingrained in the soul of each peasant and each thinker, in the mind of every soldier and every political writer, present in the memory of each deputy, each minister, each senator."[70]

Janvier's writing was direct and forceful: he wrote like he talked. He wrote especially to transcend and transform the reality on which he opined. He wanted the ink that fed his pen to be the sap that transformed the failings of the community into which he was born. His pen was always on alert; he was quick to seize it against the detractors of Haiti and the black race. In his work, he tackled the most varied themes and subjects, from anthropology to political economy, constitutional law, agrarian reform, and international relations, notably as pertained to Haiti's place in the world. *Haïti aux Haïtiens* specifically pertains to the problematic of the nation.

We must also add that Janvier was not indulging in art for art's sake. Well before Jean-Paul Sartre, for example, he theorized about the role of the committed intellectual in the city, he who published works of reflections based on the reality of his milieu, but which were also meant to contribute to the happiness of his collectivity, his community, or even the well-being of humanity. He believed that the intellectual should respond to a social cause. Which he applied by taking up for the subaltern social classes of his country, especially the peasants and the farmers of whom he declared himself the spokesperson. Janvier was thus a writer who demonstrated great social sensitivity. He conceived of an autonomous, endogenous political economy, he was a promoter of savings banks and popular credit, an advocate of social egalitarianism. He elaborated a political economy program whose integrative elements formed an autonomous and endogenous program for the renewed Haitian state and nation built on inclusive foundations.

Janvier was a social theorist, a nationalist, a harsh critic of political conservatism, a progressive author, and perhaps the most left-leaning among the social theorists of his time and even of the long Haitian nineteenth century (1804–1915). He came along with proposals on social change that were to be applied in Haiti, in different writings, year after year. For example, in the book *Haïti et ses visiteurs* (1883), he presented a socioeconomic program relating to land distribution and farmers. In *Haïti aux Haïtiens* he offered parameters of political economy while emphasizing a nation building project. Similarly, in *Les Affaires d'Haïti*

70 Janvier, *Haiti for the Haitians*, 71.

(*1884*), there is a section that he presented as "national policy." It is a government program based on national reconciliation, national reconstruction, the socioeconomic integration of peasants through land distribution, agrarian reform, political stability, and modernization.[71] Finally in 1886, in the book *Les Constitutions d'Haïti*, having analyzed the constitutions adopted in Haiti from 1801 to 1879, he again presented a project for an "ideal" constitution for Haiti that he thought capable of bringing stability and the economic project to the country. That constitution project is a true social project.

Janvier was an intellectual in all the meanings of the word at the time; he was even considered to be a genius. Yes, during his lifetime, there were already biographers who considered him as such.[72] Upon his death, a Haitian author published a melancholic article in which he bitterly wept over the passing of the genius Janvier: "In memory of the great genius and master Dr. Louis-Joseph Janvier." In my humble opinion, Janvier was given the title of genius for his extensive and diversified academic education and also because during a certain period he wrote and published in compulsive fashion on a great number of themes and subjects.[73]

In any case, Janvier's discourse was neither heard nor applied by the Haitian authorities. His discourse was marginalized, put aside, because he did not write in the manner expected by the Haitian power elite. Also, his nationalist stance, a line against the greed of foreign powers, was broken, even concealed, by a more accommodating political discourse that circulated both within Haiti and abroad. This powerful discourse fit into the realpolitik. In the end, it turned out that the discourse that came out on top was detrimental to the interests of the wounded social majority and to those of the country as a whole.

In general, ideas pertaining to state formation, nation building, and the seeds of nationalism provoke debate in the political, academic, and intellectual spheres in the societies in which they circulate. Thus, Janvier's ideas on these matters did not fail to generate knowledgeable analyses and all kinds of interpretations. If the ideas he circulated in his theorizations of sociological events were not applied, that does not

71 Janvier, "La politique nationale," in *Les Affaires d'Haïti*, 243–290.
72 Lenoir, "Biographie."
73 On the life and work of Janvier, see Watson Denis, "La Nation comme projet d'intégration socio-économique"; Yves Chemla's chapter in the present volume; Isidore, "Un patriote et un homme de parti"; Pradel Pompilus, *Louis-Joseph Janvier par lui-même. Le patriote et le champion de la négritude*, 2nd rev. ed. (Port-au-Prince: Imprimerie la Presse Évangélique, [1995?]).

mean that he lost his fight and that these ideas will never be applied. The contemporary French literary critic Yves Chemla, working in the francophone world, recognizes that the work of Janvier (who, by the way, he correctly presents as a national writer) is:

> essential [...] on at least two levels. First, in the history of ideas, a genre that is not too popular nowadays, it is resolutely inscribed within a critique of ideological patterns that were then common in the Western framework. But its radicalism is constructed gradually. Studying Janvier's oeuvre forces one to get into the history of a conscience that tears away from this framework, to which it actually owes its construction.[74]

Conclusion: Janvier the theorist, from yesterday to today

Louis-Joseph Janvier's pamphlet *Haïti aux Haïtiens* is one of those texts that marks Haitian historiography in general and Haitian social thought in particular. It both bears the mark of its time and goes beyond the ideas that characterized that time. This work is inscribed within the ideology of Haitian nationalism on the one hand, and on the other it intervenes in the premise of nation building in Haiti. It is a protest and programmatic work that goes from the formation of the Haitian state, imperfect in its exclusionary functioning, to the construction of the nation which requires the inclusion of all social groups, including "the wounded social majority." The author was a conscientious witness of his time. He also took on the role of apostle for tomorrow.

Haïti aux Haïtiens is one of those polemical works in the Haitian political sphere that has a timeless scope. However, I do not share all of the ideas put forth by this rebel-author in his text. I'd like to tease out at least two reservations here:

1) Janvier lacked realism. Wanting to defend his nationalist position, he unabashedly proposed economic autarky and political isolation in order to protect the country and its natural resources. He wrote on the matter: "[l]et us plainly state what must be done. We should withdraw into ourselves; gather ourselves."[75] That was impossible at the time. In a world marked by the internationalization of capital, dominated by European powers and the meteoric rise of the United States of America as a commercial, industrial, and financial power, it was unrealistic to

---

74 See Chemla in this volume, 111.
75 Janvier, *Haiti for the Haitians*, 61.

think that Haiti could come out on top alone. It would suffer the repercussions of the actions of the outside world;

2) Janvier was not enough of a pedagogue in his nation building project. He did not show the Haitian power elite that its short-term, middle-term, and long-term interests were served in this emancipating project of nation building. This Haitian nation building could only be a pipe dream, but based on common and fundamental interests, shared by several sectors involved in the project, who were aware of the stakes and who could thus make it possible.

Beyond these reservations, Janvier had the merit of posing the question of the nation in Haiti. At the time, the issue was also being raised in certain Western European and Asian countries. Thus, we can note that nation building began in certain countries during and following great social shocks and/or political changes. That was the case in the United Kingdom during the Industrial Revolution, in France during the bourgeois French revolution of 1789; it was the case during the unification of Germany (1868–1871) and during the long process of Italian unification (1848–1870). The same was true in Japan, during the Meiji Era or Restoration (1868–1912). We can consider then that the objective of nation building is a country's modernity and modernization. Similarly, Janvier wanted Haiti to enter into modernity and modernization—at its own pace of course. He wanted Haitians to control the natural resources driving this modernity and modernization.

In short, Janvier's social and economic ideas on the nation remain relevant. If today, over 135 years after the publication of *Haïti aux Haïtiens*, peasants in Haiti no longer represent the vast majority of the population, those excluded in rural areas, shantytowns, and ghettoes (according to the sociological terminology currently used in Haiti), surprisingly recall the living conditions of the wounded social majority of which Janvier spoke. In fact, they are the sons and daughters of peasants, formerly excluded from State affairs, transformed into the excluded and the marginalized in the scabrous cities following the waves of migration and disordered displacements that have taken place over the past fifty years. In that sense, Janvier remains our eternal contemporary!

Finally, I would rather like to emphasize that the writings of the social theorists of the long Haitian nineteenth century, as illustrated by those of Janvier, are worth their weight in gold. If we ignore the traditional eclecticism (epistemological practice of the time, dominated by Western thought) sometimes found in their texts to focus on the essential, we discover that they can be extremely useful. Perhaps it would not even be necessary to trawl Europe and North American banks to find ideological sap or some life-saving point of reference that could contribute to remaking or rebuilding a new Haitian society. All nations and all societies that are built and renewed draw upon their history, their nourishing culture, and the fertile thought of their poets and troubadours, their writers, thinkers, discoverers, and social theorists, indispensable seed for the socioeconomic flourishing of their peoples. In Haiti, we should do the same to get out of the woods and create attractive tomorrows in favor of the "wounded social majority." Using foreign social theories without discernment leads to gratuitous repetitions, confusion, and sociological non-adaptation. Fortunately Haiti, like other countries around the world, has its own social theorists, its appointed thinkers, such as Janvier. Haiti had such figures, writers, and thinkers throughout the nineteenth century. Of course, the writings and recommendations of nineteenth-century authors would need to be adapted to the circumstances of today.

CHAPTER SIX

Haiti for the Haitians

A Genealogy of Black Sovereignty

Brandon R. Byrd

> D'abord et avant tout, je suis Haïtien.
> Ayant payé très cher son indépendance: par son sang, par son argent, par sa résignation à ne pas faiblir sous les calomnies et sous l'injure, elle doit la vouloir garder complète, absolue, entière.
> —Louis Joseph Janvier (1884)

What did it mean to be "first and foremost" Haitian? For Louis Joseph Janvier, to be Haitian meant claiming as his inheritance the Haitian Revolution. He recognized his birthright as the terrifying, inspiring, worldmaking rebellion against the terrible "progress" of the slave ship and the plantation. His intellectual heritage was a more expansive humanism and a modernity disavowed.[1] Living in Paris, residing at the heart of Haiti's former "master," Janvier saw clearly the reformulations of racism and capitalism in an era when the dreams of Haiti's revolutionaries and its post-independence population were swiftly giving way to the nightmare of U.S. empire and European colonialism. He saw the growing chasm between the demand for universal equality and the realization of a complementary project: the recognition of black sovereignty.

Accordingly, in the aftermath of Haiti's civil conflicts of 1883, Janvier called on his compatriots to reflect on the price of liberty—on the enormous casualties and financial costs through which Haitians won

---

1 Marlene L. Daut, *Baron de Vastey and the Origins of Black Atlantic Humanism* (New York: Palgrave Macmillan, 2017) and Sibylle Fischer, *Modernity Disavowed: Haiti and the Cultures of Slavery in the Age of Revolution* (Durham, NC: Duke University Press, 2004).

and then tried to secure their anticolonial and antislavery revolution. He took charge of another, unfinished revolution—the fight for Haiti's very existence. Warning Haitians that their divided nation was "suspect" and threatened "from all sides," Janvier proclaimed that "Haiti must want to keep its independence, complete, absolute, and whole."[2] He implied that Haiti could live. He tried to write black sovereignty into being.

Sovereignty—*black* sovereignty—is a thorny thing. The most basic concept of state sovereignty, born out of the Peace of Westphalia (1648) and affirmed in the Charter of the United Nations (1945), is the principle that each state, no matter how small or "poor," has a right to the exclusive control over its territory without outside interference.[3] It encapsulates the contradictions of so-called Western civilization—it is a suggestion of the legal equality of states that emerged alongside the plunder of Africa and the alienation of millions of Africans from their natal lands. The transatlantic slave trade produced a new racial taxonomy in which blackness was bound, ball and chain, to subservience, servitude, and enslavement. The racial thought of the Enlightenment suggested that black people lacked the will needed for self-governance—that black muscles, not minds, were needed to make the capital of the modern world. As Janvier suggested, the aberrance of black political bodies in the age and aftermath of slavery created a unique challenge for Haiti. His country imposed itself upon slaveholding empires then inhabited a world in which the "modern," "civilized," and democratic nation-state was racialized as white. Haiti was a "black Republic" that faced more than its share of "slander and insult"—an independent state that still struggled for two conditions of sovereignty: recognition and respect.[4]

In recent years, scholars have increasingly moved beyond the Haitian Revolution towards the politics of post-independence Haiti.[5] As

---

[2] See the translation of Janvier, *Haiti for the Haitians*, 71 above.

[3] Derek Croxton, "The Peace of Westphalia of 1648 and the Origins of Sovereignty," *The International History Review* 21, no. 3 (September 1999): 569–591. On the unequal integration of states as a fundamental trait of the modern international system, see especially Adom Getachew, *Worldmaking after Empire: The Rise and Fall of Self-Determination* (Princeton: Princeton University Press, 2019).

[4] Janvier, *Haiti for the Haitians*, 71. Radhika V. Mongia, "Historicizing State Sovereignty: Inequality and the Form of Equivalence," *Comparative Studies in Society and History* 49, no. 2 (2007): 384–411.

[5] Recent books on nineteenth-century Haiti include: Matthew J. Smith, *Liberty, Fraternity, Exile: Haiti and Jamaica after Emancipation* (Chapel Hill: University of North Carolina Press, 2014); Julia Gaffield, *Haitian Connections in the Atlantic World: Recognition after Revolution* (Chapel Hill: University

historian Julia Gaffield has suggested, the early Haitian state announced its existence with a historic Declaration of Independence, which must be read not as a single, momentary proclamation but as a series of acts that reasserted Haiti's right to be as they traversed the Atlantic World.[6] Haiti, to quote historian Karen N. Salt, "rewrote the rules about who could and could not be a sovereign body, as well as how that sovereignty would be performed." In *The Unfinished Revolution: Haiti, Black Sovereignty and Power in the Nineteenth-Century Atlantic World*, a critical intervention in scholarship on post-independence Haiti and interdisciplinary studies of sovereignty, Salt argues that after Haiti's successful insurrection against slavery and its ensuing struggle against a return to French imperial control, "there was—and remains—a third, and unfinished revolution in Haiti: sovereignty." In tracking this "unfinished project" of black sovereignty, in following how a wide range of Haitian state and non-state actors tried "to (re)position Haiti in an Atlantic world fueled by Atlantic racial slavery and strategies of dispossession sown from the seeds of racialisms," Salt offers important insights into how race and racism have structured the geopolitical systems of the modern world.[7] Just as significantly, she encourages further conversation about black political thought in which post-independence Haiti, its "unfinished revolution," and other black states take center stage.

This chapter contributes to that conversation by tracing a genealogy of the phrase that Janvier used to express his imagined and world-altering

---

of North Carolina Press, 2015); Marlene L. Daut, *Baron de Vastey and the Origins of Black Atlantic Humanism* (New York: Palgrave Macmillan, 2017); Johnhenry Gonzalez, *Maroon Nation: A History of Revolutionary Haiti* (New Haven: Yale University Press, 2019); Jean Alix René, *Haiti après l'esclavage: formation de l'état et culture politique populaire (1804–1846)* (Port-au-Prince: Éditions Le Natal, 2019); Chelsea Stieber, *Haiti's Paper War Post-Independence Writing, Civil War, and the Making of the Republic, 1804–1954* (New York: New York University Press, 2020). Mimi Sheller, *Democracy after Slavery: Black Publics and Peasant Radicalism in Haiti and Jamaica* (London: Macmillan, 2000) remains indispensable as well.

6 Julia Gaffield, ed., *The Haitian Declaration of Independence: Creation, Context, and Legacy* (Charlottesville: University of Virginia Press, 2016).

7 Karen N. Salt, *The Unfinished Revolution: Haiti, Black Sovereignty and Power in the Nineteenth-Century Atlantic World* (Liverpool: Liverpool University Press, 2019), 14, 18, 40. On Haitian sovereignty, see also Patrick Bellegarde-Smith, *Haiti: The Breached Citadel* (Toronto: Canadian Scholars Press, 2004); Yarimar Bonilla, "Ordinary Sovereignty," *Small Axe* 42 (November 2013): 152–165; Robert Maguire and Scott Freeman, eds., *Who Owns Haiti? People, Power, and Sovereignty* (Gainesville: University Press of Florida, 2017).

end to Haiti's "unfinished revolution."[8] First surfacing among British abolitionists and U.S. black activists during the 1850s and later in the United States' Reconstruction era, "Haiti for the Haitians" was tethered to the fraught present of a revolutionary black state. Its use betrayed hopes and anxieties about Haiti's bearing on questions of slavery, abolition, and black potential in the Atlantic World. By the turn of the twentieth century, "Haiti for the Haitians" gained wider use among imperialists and anti-imperialists. It was, as Janvier's text suggests, linked to broader debates about the internal politics and international futures of black political bodies—from new citizens to sovereign states—in an era of U.S. racial segregation, empire, and European colonialism. Unsurprisingly, the phrase exploded into widespread use during the U.S. occupation of Haiti (1915–1934), expressing not only opposition to the violent suppression of Haitian sovereignty but also echoing the anticolonial ethos captured in the better-known "Africa for the Africans" and embraced by black intellectuals and white liberals amid the rising, radical internationalist sentiment of the World War I era. It became part of a vernacular of anticolonial nationalism still used to contest ongoing neocolonial projects, including interventions of the so-called international community in Haiti.

More than two centuries after the Haitian Revolution, Haiti remains at the heart of popular and academic debates about the practice and limitations of nationalism and state sovereignty in an age of globalization. The genealogy of "Haiti for the Haitians" reveals the deep roots and expansive routes of those recurrent debates, which have always included Haitians and non-Haitians alike. It lays bare a polyvocal discourse about black sovereignty—an overlooked body of political thought about power, democracy, political and economic independence, and their proper bearers—as it addressed, emerged from, and transcended Haiti.

As imagined by the English author John Relly Beard, Jean-Jacques Dessalines deserved more contempt than credit for first declaring "Haiti for the Haitians." In his most famous work, a hagiographic biography that remained the standard anglophone history of Toussaint Louverture decades after its first printing by a London publisher in 1853, Beard regretted that "all those brave men" who fought for Haitian independence "should be willing or should be compelled to bend the knee to the ruffian

---

8 This genealogy focuses on the phrase's anglophone and francophone history.

spirit of Dessalines." He mourned for Haiti when he remembered that an "island just redeemed from bondage [...] took to itself a new master, and gave to that ferocious soldier the power to establish laws, to declare war, to make peace, and even to appoint his successor." In a flight of historical fancy, Beard imagined that the first Haitian head of state, "[h]aving, by a show of mildness, gained the advantage which he sought, of securing time for affairs to settle, for the increase of his forces, and the acquisition of power," finally "threw aside the mask." He told his audience of English readers, many of them familiar with Dessalines's infamous despotism, that the slave turned emperor "raised the cry of 'Hayti for the Haytians,' thinking by proscribing foreigners he should effectively consolidate his own authority."[9]

Beard's reimagined declaration of Haitian independence was tied to a real revolutionary history. On January 1, 1804, Jean-Jacques Dessalines stood at the Place d'Armes in Gonaïves, a coastal town located about sixty miles from the battlefield where his men had just driven the French from Saint-Domingue. With the officers of his "Indigenous Army" around him, Dessalines, a man who like so many of his troops still bore the scars of slavery, proceeded to articulate what would become the fruits of the Haitian Revolution. "It is not enough," his declaration began, "to have expelled the barbarians who have bloodied our land for two centuries." Instead, "we must, with one last act of national authority, forever assure the empire of liberty in the country of our birth." Haitians had to establish sovereignty, not just freedom.[10]

This call for an independent black state inspired awe and fright among various audiences across the Atlantic World. The Haitian Imperial Constitution of 1805 forbid foreign property ownership in Haiti and announced that Haitians, even the white women, Germans, and Poles naturalized as Haitian citizens, "shall henceforth be known

---

9 John Relly Beard, *Toussaint L'Ouverture, the Negro Patriot of Hayti: Comprising an Account of the Struggle for Liberty in the Island, and a Sketch of Its History to the Present Period* (London: Ingram, Cooke, & Co., 1853), 291. On historical representations of Dessalines, see Lindsey J. Twa, "Jean-Jacques Dessalines: Demon, Demigod, and Everything in Between," *Romantic Circles*, https://romantic-circles.org/praxis/circulations/HTML/praxis.2011.twa.html; Marlene L. Daut, *Tropics of Haiti: Race and the Literary History of the Haitian Revolution in the Atlantic World, 1789–1865* (Liverpool: Liverpool University Press, 2015).
10 Quotations from "The Haitian Declaration of Independence," in Laurent Dubois and John D. Garrigus, *Slave Revolution in the Caribbean, 1789–1804: A Brief History with Documents* (New York: Bedford/St. Martin's, 2006), 188–190.

by the generic appellation of blacks."[11] It offered a radical reformulation of race as a political rather than biological or cultural category and introduced Haiti to the world as a revolutionary black state.[12] The emergence of what, even in its monarchical formations, became colloquially known in Europe and the Americas as the "black Republic" inspired subversive visions of freedom and nation building among free and enslaved people of African descent across the Americas, who previously attached their hopes to print news, gossip, and rumors about the Haitian Revolution.[13] European and Euro-American political leaders, citizens, and subjects committed to slavery, colonialism, and their attendant racial hierarchies responded differently. While the most famous disavowals of Haitian sovereignty came in the European and U.S. refusal of formal diplomatic recognition of Haiti, a number of white authors in Europe and the Americas popularized a narrative of the Haitian Revolution meant to undermine the legitimacy of the Haitian state. In serialized fiction and memoir that moved across the Atlantic, the Haitian Revolution became synonymous with race war in which black savages enacted wild fantasies of revenge upon innocent slaveholders, robbing their white and biracial victims of their right to life, liberty, and the pursuit of (human) property.[14]

Dessalines became the embodiment of the so-called "Horrors of Saint-Domingue." His critics, internal and external, during his lifetime and after his assassination, demonized him for ordering the execution of the French citizens who remained in independent Haiti. The first

---

11 Dubois and Garrigus, *Slave Revolution in the Caribbean*, 191–196.

12 On the Haitian Constitution of 1805, see especially Julia Gaffield, "Complexities of Imagining Haiti: A Study of National Constitutions, 1801–1807," *Journal of Social History* 41, no. 1 (Fall 2007): 81–103; Anne Gulick, "We Are Not the People: The 1805 Haitian Constitution's Challenge to Political Legibility in the Age of Revolution," *American Literature* 78, no. 4 (2006): 799–820; Philip Kaisary "'To Break Our Chains and Form a Free People': Race, Nation, and Haiti's Imperial Constitution of 1805," in *Race and Nation in the Age of Emancipation*, ed. Whitney Nell Stewart and John Garrison Marks (Athens: University of Georgia Press, 2018); Claude Moïse, *Constitutions et lutes de pouvoir en Haïti, 1804–1987* (Montreal: Éditions du CIDIHCA, 1988).

13 Alfred N. Hunt, *Haiti's Influence on Antebellum America: Slumbering Volcano in the Caribbean* (Baton Rouge: Louisiana University Press, 1988); Maurice Jackson and Jacqueline Bacon, eds., *African Americans and the Haitian Revolution: Selected Essays and Historical Documents* (New York: Routledge, 2010); Julius S. Scott, *The Common Wind: Afro-American Currents in the Age of the Haitian* Revolution (New York: Verso, 2018).

14 Daut, *Tropics of Haiti*.

Haitian head of state became the embodiment of the aberrant black political body.

The birth of Haiti and the competing representations of it provided both possibilities and problems for abolitionists, including Beard. On the one hand, the Haitian Revolution proved that slavery could be defeated. The revolution had produced a "Black Republic" that could, according to the nineteenth-century definition of the nation as a measure of racial capacity, prove the political capabilities of individual black people and affirm their collective preparedness for freedom.[15] By the 1850s, following the passage of the Fugitive Slave Act of 1850 and the guerrilla warfare over the fate of slavery in Kansas that followed the Kansas-Nebraska Act of 1854, a growing number of U.S. abolitionists, particularly African Americans, even hailed the Haitian Revolution as evidence of the political uses of subaltern violence—as a model for a violent antislavery revolution of their own. That radical position was a central but not universal aspect of transatlantic abolitionism.[16] For other abolitionists in the anglophone Atlantic world, emancipation could be secured and legitimized through legislation. To them, Great Britain's Slavery Abolition Act of 1833 was a success story while the "Horrors of Saint-Domingue" were a threat. These bourgeois reformers feared that the Haitian Revolution or, more plainly, the mass deaths of French planters and troops would discredit the tenuous project of emancipation.

Romantic treatments of Louverture and routine disavowals of Dessalines responded to reactionary movements across the Atlantic world. The standard characterizations of both revolutionaries were

---

15 Foundational scholarship on nations and nationalism includes Benedict Anderson, *Imagined Communities: Reflections on the Origin and Spread of Nationalism* (New York: Verso, 1983); Ernest Gellner, *Nations and Nationalism* (Ithaca: Cornell University Press, 1983); Eric J. Hobsbawm, *Nations and Nationalism since 1780: Programme, Myth, Reality* (Cambridge: Cambridge University Press, 1990).

16 On U.S. black abolitionists' views on violence, see especially Kellie Carter-Jackson, *Force and Freedom: Black Abolitionists and the Politics of Violence* (Philadelphia: University of Pennsylvania Press, 2019). On the politics of transatlantic abolitionism, particularly in the anglophone Atlantic world, see especially Richard J.M. Blackett, *Building an Anti-Slavery Wall: Black Americans in the Atlantic Abolitionist Movement* (Baton Rouge: Louisiana State University Press, 2012); W. Caleb McDaniel, *The Problem of Democracy in the Age of Slavery* (Baton Rouge: Louisiana State University Press, 2013); Manisha Sinha, *The Slave's Cause: A History of Abolition* (New Haven: Yale University Press, 2016).

attuned to the rise of a more nakedly racist pro-slavery ideology in the antebellum United States, the scrutiny of emancipation in the British West Indies, and the continued importation of enslaved Africans to Cuba and Brazil. They were understood as an important part of a more respectable and usable history of Haitian freedom and sovereignty.[17]

Beard's pioneering use of "Haiti for the Haitians" is thus inseparable from his era's wider ideas and debates about slavery and emancipation. Beard admitted that he wanted to "supply the clearest evidence that there is no insuperable barrier between the light and the dark-coloured tribes of our common human species" and show that "the much-misunderstood and down-trodden negro race are capable of the loftiest virtues and the most heroic efforts."[18] His goal was to prove that people of African descent could rise to the European standard of civilization. Like numerous other Anglo-Atlantic abolitionists of his day, he reasoned that the best way to do that was to elevate a genteel version of Toussaint Louverture rather than attempt to rehabilitate the fraught image of Dessalines.[19] The Haitian Imperial Constitution became a casualty of his attempts to integrate Louverture—and, by extension, Haiti and Haitians—into a usable, universal history of Western humanity. In Beard's strategic rendering, the proscription on foreign landownership in the "Black Republic" was a retrograde policy rather than a necessary extension of an antislavery and anticolonial revolution. He accepted that the degraded slave was in need of guidance once gifted freedom and put "Haiti for the Haitians" towards a typical, conservative politics of emancipation that had the effect of undermining Haitian sovereignty.

With the help of authors who were also active in transatlantic abolitionism, Beard's invocation of "Haiti for the Haitians" moved from Europe to the United States in ensuing decades. In 1863, James Redpath, a Scottish immigrant then based in Boston, published a second edition of Beard's *Toussaint L'Ouverture* in the hopes "of affording some aid

---

17 The definitive work on histories of the Haitian Revolution is Daut, *Tropics of Haiti*.
18 Beard, *Toussaint L'Ouverture*, 13.
19 Another famous nineteenth-century rendition of Louverture was Wendell Phillips's oration in which he declared that "the Muse of History" would one day rightfully place "the name of the soldier, the statesman, the martyr, Toussaint l'Ouverture" above all other "revolutionaries," including George Washington and Napoleon Bonaparte. On Phillips and other portrayals of Louverture in the antebellum United States, see especially Matthew J. Clavin, *Toussaint Louverture and the American Civil War: The Promise and Peril of a Second Haitian Revolution* (Philadelphia: University of Pennsylvania Press, 2010), 55–76.

to the sacred cause of freedom, specially as involved in the extinction of slavery, and in the removal of the prejudices on which servitude mainly depends."[20] William Wells Brown then repurposed Beard's work. Brown was a formerly enslaved U.S. black activist who once worked for the Haytian Bureau of Emigration, the organization, funded by the Haitian government and led by Redpath, that facilitated black North American immigration to Haiti between 1860 and 1862. In 1873, Brown published *The Rising Son; of, The Antecedents and Advancement of the Colored Race*. He hoped that his book would help speed the dawn of a new day of racial equality by providing an argument for the establishment of U.S. democracy and a literary blueprint for how African Americans might transition to freedom.[21] He borrowed from Beard to distinguish himself and his fellow black citizens from Dessalines's disreputable example of post-emancipation blackness. In Brown's imagined history of the Haitian Revolution, Dessalines "having, by a show of mildness gained the advantage which he sought, the acquisition of power, [...] threw aside the mask, and raised the cry of 'Hayti for the Haytians'." Dessalines, in Brown's telling, lacked the restraint of Toussaint; the "ferocious" Dessalines instead offered an example of black politics that newly enfranchised U.S. black citizens should not and would not replicate.[22]

The U.S. democracy—the cornerstone of a world remade on the principle of racial egalitarianism—that Brown envisioned did not come to fruition. By 1876, white Democrats in the U.S. South "redeemed" their region from alleged black misrule and regained control of local and state government through campaigns of election fraud, voter suppression, and relentless violence against U.S. black citizens and white Republicans. Meanwhile, white northerners at the forefront of the Republican Party became less committed to protecting the newly established political and civil rights of African Americans. Rapacious capitalism, at home and

---

20 James Redpath, "Preface," in John Relly Beard, *Toussaint L'Ouverture: A Biography and Autobiography* (Boston: James Redpath, 1863), iii. On Redpath and the Haytian Bureau of Emigration, see especially John R. McKivigan, *Forgotten Firebrand: James Redpath and the Making of Nineteenth-Century America* (Ithaca: Cornell University Press, 2008).
21 As Stephen G. Hall writes, Brown's goals were part of a larger post-emancipation political project. See *A Faithful Account of the Race: African American Historical Writing in Nineteenth-Century America* (Chapel Hill: University of North Carolina Press, 2009).
22 William Wells Brown, *The Rising Son; or, The Antecedents and Advancement of the Colored Race* (Boston, MA: A.G. Brown & Co., 1874), 174.

abroad, became their *raison d'être*. What scholars would later name "racial capitalism," a structure fundamentally connected to empire, now built on the backs of "free" black laborers from the cotton fields of Mississippi to the rubber plantations of the Congo, remained the means of accumulating wealth in the West. It was the foundation of Louis Joseph Janvier's world—the framework in which Haiti's internal politics and its interrelated foreign relations both emerged.[23]

In 1884, Janvier, born in Port-au-Prince but then living and studying in Paris, published a message to his compatriots. Recalling recent events, Janvier issued a thinly veiled condemnation of the Liberal Party, whose leaders, primarily composed of light-complexioned elites, opposed popular democracy and often undermined the power of the executive. He accused his "dubious relatives" of tearing apart Haiti's social fabric; he looked to Haiti's history for lessons on how to stitch his nation back together. Reminding Haitians that "out of all civil war, a nation should emerge strengthened, wiser, more unified, more courageous," Janvier recalled that Haiti's founders had "created the Haitian nation alone" and "left us this corner of the earth so that there would be a place in the world where one cannot spit with impunity in the face of the black race." Dessalines, Haiti's "Liberator," had, Janvier continued, left Haitians a great responsibility. To Janvier, the only way for Haiti, a country that he associated with its black majority, to fulfill the promises of the Haitian Revolution was to "uphold the traditions" and "live and grow alone." Haitians had to remember that "a nation cannot live autonomously, cannot grow on its own unless at every moment each one of its sons taken in isolation, each one demonstrates individually the haughty, proud, imperious will of the nation." They had to heed the urgent demand that became the title of Janvier's book: "Haiti for the Haitians."[24]

With his subversive reassertion of "Haiti for the Haitians," Janvier not only clarified his vision for Haitian governance but also challenged contemporary nationalisms that functioned as imperialism. As Marlene Daut notes in her essay in this volume, Janvier, like other

[23] My use of racial capitalism is informed by Cedric Robinson, *Black Marxism: The Making of the Black Radical Tradition*, 2nd ed. (Chapel Hill: University of North Carolina Press, 2000), 9–28; Charisse Burden-Stelly, "Modern U.S. Racial Capitalism: Some Theoretical Insights," *Monthly Review* (July 1, 2020), https://monthlyreview.org/2020/07/01/modern-u-s-racial-capitalism/; Destin Jenkins and Justin Leroy, eds., *Histories of Racial Capitalism* (New York: Columbia University, 2021), 1–26.

[24] Janvier, *Haiti for the Haitians*, 47, 60, 65, 71, 76.

Caribbean intellectuals, including another prominent member of the National Party, Demasvar Delorme, was responding to "America for the Americans," a slogan that represented the imperial designs of the late nineteenth-century United States.[25] One of the chief concerns expressed in his work was that his political opponents would go so far as placing Haiti under a foreign protectorate—that some Haitian elites would sacrifice aspects of Haiti's sovereignty to ensure a stronger state more conducive to their political and economic interests.[26] In response, Janvier argued that Haitians could not "abdicate our sovereignty over any point of the territory." He proposed an anticolonial nationalism founded on opposition to U.S. and European imperialism, a demand for Haiti's political independence, and an insistence on the inviolability of its territorial integrity.[27]

As the Introduction to this volume notes, Janvier's vision of national sovereignty was not synonymous with the ideas of popular sovereignty held by rural Haitians. To paraphrase Jean Casimir, many National partisans opposed their Liberal counterparts not because they valorized or shared the culture of those who Casimir calls the "sovereign people" but because they saw themselves as best positioned to speak for and act on the behalf of rural Haitians.[28] Janvier was not free from this colonial logic. He championed reforms in agriculture, finance, religion, and education that would "modernize" Haiti but were sometimes at odds with the values and cultural and social institutions of rural Haitians. His insistence on the importance of Protestantism is a case in point. To Janvier, "progress" was a fruit to be enjoyed and demonstrated by all Haitians. He offered full inclusion in Haiti's civic and economic life to rural people who prioritized their relationships with one another rather than the relations between the Haitian state and the outside world.

Yet, despite its biases and limitations, Janvier's political thought challenged the existing international order. In *Haïti aux Haïtiens*,

---

25 See Daut's essay in this volume, 129–132.
26 In fact, as David Nicholls has noted, some Liberals "attacked Janvier's conception of 'Haiti for the Haitians' as relevant only as a protest against slavery in an earlier period, arguing that in [their] own day it was a serious mistake which could lead to the increasing isolation of the country." See Nicholls, *Haiti in Caribbean Context: Ethnicity, Economy, and Revolt* (New York: St. Martin's, 1985), 114.
27 Janvier, *Haiti for the Haitians*, 50.
28 Jean Casimir, *The Haitians: A Decolonial History* (Chapel Hill: The University of North Carolina Press, 2020), 264.

Janvier not only insists that Haitians could not allow foreign annexation or colonization of their country but also warns Haitians against entering into exclusive trade deals with any foreign power, which "would be an odious measure and childish as well," or borrowing "a penny [or] a doubloon either from the United States or from any transatlantic power."[29] He even insists on breaking up the large landholdings of the Haitian state, returning "the land to the peasant's hands," and extending lines of credit to small-scale farmers, including cultivators of coffee, a crop that could be produced with relatively little capital.[30] Taken to its logical outcomes, Janvier's idea of "Haiti for the Haitians" entailed the making of a new international system conducive to the sovereignty and equal integration of a black state. Now as then, there is radical potential in this idea—in the clarion call for Haitian sovereignty—which Janvier issued in the shadow of the world's powers, in the age of empire when, in his words, the international community loomed as a state above the Haitian state.[31]

A storm of events made clear to Janvier and his contemporaries the material and discursive violence of empire. In *Haïti aux Haïtiens*, Janvier responded to the upheavals of 1883. He espoused a nationalist vision clarified by a war in which the British consul in Port-au-Prince warned the U.S.-backed Haitian president that the British would bombard the Haitian capital if he did not quell an uprising that had been funded by local and foreign merchants in Jamaica.[32]

Predictably, some prominent foreign nationals in Haiti expressed different interpretations of the events of 1883 and the saliency of Janvier's clarion call of "Haiti for the Haitians." After losing significant personal property in the fires of 1883, Joseph Robert Love, a black Bahamian clergyman and doctor who had moved from the United States to Haiti in 1881, emerged as the voice of British West Indians in the Haitian capital. Love called for a stronger British hand in Haiti

---

29 Janvier, *Haiti for the Haitians*, 64, 68.
30 Ibid., 69.
31 André-Georges Adam, *Une crise haïtienne 1867–1869: Sylvain Salnave* (Port-au-Prince: Éditions Henri Deschamps, 1982), 65. Here I employ the language of Patrick Bellegarde-Smith's classic, *In the Shadow of Powers: Dantès Bellegarde in Haitian Social Thought* (Nashville: Vanderbilt University Press, 2019).
32 Recent scholarship on the insurrection includes Matthew J. Smith, *Liberty, Fraternity, Exile: Haiti and Jamaica after Emancipation* (Chapel Hill: University of North Carolina Press, 2014).

and complained that "in Hayti the term étranger invites injustice and oppression." He later boasted of having "done more for the Jamaicans in Haiti than any other single man has done." The incendiary violence of 1883 left Love not only destitute but disillusioned with Salomon and the National Party. He saw both as embracing a politics of nation over race that left black foreigners on the margins of Haiti's political and economic life and vulnerable to discrimination. After being expelled to Jamaica by Haitian president Florvil Hyppolite, who accused him of stirring up domestic troubles, Love bitterly concluded that "I have found that Haitians have strayed so far from the true idea of a development of *race*—the idea of 1804." He complained that "I have heard authoritative voices speak of 'LA RACE HAITIENNE'"—that he had witnessed a misguided application of the doctrine of "Haiti for the Haitians."[33]

As Love hinted at a race consciousness and Pan-African sensibility that he would further develop as the editor of the *Jamaica Advocate* and in public writings that would inspire Marcus Garvey, Haiti entered the crosshairs of another British subject: Spenser St. John. In the same moment that representatives of Great Britain joined their counterparts from Europe and the United States at the Berlin West Africa Conference of 1884–1885, St. John, a career diplomat who once held his country's top diplomatic post in Port-au-Prince, published *Hayti; or, the Black Republic*. The polemic expressed the same racist ideologies used to justify the European "partitioning" of Africa. In a work that popularized common anti-Haitian tropes, St. John speculated that cannibalism was pervasive among Haitians and wrote that his time in Haiti made him less confident in "the capacity of the negro to hold an independent position." His principal hope was that readers, who were reckoning with the transition from slavery to free labor across the Americas, would accept that "as long as [the negro] is influenced by contact with the white man, as in the southern portion of the United States, he gets on very well. But place him free from all such influence, as in Hayti, and he shows no signs of improvement."[34]

---

33 Quotations found in Smith, *Liberty, Fraternity, and Exile*, 232, 256, 268. On Love, see also Rupert Lewis, "Robert Love: A Democrat in Colonial Jamaica," *Jamaica Journal* 11, nos. 1–2 (August 1977): 58–63; Joy Lumsden, "Joseph Robert Love, 1839–1914: West Indian Extraordinary," *Afro-Americans in New York Life and History* 7, no. 1 (January 31, 1983): 25; Robert A. Hill, ed., *The Marcus Garvey and Universal Negro Improvement Association Papers*, Vol. 1: *1826–August 1919* (Berkeley: University of California Press, 1983), 532–536.

34 Spenser St. John, *Hayti; or, The Black Republic* (London: Smith, Elder,

The Scottish "explorer" Hesketh Prichard was one of several Europeans writers who followed St. John's lead, inventing more tales of Haitian barbarism meant to discredit black sovereignty. In November 1899, the publisher of the London-based *Daily Express* commissioned Prichard to travel to Haiti in search of lurid stories about life in the "black Republic." Then at the outset of his career, Prichard was more than happy to comply. Upon returning to Britain from his months-long travels, he published his findings in *Where Black Rules White: A Journey Across and About Hayti*. The book achieved its goals. *Where Black Rules White* was widely and favorably reviewed then and became an enduring staple of white supremacist literature by following the blueprint set by *Hayti; or, the Black Republic*. It demonizes Vodou, deriding a community-oriented religion based on the intricate relationship among humans and spirits as nothing more than barbaric superstition, and lampoons the African physical features of Haitians. In fact, it comes dangerously—purposely—close to plagiarizing St. John. Following the example of his successful predecessor, Prichard asked his readers "how," more than a century after the Haitian Revolution, "does the black man govern himself?" In Haiti, "[w]hat progress has he made? Absolutely none." Haiti proved that "[h]e ... cannot rule himself."[35]

Attempting to prove that point, Prichard appropriated the slogan through which Janvier expressed his vision of black sovereignty. Haitian president Tirésias Simon Sam, a member of the National Party and a man of the "ultra-negro type" according to Prichard, had formed a government "black enough to delight the heart of the most advanced negro-phile." That composition was no accident, he alleged. Misusing the words of a Haitian writer who insisted that "[w]e will adopt to ourselves the doctrine of Monroe, the American—Hayti for the Haytians," Prichard insisted that "'Hayti for the Haytians,' that war-cry of the people of the Republic, means really Hayti for the negro—no mulatto need apply." In his intentional exaggeration of how color and class influenced Haitian politics, the slogan "Haiti for the Haitians" was neither a clarion call for popular democracy nor an anticolonial demand. Instead, it meant irrational color prejudice and

---

& Co., 1884), 131, 134. On St. John and *Hayti*, see especially Jack Daniel Webb, *Haiti in the British Imagination: Imperial Worlds, 1847–1915* (Liverpool: Liverpool University Press, 2020), 139–188.

35 Hesketh Prichard, *Where Black Rules White: A Journey Across and About Hayti* (Westminster: Archibald Constable & Co., 1900), 284.

the elevation of uncivilized black men "who can neither read or write" over biracial black people whose white ancestry lent them some intelligence. "Hayti for the Haytians," Prichard concluded, simply "means conservatism to savagery."[36]

This widely accepted caricature of Haitian misgovernment would provide the pretense for U.S. invasion. During the late nineteenth and early twentieth century, U.S. gunboats constantly plied Haitian waters. The warships loomed as U.S. naval officers and diplomats "negotiated" for Haitian territory and demanded concessions for U.S. citizens in Haiti. They waited for the chance to finally place the United States above the French, Germans, and Brits as the proper authority in Haiti—as the new imperial power in what eighteenth-century commentators had called the "Pearl of the Antilles." That opportunity came in July 1915. After Haitian president Vilbrun Guillaume Sam ordered the execution of more than 160 political prisoners, a crowd seized him from his hiding place in the French legation and killed him. U.S. president Woodrow Wilson then authorized an invasion of Haiti. On July 28, the U.S.S. *Washington* entered the harbor of Port-au-Prince. Hundreds of Marines landed just south of the Haitian capital and quickly assessed their surroundings before moving into Port-au-Prince. They then subdued the capital. In doing so, the Marines took the first steps towards securing the overlapping interests of the National City Bank of New York, which controlled the National Bank of Haiti, and the U.S. military, which was particularly worried about Germany's interests in the World War I-era Caribbean.[37] They, as historian Hans Schmidt noted, acted on a set of common "racist preconceptions" that "placed the Haitians far below levels Americans considered necessary for democracy, self-government, and constitutionalism."[38] In the words of U.S. secretary of state Robert Lansing,

---

36 Ibid., 237, 283.
37 On the role of finance capitalism in the U.S. occupation of Haiti, see especially Peter James Hudson, *Bankers and Empire: How Wall Street Colonized the Caribbean* (Chicago: University of Chicago Press, 2017). Other foundational scholarship on the occupation includes Mary Renda, *Taking Haiti: Military Occupation and the Culture of U.S. Imperialism, 1915–1940* (Chapel Hill: University of North Carolina Press, 2001); Hans Schmidt, *The United States Occupation of Haiti, 1915–1934* (New Brunswick: Rutgers University Press, 1995); Jeffrey W. Sommers, *Race, Reality, and Realpolitik: U.S.–Haiti Relations in the Lead Up to the 1915 Occupation* (Lanham: Lexington Books, 2016).
38 Schmidt, *The United States Occupation of Haiti*, 10.

black people of all nations were "devoid of any capacity for political organization [... or] genius for government."[39] The example of Haiti proved it.

While the cynical "Haiti for the Haitians" deployed by Prichard and his ilk captured the ideologies that motivated the invasion of Haiti, Haitian activists built on the legacy of Janvier by couching their resistance to the ensuing U.S. occupation in a new, radical iteration of that phrase. After the U.S. Marines invaded Port-au-Prince, the United States quickly tried to strengthen its control of Haiti by elevating light-complexioned Haitians pliable to U.S. interests into positions of political power, censoring the Haitian press, introducing racial segregation to Haiti, conscripting the labor of rural Haitians, reorganizing the Haitian army under U.S. command, rewriting the Haitian constitution to allow for foreign landholding in Haiti, and placing white Americans in control of Haitian politics and finances. In response, residents of rural Haiti took up arms against the U.S. Marines.[40] Other Haitian activists wielded their pens with "Haiti for the Haitians" as their rallying cry. In 1922, during a U.S. congressional hearing on the occupation brought about by the efforts of anti-occupation protests in Haiti and beyond, a participant introduced a recent article from *Le Courier haïtien*, a nationalist newspaper that frequently drew the ire of occupation authorities. Under the title "Placards," the paper listed the following demands:

1. The Haitian people are bound to her Sovereignty and her Independence, Haiti to the Haitians.
2. Live free or die [...]
6. Long live free and independent Haiti [...]
8. Haiti to the Haitians.

---

39 Laurent Dubois, *Haiti: The Aftershocks of History* (New York: Metropolitan Books, 2012), 214.
40 Recent and foundational scholarship on Haitian resistance to the occupation includes Roger Gaillard, *Premier écrasement du cacoïsme* (Port-au-Prince: R. Gaillard, 1981) and *Charlemagne Péralte: le Caco* (Port-au-Prince: R. Gaillard, 1982); Suzy Castor, *L'Occupation américaine d'Haïti* (Port-au-Prince: Société haïtienne d'histoire, 1988); Marvin Chochotte, "The Twilight of Popular Revolutions: The Suppression of Peasant Armed Struggles and Freedom in Rural Haiti during the US Occupation, 1915–1934," *The Journal of African American History* 103, no. 3 (Summer 2018): 277–308; Yveline Alexis, *Haiti Fights Back: The Life and Legacy of Charlemagne Péralte* (New Brunswick: Rutgers University Press, 2021).

A Genealogy of Black Sovereignty 235

Below these (and thirty others) written in French, came eight more "English Inscriptions" including

38. Give us liberty or give us death.
39. Shall Haiti be your Ireland?
40. Shall Haiti be your Belgium?
41. Shall Haiti be your Congo?
42. Self determination for Haiti.[41]

The appropriation of Patrick Henry's words highlighted the hypocrisy of the United States, a country committed to imperialism despite its birth in anti-imperial revolt. Still, the allusions to Ireland, Belgium, and especially the Congo were more telling of the anticolonial nationalism implied in the protestors' use of "Haiti for the Haitians." For the editors of *Le Courier haïtien* and other Haitian activists, the struggle for Haitian sovereignty was part of a moment, a struggle, in which shared experiences of Western imperialism, capitalism, and militarism linked ostensibly disparate nationalist insurgencies. Haiti's second war for independence was linked to events in Europe, where the Irish had just concluded a prolonged fight for their independence while the Belgians had only begun to rebuild following the violence inflicted upon them by Germany at the outset of World War I. Certainly, occupied Haiti was connected to colonial Africa, where the effects of the Belgian king Leopold II's genocide in the Congo continued to afflict a population now under the rule of the Belgian state. It was not exceptional. Instead, Haiti's plight was illustrative of global structures of inequality and power.

As Haitians articulated a radical internationalist politics through the call for a "Haiti for the Haitians," their U.S. allies adopted the phrase and put it to similar use. At a time when the United States occupied not only Haiti but also Nicaragua, Cuba, and the Dominican Republic, *The Nation*, a progressive journal published in New York, proclaimed that U.S. citizens had to ask themselves "what shall be American policy toward these Caribbean republics whose independence we have

---

41 *Le Courier haitien*, published at Port-au-Prince, Haiti, November 29, 1921 in U.S. Congress. Senate, Select Committee on Haiti and Santo Domingo, *Inquiry into Occupation and Administration of Haiti and Santo Domingo: Hearings before a Select Committee on Haiti and Santo Domingo, United States Senate, Sixty-Seventh Congress, First and Second Sessions, Pursuant to S. Res. 112 Authorizing a Special Committee to Inquire into the Occupation and Administration of the Territories of the Republic of Haiti and the Dominican Republic* (Washington, D.C.: Government Printing Office, 1922), 1550–1551.

taken …?" Its answer was a simple yet remarkable call for solidarity. Put simply, occupation should—had to—"give way to the old rule of Haiti for the Haitians."[42]

U.S. black Marxists also deployed the phrase, imbuing it with the same urgency and a similar meaning as "Africa for the Africans," the slogan popularized by Garvey, who drew inspiration from Robert Love.[43] In July 1925, local branches of the Workers Party of America (WP), the political organization of the Communist Party USA (CPUSA), and the Young Workers League (YWL), the youth affiliate of the WP, held a series of rallies and a "huge mass meeting" at the South Side Community House in Chicago, Illinois. Speakers, including Lovett Fort-Whiteman, a black Texan who became known as the "Reddest of the Blacks" after founding the CPUSA and organizing the American Negro Labor Congress, preached to the crowds while WP and YWL workers distributed thousands and thousands of pamphlets containing a "special appeal to the Negro youth to join the Y.W.L." That appeal struck a similar tone as the demands published in *Le Courier haïtien*. "Negro Workers!" the leaflets announced,

---

[42] "What to Do in Haiti," *The Nation* (November 3, 1920). See also Ernest Gruening, "Haiti for the Haitians," *Current History* 40, no. 4 (July 1934): 418–424. On U.S. "interventions" in Latin America and resistance movements to them, see especially Alan L. McPherson, *The Invaded: How Latin Americans and Their Allies Fought and Ended U.S. Occupations* (New York: Oxford University Press, 2013).

[43] For instance, Robert Love wrote in 1901 that "'Africa for the Africans' is the new shape of an old cry […] This cry will waken the so-called civilized world to a consciousness of the fact that others who are not accounted as civilized, think, with regard to natural rights, just as civilized peoples think." *Jamaica Advocate* (April 20, 1901), quoted in Lewis, "Robert Love," 62. Recent histories of black Marxists in the internationalist moment of the post-World War I era include Brent Hayes Edwards, *The Practice of Diaspora: Literature, Translation, and the Rise of Black Internationalism* (Cambridge, MA: Harvard University Press, 2003); Michael O. West, William G. Martin, and Fanon Che Wilkins, eds., *From Toussaint to Tupac: The Black International since the Age of Revolution* (Chapel Hill: University of North Carolina Press, 2009); Minkah Makalani, *In the Cause of Freedom: Radical Black Internationalism from Harlem to London, 1917–1939* (Chapel Hill: University of North Carolina Press, 2011); Raphael Dalleo, *American Imperialism's Undead: The Occupation of Haiti and the Rise of Caribbean Anticolonialism* (Charlottesville: University of Virginia Press, 2016); Margaret Stevens, *Red International and Black Caribbean: Communists in New York City, Mexico and the West Indies, 1919–1939* (London: Pluto Press, 2017).

> Smash Imperialism Abroad!
> Africa for the Africans.
> China for the Chinese.
> Haiti for the Haitians.
> The world for the Workers.
> Fight oppression at home!
> Down with Jim Crowism.[44]

Down with the status quo. For Fort-Whiteman and his fellow black Marxists, "Africa for the Africans" was not the property of Garveyites. It was neither exclusive nor exceptional. Instead, similar slogans, including "Haiti for the Haitians," captured their expansive hopes for universal emancipation from capitalism, racism, and imperialism and expressed their solidarity with other people subjected to the slavery of colonialism.[45] The Russian Revolution certainly encouraged those hopes of anti-imperial internationalists but so, too, had the occupation of a black nation.

Haitians, aided by their allies abroad, liberated Haiti in 1934. But the long years of military occupation had made a lasting impact on Haitian politics and thought. Novels were one venue in which Haitian writers explored the themes of patriotism and national identity and articulated the affective and psychological condition of military occupation.[46] L'Union patriotique, an anti-occupation organization established with the support of U.S. black activists, was a more overtly political expression of Haitian nationalism. Its members included Sténio Vincent, the president who would declare Haiti's second independence. Jean Price-Mars was also part of the Patriotic Union and perhaps the leading intellectual of Haiti's national resistance. During the occupation,

---

44 "Mass Meetings to Rally Negro Workers against Imperialism," *Daily Worker* (July 3, 1925).
45 Those similar slogans would encompass other anticolonial struggles in the Caribbean. For instance, in the early 1960s, the Organisation de la jeunesse anticolonialiste de la Martinique (OJAM) adopted the slogan "Martinique aux Martiniquais." Yarimar Bonilla, *Non-Sovereign Futures: French Caribbean Politics in the Wake of Disenchantment* (Chicago: University of Chicago Press, 2015), 28.
46 See Nadève Ménard, "The Occupied Novel: The Representation of Foreigners in Haitian Novels Written during the United States Occupation, 1915–1934" (PhD diss., University of Pennsylvania, 2002).

Price-Mars accused the Haitian elite of a "collective bovaryism"—as seeing themselves as "colored Frenchmen" rather than people of African descent. He was a prominent voice of *indigénisme*, a literary, cultural, and intellectual movement that demanded a stronger Haitian national identity rooted in Vodou, folklore, and other cultural traditions of Haiti's peasants.[47]

While the crisis of occupation inspired new modes of thinking about race, culture, and Haiti's national consciousness, it also fundamentally altered the political conditions in which the theory and practice of Haitian nationalism and governance took shape. During the occupation, the United States had created the Gendarmerie, a new military commanded by U.S. Marines and capable of controlling Haiti's rural population. Haitian presidents would then use the more robust military, renamed the Garde d'Haïti, to consolidate their authority within a more powerful central government. From 1934 to the end of his second presidential term in 1941, Vincent, part of Haiti's light-complexioned elite, used the Garde to support his increasingly authoritarian nationalism.[48] He banned the Parti Communiste Haïtien and exiled its leader, Jacques Roumain. He also censored leftist periodicals that criticized his government's continued economic ties with the United States. In turn, the Haitian press became more and more reactionary by the late 1930s. As Chelsea Stieber notes, the advancement of authoritarianism against competing communist, feminist, and democratic impulses should be understood as an outcome of Haitian intellectuals' engagement with right-wing political ideologies that emerged in France but traversed the Atlantic World. These reactionary politics were the product of an era in which Haitian elites saw a need to reestablish Haiti on a different foundation, one capable

---

[47] J. Michael Dash, *Literature and Ideology in Haiti, 1915–1961* (London: Palgrave Macmillan, 1981); Jean Price-Mars, *So Spoke the Uncle*, trans. Magdaline W. Shannon (Washington, D.C.: Three Continents Press, 1983); Magdaline W. Shannon, *Jean Price-Mars, The Haitian Elite and the American Occupation, 1915–1935* (New York: St. Martin's Press, 1996).

[48] On the politics of post-occupation Haiti, see especially Smith, *Red & Black in Haiti: Radicalism, Conflict, and Political Change, 1934–1957* (Chapel Hill: The University of North Carolina Press, 2009); Grace Louise Sanders, "La Voix des femmes: Haitian Women's Rights, National Politics and Black Activism in Port-au-Prince and Montreal, 1934–1986" (PhD Ddiss., Unviersity of Michigan, 2013); Chantalle F. Verna, *Haiti and the Uses of America: Post-U.S. Occupation Promises* (New Brunswick: Rutgers University Press, 2018).

of withstanding the domestic and international conditions that had caused the occupation.[49]

The occupation would continue to cast a shadow on Haitian politics in the 1940s and '50s. Haiti strengthened its economic and political relationship with the United States during the presidency of Elie Lescot, a man who shared the class and color background of his predecessor, Vincent. Lescot would, for instance, initiate the Société Haïtiano-Américaine d'Exploitation Agricole (Haitian-American Society for Agricultural Development), a development project that cleared millions of trees, appropriated thousands of acres of land, displaced hundreds of thousands of Haitian peasants, and enriched its financiers in the U.S. and Haitian governments.[50] He notably launched this initiative while fighting an "anti-superstition" campaign against Vodou. While Haitian Marxists and feminists clamored for more say in Haiti's governance and society, sometimes through their own oppositional uses of "Haiti for the Haitians," other voices, namely those of the advocates of black consciousness known as *noiristes*, argued that Lescot's policies proved the problem of the *mulâtre* monopoly on power. Taking Price-Mars as their idol but undermining *indigénisme*'s call for national unity, they demanded *noiriste* control of the state.[51]

The ascension of Haiti's black middle class began in the presidential administrations of Dumarsais Estimé and Paul Magloire; its "triumph" came with the election of François Duvalier. In September 1957, Duvalier, a respected doctor and a leading theorist of *noirisme*, won a heated presidential election with the support of the Garde and likely a good deal of electoral fraud. He immediately began erecting the foundations of a dictatorship. Having declared that his opponents were "enemies of the nation," Duvalier created a civilian militia and a private police force.[52] The members of both groups, the Tonton Makouts, crushed political dissent across Haiti.[53] Through targeted and random acts of violence by his armed forces, Duvalier censored

---

49 Chelsea Stieber, "'Camelots du roi ou rouges': Radicalization in Early Twentieth-Century Haitian Periodicals," *Contemporary French Civilization* 45, no. 1 (2020): 47–69.
50 On SHADA, see Myrtha Gilbert, *Shada, chronique d'une extravagante escroquerie* (Port-au-Prince: Éditions Université d'État d'Haïti, 2012).
51 Price-Mars had, in fact, argued that "a politically radical black consciousness could ultimately lead to despotism." See Smith, *Red and Black in Haiti*, 27.
52 Dubois, *Haiti: The Aftershocks of History*, 325.
53 Marvin Chochotte, "'Making Peasants Chèf': The *Tonton Makout* Militia and the Moral Politics of Terror in the Haitian Countryside during the Dictatorship

the press and criminalized labor unions, communist organizations, feminist groups, and the Catholic Church. He enriched himself at the expense of Haitians, pocketing state funds, which included initially millions of dollars of U.S. aid delivered in support of his anti-communist regime.[54]

Duvalier used a range of rhetorical and cultural tactics to vindicate his dictatorship, including the appropriation of a familiar phrase.[55] On January 2, 1963, he delivered an address to Haiti. As he would on other celebrations of Ancestors' Day, the annual holiday when Haitians celebrate the success of the Haitian Revolution and their founding fathers, Duvalier took the opportunity to legitimize his violent rise to power and exaggerate his regime's achievements. Characterizing the "Duvalier revolution" as the heir to the Haitian Revolution and suggesting that he was the successor to Dessalines, Duvalier proclaimed that his efforts to strengthen state control over Haitian economic and social life was launched in an effort to secure an independent and sovereign future for Haiti. He equated himself with the nation and credited his power with reviving Haiti's self-respect and strength after the humiliation of the occupation. It was his mission, like those of Haiti's founding generation, Duvalier announced, "to implant and embed the consciousness that Haiti is for the Haitians." His revolution, too, was an affirmation that it was the duty of Haitians, and Haitians alone, to build their nation through dignified struggle.[56]

---

of François Duvalier," *Comparative Studies in Society and History* 61, no. 4 (October 2019): 925–953.

54 On the dictatorships of François Duvalier (1957–1971) and his son Jean-Claude Duvalier (1971–1986), see Michel-Rolph Trouillot, *Les Racines historiques de l'État Duvalierien* (Port-au-Prince: Henri Deschamps, 1987) and *Haiti, State against Nation: The Origins and Legacy of Duvalierism* (New York: Monthly Review Press, 1990); James Ferguson, *Papa Doc, Baby Doc: Haiti and the Duvaliers* (Oxford: B. Blackwell, 1988); Bernard Diederich, *L'Héritier* (Port-au-Prince: Henri Deschamps, 2011); Claire Antone Payton, "The City and the State: Construction and the Politics of Dictatorship in Haiti" (PhD diss., Duke University, 2018).

55 Duvalier's use of Vodou in service of his dictatorship has garnered significant scholarly attention. In particular, see Michel S. Laguerre, *Voodoo and Politics in Haiti* (London: Palgrave Macmillan, 1989), 101–120; R. Anthony Lewis, "Language, Culture, and Power: Haiti under the Duvaliers," *Caribbean Quarterly* 50, no. 4, special issue: Essays in Honour of the Bicentenary of Haitian Independence, 1804–2004 (December 2004): 42–51.

56 "Message De Son Excellence l'Honarable Docteur François Duvalier, President de la Republique à l'occasion du Jour des Aïeux, le 2 Janvier 1963," Ministere des

A Genealogy of Black Sovereignty 241

While Duvalier used "Haiti for the Haitians" as propaganda, some foreign observers once again used the phrase to accuse Haitians of an incapacity for democratic governance. In April 1964, the *New York Times* criticized the upcoming confirmation of Duvalier as Haiti's "president-for-life." "Haiti does not need Emperors, or Kings, or Presidents for life," the leading U.S. newspaper insisted. "She needs good, honest government." Rather than stopping with that accurate statement, which affirmed the popular sentiments of Haitians, the *Times* proceeded to blame Haitians for a dictatorship that, in one year alone, had received 13.5 million dollars, half of its entire budget, from the U.S government. "Duvalier may seem like a monster to us, but an overwhelming number of Haitians are willing to put up with him, as their ancestors did with equally brutal and tyrannical rulers," the *Times* argued. He was no different than Dessalines or any other Haitian despot. And so, the paper concluded, it was simply "a case of 'Haiti for the Haitians' until the Haitians decide that they want no more Presidents like François Duvalier."[57]

Published at the height of the modern U.S. Civil Rights Movement, the *Times*' flippant, mocking allusion to "Haiti for the Haitians" was indicative of the broader ahistoricism that plagued mainstream discourse during the era of desegregation and decolonization. As black people and former colonial subjects in the Global South rose up from under Jim Crow and colonialism—as they claimed citizenship and national independence—liberal white writers and pundits in the United States and Europe tended to characterize these momentous events as if the preceding centuries of racial and economic oppression had never happened. They elided whole histories of occupation in their rush to herald a new day for what the white world had finally accepted as human rights. While the ink on the Voting Rights Act of 1965 was still drying and red lines continued to divide American maps, African Americans were told to achieve the American Dream and accused of a whole host of pathologies when they did not. The world's first postcolonial black state suffered a similar fate. In its superficial empowerment of Haitians, which dismissed geopolitical structures of power, the *Times* presaged the paternalistic tones in which the U.S. and European press would cover postcolonial Africa. It implied the need for outside intervention to "democratize" Haiti, writing of Haitians' supposedly innate

---

Affaires Etrangeres, Port-au-Prince, Série B, 524PO/B/85, Centre Diplomatiques, Nantes, France. Thanks to Erin Zavitz for her generosity in sharing this source.
57 "Haiti's President for Life," *New York Times* (April 3, 1964).

preference for "brutal and tyrannical rulers" as if the disaster of recent U.S. occupation had never happened.

Of course, this ahistoricism butted up against subaltern political thought about black sovereignty informed by a long history of oppression. In March 2000 this became clear to Daniel Whitman, the counselor for public affairs at the U.S. Embassy in Port-au-Prince. That month, Whitman took John Conyers, the founder of the U.S. Congressional Black Caucus, to Pétionville, the suburb of Port-au-Prince in which many foreign NGO workers reside. No Haitians were willing to talk to Conyers. In the midst of a heated election pitting presidential candidate Jean-Bertrand Aristide's Fanmi Lavalas (Lavalas Family) against several opposition parties, suspicion of foreigners ran high. There was good reason for those misgivings. Aristide held the presidency years earlier before a military coup displaced him. His ouster and exile resulted in a devastating embargo that merged with political repression in forcing countless Haitians to flee their country. The subsequent U.S. intervention to restore Aristide to power worked—to a certain extent. Back in office, Aristide conceded to U.S. demands to lower taxes on foreign trade, a move that aided U.S. corporations with investments in Haiti and brought attendant harm to Haitian peasants undermined by cheap imports and unfavorable land policies. Now, the 2000 presidential election would have dramatic consequences. What those effects would be was uncertain but it was obvious to Haitians, well-aware of their ongoing history of foreign occupation, that there was little to gain from being identified as voters or in talking to high-ranking politicians from the United States.[58]

The residents of Port-au-Prince found other ways to voice their frustrated hopes for a type of sovereignty rooted in popular democracy. That tumultuous March, as Whitman and Conyers witnessed mounting disillusionment in the wake of the continued postponements of the pivotal election, Haitians took to the streets of the capital to celebrate Carnival, the annual festivities leading up to Mardi Gras. There, bands played their prepared music while the voices of the crowd rose as one:

> *Piye neg yo, piye neg yo*
> *Nou mele, nou mele [...]*
> *Ayiti peyi nou li ye*
> *Ayiti pou Ayisyen [...]*

---

58 Daniel Whitman, *A Haiti Chronicle: The Undoing of a Latent Democracy, 1999–2001* (Victoria, British Columbia: Trafford, 2005), 107–109. On Aristide, see especially Alex Dupuy, *The Prophet and Power: Jean-Bertrand Aristide, the International Community, and Haiti* (Lanham: Rowman and Littlefield, 2007).

"They're pillaging us, they're pillaging us," the crowd cried out. "We're in a mess, we're in a mess [...] Haiti is our country. Haiti for the Haitians."[59]

Western writers often struggle to write about sovereignty in a way that does not depict Haiti as odd or exceptional. That does not treat the liberal democracies of the North Atlantic as the standard international body. That does not assume that the black body is wrong or aberrant.

Yet, as anthropologist Yarimar Bonilla suggests, sovereignty and the geopolitical contexts in which it is said to exist are best understood from the position of bodies denied it.[60] Rather than revealing the unique instability of Haitian politics, the recent occupation of Haiti by the International United Nations Mission for the Stabilization of Haiti, which received support from the World Bank and the International Monetary Fund, demonstrates the neoliberal impulse of modern-day "humanitarianism."[61] It laid bare the standard experience of nominal sovereignty across much of the postcolonial world. In protesting the Haitian government's theft of funds accumulated through Petrocaribe, Venezuela's oil-purchasing and development program, Haitians renewed a longer struggle for government accountability to them, the people. They redefined political sovereignty as a starting point, not an end—as a condition incompatible with "humanitarian" interventionism, neoliberalism, and current international institutions; as a basic foundation on which political, economic, and social justice might actually, finally, exist.

This genealogy of "Haiti for the Haitians" locates the roots and routes—the historical denials and assertions—of that aspirational idea. From the nineteenth century to today, activists, intellectuals, and political actors of all kinds have used the phrase to express their ideas about slavery and abolition, colonialism and imperialism, democracy

---

59 Whitman, *A Haiti Chronicle*, 108–109.
60 Bonilla, "Ordinary Sovereignty," 164.
61 On the role of the international community in contemporary Haiti, see especially Paul Farmer, *The Uses of Haiti* (Monroe: Common Courage Press, 2005); Jonathan M. Katz, *The Big Truck That Went By: How the World Came to Save Haiti and Left Behind a Disaster* (New York: St. Martin's Press, 2014); Mark Schuller, *Killing with Kindness: Haiti, International Aid, and NGOs* (New Brunswick: Rutgers University Press, 2012); Mamyrah Dougé-Prosper and March Schuller, eds., "End of Empire? Racial Capitalism, Forced Migration, and State Violence in Haiti," *NACLA Report on the Americas* 53, no. 1 (Spring 2021).

and, importantly, sovereignty. They have ranged from reactionary to revolutionary. They have looked to and from Haiti, and sometimes beyond. Accordingly, the diverse iterations and reverberations of "Haiti for the Haitians" have expansive implications. Together, those words offer insights into Haiti's domestic politics and point to its transatlantic connections. They speak to an ongoing history of postcolonial and post-slavery struggle as it has unfolded at the local, national, and international levels.

Afterword

The Elusive *Habitant*[1]

Jean Casimir
Translated from French by Chelsea Stieber

The English edition of Louis-Joseph Janvier's *Haïti aux Haïtiens*, translated by Nadève Ménard and edited by Brandon Byrd and Chelsea Stieber, includes a variety of notes highlighting the complexity of the author's thought and the underlying elements of his era. It is one of the jewels of late nineteenth-century Haitian thought, a period during which the country produced probably its richest crop of intellectuals. The text is preceded by a remarkable introduction by Byrd and Stieber that analyzes the repercussions of these ideas in the sphere where local inequalities were taking shape, and the research itinerary that complements findings from the period. It is followed by six essays on Janvier's life, work, and times, as well as the issues that he raised with regard to the European continent. The following reflections aim to point out Janvier's limitations—limitations that he shared with his different audiences.

I

Modern-day Haitians were born at the crossroads of two trajectories: the first, charted by prisoners unaware of the reasons for their captivity and who strove relentlessly to rectify things and return to normalcy; and the other, charted by the guarantors of a public order who scarcely thought of relinquishing the benefits conferred to them by a proslavery state. The first, in their quest for autonomy—and thus sovereignty—created the nation against the designs of colonial power. The other

---

[1] Settler; *abitan* in Haitian Creole.

was forced to join this quest for autonomy in self-defense, after the metropole in disarray planned to deport them and exterminate those they had been anxious to use as *cultivateurs*.[2] Devoid of any sympathy towards one another, these two social classes unwillingly forged a modicum of understanding in order to expel the murderous troops from the country. The state of Haiti proclaimed its independence, but its feeble government would develop in the midst of a community of soulless, lawless nation-states.[3]

The essays that accompany the translation of Louis-Joseph Janvier's *Haïti aux Haïtiens* in this volume show how towards the end of the nineteenth century the author was thinking within the constraints placed upon political authorities negotiating their autonomy in a time of rampant imperialism. They were fragile and vulnerable. The author advised turning inward.[4] His trajectory is the culmination of an itinerary charted by the (institutional) fathers of the nation, *the Black Jacobins*, along with the Abbé Grégoire, the abolitionists of their time, and the Society of the Friends of the Blacks. They set out to integrate Haitians into the international community by "civilizing" and "developing" them, without accountability to anyone. This *mission*—which was not benevolent—was tainted by injustices that Louis-Joseph Janvier only obliquely critiques.

The Haitian state and its bureaucracy demonstrate France's presence in the colony. The governmental organizations that took over after 1804 maintained colonial officials' roles and reinforced their attendant privileges. Byrd and Stieber's Introduction asks pertinent questions: "Who were the Haitians who had the implied, inviolable claim on Haiti? To whom did Haiti not belong? And what then defined that place declared for Haitians? What was Haiti and what could it be?"[5]

The mutual lack of comprehension and low esteem between the two contradictory colonial classes, namely the *anciens affranchis*[6] and the former captives, was hardly suitable for even a short-lived alliance. Nevertheless, the threat of death and the pride and contempt of the

---

2 Agricultural workers, as distinct from self-employed peasants.

3 See Jean Casimir, *Une lecture décoloniale de l'histoire des Haïtiens: du traité de Ryswick à l'Occupation américaine (1697–1915)* (Port-au-Prince: Jean Casimir, 2018); Jean Casimir, *The Haitians: A Decolonial History*, trans. Laurent Dubois (Chapel Hill: University of North Carolina Press, 2020).

4 Louis-Joseph Janvier, *Haiti for the Haitians*, 61 above.

5 See the Introduction, 32 above.

6 People emancipated prior to 1793.

international community drove them to solemnize a sort of non-aggression pact that became the Haitian state. To grasp the problem that *Haïti aux Haïtiens* tries to resolve, it is important not to get distracted as the author does by the divisions between officials governing a public order that is colonial in origin. The problem, born of the divergence between the Liberal Party and the National Party, does not stem from the local universe. Their famous mottos, power to the most capable (the Liberals) or power to the greatest number (the Nationals), can easily lead us astray.

When the crisis in the colony reached its peak in 1791, the slaves freed by France along with men of mixed race born of free parents ended up in the (French) Legions of Equality, where they were responsible for reestablishing the colonial order. Following the General Insurrection a short time later, another group of people reduced to slavery, mostly slave drivers,[7] took charge of negotiating the insurgents' return to the plantation gangs[8] in exchange for the freedom of a number of organizers of the uprisings. Some received their freedom as a privilege resulting from their assistance maintaining the pro-slavery order and, generally speaking, were very pleased about their much greater proximity to their benefactors than to the captives. Others negotiated their freedom following discussions they conducted on behalf of the rebels, with whom they maintained greater familiarity. Yet both intermediary factions endorsed their differences with the people freed by the general emancipation decree of 1793 and detached themselves from the masses by acting as a hinge between exploiter and exploited.

The role of those responsible for public order in the police force and the militias, resulting from intermediaries' outside relationships, was threatened during the rise in imperialism at the end of the nineteenth century. Indeed, in the century that followed independence, these strata could not take over the dominant role held by capitalist planters. Thus they lived with the urgent need to preserve the limited administrative functions at their disposal.

Janvier is adamant: "It is through the mind that man is conquered. We entrust the minds of our children to France, which it seeds with its ideas. That is enough. It is up to us to do the rest."[9] But, he continues elsewhere: "When you live surrounded by enemies and all kinds of

---

7 In French: *commandeurs*.
8 In French: *ateliers*.
9 Janvier, *Haiti for the Haitians*, 65.

pitfalls, you cannot guard against surprises too carefully."[10] He goes further still: "They say it everywhere, our dear friends and dubious relatives, that they have obtained important concessions due to your gullibility, and that they can get all the concessions they ask for. They even say it in our own newspapers."[11]

In this environment, oligarchs worried about international pressures and not about the impact of internal contradictions forestalled or mitigated by the retreat of the bulk of the population and its never-ending evasion of governmental directives. Hence the prevalence of modern-world objectives in politics, which leads Janvier to want to integrate a so-called *paysan*[12] by means of an agrarian reform that popular movements were not asking for. The oligarchy's awareness of its subordinate position is hardly surprising. But the search for a way out of their awkward position is held in check by their validation of Western Europe's hegemony and their misinterpretation of the identity of most inhabitants of the country.

We find the following sentence in Louis-Joseph Janvier's text: "Let us not forget that when the buccaneers settled on that island [La Tortue], at the beginning of the seventeenth century, they only did so because it had been abandoned by the Spanish, the only ones who could have claimed legitimate ownership at the time."[13] The values of modernity lead a thinker of this caliber astray with regard to the meaning of "legitimate." The weight of the right of conquest creates a straightjacket that excludes ethics and morality from any governance. While Western Europe was plundering Central Europe, Africa, and Asia with impunity (which Janvier addresses), Haitian oligarchies inspected and robbed the state without restraint.

According to *Haïti aux Haïtiens*, we must unilaterally curb the pernicious appetites of these church mice[14] albeit without addressing their damaged compass that deems stolen property legitimate. The victory of the Indigenous Army over the French established the territory's property rights and thus, a sovereignty equal in its legitimacy to Spain's claim over the Taïno's territory. Louis-Joseph Janvier's oeuvre reads like a stubborn defense of property hijacked and confiscated in this way. It then becomes necessary to prohibit foreigners' access to this

10 Ibid., 72.
11 Ibid., 76.
12 Peasant. Janvier and most French-speaking observers called the person in question a *paysan*. S/he calls him/herself a "settler": *habitant* or *abitan* in Haitian Creole.
13 Janvier, *Haiti for the Haitians*, 73.
14 Ibid., 48.

Afterword 249

property at all costs and, to make things easier, to plan the sharing out of it to the greatest number of *paysans* thanks to agrarian reform.

Independence and, consequently, Haitian sovereignty, were mainly decided on the international stage. By reinforcing national unity, Louis-Joseph Janvier hoped to defend both in the face of the abuses originating in the right of the strongest and instrumental reason, undisputed substitutes for the justice system. As a counterpart to this world, divided up by greedy imperialists, was a state surrounded by an oligarchy of large landowners dominating a mass of destitute *habitants*. Janvier maintained the attribution of propertied or dispossessed classes without referring to this fissure's origin in the right of conquest—of Spain, of France, and of the Haitian state. Presumably, access to landownership would bring the *paysans* closer to local oligarchies. By satisfying this objective suddenly within reach, the oligarchies would develop a nationalism that was attentive to the international context[15] in which their scrawny government would establish and defend its dubious version of sovereignty.

It is unclear whether the path Janvier mined is passable or opens onto a solution. Wanting to strive for "an equal place in the international order" for Haiti[16] implies replicating the imperial state and its definition of sovereignty. The odds of success in such a battle are slim, as evidenced by the examples of Poland and Egypt that Janvier cites.

Recruiting *paysans* to a fight against imperialism seems even more problematic, for we have to ask ourselves why political authorities were never able to undertake a proper agrarian reform. The sudden realization that the *paysans* were entitled to landownership because this policy rescued the ruling classes does not necessarily imply that they would rush to take the pieces of land offered to them. They did not disperse throughout the territory, despite being faced with an abundance of land in the west and east of the island throughout the nineteenth century, and nothing indicates that landownership was of paramount importance to their life plans.

II

Poland's and Egypt's difficulties demonstrated that the political landscape was not broken up into discrete units made up of nation-states. The desire to correct the distribution of landownership in Haiti while forcing new landowners to produce export commodities, as per

---

15 See the Introduction, 39–42 above.
16 Ibid., 40.

the law issued by Salomon's government, seems to retain the designs of the hand responsible for unequal land distribution in the first place. Why did this hand create a destitute majority to begin with? Or to return to the questions from the Introduction, "Who were the Haitians who had the implied, inviolable claim on Haiti?"[17]

A common thread runs from the colonialism of the eighteenth century to the imperialism of the late nineteenth, from slavery to the civilizing mission of France and her peers. To ensure that the history of France structured that of its colony, officials established a staggering equivalency between liberation and liberty when the custodial institution of metropolitan interests, plantation slavery, was being abolished. This wicked confusion enabled France to hide the common denominator between royalist and republican factions, as well as between abolitionist and pro-slavery factions, or between the *affranchis de l'ordre* and those *de la négociation*.[18] The social categories invented by French history cannot detect the insurgents' thoughts and feelings because colonial logic dictates that they are nonexistent or futile. Those who do not have the right to possess anything that belongs to their master possess no thoughts, knowledge, or spirituality worth mentioning.

Despite its monopoly on modern wealth, by the end of the eighteenth century France was unable to maintain the daily war required to transform the people it shackled into slaves. France did not have a monopoly on power. Its weakness required it to fall back on the illusory figure of the *cultivateur* or *nouveau libre*,[19] thus on a *liberated* person.[20] This superficial change in status was not enough to subjugate the insurgents and lock them up on commodity plantations. Nor did it calm the civil wars in the colony, so France decided to exterminate or deport the protesters. It failed in this task.

The ensuing ephemeral pact sealed in 1804 between a few *affranchis* and those they called the *nouveaux libres* disappeared as soon as the governments that were counting on the social death of the *nouveaux libres* took power. Despite their opposition to slavery, these governments only institutionalized the political participation of the minority whom they showered with land. Formal power remained limited to the concept of sovereignty founded on the right of conquest.

---

17 Ibid., 32.
18 The term *affranchis de l'ordre* refers to those people freed before the decree of general emancipation, hence by the slave owners; *affranchis de la négociation* refers to those freed in the ensuing negotiations after 1791, by the state itself.
19 People freed as a result of the 1793 and 1794 emancipation decrees.
20 In French: *personne libérée*.

The country's governance copied the colonial administration as best it could and exhausted itself reactivating the role of agricultural laborers. In fact, the Haitian legal system is to this day unable to find *paysans* in the national territory. The small agricultural producer has no reason to exist if he is not producing export commodities. The Executive is not thinking about how to center agriculture on the norms and values that define the *habitant*'s well-being, and thinks even less about the actual presence of the local language in the judicial system or in public administration. It matters little whether *cultivateurs* understand the law, so long as they do as they are told.

It is worth remembering that two-thirds of the population in Saint-Domingue disembarked as adults in the fifteen years leading up to the general insurrection of 1791. This overwhelming majority originated from a universe of free people. They could not shed their first education overnight, especially since they were being socialized in a colony torn apart by the crises of a metropole incapable of impressing them. On the other hand, the minority of *affranchis* who had never known a world without slavery could not conceive of incorporating a practice of freedom into the state that went beyond general emancipation and would express the captives' profound desires. For this minority, the integration of prisoners began at the lowest rung of a society governed by modernity.

In the end, the Indigenous Army forced the French expeditionary army to surrender. Traditional history attributes the victory to emancipated slaves who had been formed by the Enlightenment and dispenses with the feelings of almost all of the revolutionary insurgents. The enormous distance between the *anciens affranchis* and the *anciens captifs*,[21] as defined by the colony, lurks behind the need to militarize agriculture in order to protect against a French counteroffensive. Provisioning certain essential goods from the international market, including arms and munitions, would require the reactivation of an economy centered on foreign trade.

And yet the whole of the nineteenth century refutes this falsehood. During this period, the provisioning of essential goods defied the revival of the plantation. There were no grounds for the militarization of agriculture,[22] apart from the minority interests of the *anciens libres*.[23]

---

21 Captives (that is to say, people the colony referred to as slaves) prior to general emancipation.
22 In French: *caporalisme agraire*.
23 Georges Anglade, *Atlas critique d'Haïti*, http://classiques.uqac.ca/contemporains/anglade_georges/atlas_critique_haiti/atlas_critique_haiti.html. *Anciens libres* is a term synonymous with *anciens affranchis*—people freed prior to 1793.

Their insistence on reviving the commodity-producing plantation introduced the figure of the *cultivateur* into all of the laws issued by the Haitian state in place of the *paysan*, not to speak of the *habitant*. The two groups of freed people who agreed on the necessity of militarized agriculture—the original *affranchis* of the colonial order, and the new crop of *affranchis* who negotiated their liberation after 1791[24]— maintained and promoted the incompatibility of their interests with those of agricultural workers.

To this end, society criminalized the insurgent's behavior before and after the general insurrection of 1791: he was made a deserter and a bandit in the eighteenth century, and a vagabond and an outlaw in the nineteenth. This is the person, exiled from economic and political decision-making, to whom Louis-Joseph Janvier proposed distributing land. But the captives, forcefully removed from Africa, revolted against their enslavement by gradually capturing the position of the *habitant*. They did not dream of being inserted into the lowest rung of commercialized agricultural activity. Having come from a world that evolved outside of the plantation system, they wisely positioned themselves outside of that sphere. In fact, they called themselves *moun an deyò*, people from the outside, regardless of the metropole's supposed needs or the post-independence governments' fabricated urgency to reactivate export agriculture.

Beginning in 1793, political authorities thought that they could thwart the uncompromising attitude of the *nouveaux libres* by assigning them the status of passive citizens. Solving the economic stagnation that resulted from authorities' casual treatment of the *nouveaux libres*' interests required a kind of brute force that governments after 1804 did not possess. They could not prevent the so-called *cultivateurs* from settling independently and autonomously in their gardens, and thus, from being active citizens.

Slavery, the *cultivateurs*' confinement, and the commodity-producing plantation are all French institutions. To revive them in one form or another is to continue the history of France in Saint-Domingue or in Haiti, and requires relying on military force or an expeditionary army. The essential question for a Haitian was not to optimize the efficiency of French institutions. It was to optimize the institutions that the captives designed to get out of slavery. For it wasn't French institutions or French thought that broke their chains. It wasn't a question of how

---

24 Jean Casimir, *Haïti et ses élites, l'interminable dialogue de sourds* (Port-au-Prince: Les Éditions de l'Université d'État d'Haïti, 2009), 205ff.

Afterword   253

to convert captives into peasants and undertake agrarian reform, it was a question of how the captives presented themselves to the world and with what aspirations. Why did the captives retain their identification as *habitants* and not *cultivateurs*? What does the choice of the word *habitant* reflect? Why from Goman (1807–1819) to Acaau's Piquets (1843–1844) and from Salnave (1867–1869) to Charlemagne Péralte and Benoit Batraville's Cacos (1915–1920) does the Latin American demand for land and liberty not feature prominently in their protests?

Both the colonial and national governments discriminated against the African deportees and forced them back towards a capitalist agricultural regime that the state could not maintain without a relentless war against an unarmed population. The false pretext of their lack of education, civilization, and spirituality justified their appalling treatment, even as their torturers displayed unprecedented barbarity towards the most vulnerable and the most fragile: the elderly, adults, and babies at their mothers' breasts. In addition to a range of colonial torments, abuses and punishment of all sorts, the post-1804 executive power added to its arsenal of repression the monopolization of fertile land and the lack of health services, education, public procurement, and leisure time. Such a lack cannot be explained by the scarcity of government funding, as the treatment of laborers in the "pearl of the Antilles" demonstrates.

Upon their arrival in the colony, these social actors were deprived of the right to possess anything at all. To carve a path towards their goal of self- and communal fulfillment, they invented a world unknown to modernity: a world where private property was not confused with the right to use and abuse nature's gifts, including human beings. Rather than constructing a universe for themselves in the dregs of society, they discovered that *tout moun se moun* ("every person is a person") and identified as inhabitants or settlers or colonists, ready to live as they saw fit.

The post-1804 oligarchies never questioned the monolingual Creole-speakers' choice of the term *habitant*. There were no *paysans* in Saint-Domingue and the Creole language could not adopt a concept without a lived experience of that reality. The refusal to recognize the rationality of the *moun an deyò* is the common denominator of the Nationals, the Liberals, and all modern people. They did not realize that captives doomed to perpetual poverty would sidestep private property in favor of relationships grounded in solidarity and reciprocity, which sheltered them from the abuses of plantation society. From these relationships emerged a community of peers, a source of care, affection, exuberance, and happiness, as well as protection from the unspeakable abuses of the modern state. This community revered human beings and from its cradle, the *lakou*, and enjoyed a sovereignty that dispensed with the supremacy of private property and the ideologies of the modern state.

The *habitants*' world bloomed out of morality and ethics. From their viewpoint, the law of nations formulated by the local government and the international community to justify their existence excluded any justice from modern political life, along with any celebration of the lives of the majority. Under the aegis of its modernity, colonial society was unable to reproduce the population during over a century of colonization. Conversely, in their isolation and solitude, the population of the *habitants* quintupled during the nineteenth century.

Haiti for the Haitians indeed. But the population is not a homogenous totality. The modern world differentiates it into races, white, mixed, and black; or into social classes, bourgeois, proletarian, and enslaved. These categories did not emerge from the Haitians' fight against the infernal institution. How could they invent a free and autonomous society with instruments of thought derived from colonialism, that is to say, with the instruments used to think by those who insisted on placing and replacing their shackles?

Haiti's oligarchs experienced an independence and a sovereignty fraught with uncertainty. For Louis-Joseph Janvier, introducing what he calls the *paysan* into the country's political and economic life was a way to balance the social structure visible to him. But the *paysan* he speaks of exists neither in the colonial mentality nor in the mentality of the *cultivateurs* turned *habitants*. Only the French-educated oligarchs wanted to import them to the country. The *habitants* they imagined did not coincide with those who lived in the territory. For the oligarchs, society was founded upon *anciens esclaves*[25] or *cultivateurs*: a point of departure that dispenses with the Haitian *habitant*'s autonomous process of construction. The oligarchs set aside and ignored the national community's local experiences, the paths and the means they utilized to break their shackles, and, above all, the institutions they invented along the way.

The belated centrality that Louis-Joseph Janvier offers to the *paysan* reproduces the *habitant*'s invisibility and abandons leaders to the mercy of imperialism. To avoid thinking of the *habitants* as colonists in the literal sense of the term, "settlers," we must maintain the racialized terms

---

25 People whom the colony referred to as slaves, prior to general emancipation.

of human relations. On these grounds, the *habitants* were consigned to the lowest echelons of society, which only an external support could help to achieve.

III

The *habitants* of Haiti seized their own sovereignty in 1791 without asking for the consent of the modern world. So long as their sovereignty is ignored, the sovereignty of the entire nation remains suspended indefinitely. One cannot perceive sovereignty under the weight of modernity's hegemony and under a national autonomy managed by means of the law of the strongest. When Janvier wrote his pathbreaking book, nowhere were modern intellectual elites addressing themselves to the rural masses. In the case of Haiti, these masses constituted nearly the entire population and they were not using the language or the thought forms of these intellectuals. Their will to live as they wished determined the scope of a space that they alone controlled, without the assistance of professional thinkers.

The majority of the population were not converted into representatives of the modern world because they did not have to entrust the minds of their children to France to be seeded with its ideas.[26] The charms of the capitalist universe did not impress them. To rely on them for any modernization project—for any civilizing mission—inevitably requires authoritarianism, which for more than two hundred years has ended in failure.

Haiti aux Haïtiens offers the reader, on the one hand, the course charted by Haiti's intellectual elite to keep from being swallowed up by the racist and imperialist ideologies of the era and, on the other, the yawning gap that separates this intellectual elite from the masses out of which it emerged. The elite's small world at the heart of the Atlantic Ocean has not yet freed itself from the pitfalls of established political powers, which sterilize its efforts at emancipation. This elite remains incapable of freeing itself from the metropolitan system, while the *habitants* have created a world for themselves beyond that universe, for over two centuries.

Likewise, Louis-Joseph Janvier's oeuvre demonstrates the obstacles that local history imposes on thinkers' ability to dialogue with their natural allies abroad. These thinkers were socialized in the prison of modernity and few among them can imagine a universe other than the

---

26 Janvier, *Haiti for the Haitians*, 65.

one offered by Western Europe. So long as Haitian intellectuals and their natural allies remain under the spell of modernity, their exchanges will but hobble along.

Jean Casimir
Delmas, April 4, 2021

Index

abolitionism 2–3, 115, 119–20, 222, 225–26, 246, 250
   see also abolitionists
abolitionists 226, 246
   African American 225
   British 37, 222
   French 67n42, 154n61
   United States 50n8, 59n26, 115–16, 127
   see also abolitionism
Acaau, Jean-Jacques 10–11, 12, 206, 253
Adams, John Quincy 57n21
affranchis 246, 250–52
Africa 3, 15–17, 25, 38, 133, 157, 252
   children of 89, 126
   civilizing mission and 164–65n6, 169
   colonial 235
   for the Africans 38, 222, 236–37
   Haitian experience and the people of 35
   origins as condition of Haitian citizenship 49n7
   partition of 63n35, 231
   plunder of 220, 248
   political ideologies 4
   postcolonial 241
   scramble for 182
   and Vodou 70n48, 195n23
   see also colonialism; enslavement; imperialism; neocolonialism; Pan-Africanism
Afro-diaspora 124, 126
Age of Revolutions 3
agriculture 54, 64n38, 65, 75, 253
   laborers 6, 10, 12, 53, 54n15, 207, 251–52

   production 3, 5, 20, 152, 175, 194
   taxation on 206n58
   theories on 125
   see also cultivateurs; farmers; *habitants*; industrialism; labor; land; *paysans*; peasants; proletarians; property
d'Alembert, Jean le Rond 96
Alexis, Jacques Stephen 95
Ali, Mehmet 52
American Dream 241
American Negro Labor Congress 236
Americanness 134–35
Ancestors' Day 240
Ancien Régime 167
anciens affranchis see affranchis
anciens captifs 251
anciens libres 251–52
annexation 26, 59, 78, 142, 152, 199, 201, 230
Anthropology Society of Paris 86
anticolonial 141, 165, 235, 232
   confederation 26
   dissent 33
   independence 28
   movements 127
   nationalism 35, 38, 52n11, 222, 229, 235
   politics 27, 40
   project 24, 30
   resistance 150
   state 184
   struggle 2, 41, 102, 237n45
   thought 36, 119–20, 177
   revolution 13, 37, 220, 226
   writing 173, 179n39, 181

258 Index

anti-Haitian tropes 231
anti-imperialists 38, 222
Antillano, El *see* Betancès, Ramón Emeterio
antislavery
  efforts 115–16
  independence 26n63, 28
  movements 127
  project 24
  revolution 13, 37, 220, 225–26
  state 182, 184
  struggle 2
  thought 120
  tradition 67n42
  see also abolitionists; anticolonial; solidarity
Ardouin, Coriolan 149
Aristide, Jean-Bertrand 242
aristocracy 6, 105, 180n40, 205
armée indigène 5
Army of Sufferers 11, 206
  see also Acaau, Jean-Jacques
Auguste, Jules 86
authoritarianism 238

Báez, Buenaventura 26
Bahamas 1
Banque Nationale d'Haïti (BNH) 54n15
Barrès, Maurice 100
Batraville, Benoit 253
bazelaisistes 28
  see also Boyer Bazelais, Jean-Pierre
Berlin West Africa Conference of 1884–1885 16, 63n36, 231
Bernabé, Jean 134
Betancès, Ramón Emeterio 37, 86, 118, 127–30, 132, 165, 176
Bibliothèque Nationale 100
Bidlack Treaty (Treaty of New Granada) 74n55
Black Atlantic humanism 28, 154
  see also humanism
black internationalism 114, 237
black political bodies 220, 222
Blaine, James G. 57–58, 136
Boisrond-Canal, Pierre Théoma 28
Boisrond-Tonnerre, Louis-Félix 114
Bonaparte, Napoleon 5, 52n11, 91, 226n19

Bordier, Arthur 143
Bourbon Restoration 168
bovarysme collectif 107, 133
  see also Delorme, Demesvar; Janvier, Louis-Joseph; Price-Mars, Jean
Bowler, Arthur 86, 152n50, 165, 176
Boyer, Jean-Pierre 3, 6, 11, 12, 26n63, 110
  actions as president 7–8, 72n52
  and colonialism 128
  color prejudice 97–98
  indemnity 79n63
  laisser grainnin "laisser faire" 19n42
  opposition to his presidency 9–10
  rural code 21, 206n58
  on unification of Haiti 24–25
  see also Acaau, Jean-Jacques; indemnity treaty; Guerrier, Phillipe; Piquets
Boyer Bazelais, Jean-Pierre 1, 4, 11, 12, 28–30, 191n10
Brazil 63, 126, 204, 226
Brown, William Wells 227

Cacos 99
  see also Batraville, Benoit
Cambodia 62
canalistes 28
  see also Boisrond-Canal, Pierre Théoma
capital 10
capitalism 5, 137, 139, 219–20, 227–28, 233n37, 235–37
Caribbean Confederation 130
Caribbeanness 135
de Caritat, Marie Jean Antoine Nicolas 66–67
Catholic Church 97, 99, 167, 240
Catholicism 70, 94, 99, 167, 169, 195
Les Cayes 10
Cenacle of 1836 209
Césaire, Aimé 53n14, 114, 126, 140, 164n5, 179n39
Chamoiseau, Patrick 134
Charter of the United Nations 220
Christianity 16, 167
  see also civilizing mission; colonialism

Christophe, Henry 6, 31, 89, 97, 110, 115, 128, 208
citizenship 11, 91, 188n4, 222
　birthright 59–60n26
　Boyer Bazelais, Jean-Pierre on 7
　claims on 241
　emergence of 98
　French 2, 166, 168n14
　Geffrard, Fabre and 12
　global 140
　limitations to 22–23n55, 49n7
　rights 134
　Salomon, Lysius Félicité and 10
　transnational 135
civilization 52, 93, 108, 174, 178, 185, 220, 253
　abolition and 168
　Antillean 155–56
　Black Latin 142, 198
　creolization and 159
　debates 35
　European standard of 226
　and the French empire 15, 165, 167, 179, 181
　and inferiority 163–64
　as monetary meaning to United States 137–38
　and political ascendance 12
　religion and 14, 16, 70n48
　science and 87, 97, 143
　Western conceptions of 170–71, 175, 220
　and whiteness 24, 55n18
　see also universal brotherhood
civilizing mission, the 15–16, 169, 250
　and authoritarianism 255
　defiance of 151
　and French Third Republic 143, 183, 185
　and Haitian sovereignty 36
　inconsistencies of 171
　and fundamental inequality 164–66
　see also colonialism; France
civil war (Haiti) 1–2, 6, 47, 87, 99, 191n10, 192
　of 1868–1876 78n62
　of 1883–1884 28, 30–31, 38, 208
　calming of 250
　and color prejudice 127

　condemnation of 202
　erasing traces of 69, 201
　exploitation and 205
　and the nation 228
　and peasant condition 95
　post-independence 11, 13
　publishing as militancy during 193
Civil War (U.S.) 17, 119, 127
class 19n43, 22, 232, 239
　color and 148
　divisions over 39, 48n6
　political 92
　social 187, 189, 193, 207, 210, 212
　struggle 205
　unity 125
Clayton-Bulwer Treaty (1850) 74–75n56
Clemenceau, Georges, 171–72n23
Clément, Jean-Baptiste 108
coffee 8n21, 13, 20–21, 62–63, 230
colonialism 111, 250, 252, 254
　age of 40–41
　as aspirational idea 243
　combating 116, 126
　critiques of 53n14, 142
　debt and 31
　defiance of 37, 241
　European 63n36, 179n39, 219, 222, 224
　French 62n32, 167, 176–77
　and land ownership 22–23n55, 49n7
　missionary 171
　nationalism and 36, 42
　scientific 147, 150
　shared experience of 25
　slavery of 237
　transnational debates 121
Colonial Pact, the 62
Columbus, Christopher 26n63, 86n7, 110, 150
commerce 16, 30, 59, 64, 197
commercial 7, 8n21, 23, 58n22, 61–62, 78n62, 152, 175, 199, 215
　see also agriculture; commerce; commodities; farmers; plantation economy
commodities 249–251
commodity plantation see plantation economy
communism 238

Communist Party USA (CPUSA) 236
de Condorcet, Nicolas *see* de Caritat, Marie Jean Antoine Nicolas
Confiant, Raphaël 134
conquest 76, 94, 112, 128, 248–50
contagionist doctrine 145–46
  see also prejudice; tuberculosis
Conyers, John 242
Cook, Mercer 126
Coppée, François 85, 132
cotton 12, 64, 228
counter-plantation system 5, 69n45
  see also lakou
courtyard *see* lakou
CPUSA *see* Communist Party USA
Creole 3, 134, 144, 156, 253
Creoleness 134, 157n69
créolité 134–35
creolization 125, 145, 156–60
critical race theory 121, 155
Cuba 18, 114, 226
  anticolonial Caribbean Confederation 26, 130–31
  emigration to 20
  liberation of enslaved 119
  occupation of 235
  Spanish colony 24
cultivateurs 4, 246, 251–54
  see also farmers; *habitants*; *paysans*; peasantry

Darwin, Charles 15, 154, 159–60
decolonization 35, 160, 241
Delorme, Demesvar 99, 113, 121
  as Afro-diasporic activist 126–27
  anticolonial movements 120
  black nationalism 34, 118, 140
  on colonialism 116
  on domestic racism 119, 128
  on governance 21
  on Haitian sovereignty 135
  and Haiti's intellectual tradition 37, 131–32, 209
  as novelist 102, 133, 190n8
  on racial uplift 139
  on United States expansionism 57–58n21, 122–24, 129, 137–38, 229
democracy 210, 243
  and black sovereignty 124, 222
  according to Delorme, Demesvar 21
  human rights and 171–72n23
  and land 10
  meaning of 123
  popular 228, 232, 242
  U.S. notions of 139, 227, 233
Denis, Clément 86, 152n50, 165, 176
Depestre, René 114
deportees 246, 250, 253
Dessalines, the 29
Dessalines, Jean-Jacques 5, 14, 119, 128, 195, 197
  assassination 211
  criticism of 222–24, 241
  as hero 89, 240
  as leader 97, 110
  as liberator 114, 228
  in reimagined history 225–27
  unification 24
Dévost, Justin 86, 165, 176
dictatorship 239
Diderot, Denis 63n35, 66–67, 96
Domingue, Michel 8n21, 28, 78–79n62, 110
Dominican Republic 13, 61n30, 72–73n52
  and the Caribbean Confederation 130
  and immigration 20
  independence 24–26
  neutrality 195
  and the United States 18, 59–60n26, 122n29, 199n35, 235
  see also Haiti; Hispaniola; Saint-Domingue; Santo Domingo
Douglass, Frederick 59, 199
Du Bois, W.E.B. 124–25, 140
Dumas, Alexandre 132
Durand, Oswald 149
Dutrouleau, Auguste-Frédéric 148
Duvalier, François 239–41

École Médecine de Port-au-Prince 14
education 65–66n41
egalitarianism 21, 59–60n26, 166–68, 213, 227
  see also liberal egalitarianism

Egypt 40, 52, 56, 78, 102, 108, 249
elites 9, 19, 24–25, 39, 65–66n41, 72–73n52, 228–29, 238, 255
emancipation 255
    debates 225–26
    from foreign servitude 182
    Haitian influence 126
    in Santo Domingo 72n52
    and land reform 11
    nationalism and 42
    political 187, 211
    social 204
    Sonthonax decree of 1793 2, 4n8, 247, 250nn18–19
    universal 115, 237, 251
empire 128
    American U.S. 17–18, 58–60nn24–25, 135, 219, 222
    debates 35, 165–66
    French 15–16, 27n64, 167–71
    and Haitian nationalism 185, 223
    and racial capitalism 228
    racism and 127, 137
    Roman 181, 211n68
    science and 146–47
    violence of 230
    see also colonialism; France; Great Britain; United States
Encyclopedia, The 14, 63
enfranchisement 59–60n25, 227
Enlightenment, the 35, 63n35, 67n42, 96, 183, 220, 251–52
enslavement 2, 24, 41, 69n45, 99, 150, 178, 184
    autonomy from 5, 183
    and blackness 220
    and citizenship 127
    colonial dependence and 31
    commodities 63
    and indemnity 8
    liberation from 119
    and notions of freedom 3–4, 224
    ongoing 226
    and revolt 252
    as social class 254
    solidarity and 25
    see also Catholicism; genocide; slavery
Estimé, Dumarsais 239

exile 3, 129, 132
    Aristide, Jean-Bertrand 242
    and Jamaica 10–11, 29
    Janvier 85, 111
    Liberal members in 28
    political 12–13
    as theme 102–3
expansion
    and biological racism 171
    colonial 104, 143, 147, 168–69
    corporate 17
    European 16
    German 170
    Haitian 64, 197
    United States 18, 50n9, 59–60n26, 128
    see also colonialism; France; imperialism; racism; United States

Faculté de Médecine, Paris 15, 143, 145
Fanmi Lavalas (Lavalas Family) 242
farmers 207
    agrarian reform and 205–8, 230
    guano and 67–68n44
    and infrastructure 92
    and national theory 211–12
    as social class 187, 204, 210, 213
    tenant 20
    see also cultivateurs; habitant; paysans; peasantry
feminism 107, 238–39, 240
Ferry, Jules 16, 169–71, 176
Firmin, Anténor 34, 111, 117–18, 127, 190n8
    and agro-industry 210
    and formation of public opinion 165
    on racial inequality 83–84, 181
foreign intervention 23–24
Fort-Whiteman, Lovett 236–37
France 15, 19, 65, 88, 96, 121, 169
    anti-parlementarism 106
    colonial empire 7–8, 123, 131, 162, 164–65, 169, 250
    as commercial power 62, 64
    diplomatic relations 12, 189
    and exile 3, 83, 103
    First Empire 168
    First Republic, the 167–68
    geographic imaginary and 122
    Haitian civil war and 30, 247
    Haitian debt 50n9, 54n15

Haitian writers in 27, 32
in ideological context 95
as missionary nation 167, 170–71
neocolonial discourse 183–84, 185
political discourse 100, 165, 211, 216
protest 250
racial inequality 166, 179–81
reactionary politics 238
Republican 91, 168
tuberculosis and 145
veneration for 133
see also French secular universalism; Third Republic France
Franco-Prussian War 63n36
fraud 227, 239
freedom 3–4, 25, 55n17, 173, 225–26, 247
betterment of the black race through 90–91
economic 204
enslaved demand for 167
Haiti's fight for 114, 183
as a human right 40
and modernity 251
and nationalism 135
as sacred cause 227
sovereignty and 223
subversive versions of 224
Freedom Tree 83, 119
French Atlantic triangle 123
French Directory 5
French imperialism 147, 167–68
see also colonialism; empire; France
French Indochina 15
French Revolution (1789) 63, 67n42, 121, 166, 171–72n23, 216
see also revolution
French secular universalism 15–16, 164, 166–67, 169
see also civilizing mission; colonialism
French West Indies 15
Fugitive Slave Act of 1850 (US) 225

Garde d'Haïti 238–39
Garvey, Marcus 231, 236
Garveyites 237
Gautier, Judith 85, 132
Geffrard, Fabre 12–13, 84, 89, 99, 110

Gendarmerie 238
General Insurrection 247, 251–52
Germany 8–9n21, 16, 64, 70n48, 170, 197, 211, 216, 235
global intellectual tradition 40, 118
Global South 16, 41, 241
Goman (Perrier, Jean-Baptiste) 206, 253
la Gonâve 48–49, 67, 72–73, 75, 198, 203
Grant, Ulysses S. 26, 57, 59, 199
Great Britain 2, 12, 16, 30, 52n11, 62n32, 67n43, 70n48, 77n61, 231
see also Clayton-Bulwer Treaty
Grégoire, Henri 66–67, 246
guano 23, 67–68n44, 72–73
Guerrier, Phillipe 11, 110

habitant 248n12, 251–53
see also cultivateurs; farmers; *paysans*; peasantry
Haitian-American Society for Agricultural Development 239
Haitian Atlantic humanism 35, 119, 140
see also Black Atlantic humanism; humanism
Haitian Creole 19n42, 253
see also Creole
Haitian Imperial Constitution of 1805 223, 226
Haitian independence 3, 5–6, 24n58, 28, 65–66n41, 77n59, 115, 117, 142, 222–23
Haitian intellectual tradition 24, 34, 37, 119, 152
Haitian Republic 6, 154, 171, 173, 178, 199
Haitian Revolution 3–4, 10, 42, 177, 220, 222, 227
as anticolonial project 24
and diplomatic relations 8
as emancipatory project 40, 223
as inheritance 184, 219
meaning of 225
promises of 31, 228
rumors of 224
success of 232, 240
as symbol of black humanity 114
see also Dessalines, Jean-Jacques; Haiti; Saint-Domingue

Haiti as black Republic 117, 184, 189, 220
Haïti aux Haïtiens 2, 23, 26, 31, 191, 248, 255
  as challenge to existing order 229
  context 190
  as criticism of United States political leadership 136
  as critique of US colonialism 199
  and discursive violence of empire 230, 246
  and Haitian peasants 39
  influence 131, 192
  as idea 37, 135, 222, 236
  nation building 32, 36, 132, 165, 188–89, 202, 213, 215
  as patriotic work 208
  relevance 41, 216
Harlem Renaissance Movement 114
Haytian Bureau of Emigration 227
Henry I (Haiti) *see* Christophe, Henry
Hispaniola 26n63, 50n9, 72–73n52, 86n7, 110–11, 139
  see also Dominican Republic; Haiti; Saint-Domingue; Santo Domingo
Horrors of Saint-Domingue 224–25
de Hostos, Eugenio María 130
Hughes, Langston 126
Hugo, Victor 132
humanism 40, 134, 165, 170, 179n39, 219
  see also Black Atlantic humanism; Haitian Atlantic humanism
Hyppolite, Florvil 110, 231

identity 25n59, 67n43, 166, 178, 181, 237, 238, 248
immigration 7, 227
imperialism 42, 135, 185, 222, 243, 246, 249–50, 254
  French 147, 168–69, 182
  and global white supremacy 137
  nationalism that functioned as 38, 228–29
  North Atlantic 142
  republican new 16, 164, 171–72, 180, 182–83
  rise in 189, 247
  slogans against 237
  and transatlantic abolition 120

United States 17, 35, 37, 67–68n44, 121, 128, 138–39, 235
  and universalism 167, 184
  see also colonialism; empire; France
indemnity treaty (1825) 7–9, 55n17, 77n59, 79–80n63
indigénisme 65–66n41, 238
Indigenous Army 223, 248, 251
  see also armée indigène
indigenous population 110, 143, 150, 156, 164–65n6
Indochina 15, 169
industrialization 52n11, 54, 175, 194, 209
Industrial Revolution (United Kingdom) 216
inequality 95, 235
  and civilizing mission 164, 176–77
  global structures of 235
  of human races 27, 35, 53n14, 171, 174–75
  racial 151, 185
  refutation of 178–81
  scientific dogma 83
  social 96
  see also Ferry, Jules; Quesnel, Léo; racism
insurgents 1, 29, 247, 250–51
insurrection 2, 6, 69, 139, 201, 221
  see also General Insurrection; Liberal Insurrection of 1883
International Colonial and Export Exhibition 63n36
internationalism *see* black internationalism
International Monetary Fund 243
International United Nations Mission for the Stabilization of Haiti 243
Italy 211, 216

Jacques I *see* Dessalines, Jean-Jacques
Jamaica 1, 10, 24, 28–29, 79, 230–31
Janvier, Louis-Joseph 16, 24, 190
  anti-imperial resistance 26–27
  and Black Atlantic humanism 28
  on civil war 13, 47
  constraints upon autonomy 246
  economic policy 65, 75
  education 14–15, 145, 247

in France 27, 35, 37, 103, 121, 174
on Haitian debt 8, 31
and Haitian national sovereignty 34, 123, 183–85, 196, 216
on Haitian politics 18, 19–20, 30
land policy 21–22, 54n15, 207, 252
intellectual construction of Haiti 36
on internal division 31
and the Liberal Insurrection of 1883 1, 29
pessimism 99
scope of work 33, 212
self-identity 32
on trade 23
see also France; *Haïti aux Haïtiens*; Paris; Third Republic France
Jim Crow 237, 241
July Monarchy 168

Kansas-Nebraska Act of 1854 (US) 225
kingdom 6, 52n10, 111, 208–9
kinship 4–5, 119

labor 3–6, 9, 12, 16, 73n53, 136, 211, 231, 234, 240
see also agriculture; enslavement; land; peasantry; slavery
Lafitte, Pierre 66–67, 158
lakou 4–5, 254
de Lamartine, Alphonse 132
land 3, 9, 25, 93, 96, 110, 250, 253
appropriation 239
and citizenship 98, 151
concessions 54
distribution 10, 205, 213, 230, 252
and economic freedom 204, 211
and foreigner ownership 197
free 56
Haitian debt and 88
Haitian history and the 223, 228
inheritance 4–5
policies 6–7, 242, 249–50
reform 11, 20–21, 23, 27, 29
rightful claims to 39, 69, 206–7
taxes 22
and territory 94, 203
see also landownership; property
landholding see landownership

landownership 4, 19, 20–22, 49n7, 60, 207, 226, 234, 249
Land Reform law 1883 29
Lansing, Robert 233–34
latifundia see property
Latin America 120, 132, 135n78
Latin American Age of Independence 117, 133
see also Firmin, Anténor
Legions of Equality (French) 247
Leopold II (Belgium) 235
Lescot, Elie 239
liberal egalitarianism 166–67, 168n14
see also egalitarianism
Liberal Insurrection of 1883 1, 29, 39, 47n2
Liberal Party 19–20, 23, 28–29, 32, 191n10, 208, 228, 247
liberation 117, 119, 195n21, 204, 207, 250, 252
liberty 11, 114, 119, 128, 131
demands for 235, 253
and equivalency with liberation 250
ideals of 210, 223
price of 219
and revolution 224
symbol of 169
values of 171
de Lisle, Leconte 15, 132
Louverture, Toussaint 3, 5–6, 24n58, 127
and Freedom Tree 83
as Haitian hero 89, 97, 222, 225–26
as patriarch to all Black people in the Americas 126
Love, Joseph Robert 230–31, 236
Lycée National 14, 116
Lycée Pétion 174

Magloire, Paul 239
Mallarmé, Stéphane 132
Manouvrier, Léonce 152
Maran, Réné 124
Marcuard André et Cie. 8n21, 78n62
maroon see marronage
marronage 4, 145, 150–51, 156
see also freedom
Martí, José 34, 117–18, 127
Marxism 236–37, 239

McKay, Claude 124
Meiji Restoration (Japan) 216
métissage 157, 159
metropole 16, 116, 147, 169, 190n8, 246, 251
Michelet, Jules 66–67, 84, 89, 149
militarism 235
militia 239
minifundia see property
Miragoâne 1, 19, 30
missionary 14, 167, 169, 171
   see also civilizing mission; Catholicism; colonialism; empire
modernity 14, 70n48, 101, 151, 216, 219, 251, 253
   colonial vision of 12, 254
   and the nation-state 41
   prison of 255–56
   values of 248
Monroe, James 57n21, 128
Monroe Doctrine 18, 58, 127, 135–36, 192, 232
morality 95, 101, 163, 179, 248, 254
moun an deyò 252–53
mulâtres 90, 98
"mulatto" 1, 19n43

National Bank of Haiti 233
National City Bank of New York 233
National Constituent Assembly 67n42
National Convention (French Republican) 3, 67n42
nationalism 32, 35–37, 183, 188, 249
   anticolonial 38, 40–42, 52n11, 222, 229, 235
   and the civilizing mission 166–67, 169
   Creole 134–35
   economic 19, 23, 27
   global black 34, 140
   Haitian 215, 237–38
   and nation building 189, 214
   plebiscitary 179, 184
   transnational debates 121, 163
   United States 58–59n24
National Party 19–20, 28, 28–29, 190n8, 205, 212, 229–32, 247
   see also Domingue, Michel; Saget, Nissage; Salomon, Lysius Félicité

natural hierarchy of man *see* Renan, Ernest
naturalization 49, 54
natural resources 197, 201, 212, 215–16
Nau, Emile 208–9
Nau, Ignace 149
Navassa Phosphate Company 72, 73n53
Negrismo 114
négritude 85, 89, 114, 118, 134–35
Negro Renaissance Movement *see* Harlem Renaissance Movement
neocolonialism 38, 178, 183, 185, 222
new imperialism 16, 169, 171, 180, 182–83, 185
   see also civilizing mission; colonialism; Ferry, Jules; France; Third Republic
noirisme 239
noiristes 38, 239
nouveau libre 250, 252

Oceania 169
occupation 38, 222, 237
   ahistoricism of 241–42
   Boyer's unification as 25
   of Egypt 52n11
   "Haiti for the Haitians" slogan 222, 236
   humiliation of 240
   reactionary politics due to 238–39
   resistance to 234
   United States 8–9n21, 18, 22–23n55, 38–39
   vocational education during 65–66n41
   warning of 31
oligarchs 248–49, 253–54
   see also cultivateurs; farmers; *habitants; paysans;* peasantry
Opportunist Republicans 16, 169, 173
opposition 3, 8–10, 12, 22–23, 41, 128, 229, 250
   to occupation 38
   parties 242
   systematic 99
   violent 29, 222
oppression 231, 237, 241–42
Ottoman Empire 16, 52n11

Pan-Africanism 34, 114, 117, 120–21, 231
Panama Canal 74
Pan-Americanism 34, 58n22, 59–60n26, 117–18, 120–21
Pan-Caribbean 118
Paris 1, 16, 35, 38, 84–85, 111, 219
   as audience for Janvier's writings 32
   and Banque Nationale d'Haïti (BNH) 54n15
   as fictional setting 101–3, 107
   Haitian colony in 190n8
   Haitian mobilization in 176
   Janvier's activism in 228
   as locus of civilizing mission 15
   as locus for writers 132, 165
   site of Janvier's death 112
   study of pathological anthropology 86
Parti Communiste Haïtien 238
paternalism 22, 151, 241
Patriotic Union 237
patriotism 36, 78, 93, 237
paysans 188, 249–51, 253
   see also *cultivateurs*; *habitant*; farmers; peasantry
Peace of Westphalia (1648) 220
peasantry 10–11, 12, 14, 19, 20n45, 54, 69n45, 151
   see also agriculture; *cultivateurs*; *habitant*; farmers; labor; land; *paysans*
Péralte, Charlemagne 253
Perin, Georges 171–72n23
Perrier, Jean-Baptiste (aka Goman) 253
Pétion, Alexandre 3, 6, 11, 14, 31, 84, 89, 97, 110, 116–17
PetroCaribe 41, 243
Phillips, Wendell 127, 226n19
   see also abolitionists; Louverture, Toussaint
pigmentocracy 156
Piquets 11–12, 99, 205n55, 206, 253
plantation economy 2, 3, 5–6, 69, 219, 250–53
plantation slavery 247, 250
   see also enslavement; plantation economy; slavery
police force 239, 247
political science 84, 94, 97, 104, 112

Polk, James 128
populism 10, 26
Positivism 177
postcolonialism 122, 241
   Atlantic world and 133, 243
   creolization and 145, 159
   frustrations of 13
   independence and 165, 175
   modernity and 151
   ongoing history of 244
   statehood and 40–41, 42
poverty 55, 70n48, 86, 139, 141, 151, 183, 253
prejudice 28, 86, 114
   Catholic 99
   color 102, 119, 123, 180, 232
   contagion as 145
   racial 177
   transformation under Boyer 98
   the United States and 127–28, 155–56
   and the Western gaze 90
Price-Mars, Jean 65–66n41, 127, 237, 239
   on afro-diasporic Americas 124
   and *bovarysme collectif* 133, 238
   collaborations 125
   and Haitian representation 95
Prichard, Hesketh 232–34
proletariat 12, 19, 98, 205, 207
property 22, 101, 207, 203
   claims by the United States 72
   the enslaved as 8, 224
   and foreigner ownership 49n7, 223
   large (*latifundia*) owners 205
   -owning classes 104
   price of 94
   private 253–54
   small (*minifundia*) owners 69, 98, 204
   stolen 248–49
pro-slavery 116, 226, 247, 250
Protestant ethic 14, 70
Protestantism 14, 70n48, 83–84, 195–96
Puerto Rico 18, 26, 126, 130–31, 200n39
pulmonary phthisis *see* tuberculosis

de Quatrefages, Armand 156–57, 158n71
Quesnel, Léo, 87, 173
   criticism of 176–77, 178, 182
   and inequality of human races 27, 174
   racist portrayal of Haiti 150–51, 175

race 48, 55, 65–67, 70n48, 89–90, 96, 231
    consciousness 231
    and creolization 157–58
    crisis of occupation and 238
    debates on 156
    defense of 213
    in defiance of colonialism 37
    essentialist concepts of 163–65, 171, 173, 184–85
    and evolution 154
    and geopolitics 221, 224
    and Haitian citizenship 49n7
    as marker of inferiority 53n14, 108, 152, 176–80
    and nation 15, 136, 141–42, 195, 198, 226, 228
    pathogens and 144, 146–47
    and persecution 119, 137
    and religion 70, 99
    social justice and 125–26, 130
    as topic of essays 32–33
    see also critical race theory; race man, the; racial inequality; racism
race man, the 120
racial inequality 53n14, 151, 174–76, 178–81, 185
racialization 146, 220
racial taxonomy 220
racism 25, 35, 175, 208, 237
    biological 170–71
    and capitalism 219, 237
    challenges to 28, 36, 42
    domestic 128
    and empire 127, 137
    eradicating 119
    and geopolitics 221
    scientific 17, 86–87, 146
    transnational debates 121
    Western 94
    see also race; racial inequality
Raybaud, Maxime 175
Raynal, Guillaume Thomas François 96
Reconstruction (U.S.) 17, 59–60n26, 73n53, 222
Redpath, James 226–27
religion 5, 33, 53, 70n48, 99, 178, 212, 229, 232
    see also Christianity; Protestantism; Vodou

Renan, Ernest 84
    critiques by Janvier 164, 178–79, 181
    debates on nationalism 163, 211
    on hierarchy of nature 53n14, 95–96, 180
    reason as object of faith 108
republicanism 12, 124, 164–65, 169, 185, 210, 250
Republican National Convention (U.S.) 58n22
Republican Party (U.S.) 59n25, 227
revolution 92, 150, 222
    anticolonial 13, 226
    antislavery 24, 37
    Duvalier 240
    and Haitian Atlantic humanism 140
    liberal 10
    as model 225
    social 211
    "true" 6
    unfinished 220–22
    see also French Revolution
La Revue Indigène 114
Rigaud, André 3
Roumain, Jacques 95, 112, 126–27, 238
royalists 93, 250
Rural Code of 1826 7, 21, 97
Russian Revolution 237

Sabourin, Dantès 165
Saget, Nissage 28
Salnave, Sylvain 12
Salomon, Lysius Félicité 1, 10–12, 20–21, 54n15, 65n40, 66, 110, 190n8, 250
    and agrarian reform 69n46, 205
    and elected office 28–29, 60n27
    the Liberal uprising and 30, 191n10, 192n12, 231
    US-Haitian relations and 50n8, 200
Sam, Vilbrun Guillaume 233
Saint-Domingue 2, 7, 62n34, 91, 175, 196n25, 223, 251, 253
    and the enslaved 4, 63n35, 252
    Horrors of 224–25
    political leadership 3
    prosperity 69
    see also Haiti; Hispaniola

Santo Domingo 24n58, 72
  see also Dominican Republic; Hispaniola
Schœlcher, Victor 66–67, 86, 176
  see also abolitionists
science 15, 96, 105, 108, 143, 146
scientific racism see racism
Second Empire 168–69
Second Republic 168
segregation 222, 234
self-governance 17, 220
slavery 5, 73n53, 93–94, 222, 243, 250–52
  abolition and 3, 59–60n26, 115, 119, 166, 168
  aftermath of 220–21, 224
  colonial 28, 35, 38, 40, 49n7, 126, 144, 237
  of color prejudice 128, 180
  extinction of 227
  Haitian Revolution and defeat of 225–26
  land redistribution 21, 69
  questions of 222
  reestablishment of 91, 247
  resistance to 4, 26
  scars of 223
  transnational debates about 121
  see also plantation slavery; racism
Slavery Abolition Act of 1833 (Great Britain) 225
Société d'anthropologie de Paris (SAP)15, 143, 145, 152–53, 155–56, 161
Society of the Friends of the Blacks 246
solidarity 253
  emancipation from colonialism and 236–37
  hemispheric 118, 129
  and racial uplift 139
  social 125
  trans-island 25, 130
  and transnational "black" sovereignty 34
  see also colonialism; Marxism; Pan-Africanism
Sonthonax, Léger-Félicité 2, 167
Sorbonne 163, 178
Soulouque, Faustin 11–13, 24n58, 84, 98, 110, 175

South Side Community House (Chicago) 236
Sri Lanka 63n36
St. John, Spenser Buckingham 55n18, 231–32
Stowe, Harriet Beecher 115
subaltern 213, 225, 242
  see also class; violence
sugar production 4, 6, 48, 62, 86n7, 198

Third Republic France 15, 32, 35–36, 63n36, 163, 173
  biological racism and 170–71
  imperial politics of 37, 176, 180, 185
  monarchists and 169
  and universalism 166–67
  as watershed moment 164–65
  see also civilizing mission; colonialism; Renan, Ernest; universalism
Tonton Makouts 239
la Tortue (Tortuga) 75, 248
trade 23, 58n22, 62n34, 63–64, 170, 197, 230, 242, 251
transatlantic slave trade 220
tree of liberty see Freedom Tree
tuberculosis 145–46
  hygienist assumptions 85
  Janvier dissertation 15, 35
  as miasmatic disease 147–48
  and poverty 151
Tuskegee Institute 65–66n41

L'Union patriotique 237
United States 41, 70n48, 94, 113–14, 133, 152, 193–94
  "America for the Americans" 136, 229
  antebellum 226
  and the Atlantic world 118, 122–24
  Blacks in the 125
  color prejudice 127–29, 156
  criticism toward 198–99
  decolonization 241
  diplomatic crisis with Haiti 78–79n62, 189
  diplomatic recognition from 12, 36n80
  emancipation 126
  and empire 16–18, 23–24, 26, 67–68n44, 70n48, 72, 135

exports 64–65
foreign policy 57–58, 59–61
and money 138
occupation 38, 49n7, 50nn8–9, 175, 233–35, 236, 239
political economy 196
as protectorate over Haiti 13, 137
treaties 74–75n55
universal brotherhood 167
universalism *see* civilizing mission; Ferry, Jules; Renan, Ernest; Third Republic France
U.S. Civil Rights Movement 241
U.S. Congressional Black Caucus 242
U.S. Marines 234, 238

de Vastey, Baron 28, 30–31, 115, 139–40, 181, 208
   see also Black Atlantic humanism
Vatican, the 12
vaudoux see Vodou
Vaval, Duraciné 83, 85, 89, 100, 109–11, 192
Villemin, Jean-Antoine 145
Vincent, Sténio 237–39
violence 89, 91, 227, 231
   colonial 28, 150, 175
   of empire 230

random acts of 239
subaltern 225
and war 235
Vodou 5, 11–12, 70n48, 91, 195n23, 232, 238–39
Voting Rights Act of 1965 241

War of Knives 3
War of Restoration (Dominican Republic) 26
Washington, Booker T. 65–66n41, 125
Washington, George 122
Wesleyan Church 14
Western liberalism 5
West Indies 15, 61, 86n7, 122, 135, 226
white supremacy 17, 59n26, 137, 153–54, 166, 175n28, 232
   see also colonialism; empire; racism
Whitman, Daniel 242
Wilson, Woodrow 233
Workers Party of America (WP) 236
World Bank 243
World's Fair 1878 (L'Exposition Universelle de 1878) 63n36
World War I 38, 222, 233, 235

Young Workers League (YWL) 236